LOOSE ENDS

A NOVEL BY

JOHN LAROCQUE

"HIC SUNT DRACONES"
(HERE BE DRAGONS)

Merritt Island Publishing
Copyright 2016

Merritt Island Publishing
2409 Willowbrook Road
Merritt Island, Florida 32952

WE SHOULD NOT DO EVIL SO THAT GOOD WILL COME OF IT
Christian Maxim (Derived from Romans 3:8)

EVIL IS IN THE EYE OF THE BEHOLDER
Apakoh

Acknowledgements:

- Leonard LaRocque – Dad ("There are no strangers, only friends you haven't met.")
- Charlotte LaRocque – Mom ("What are you boys doing up there?")
- Jim LaRocque – Brother/Advocate/Political Advisor/Car Enthusiast
- Mary LaRocque-Brandabur – Niece/Animal Trainer/Purchasing
- Jack Brandabur – Brother/Weapons + Hunting Advisor
- Jane Dallet – Sister/Reviewer/ Cheerleader/Spiritual Advisor
- Pat Dallet – Brother/Cheerleader/Partner in Crime
- Charlie LaRocque – Brother/(PITA)/ Partner in Crime
- Julie LaRocque – Sister/Spiritual Guidance
- Carrie Kendig – Support/Patience
- Don and Patti Petrich - Inspiration
- Doug Vliet – Partner in Crime
- Laurie Martin – Partner in Crime
- Bonny Melby – Partner in Crime
- Cindy Davis – Editor/Teacher
- Denver – Friend

Chapter 1

The view from the blind was spectacular. Artic winds had sculpted snowdrifts across the Methow Valley's mile-wide expanse. Reeds poking above the snow hinted where the alfalfa fields ended and the ice-encrusted river began. Thousands of Canada geese gathered along that line waiting for their day in the sun.

Brian stepped into the moonlit darkness and stretched his six-foot frame against the brisk winter breeze. He was three-hundred miles and a world away from his office overlooking the state capitol. The geese were stirring. Soon, they'd take to the air, and he needed to be ready. Now, his bladder demanded relief. Embracing Jim Croce's advice about not *spitting into the wind*, he turned away from the shelter and came face-to-face with a man pointing a pistol at him.

"Don't bother lowering the zipper. We don't have time for that. Get inside."

Brian reentered the blind, followed closely by the stranger. The intruder picked up the prized shotgun, released its safety, and prodded his captive out the door towards the river. It took five minutes trudging through knee-deep snow to reach the reeds. Brian's mind leaped from thought to thought: *Do I know this guy? I've really got to pee. Where the hell is he taking me? I'm going to wet my pants. I should've listened to Don. I'm going to hit this bastard in the mouth.*

But Brian asked only two questions, "Who are you, and what do you want?"

The man didn't reply, just pointed east with the shotgun. A few minutes later, he stopped among the reeds but directed Brian onto the wind scoured ice. Five steps farther, Brian turned and faced his captor. He was ten feet from shore and had as many feet of bone-chilling water beneath him. There was no guarantee two-inches of ice would hold his one-hundred-ninety pounds from a torturous death.

Brian summoned his courage. With the bravado he used to send overpaid lobbyists scurrying and arrogant department heads back to their offices penniless, he demanded, "Shoot me or let me get the hell out of here. I've got to pee."

The man smiled. Brian thought his ploy had spared him from being torn in half by birdshot from his mint-conditioned Parker. He wasn't entirely wrong.

Chapter 2

Be Prepared is the simple yet compelling motto that served Major Donald Rowland well throughout his twenty-year career with the Army. Two tours in Iraq had frequently tested his preparedness. After the last tour, when his primary duty was delivering sacks of money to warlords, he concluded it was time to retire. He chose to put down roots in Olympia, a city he'd come to know while training with Fort Lewis's 2nd Ranger Battalion.

For a few months, retirement suited him. He set up housekeeping, became a fitness club regular, and volunteered at the veteran's center. In May, two separate but linked events shattered his complacency and forced a new occupation on him.

The first happened in Seattle, eighty miles to the north. Jacqui Moore, a twenty-three-year-old, single mother was nearly killed by Samuel Germain Lavel, a man who'd done the same thing a year before to a University of Washington co-ed. Lavel was caught and charged in the co-ed's assault. According to the media, the case against him was ironclad, but it fell apart when the defense team revealed a lab technician hadn't signed a form after processing the knife Lavel used to stab the co-ed seven times. The technicality set him free, much to Don's dismay.

A year later, when Lavel was arrested for assaulting Jacqui Moore, Don's frustration turned to anger. After a few days, the anger abated, replaced by a commitment to action. He wrote a check to help with Ms. Moore's medical costs and brought a bouquet of flowers to bolster the young woman's spirits. The charge-nurse was taken with Don's sincerity and asked if he'd like to speak with Ms. Moore. A few minutes later, he was ushered into her room. The bruises on her face, neck, and arms reminded him of battlefield trauma. It'd be months before her eyesight returned to normal, her jaw worked properly, and her legs mended well enough to stand.

Over the next hour, Don was moved to tears by Jacqui's irrepressible spirit, her belief that something good would come from her suffering, and that in the end, her attacker would be suitably punished. She bore no animosity towards the justice system that had failed her and the co-ed. She even hoped Samuel Germain Lavel would turn his life around.

Jacqui's sister was caring for her little girls, and her dad was making her apartment wheelchair-friendly, something she hoped she'd need for only a few months. She thanked Don for his concern and the donation, assuring him it would be put to good use. He left buoyed by the woman he'd come to cheer up. Two days later, Don's outlook crashed to the ground when blood clots escaped from Jacqui's broken leg and caused the heart attack that killed her. Her death at the hands of a career criminal confirmed Don's misgivings about America's judicial system. Lavel preyed on vulnerable people: stealing, assaulting, and now murdering them. The system protected him, allowing, if not necessitating, more of the same.

Don was struggling with what to do when a second event set his course. On a September evening ideal for running, he slipped into his shorts, laced his well-worn sneakers, and drove to Capitol Lake. To take advantage of the remaining light, he ran the course backwards. Forty-minutes later, he approached the deserted parking lot and noticed the dome light was on in his Jeep. Initially, he was angry at himself for being careless, but movement in the car refocused his anger. Someone was rifling through the glove box, periodically glancing to the east, the usual direction for returning joggers. The man didn't notice Don approach from the west.

The Ranger grabbed the thief's belt and yanked him onto the pavement. A frustrated and seething six-foot-four inch Ranger with two-hundred-forty pounds of highly trained muscle at his command stood over a trembling wisp of a man. Don's instinct was to tear into the thief, teach him a lesson he'd never forget. He forced that notion from his mind and replaced it with one that would be far more satisfying. "Stay down or I'll break you in two."

Don retrieved a roll of duct tape from his tool box, and soon the twenty-something-year-old was bound, blindfolded, gagged, and resting uncomfortably in the back of the Jeep. Don drove to a golf course a few miles south of the lake, parked by the mower shed, and rummaged in his toolbox before removing the man's blindfold. Unadulterated terror showed across the man's face, exactly what Don wanted from his captive. The camouflage paint left only Don's eyes visible. The taillights' red glow made Don appear insane, unhinged. He collected his captive and carried him into the darkness. The would-be thief mumbled incessantly; begging for mercy. Don found a tree and taped the man to it.

After allowing the thief time to ponder what the maniac with the enormous knife would do next, Don explained the situation, "You have two options. One, tell me about a crime that's going to happen: who what, where, and when. If you choose this path, I'll cut the tape, and you walk away. Option two is you keep your mouth shut, proving there is honor among thieves, and I cut off your balls. You won't be found until tomorrow, and by then you won't need them. It's up to you. I can live with either option. You, on the other hand, can only live with option one. If you pick it, and I strongly recommend you do, then you can't warn anyone. If you do, I'll find you and hang your nads in my garage."

The thief took Don's suggestion. Don wrote quickly but several times had to ask his captive to slow down or repeat a detail. Good to his word, Don freed the man and watched him sprint into the night.

❖

A month after the interrogation on the golf course and two months before the event on the Methow River, a late October evening witnessed the culmination of Don's meticulous intelligence gathering, planning, and preparation. If all went well, his mission would succeed at *Level-Alpha*, all objectives accomplished – no casualties. If all didn't go well, the success level would likely plummet.

The sun was sinking when Don crested Prather Road. Its forest-lined intersection with Michigan Hill Road was less than a mile from his destination. He turned onto Langworthy Way. Checking to be sure nobody was behind him, Don made a hard right, pushing the Jeep through a thicket of old growth blackberry stalks. The vehicle emerged in front of a long abandoned homestead. The thorny gate closed behind him, obscuring the entry point. Don spun the Jeep so it faced the invisible exit. He cut the engine and listened. All quiet, so far so good.

It'd been a beautiful day in western Washington, and the night promised to be dry and warm. He opened the hatch, revealing an empty cargo area. Flicking the toggle switch he'd installed on the door panel, the floorboard rose noiselessly. The hidden compartment held an array of military gear. He slipped on a camouflage jacket and blackened his face. A watch cap covered his shaved head. He strapped a holster under his arm, picked up the Glock, checked its magazine, and chambered a round. Setting the safety, he holstered the weapon. The Ka-Bar knife was secured to his left thigh. If the plan worked, he wouldn't need the Glock or the Ka-Bar. If it didn't, they'd get him out of most compromised situations. Don opened the backpack and inspected its contents. He slung the Ruger Nighthawk over his shoulder. Lightweight and sturdy, the rifle was perfect for close-quarter assaults. He locked the Jeep and walked into the woods. After a few steps, he stopped, turned, and electronically unlocked the doors. Having the Jeep ready to leave might be the difference between a clean get-away and an awkward moment with the authorities. All was in order. Ranger Special Operations taught him well.

An abandoned Christmas tree farm separated him from his objective. Spindly noble firs rose to the sky. He made his way through them in stealth-mode and found the fence separating the homestead from Doug Hansen's ranch. He stashed his gear behind a hawthorn bush at the turn in the driveway. With an unobstructed view of the property, it'd be his observation post. Nobody could enter or exit without being seen from the shrub.

He was early, a trait his parents instilled in him when he was growing up in the Adirondacks, but time slipped by quickly. Hansen's front door opened, a man emerged, and disappeared into the detached garage. The double-wide door lifted along its track. Doug Hansen backed his SUV onto the apron, and the door slid back into place. Don expected Hansen to lean on the horn, attempting to hurry his wife and daughter, but instead, the man walked to the front door and played a tune with the doorbell. Don recognized the beat, *Innagaddadavida*. Soon mother and daughter rushed out, got into the car, and buckled their seatbelts. Hansen went through the house turning off lights. Room after room went dark.

Doug drove his ladies to Michigan Hill Road and turned left. It was opening night of Rochester High's production of *Finian's Rainbow*. Katie Hansen was playing Sharon McLonergan, the leading lady Petula Clark made famous in1968. After Hansen's taillights disappeared, Don walked briskly to the house; no lights came on, no dogs barked, no geese honked. He tried the door. It opened. No alarm sounded. Hansen believed if a burglar wanted in, he'd get in. Nothing would prevent it. Leave the door unlocked, and there's less damage. Don sprinted to the barn and deposited his gear in the tack room. He exited through the hay door, leaving it ajar. Satisfied he had a feel for the place, he settled in behind the hawthorn. If his source was correct, a truck would soon pull into the driveway, and a number of men would pillage the ranch. To pass the time and set the mood, Don played Jimmy Buffet's *Gypsies in the Palace* on his iPod.

As predicted by the man taped to a tree on a golf course, headlights illuminated the driveway. The truck slowed. Two men swung out of the back and ran across the field. The leader was savvy. Deploying scouts in advance of an assault was a sound military tactic. The thirty-foot van stopped in front of the house. A man got out, went to the door, and rang the bell. No answer. He opened it, stuck his head in, shouted something, listened, and then waved to the driver. The engine went silent, and two more men got out. The party of five had arrived.

The burglars huddled around the truck's headlights. The leader pointed to the barn, and one of the thieves walked off. Another went to the garage; lights came on and the door rose again. The driver got back in the truck and turned it around. He opened the tailgate and joined the men in the house. Room after room lit up.

Don squeezed through the hay door and positioned himself in the stall opposite the tack room. The barn-thief made three trips depositing high-end rodeo gear in the hallway. On his fourth, Don shot him in the neck. The man reached for the wound but was unconscious before his fingers found the dart. He collapsed behind the saddles, out of sight from the house and garage. Don gathered up the man and carried him into the tack room. The drug wouldn't wear off for hours, but Don took no chances. He tied the man to the table and found a rag in the neighboring stall.

"A little horse poop never hurt anyone, and it keeps you regular." Don stuffed the cloth into the thief's mouth.

Someone called from the house, "Sam, you okay out there?"

"Doing fine," Don replied in a muffled voice.

"We'll be done in twenty minutes. Then we'll get you and the gear."

"On it." Don wondered if the man noticed anything unusual. Nothing. So far, so good.

Don had twenty minutes to subdue four men scattered around two buildings. Shouldn't be a problem, but in case something went wrong, he didn't want the truck to become a getaway vehicle. He loaded the Ruger with a pellet, cocked it, and shot the front tire. The rifle's discharge was barely audible, and the tire hissed softly until it was flat.

After duck-walking across the driveway, Don knelt behind a fencepost opposite the garage. Hansen's woodworking lights silhouetted the next target brilliantly. The garage-thief was running tools out to the apron. He put down a lathe, heard a muffled sound, and felt a sting under his chin. His arms went limp, allowing his nose to break his fall. Blood gushed from both nostrils.

Don grabbed him by the shoulders, dragged him into the night, and zip-tied the burglar to a gate. The man's nose continued to bleed, staining his Hawaiian shirt a deep red. Don moved into position; two down, three to go. Odds had improved dramatically.

A third man came looking for the garage-thief. "Harry, where the hell are you? We've got no time for breaks."

The third thief joined Sam and Harry; darted, unconscious, and tied to something immovable, this time the wheel of an ancient Yanmar tractor. Before Don could get resituated, he heard, "Bert, get out here. There's blood on the ground, and I can't find Harry or Jeff."

Uh-oh, Don thought. The fourth thief was outside the garage, pointing a gun everywhere he looked. The fifth was elsewhere, waiting, probably armed. So far nobody had been seriously injured. Darts, not bullets, were flying through the air. Don didn't want to turn this into a true firefight.

"Bert, where are you? Am I it? Are all of you assholes gone? What the hell's going on?" He turned towards the house and continued to rant.

Don reloaded and shot him in the ass.

"Ouch. Mother fu…" were the last syllables the thief uttered. He corkscrewed onto the pavement. Don reloaded the rifle.

"Drop the gun." The leader of the band emerged from the darkness. "You got a silencer?"

"It's an air-rifle. No need for a silencer."

"Drop the damned thing and move to the garage. Any more of you out here?"

"Just me." Don walked to the garage, turned, and met Bert. He was Don's size, around two hundred-forty pounds, holding a pistol.

"This ain't an air gun. It shoots real bullets, and if you do anything stupid, I'll show you how well it works." The man approached Don. "You a Marine?"

"A Ranger."

"Well Ranger, you're a POW now."

"Not for long."

Ignoring Don's comment, "You've taken out my help, so someone with a strong back and weak mind has to load this stuff. You fit the bill, asshole. Start with the house. Get moving."

Don had encountered men like Bert in his days with the military police: brutes among people they could intimidate, using their strength liberally, pushing whenever the situation called for it, and the situation always called for it. Don stood his ground. When the thief shifted his weight to shove Don, the Ranger moved back. Without Don's body to absorb his momentum, the man stumbled forward. Don assisted the unbalanced man find the concrete, knocking him unconscious. He moved the drugged and dazed men to the barn, lining them up outside the tack room. He administered the antidote to the four who'd been darted and poured water on the fifth. They all regained a semblance of consciousness.

"Here's the drill." Don got their undivided attention. "I'm going to take each of you into that room for a chat. If you tell me what I want to know, you'll come out mostly intact. If you don't cooperate, you'll experience pain like never before. Sam, let's start with you."

Don tossed Sam over his shoulder and went into the room. The men heard muffled screams, a thud, and a loud slam. Soon, Don carried Sam's unconscious body into the hallway then tossed a bloody mass onto the barn-thief's chest.

Don towered over the men on the floor. "Sam cooperated but not without a little persuasion." He pointed to the blob. "I let him keep his right nut. He might want kids. Harry, you're next, and I'm no longer in a good mood."

Harry went in standing, but came out in Don's arms, as did Jeff, only there was more blood. Bert was next, stayed in longer, and was dragged out.

"That's it for Bert." Don sat next to the last thief. "I didn't catch your name. Please don't tell me it's Ernie."

"It's Pete. I'll tell you anything you want to know. You don't have to hurt me. I've got a wife and two kids."

"They must be real proud. Let's see what you've got. If it's good, I'll just knock you out. Most of the time, the jaw can be set without surgery."

For ten minutes, Don asked questions and got answers. Pete answered questions Don didn't have time to ask.

"Pete, you've done well. I have all I need."

"What are you going to do?" Pete's eyes were wide with fright.

"Get you boys a ride. No need to put you under." Don took the bloody blob from Sam's chest. "I'm going to give these guys the antidote so the medics don't have to figure all that out. Your friends will come around soon with massive headaches but no permanent damage. And Sam still has both his balls. Now, I'm taking a collection to pay for the damage you've done to this nice family's home."

Don was pleased with the amount they contributed and placed an envelope in the tack room. He wrote a short note. "They're sorry for what they did."

Don tended to one last detail, slipped off his gloves, and left the barn laughing. "I crack me up."

He heard sirens long before red and blue strobe lights bedazzled the night. Two Thurston County patrol cars tore up the driveway. From the hawthorn, Don watched deputies search the property. While they were busy, a car sporting a television station's emblem pulled alongside a squad car. A third cruiser arrived shortly after.

"Saying *shots-fired* does get their attention. And technically shots were fired, just not the usual kind. I'd go with Level-Alpha tonight. All objectives met – no casualties, at least among the good guys." Don disappeared into the night.

Chapter 3

Don watched Kelly Swann, KMML's South Sound reporter, describe the situation. "I'm at the Hansen ranch, fifteen miles south of Olympia, the morning after a burglary was stopped here. Last night, sheriff's cars and a moving van next to a pile of tools confirmed the anonymous tip I got about a burglary in progress. Police are still not sure how five armed men were literally caught with their pants down."

Swann's video tape of last night's action showed sheriff deputies cautiously searching in and around a rural house and garage. Noise from the barn caught their attention, and several officers, weapons drawn, entered the structure. A few minutes later, light from the camera illuminated a parade of men staggering from the barn under the watchful eyes of the deputies. The first four wore underwear and handcuffs. The fifth held a horse blanket around his waist. Kelly postulated he'd come commando style.

The live feed returned. "This burglary went terribly wrong for the burglars. The sheriff's office won't speculate on how they were captured other than to say someone with exceptional skill turned the tables on five able-bodied criminals. Blood-soaked bandages found in the barn indicate the man who interrupted the robbery may have been seriously injured. Finally, information recovered here is expected to solve several other recent crimes."

Don's cell phone rang. He turned off the news.

"So you finally put Operation Death Wish in motion." Justin Clarke was on the line. "I thought you were blowing smoke when you said you were going to go all Charles Bronson out there. Even stations here in

Syracuse picked up the story. *Naked thieves meet their match in Washington State*. How badly were you hurt?"

"Justin, you old war horse, good to hear from you. I'm well. No injuries. The blood was ketchup. I'm surprised they're playing it up so much."

"The good guys won for a change." Justin was pleased with his friend. "I assume the information they recovered was left by you? Did you have much trouble getting it out of them?"

"Not after I tossed the first guy's left nut on the ground. You should've seen their faces." Don enjoyed recounting the adventure. "After that, it got easier and easier. I had to shut the last guy up or I'd still be there. I've got tons of intel but haven't sorted through it yet. One name keeps coming up though: Bryce Williams. He's a local barber, seems to be at crime-central, at least for these guys. I could use your help. Up for a trip to the Pacific Northwest?"

"You know me. Ride to the sound of gunfire." Justin paused. "Oh, that's right, your gun goes *poof* now instead of *bang*. You holding a toy doesn't project that same John Wayne image I have of you."

"It's not a toy. It's a high-powered air-rifle. I'll send you a ticket?" A smile crept across the major's face. "Will Margie be upset with you leaving on such short notice?"

"No. She's at her mom's in Florida, and she may bring the old bat back to live with us. If she does, I'm moving in with you. The Pacific Northwest should be far enough away from the bloodsucker. How soon do you want me?"

"Next couple of days would be great. I've a lot of surveillance to do and intel to gather." Don pumped his fist, delighted his friend would join him. "I'm not sure how to approach this next step. We'll have to chat."

Chapter 4

Saturday evening outside of session was an especially odd day and time for a state senator to be in his office. The capitol was empty except for cleaning crews. Senator Samuel Bernard waited impatiently for information that would ruin his career and send him to prison. The phone rang at six-thirty. Andrei was punctual. The senator pushed the intercom, informing security his appointment was at the service entrance.

Andrei Clemmens signed the log. The name of the interior design company he scrawled on the registration sheet was indecipherable. He told the officer he knew the way and didn't want or need an escort. The elevator deposited him on the fourth floor. Most financial decisions for the State of

Washington were made on this floor; many of them in Senator Bernard's office. The senator stood in the hallway.

"Good evening, Andrei. Do you have good news for me?" Bernard led his *interior designer* into the office.

"No sir, I don't." Andrei came right to the point. "Crane's looking into the North-South Interchange and the Delvion Bridge projects. It won't be long before he moves past the overviews and gets into the details. If he keeps pushing, he'll have all the puzzle pieces before long. Then it's only a matter of time before he puts them together, leading him and the state patrol to this office."

"We should consider the alternatives." The senator grimaced.

"All of them, Senator?" Andrei asked, hopefully.

"Unfortunately, yes. If we can't stop him, we'll bury him."

"I'm glad you agree with Apakoh. Say the word, and Crane's investigation halts."

"I hope I can redirect him. He's a nice guy and has helped me many times deal with those idiots in the House. Let's get out of here." The senator ended the conversation about terminating Crane. He'd put that decision off for as long as he could, maybe until after the holidays. It all depended on how fast the analyst collected evidence about the senator's role in a well-orchestrated cash-extraction scheme. The senator counted on Brian's pride preventing him from bringing in the state patrol until he had everything figured out; until it was too late.

"Andrei, let me walk you to your car."

Chapter 5

Apakoh was the name members of Spokane's Bratva had given to their leader, Taras Revoldi. For appearance sake, Revoldi owned a small construction company in Spokane. His primary job was running the Russian criminal organization operating well below the radar in eastern Washington. The Dragon had learned how to govern such an organization from his mentors in Pskov. Their first rule was to stay out of day-to-day activities. Tonight, Revoldi was purposefully breaking that rule.

Anton Breshnon had betrayed Apakoh and the Bratva. Drugs, gambling, a woman, something had enticed the highly trusted man to steal from the organization; an incredibly stupid thing to do. Revoldi took a month to identify him as the thief and calculate the amount he'd taken. The theft angered him, but Anton's efforts to protect himself provoked the Dragon's rage. Apakoh would personally extract his due. The night of torment began.

"Anton, you disappoint me." Revoldi surveyed the man tied to a chair in the middle of a dimly lit warehouse.

"Apakoh, I didn't do anything."

"Don't call me that. You've lost that right." Revoldi's voice was deceivingly calm. "And don't lie. Lying makes this worse."

"I needed money and didn't have any way to get it." Anton's head bowed.

"You didn't come to me." The Dragon circled. Levi and Dimitri remained in the shadows.

"I was ashamed. You'd want to know why I needed it."

"I do want to know why you stole over a hundred thousand dollars from me. What were you going to do with it?" Revoldi slammed his hand into a locker, sending a shockwave across the empty room and a shiver down the captive's back.

"I was being blackmailed. A hooker was going to the cops if I didn't pay her."

The Dragon turned towards Anton. "To tell them what? What does she know?"

"She knows about the money we take from restaurants."

"How does she know?" The Dragon hovered over Anton.

"One night, we were having a good time, and it got late. So I took her on a collection run."

"You idiot! You took a prostitute with you." Revoldi was stunned at the man's miscalculation. "Does this hooker have a name? Is she one of ours?"

"Charlene." Breshnon stammer. "I don't trust our girls. I found her on the internet."

"Where is she?" Disbelief was etched in the Dragon's face.

"At the Winslow Motel, room 117."

"Levi, get Charlene." Apakoh turned to the man strapped to the chair. "Does she have the money?"

"No. I was waiting until I had it all. It's under the spare tire in my car."

"Dimitri, get the money. Count it when you get back."

The door closed behind Dimitri, leaving the Dragon alone with the terrified man. "Anton, you were stupid. This whore would bleed you, bleed us, for years. You should've come to me. I would've shown you how to deal with blackmailers."

A few minutes later Dimitri appeared with a stack of bills. He reported all the money was there.

"You didn't lie. That's good." Revoldi sat alongside Breshnon. "Soon Levi will be back with your whore. Then we'll continue."

"Don't hurt her. Do what you will with me, but leave her alone."

13

"Anton, you didn't fall for this woman, did you?" Revoldi was incredulous.

The room fell silent. Anton remained secured to the chair, his wrists bleeding from zip-ties cutting into his flesh. The Dragon paced, waiting for Levi and the whore. The gate-alarm announced their arrival. The warehouse's personnel-door opened, and Levi shoved a woman into the room. She was wearing next to nothing. Revoldi stared at her. "Anton, you have excellent taste. I assume from her lack of clothes she was entertaining someone?"

"She was," Levi answered. "He pissed his pants and ran home."

Revoldi grabbed the woman's arms. "Did you think you could extort money from the Bratva?"

She looked the Dragon straight in the eyes. "I don't have a fucking clue what you're talking about. I don't steal money. I earn it. I'm not proud about how I earn it, but it's what I do. Who the hell is Bratva? What the hell did you tell them, Anton?"

"I told them…" Anton began.

Revoldi cut the small man off. "You want money for your silence."

"Silence? Silence about what?" Charlene flipped her hair behind her head. "That he can't get it up unless I talk dirty?"

Dimitri snickered, drawing a disapproving glance from Revoldi.

"Silence about the restaurants."

"I don't know anything about restaurants, and if he told you I do, then he's lying." Levi zip-tied the woman to a chair.

"Anton, Charlene doesn't seem to know about the money you've stolen."

Charlene's eyes again met Revoldi's. "What are you talking about?"

"Either you are very clever or Anton's lied about why he wanted over one-hundred thousand dollars." The Dragon walked between the couple.

"I got it for her," Anton stammered. "So she'd keep quiet."

"That's not what I see in her eyes." Revoldi turned from the woman. "Dimitri, bring me the money. Levi, get our guest something to wear."

Levi draped a coat over Charlene's shoulders and bunched it around her knees. The Dragon took three bundles of money to the woman. "Here's twenty-five thousand dollars. Will it keep you quiet, Charlene?"

"Depends on what I know and who's asking."

The Dragon laughed. "Excellent answer. I like brashness in the face of death. Will it keep you quiet if someone asks you what happened to Breshnon?"

"Who's Breshnon?"

Pointing to the man tied to the chair. "Your lover and my thief is Anton Breshnon, and he's about to die. Will twenty-five thousand dollars keep you quiet?"

"If I can walk out of here, I'll forget everything." Fear showed brightly in Charlene's face.

"I don't want you to forget *anything* that happens tonight. I want you to remember every detail so you know what we'll do to you." Revoldi circled behind Charlene and grasped her shoulders hard.

Wincing from pain, she replied, "I get it. I'll take the money and shut up."

"Good. Dimitri, get the pipes."

Anton strained against his ties. "No, Apakoh. I took the money to protect the Bratva, to protect you. She's a liar. Don't kill me for stealing a few dollars."

"We're going to beat you for taking the money, Anton. I'm going to kill you for trying to sell us out to the police."

"I wouldn't do that, never. I promise. Whoever told you I would, lied."

"My source wouldn't lie. He has nothing to gain. Anton, you approached the wrong cop." Revoldi picked up a four-foot pipe. "Charlene, watch closely to what happens to someone who betrays me. You never want to be in Anton's chair."

With that, Apakoh brought the pipe through a long arc into Anton's left arm, pulverizing the man's ulna and radius. Anton screamed and passed out. Dimitri poured water over him. When Breshnon came around, Levi lifted his pipe, but the Dragon held him off. "Anton must experience the pain of each blow. Let him realize the horrible price he's paying."

Tears ran down Breshnon's face. Revoldi signaled Levi. The downward force of the second blow drove Anton into his chair. The snap of the collar bone reverberated across the room. Breshnon blacked out again. A bucket of water woke him to immeasurable pain. Charlene looked on in terror.

Over the next hour, every bone in Anton's extremities was shattered. Each blow directed by the Dragon to cause maximum damage and inflict the greatest pain. Apakoh delivered the final blow to Anton's neck.

Revoldi cut Charlene's ties. "You have your life, twenty-five thousand dollars, and a job. You work for the Bratva now. Will anyone care if you disappear?"

"No," Charlene said matter-of-factly, sadly.

"Levi, clean out her room. Toss her old life into a dumpster." Apakoh put his arms around Bratva's newest asset. "Tonight you start a new life. Do I need to show you Anton again? To remind you not to say anything?"

"No. I'm good."

"Levi, take Charlene to the apartment." The Dragon surveyed Anton's battered corpse. "Dimitri, we need to dispose of this pile of *nomet*, this pile of dung."

"The river's running strong, Apakoh."

"Load him while I tell Zoya I'll be late for dinner with Monsignor Bartosz. She will not be pleased."

Levi escorted Charlene to the car and drove off. Dimitri tossed Anton's body, rope, and five cinderblocks into the company's van. An hour later, Charlene was in red-flannel pajamas eating a pizza she'd found in the apartment's freezer. She didn't offer any to the Russian goon watching her. Thirty-miles south, Anton's body was under fifty-feet of water.

The Dragon drove home, not convinced Anton had lied or Charlene had been truthful, but he was sure Anton intended to talk to the police, and Charlene would be far more useful than the snitch. When he arrived home, he kissed his wife, made his apologies for being detained at work, and shook Monsignor Bartosz's hand, certain Zoya had already doubled his pledge for the new rectory.

Chapter 6

The title on the door read *Capital Budget Committee - Brian Crane – Chief of Staff.* Crane attained his rank through hard work, tenacity, and brilliantly honest assessments of budget requests. The upcoming session would be his third as chief, and it promised to be more contentious than the previous two combined. Revenue was down and demand for services up, the perfect budget storm. Senator Bernard, the committee's chair, expected him to separate *the wheat from the chaff;* meaning agency heads, lobbyists, and more than a few legislators would hate Crane even more than they already did.

Andrei arranged for Bernard to meet with Crane from noon to one. He'd use the hour to search Crane's office, see how deep the analyst's inquiries had gotten, and determine if Revoldi's name appeared anywhere. At 11:50, Brian answered his phone and hustled out of the building.

The Russian walked past the vacant reception desk into Crane's office. He turned on the computer and quickly by-passed its security measures. Andrei found nothing regarding the contracts, concluding Crane was working the analysis on his home computer. He was disappointed but not surprised. Everything he'd heard about Crane led him to believe the man was committed and not easily deterred. He spent a few minutes sifting through paper strewn around the office but found nothing of interest. He'd visit Brian's home later in the week.

Once outside, he dialed the senator's private line. Bernard's cell phone rang, interrupting Brian's presentation. Instead of taking the call, the senator signaled Brian to continue. Crane was surprised and pleased his report on park funding trumped a personal call to one of the most powerful senators in state history. Bernard tried to appear interested in the drivel coming from his chief of staff's mouth.

Chapter 7

Harry, the thief with an affinity for avoiding underwear, told Don the path from Evergreen College's library to the main parking lot was ideal for mugging someone. A man named Dwayne was planning such a robbery for this week. On Monday, Don confirmed Harry's assessment of the path but concluded it'd take two people: one to stand watch while the other subdued the victim. Dwayne would have an accomplice.

Tuesday, Don wandered among the library's stacks and watched the flow of people. At dusk, he left the building and strolled down the path towards the parking lot. When he was sure no one could see, he disappeared into the underbrush. The evening passed without incident. Don went home disappointed but still convinced Harry had told the truth about an imminent robbery. Holding a hammer over a man's scrotum usually elicits the truth.

Don returned Wednesday, wearing a black, all-weather hoody. He loitered at a kiosk reading ads for roommates and books for sale. When the path was empty, he moved quickly, concealing himself in the spot offering the best view. He waited in Washington's torrential drizzle for someone to set up an ambush.

At seven, two young men approached from the parking lot. Nothing they did concerned a passing security officer, but to Don they were suspicious, moving their heads from side-to-side, scanning for opportunity and opposition. They passed Don, unaware of his presence. Neither spoke, unusual behavior for friends, even acquaintances, walking to a library. They entered the building, ostensibly to find their victim. If this was Dwayne and his associate, they'd be back soon. And they were. This time their pace was quick but deliberate. They'd spotted their prey, probably a woman, noting something to identify her in the near darkness. They entered the tree-lined path. Immediately, one eased into the bushes. The other walked fifty yards to the edge of the parking lot and lit a cigarette. He read the ads Don had scanned hours before.

The trap being set quickened Don's pulse, but he had to wait until they did something. If he intervened prematurely, he'd be charged with assault. He was counting his heartbeats when a chirp came from the library-end of the path. A confirming whistle replied from his right. Don watched a young woman walk by the man in the bushes. Judging from the light in her hand, she was busy with an electronic device. Don understood why they'd picked her. She was slender, almost skinny, tall, and distracted. She couldn't protect herself from an elf. The trailer slipped in behind her.

After the small parade passed, Don stepped out, tapped the stalker on the shoulder, and punched him, immediately silencing him. Don fell into place behind the girl. She didn't notice the change in companions, so the man waiting to ambush her didn't have a clue his plan had gone to shit. When she rounded the corner, the lead man stepped out, threatening, and to the point.

"Hey babe, you're being robbed. Hand over your purse, jewelry, and phone. Otherwise, my partner's going to hurt you, and we'll still end up with your stuff."

Don spoke on cue, "Sorry pal, your partner's pretty much unconscious."

The man, startled by the intimidating voice coming from the dark, turned to run. The woman sprang. With a gymnast's agility, she wrapped her arms around his neck and rode him to the ground. She put one of his arms behind his back and pulled hard. "Stay down asshole. Give me a reason to break off this arm and beat you with it. And you're under arrest."

Don was taken aback. The woman he was rescuing turned out to be Rambo.

"Mister? Round up that other turd and bring him here. There's an extra pair of cuffs in my purse."

"Sure," was all Don could muster. He pulled out the handcuffs and found the man he'd disabled. The punk wasn't able to stand, much less walk. Don tossed him over his shoulder and carted him to the kiosk. The officer had secured her attacker and was calling for backup when Don arrived. "Where do you want him?"

"Over there by the post." The cop shook her head. "What the hell did you use on him, a sledgehammer?"

"My fist. He wasn't expecting it I guess."

She checked the man. "He's alive. That's good. He was in the bushes on my left, but I don't remember seeing you in there. Did you follow me out of the library?"

"No. I was in the bushes. You both walked by me."

"You're good. What are you doing here? Waiting your turn to assault someone?"

Don stepped back into the shadows. "I was taking a whiz when I saw him sneak up behind you."

"Right, and my name is Helen Keller. You a cop? Security?"

"No, just a guy passing by, Helen." Don liked this woman. She was a wiseass.

"I'm going to need your statement. By the way, what's your name?"

"Bart. Bart Simpson." Don chuckled, thinking he was being rather cute.

18

"Just what I need, a comedian. Come here and give me your ID."

"I can't do that. I'm late for dinner, and Homer's going to be pissed if I don't show up soon. Have a nice evening. By the way, you're good at close-quarters combat. Glad you're one of the good guys. Um, good gals? Good women?"

"The first rule of getting out of a hole, Bart, is to quit digging." The cop approached Don. "Best you button up before you reach China. Let's see some ID."

"You'll have to take my word for it, ma'am. Gotta run."

"Ma'am? Did you just fucking call me *ma'am*?" the officer asked, more than a little irritated.

"No offense, but we weren't formally introduced." Looking at the two men, Don asked, "Which one of you is Dwayne?"

The man who'd lost his ability to speak pointed to the other.

"Harry sends his regards." Don walked towards the library.

The cop couldn't follow. She had two criminals, one apparently named Dwayne, to keep track of until help arrived.

Don ditched the path soon after he rounded the corner and waited until the police and their prisoners left to return to his car. Helen was an interesting woman. He hadn't seen her all that well, but she seemed attractive, definitely a wiseass. He wished he'd gotten her real name, but neither of them seemed inclined to share that tonight.

When Detective Linder briefed her sergeant, she couldn't recall much about the man who'd helped her. He was white, but otherwise not much stuck. He'd stayed far away and in the worst light possible; hidden in plain sight.

It was only by chance Patti had been at the library and, by even greater coincidence, she spotted the thieves' *tells* as they canvassed the tables and stacks for a victim. Well trained at undercover work, spotting criminals had become second nature. She made herself the ideal target: ditsy, distracted, and burdened with too many bags and books. When she left the building, she flashed her badge and directed the librarians to slow anyone who wanted to leave, putting her alone in harm's way with two determined predators. She preferred that than having the men find someone who truly couldn't defend herself.

While she was sure she could've taken both would-be robbers, she appreciated Bart's help. She liked his Joe Friday approach, except for the *ma'am* comment. He could've left that out altogether. She filled out the report and wondered if she'd meet him again.

Don was home wondering the same thing about her.

Chapter 8

Morning broke as many do in western Washington with heavy mist covering the landscape. Pre-dawn hours were Don's favorite part of the day. Today they'd be spent gleaning more from the Hansen tapes. A little discouraged at not getting the cop's name, he wondered if the newspaper had a story about his exploits. He spotted the *Olympian* halfway down the driveway, put on his sneakers, and fetched the paper. His neighbor was doing the same.

"Morning Brian. Looks like a few more days of rain." Don picked up the plastic-sheathed newspaper.

"Only two-hundred fifty more before we have our three days of summer. What've you been up to? Haven't seen you around." Brian got back to his porch first.

"I tried exercising in the evening, long walks and running. Didn't enjoy it much." Don extracted the paper from its shroud. "Aren't you seeing Deirdre anymore?"

"Yes, but she's been busy, something about work. I stopped listening after she said she wasn't coming over this weekend. I guess I was being insensitive."

Don laughed. "Nope, just being a guy. I'm sure the ladies tune us out even faster."

"You're right about that. Got to run." Brian went inside.

Don retreated to his house, wetter than he planned, but it was always nice talking with Brian. The paper's local section provided the information Don wanted. An article described how *two would-be muggers were stopped by the decisive action of Detective Patti Linder.*

Don wondered if Detective Patti Linder was married.

With coffee in hand, he watched Brian's car clear the driveway and head north towards the capitol. A black SUV approached from that direction moving slowly towards him. In Iraq, someone driving this purposefully would bring out weapons. Don looked, but the driver was hidden behind heavily tinted windows. The car passed, turned right at the corner, and disappeared. On the way upstairs to put on his sweats, Don shook his head. "Apparently, crime-fighting makes you paranoid."

Ten minutes later, dressed in an *Army* emblazoned running suit, Don glanced out his staircase's cubby-window into Brian's living room. A man was rummaging through papers on his neighbor's coffee table. Before Don could focus, the man moved out of sight. Don waited, looking intently into Brian's house. The man, dressed in black, reappeared, crossed the floor, stopped at a credenza, and opened its drawers. Brian hadn't mentioned a guest.

Don wasn't sure what to do. If he called the cops and the guy was Brian's brother or an old friend, everyone, especially Don, would be embarrassed. The best course of action was to determine if the guy belonged in the house. When Don saw Brian's backdoor open, something his ultra-energy-conserving neighbor would never allow, he knew a burglary was in progress. He dialed 911.

"This is Don Rowland at 2513 Noble Drive. My neighbor's house has been broken into, and the thief's still there. That's right, a break-in. One man as far as I can tell. The address is 2511 Noble Drive. Right, I'll wait here."

Don hung up with no intention of abiding by his commitment to the dispatcher. He went out his front door to search for the black car with tinted windows. When he got to the sidewalk he stretched, making sure if the intruder was watching, he'd assume Don was going jogging. Don's route followed the SUV's path. After two right turns he came across three similar looking black cars parked on the street behind Brian's house. *Clever*, he thought, *hide it in plain sight*. In the distance, Don heard sirens. Olympia's finest were on their way and letting everybody know it. *Idiots! Why not just call ahead and tell him you're coming by to pick him up?*

Halfway up the street, the man in black emerged from a driveway. He moved quickly, not running but walking at an ever-increasing pace. Picking up speed, he developed a noticeable limp. When he saw Don, he broke into a sprint, disappearing down an alley. With seventy-five yards between them, Don gave up the futile chase and jogged back to his house. He met the first officer on the scene and explained what had happened. When they returned to check out the cars, Don wasn't surprised to find one of them missing.

"The bastard doubled back and got his car. He had to move it or we'd have had him. Damn!" Don was upset. "The guy has balls and brains."

Don found Brian's business card and called him. A short while later, Brian, Don, and a patrolman walked through the house. Brian found nothing out of place much less missing. The officer said that was highly unusual. If Don hadn't seen the intruder, there'd have been no evidence anyone had been in the house. The police report showed a botched burglary, but Don suspected the man was looking for something, not stealing something. He didn't want to worry Brian and, without proof, kept his suspicions to himself. Brian locked up and went back to work.

Don settled in to review the Hansen tapes and realized he was disappointed Detective Linder hadn't been among the responders. It surprised him. He was smitten with a woman he'd met fighting crime. That he hadn't expected.

❖

Andrei, now across town, was angry. He'd been spotted, and, worse, his search had been interrupted well before it was done. What he'd seen made him certain Crane was farther along in his investigation than Bernard thought. The North-South Interchange's contract on Crane's kitchen table indicated the analyst was getting into the details. But there were several other unrelated contracts on the table, and it could've been a coincidence. Andrei called Revoldi to report the day's events. He noted a neighbor, a quidnunc, had prevented a complete search, but if he went back, he'd make sure the army-guy wouldn't interfere again.

Chapter 9

Five hours later, Don approached the airport to pick up his friend. He hated the name *Sea-Tac International*. It had no pizazz. Jimi Hendrix International would've been much more to his liking. While the airport's designers failed miserably at naming the facility, they excelled in making it navigable. Don easily found Justin standing under the United Airways baggage claim sign in a bright pink polo shirt. Don got out of the car. "Nice shirt."

"I'm in touch with my feminine side." Justin embraced his friend.

"Too much information, way too much. How does it feel to be an ex-Marine?" Don set the bait.

Clarke took it hook, line, and sinker. "There are no ex-Marines, except for that bastard Lee Harvey Oswald and a couple of other assholes we've kicked out. I'm a very happily *retired* Marine."

Don tossed Justin's duffle bag into the backseat. "That all the luggage you got? You better have plenty of undies because you aren't borrowing mine."

"They'd be too small in that all important area."

"Get in before you start comparing private parts out here in the street. It's good to see you." Don started the car and waved at the approaching airport cop. "Hungry? We can stop at Jack in the Box."

"You always did go top drawer, and apparently money's still no object?"

Don pulled into traffic. "I never said I was buying."

"Right, I fly three thousand miles to help, and you can't spring for burgers and fries." Justin felt at home. "Just like the old days. Marines save the grunts, and what thanks do we get?"

"All the thanks you deserve. Shut up and fasten your seat belt."

Twenty minutes later, Don stopped in front of the *Blue Mist Bistro*. Its storefront location belied the sensational dining experience waiting behind its doors.

"Whoa there, partner." Justin unbuckled his seatbelt. "You better have some serious shekels if we're eating here. The guy next to me raved about this place all the way from Chicago."

"If I run out of money, I'll use my good looks." They entered the dimly lit restaurant. "Booth or bar?"

They savored Argentinian steaks and Idaho baked potatoes and talked about their lives. Both were doing well. Civilian life wasn't bad, but it lacked the rigors of training and the adrenaline rush of combat. Don wanted to share details about his vigilante work, but the open-air restaurant wasn't the place.

The Ranger saw the surprise in his buddy's face when he mentioned he might have a crush on Detective Linder, a woman he'd barely met. Justin asked the standard questions: was she married, was she good looking, could she shoot straight? Don couldn't answer any of them. "She's a smartass and can hold her own in a fight."

Getting into the Jeep, Justin thanked his pal for the meal, then asked, "How do you plan on using a forward observer out here in the Evergreen State?"

"I don't need an FO. I need you to bug a barbershop. How long do I have you?"

"Margie says I can stay a week."

"She has you on a short leash, lad." Don headed south with his reinforcement.

"You should try it sometime, Major. The benefits definitely outweigh the costs."

Chapter 10

Revoldi grew up in Pskov, a city four-hundred miles northwest of Moscow. He joined the Bratva with high aspirations and the skills to achieve them, but competition became deadly after the collapse of the USSR. He heard Spokane Washington welcomed Russian immigrants, and by the time he was ready to move there, the eastern Washington city had eight thousand people of Russian descent. Revoldi brought his Bratva forged dreams and methods to Washington State.

Taras met Zoya shortly after she arrived from Chernobyl, a small town northeast of Kiev in the Ukraine. He was thirty, and she was in her twenties. They fell in love, married, and soon had a daughter. Zoya named their bundle of joy Lara, after *Dr. Zhivago's* lover. Lara was a talented, beautiful child who quickly acquired the character's headstrong manner. If Lara wanted something, she was relentless. She learned early to pit mother against father. Taras referred to her as his little Stalin. Maria, the couple's second child, was Lara's polar opposite. While equally captivating, she used a smile and guile to get what she wanted.

The Revoldis were constantly challenged by their daughters, especially when encouraging them to embrace Russian culture. However, both girls readily adopted American customs, often to their parents' dismay. Today the girls were celebrating Halloween, the most vexing of all American traditions. Honoring ghosts was counter to their religious beliefs. Having strangers beg at their door was counter to their cultural beliefs. Having their children enthusiastically participating in such nonsense was counter to their parenting beliefs. But years ago, the girls convinced them to set aside their objections and accept, if not embrace, Halloween.

Zoya's current dilemma had nothing to do with Halloween. It had everything to do with her daughter wanting to spend a ski-weekend with a boy. Exasperated by Lara's unwillingness to see why she was reluctant to let her go, Zoya sent her child to Taras with the familiar admonition, "If your father allows it, I'll allow it."

Revoldi began where Zoya left off. "Lara, we don't know this boy. He isn't from one of our families."

"But Dad…"

Taras hated discussions starting with *but Dad*. He'd likely lose this one too.

"Warren's on the basketball team. He's a good student. And he's Catholic."

"Lara, I was on the basketball team. I was an A student. And I'm Catholic, but I'd never let you go out with me. I wasn't good to girls until I met your mother."

"Dad, you're making that up. You don't know anything about basketball, and you never got an A in your life."

"That's not true. I did very well in physical education." Taras flexed his arms.

"They don't even teach that anymore. And all I want to do is go skiing with Warren, not marry him." Lara rubbed her father's shoulders.

"I *know* what Warren wants to do."

"Dad! You're so bad." Lara wrapped her arms around his neck. "Not all men think like you."

"The gay ones might not, but all the others do. When I was twenty-one it was all I thought about." Taras stood, knowing he'd already lost this debate.

"Warren and I are just friends, and we're going to be with a bunch of other people. The girls have their room, and the guys have theirs. Nothing's going to happen. I promise. I could've lied and told you only girls were going."

"You'd never lie to me. Not about important things. And I'd have found out anyway." Taras hugged his daughter. "If I allow this, your mother won't be happy. I'll pay for this decision."

"Mom will be fine. She knows you'll protect me. And I'm twenty years old. I can take care of myself."

"We should meet this Warren." Taras already dreaded his next conversation with Zoya.

"Dad, you're wonderful. I invited him to dinner tomorrow night." Lara kissed him on the forehead. "He's nervous, so you have to be nice to him. I mean really nice, not that Russian *trust me, I'm not going to invade your country* kind of nice, but really nice."

Much of his reluctance dissipated when he saw the joy in Lara's eyes. He no longer had, if he ever did have, any control over his precious daughter. "Tell your mother it is okay with me. Levi will drive you."

"He doesn't have to, Dad. I told Warren you'd let him borrow the BMW." With a smile generated by total victory, she added, "It has a really small backseat, so there won't be any sex there."

She was out the door before Taras could respond. Lara took after him in so many ways, except she was an excellent student and willingly went to Mass every Sunday. He trusted her judgment implicitly.

Revoldi was ready to leave when Levi stepped into the office, already knowing the answer to his question. "How did it go with Lara?"

"As always. I'll have to explain my decision to Zoya. You may be fishing me out of the river tomorrow. Now tell me, did you get our new girl set up at the house?"

"Keeping this Charlene woman alive is a mistake, Apakoh. She is headstrong and not afraid. She will hurt us if she has the chance."

"You may be right. She let Anton suffer without a care. But she knows what we will do to her if she doesn't comply. She saw that firsthand."

"That's true, but I don't trust her."

Levi's mistrust was well placed. Across town, in an apartment overlooking the river, Charlene barked into her phone. "I don't care if you're afraid of the Russians. I've dealt with scarier people. I'll call you when I need you."

Bryce's barbershop, mentioned repeatedly in Hansen's tack room, was in the heart of downtown Olympia, an area struggling for an identity. Young people with tattoos and piercings congregated there. Homeless men and women roamed the streets asking for change; irritating patrons of theaters, art galleries, and restaurants. Business owners demanded the city take back the night from vagrants and panhandlers. The *Olympian's* editorial page called for a cleaner, safer, and more family-friendly downtown. Without a vision, the city stumbled from one plan to another, but the area was improving despite itself. New owners refurbished the restaurant next to the barbershop, and Bryce's business increased immediately.

The barber was young, affable, generous, and involved in the community. He cut the hair of businessmen, attorneys, legislators, state employees, and police officers. And, given what Don learned, he played a pivotal role in Thurston County crime. He didn't organize crime. He facilitated it. A customer mentions being out of town, and Bryce contacts people willing to pay for that information.

Two weeks before the Hansen burglary, Bryce cut Doug Hanson's hair and listened to the proud father talk about his daughter's upcoming opening night. The family would go to the play then to dinner, giving burglars plenty of time to rob them blind. Bryce sold the information to Bert for ten percent of the take which now amounted to nothing.

With Justin's help, Don was confident he'd find out exactly how Bryce's operation worked and who else was involved. He wasn't sure what to do with the barber; shut him down or intervene in the crimes he set in motion. Don would discuss options with Justin at a later time. Tonight, they were doing recon.

Downtown Olympia was perfect for celebrating Halloween. Costumes, some created for the night, others normal street attire, were eye-catching. Justin looked like a homeless veteran, one of many in the area. Passing the barbershop, he noted the minimalist operation: two couches, two chairs, mirrors, high ceilings with hanging lights. He circled around to the alley. The rear of Bryce's shop looked like all the others on the block: a metal door with no windows in a reinforced frame. It'd stand up well against brute force but would give way quickly to a master lock pick. He finished his reconnaissance and headed to the pizza shop.

While Justin spied, Don found a table and ordered a pitcher of locally brewed pilsner. Justin arrived soon after the beer was delivered. Customers nodded their approval of Don feeding a down and out veteran but weren't pleased he was providing alcohol to *such a man*. The place was crowded and loud. Led Zeppelin's *Stairway to Heaven* blared from speakers over the pickup window.

"I won't have any trouble getting in and out, and there are plenty of places to hide bugs. Did you want a web cam?" Justin leaned towards Don to be heard.

"That might be useful, but let's hold off. What're you going to need?"

"I'll put together a list." Justin arranged his utensils. "We should split up the purchases. Buying it all at one place might attract attention. They'd think we're stalking someone."

"They'd be right." Don chuckled.

26

"Yeah, that's even worse. Once we have the stuff, it'll be easy to get it installed." Justin sipped the beer. "What kind of range do you want, a half mile?"

"That should be plenty. I'll set the receiver on the roof across the street. It's easy to get up there. We should test the equipment at my place. It'd suck if we did all the work and then realized some fish-bait, jarhead forgot the batteries."

"Like that's going to happen." Justin pointed to the order-line stretching out the door. "Speaking of fish, did you get us any food?"

"I got the Hawaiian with extra pineapple. Okay?"

"Perfect, but I'm not sure about them calling their pizza *New York Style*."

"Wait and see." Don grinned. "You forward observers…well those of you who didn't get blown up by one side or the other…are so judgmental."

"I'll give you judgmental, mud thumper."

"Pie for Jarhead. Pie for Jarhead." A voice screamed over the loud speaker.

"Wanted to make you feel at home." Don signaled the server.

"Hope you got a large." Justin checked out the pie.

"Shit howdy! A Marine who's hungry when somebody else is footing the bill? That's headline news." Don got napkins, forks, hot peppers, and parmesan cheese.

"Do they have oregano?" Justin asked.

Don returned to the condiment table and brought back a shaker. "Anything else?"

"Nope. Looks like New York style. Smells like New York style."

"Eat the damned thing," Don yelled, trying to be heard over the Doors.

A smile crept across Justin's face. "This is good, Don. We'll come back."

"Good thing it's cheap, or I'd have to sell a kidney to feed you." Don sat up straight when he recognized the woman walking up to the order window. Detective Linder stood fifteen feet from him. He knew it was her but doubted she'd recognize him, certainly not his face. She might remember his voice.

Justin noticed the change in Don's demeanor and looked to his right. "Is that *the* Detective Linder? You gonna introduce yourself?"

"No, and shut the hell up. Wait. Go ahead and talk. Tell me a story. Tell me about Syracuse or the Marines."

Justin understood and accommodated his friend. While he would've loved to force the situation, he knew if the detective recognized Don, there'd be questions with no easy answers. Justin took stock of the female officer. At five-foot-seven, she presented an imposing figure. Shoulder length, blonde hair framed her face. Her smile commanded attention. Justin couldn't make out her eye color but bet on blue. Her figure was masked by a jacket, but from what he could tell, she was built, as the Commodores sang, like a *brick…house*. He pulled his eyes away, and told Don he had excellent taste in women, and, given she was ignoring him, she had excellent taste in men.

For the next few minutes, while the policewoman waited for her food, Justin had a free field of fire. He told Don how lazy Rangers were. How Marines were constantly saving their pitiful asses. How forward observers were the angels of death. Don glared. Justin poured it on.

When the detective left, Don leaned towards his friend. "I'm going to wring your scrawny-ass neck."

"You and whose army? Oh, that's right, you are the army. Bring it. I'll just ask a police officer to intervene. Maybe her. Do you think she's packing?"

Don just shook his head.

Chapter 11

"How was Halloween, Mr. Crane?" the intern asked.

"Absolutely record setting, Ben," Brian answered with a hint of a smile. "Tossed the last *Milky Way* into Batman's pillowcase around nine and called it a night. I was pooped, had a hundred kids."

He walked into his office ready to do what he did best: save the state massive amounts of money by condemning poorly conceived or poorly written legislation to the shredder. Over the years, Brian had displayed a uniquely irritating way of delivering devastating reviews of proposed spending packages at the most inopportune time for their sponsors. His analyses were thorough and his recommendations compelling. His support had become critical, if not essential, to a bill's passage. Lobbyists and agency directors chafed at Brian's influence, complaining *Senator Crane* often held the deciding vote. Responding to their disdain, Brian claimed he was merely safeguarding the integrity of the state's constitution and its legislative process. For the most part, he was being truthful, but occasionally the chair would ask him to adjust his presentation so the committee's vote might be swayed to serve a *higher good*. His willingness to do so galvanized Brian's status with Senator Bernard.

Brian didn't like Senator Bernard, thought him dull and dimwitted, but ten years staffing one of the hill's most powerful committees had trained the chief-of-staff well. Committee chairs, especially the less competent ones, liked to be stroked, deferred to, and, most of all, *kept informed*. Bernard demanded all of these.

Today, Brian was assessing a piece of legislation sponsored by the senator, the same bill his boss had single-handedly killed the previous session. Back then, Bernard stated his committee was caught unaware by the House's *Liquor Sales Privatization* bill and refused hear it. Without a hearing, the committee couldn't recommend the bill, and without the recommendation, the senate wouldn't pass it. Bernard's inaction sent a message; "You fucked up not getting my support first."

The sponsors learned their lesson and worked with Bernard to introduce a revised bill. Before he'd introduce the new piece of legislation and accept their generous campaign contributions, the chair wanted Brian to assess its implications. What he really wanted was Crane's unfettered support. While the senator never put it quite that way, Brian got the message. But to deliver a ringing endorsement, Brian had to be certain the bill was, to some extent, in the state's best interest.

The Liquor Control Board, commissioned to oversee the state's monopoly on liquor distribution and sales, emphatically and actively opposed the House's bill and would likely do the same with Bernard's legislation. Brian felt the Board *doth protest too much*. The revised bill might generate additional state revenue and, therefore be worthy of passage. With the Board's meticulous records of the outflow of booze and the inflow of cash, Brian initiated his research, confident Bernard would be pleased with his results.

While he'd prefer digging into the suspiciously expensive Spokane-area road contracts, this project was important to his chair and, thus, became his priority. He'd devote his daytime job to liquor and his nighttime hobby to roads.

❖

"Hey Don, how about some fishing today? The Chinook are running."

"Justin, we can go to the market. They have all kinds of fish, even squid."

"I want to catch my own. Like to know where it's been." Justin adjusted a dial on the receiver.

"You love steak, but you don't raise cattle in your backyard."

"That's the kind of logic I'd expect from a Ranger. So no fishing, huh?"

"Sorry buddy, we don't have time." Don bit into his sandwich. "We've got to get you into the barbershop and me on the roof. Do you have everything you need?"

"We are good to go. Your bag has the receiver-transmitter. I've dialed it into the bugs' frequency." Clarke put three microphones into a pouch. "The only limitation is range. Fifteen-hundred feet max, or we lose intensity and clarity."

"Sounds a lot like your love life." Don initiated the battle.

Justin was quick to respond, "At least I have a woman. You're here in the Wild West with Patti Oakley, and you don't have the balls to ask her out."

Don took up the gauntlet. "I have plenty of balls, just no intel."

"Okay, I'll leave it alone, but you're burning daylight. Time to get serious."

"Really? Now it's time to get serious because you say it is?"

"One of us has to be the adult. May as well be the Marine, like always."

Chapter 12

That night, Andrei sat in a cold car with two men he didn't know, didn't like, and didn't trust. Voytek, as his parents named him, had always been tough and a loner. Post-cold-war Russia had been a brutally hard place to grow up. He broke his leg when he was five. Without money for a doctor, his father set it but misaligned the knee. As a result, Voytek limped when he walked quickly or ran. Kids mimicked his awkward gait until he smashed a rock into the side of a bully's head. The gush of blood astonished the gang of boys and intrigued Voytek. He came to appreciate, if not like, violence. Voytek enforced his rules: don't make fun of me, don't steal from me, and don't stop me from what I want to do. Those who violated these rules paid dearly, and Voytek's reputation grew to legend in Pskov.

He became a wiry, strong young man, and several Bratva members recognized his potential and enlisted him. By the time he turned twenty, police suspected he'd killed a woman for informing on her abusive husband. Unfortunately for the woman, her husband was a Bratva chief and a friend of Voytek. Unfortunately for Voytek, the woman's uncle was a colonel in the Russian army. A deal was struck to keep Voytek from a gulag. At age twenty-four Voytek accepted Revoldi's invitation to join him in Spokane. After he arrived, he changed his name to Andrei.

Andrei was aloof, not interested in the Bratva community. Many members didn't trust him, but all feared him. For good reason, he excelled at his craft, and Revoldi used him ruthlessly. People, regardless of age or gender, who crossed Revoldi were beaten. Some disappeared. Over time, Revoldi transitioned his business approach from brute force to diplomacy, and he had considerably less need for Andrei's talents. He encouraged his protégé to start his own enforcement-for-hire enterprise; making it abundantly clear, nothing Andrei did was to adversely affect him or the Bratva; an immutable rule.

Tonight found Andrei engaged in one of those contracts. He'd been hired to recover money from and make an example of a man who'd stolen from the White Pines Casino. Mickey Thomlinson had been stealing from the mob for months. The amount was small, worthy of a repayment plan and pink-slip, but Thomlinson had violated the trust of the manager who'd personally vouched for him. He'd stolen from his benefactor shift-after-shift, skimming more and more each week. Mickey became bold enough to employ two lackeys.

The manager contacted Howard Jenkins, an Olympia businessman who specialized in collecting debts and sending messages. Their arrangement was simple: Thomlinson would be allowed to steal thirty-thousand dollars, and Jenkins would pay the casino fifty-cents on the dollar. Once the marker was paid, Jenkins could do as he wished with Thomlinson. The businessman was certain he could extract far more than fifteen-thousand dollars from the dealer and his sister. It was Liz Thomlinson's potential that attracted him. She would do well in his Portland brothel, likely making him four or five times his investment before he let her go.

Thomlinson crossed the thirty-thousand dollar threshold just before Halloween. Jenkins delivered fifteen-thousand dollars in cash to Kevin Harland, and two days later, Andrei waited off Moon Road with the dimwits. Jenkins told him he could do what he wanted with Mickey and the boyfriend, but he was to leave Liz undamaged and willing to work for him. The cell phone on the dashboard rang. Andrei listened, hung up, and tossed it out the window. "Thomlinson's left the casino. In twenty minutes, he'll drive past us. We'll wait until he gets home and then visit him."

Almost to the minute, Mickey's drove by them. They watched the Saturn turn into the cul-de-sac a quarter-mile down the road. Andrei signaled Smith to follow their prey. Thomlinson's mobile home was the only structure in the once promising neighborhood. Smith turned off the headlights and coasted to Mickey's driveway.

Andrei turned to the man in the backseat. "Thomas, make sure Mickey's car won't go anywhere tonight."

The bear of a man took a hunting knife from its sheath and eased into the chilly night. Thomas Welch made quick work of the Saturn's tires.

Andrei surveyed the trailer. "Jeremy, there should be three people inside. Get a read on their locations. Do it quietly."

Smith joined Welch outside the car. A few minutes later, he returned. "It's like you thought, a woman and two men. The guys are in the living room. The woman's in the bedroom watching television."

"Jeremy, that bedroom has an exterior door. Find a way to block it." Andrei got out of the car. "Thomas, it's time."

The two men walked up to the small porch. Andrei knocked on the metal door; a pleasant, non-urgent rap. The porch light came on, and an African-American man opened the door. "What do you want?"

Andrei punched Harvey Campbell in the throat. Harvey slumped to the floor; breathing became his only concern. They entered the living room.

Mickey sat down at the sight of the intruders. "What did you do to Harvey?"

"Harvey will be okay in a few minutes. Call your sister out of her room so we can talk." Andrei sat across from Mickey.

Mickey summoned his courage. "You can't kick the shit out of Harvey and order me around? Get the hell out of my house, or I'll call the sheriff."

Andrei showed Thomlinson his semi-automatic. "This says I can do what I want. There'll be no calling or swearing, and what I did to Harvey was necessary. Everything I do will be done out of necessity. How much I do is up to you. Thomas, collect Liz. Be gentle but firm."

Welch deposited Harvey at Andrei's feet and left for the bedroom.

Andrei's voice was calm; almost soothing. "Mickey, our third associate will join us shortly. Then I'll begin."

"Get your hands off me, asshole," Liz screamed at Welch.

"Then don't try to get away."

"What did you do to Harvey?" Liz slid to her knees and cradled her boyfriend's head in her lap. "Are you okay, babe?"

Harvey coughed and nodded. Liz helped him to the couch. Jeremy entered the trailer and closed the door behind him. Andrei began. "Now that we're all here, I want to know if you have any guns or other weapons in the house."

Liz volunteered, "There's a pistol in the drawer and a shotgun in the hall closet."

Mickey glared at her.

"Good girl, Liz." Andrei stood and patted her on the shoulder. "I knew about them. Wanted to see if you'd be helpful and honest, rare traits these days. Mickey, let's get down to business. Counting the three-hundred dollars you pocketed tonight, you've stolen $32,565. With interest and penalties, you owe $100,000. So if you'll get the cash, we'll be on our way."

"Mickey, what's he talking about?" Liz held a still dazed man in her arms.

The Russian looked from Liz to Mickey. "Mickey's been stealing for months. Not very skillfully, I might add. We let him go to see if he'd stop. Sometimes people take a few bucks then quit while they're ahead. Not often, but it happens. *Management* doesn't want to punish someone who needs medicine or shoes for the kids. Those folks pay us back and get fired. But Mickey's been at it since July."

Mickey realized how much trouble had walked in the door.

Andrei pointed at to Thomlinson. "Mickey, you and I have to deal with a couple of things tonight. First, I want $100,000. Second, I need to know who's working with you and where to find them.

Liz and Harvey wondered what Mickey had gotten them into.

Andrei circled, ending up behind Liz and her boyfriend. "It's not your sister and Harvey. *Management* knows what your partners look like, but nobody knows who they are. Who are they, Mickey?"

"Are you going to hurt them?" Fear oozed from Mickey.

"I'd be lying if I said no. I'll punish them, but they'll be able to walk when I'm done. I can't guarantee you the same fate, but if you cooperate it'll go easier."

Mickey thought for a moment. "Sarah Geld and Charles Coley. He's an old friend. Sarah dates him. They live in Oakville."

"What was the arrangement?" Andrei wrote down the names.

"Sarah has a great body and doesn't mind showing it off. When she was at the table the pit bosses, security guys, and customers watched her instead of me. I figured out a way to slip her extra chips. It was just a few bucks a night. She'd cash out the chips, and we'd split the money. They got half, and I got half."

Andrei lifted Mickey off the couch. "Get the stash from your bathroom, and don't run. If you do, I'll have Thomas break your legs."

The beleaguered man, no longer surprised by what the enforcer knew, went to the cabinet, pulled out a wad of hundred dollar bills, and handed it to Andrei.

"Jeremy, add the three hundred Mickey has in his pocket and count this." Andrei tossed the bills to his associate.

"Three-thousand four-hundred dollars," Jeremy announced.

Andrei was surprised and pleased the little man could count that high. "You're $96,600 short. I'll need that now, Mickey."

"I don't have it. If I had that much money, I wouldn't need to steal." Mickey sat on the couch.

"I assumed that'd be the case. It leaves us with a bit of a dilemma." Andrei hovered. "My boss wants $100,000 or a guaranteed means of getting it. What's your plan?"

"I only stole $32,000. Why do I have to come up with $100,000?"

"Consider the difference my collection fee." Andrei joined Mickey on the couch. "Let's explore options. Your car's worth $10,000. So we're up to $14,000. If I take everything of value from the house, I get another $2,000; $16,000 total. All I need is $84,000 more."

"What about money they have in the bank?" Thomas offered.

Andrei was delighted Welch was paying attention. "An excellent thought. What do you three have in the bank?"

Harvey collected himself. "Why ask us? He took the money."

"True, but you all benefitted. So you're all part of the payback."

"That's not true or fair," Harvey retorted.

Andrei spoke slowly, "We can't prove that either way, Harvey, and, frankly, you can work out the details with Mickey later. What's the figure on bank accounts?"

Another $3,000 was added to the pot.

"Mickey, we are very far away from that $100,000 figure. So what else do you have to offer?" Andrei became very direct. "Give me a plan and your guarantee to follow it, and I'll leave with my associates. Your life returns to normal."

"You've taken everything. There isn't anything left," Mickey pleaded. "I'll work double shifts, and you can keep my pay."

"You have to be kidding. You were fired the minute you walked out of the casino. You don't have a job or a paycheck." Andrei became impatient. "We're looking for a solution and collateral. I'll make you an offer. First, let's settle on $75,000 as the amount you all still owe. Agreed?"

Three heads nodded unsurely.

Andrei looked at Liz. "At a thousand dollars a night, that'd be seventy-five nights."

"Seventy-five nights of what?" Mickey asked.

"Seventy-five nights of Liz's sexual services in Portland." Andrei saw the shock register in the woman's eyes. "We have a house for you, Liz. One we use for these types of arrangements."

"No fucking way, assholes," Liz exclaimed. "I'm not a whore."

"A whore is the last thing we want. We want a good-looking, self-respecting woman to prostitute herself. Men pay well for clean, girl-next-door types. You are enthusiastic, color blind, and feisty. At five or six men a night, at one-hundred dollars a throw, you'd have the debt paid off in no time."

"I'd have to sleep with 750 men."

"Probably not that many different men. Our girls have regulars, same number of events but with fewer guys. And there's higher pay for more, shall we say, exotic services." Andrei stood before Liz. "If we're doing this, we leave tonight, and you'll be back in four months."

"No way. I won't do it. We'll come up with another plan." Liz looked at her brother.

"I'm all ears." Andrei put his hands on Harvey's shoulders. "There's no demand for the guys in Portland. Well maybe some demand, but not nearly enough. We aren't set up for gay sex, and it makes the bosses nervous. They're homophobic. You have two minutes to make me an offer."

The intruders retired to the kitchen. Jeremy found a soda. Thomas kept an eye on the door, and Andrei sat in one of the dining chairs. He hummed the *Jeopardy Show's* theme song. At its conclusion, he returned to the living room. Liz was crying, visibly shaken at what was about to happen. "Do we have an agreement?"

"Yes." She stood, defiantly facing Andrei. "I'll do this, but for $37,000 and thirty-seven nights of hell."

"Nobody's ever had the balls to haggle. I have to hand it to you, girl, you've got guts." Andrei walked over to Mickey and punched him in the face. "That's for your sister's balls. Ms. Thomlinson, you'll spend seventy-five days in our house. To seal our deal, you'll have sex with Thomas and Jeremy before we leave. You can do them together or separately. If they're satisfied, you'll be one of our girls until your brother's debt's paid. If they aren't, then we have a real problem."

Liz cried. Harvey wanted a gun. Mickey looked at his shoes.

"What'll it be, Liz? One or both? We're running out of time."

Thomas beamed. Jeremy was confused.

"I'll take the big ugly one." Liz looked at Welch. "You know the way. I'm going to bathroom to puke."

Thomas ran to the bedroom tossing his shirt on the kitchen counter. Liz stepped into the small bathroom. A few minutes later, she walked down the hall. The bedroom door closed behind her.

The men in the living room were wrapped in their thoughts. Mickey was angry, ashamed, and scared. His broken nose hurt. Harvey wanted to kill Mickey, Andrei, Jeremy, and, especially, the man raping his girlfriend. Andrei considered how much pain he'd levy on Mickey before he left. Jeremy was wondering if he could perform with people listening. A scream shattered their thoughts. Sounds of a struggle came from the bedroom. Thomas exploded through the door, his arm bleeding. Rage spewed from his mouth. "The bitch stabbed me."

Andrei looked into the room. Liz was sprawled on the bed, scissors protruding from her chest. "She had so much potential. You had a brave but foolish sister, Mickey." Andrei shot Harvey in the forehead. The boyfriend died before hitting the carpet.

The Russian put a bullet in Mickey's knee. He screamed and fell to the floor.

"Ask your sister for forgiveness when you see her." Andrei shot him in the other knee. Andrei's third bullet ended Mickey's pain. "Find gasoline, kerosene, anything that'll torch this place."

"Are we in trouble for killing these folks?" Jeremy asked.

Andrei shook his head. "Not unless you mention it to the police."

As Andrei drove away from Thomlinson's funeral pyre, Don and Justin began their work. Don climbed the ladder to the Mottman building's roof and looked into the barbershop. All he could see was the front room, but he didn't need to see anything. The electronics Justin was installing would do the surveillance. Don fit the receiver-transmitter snuggly between an air vent and the rim wall. He flipped the switch, lighting the dials. The unit reported a full battery charge. Since the bugs weren't transmitting, the reception-intensity dial was flat-lined. He wondered if Justin was on schedule. Justin was wondering the same thing. Two drunks were relieving themselves in the alley, delaying his entry into the barbershop.

"What's wrong with the commode in the bar?" Justin muttered. After they left, he picked the lock and went inside. Light sneaking under the door to the shop broke the storeroom's intense darkness. He switched on his headlamp and emptied the grocery bag that served as part of his costume and his toolbox. He turned off his lamp and opened the door to the front room. Streetlights illuminated the room. He put the first bug in the fold of the couch's armrest and the other under the counter near the barber chair. He secured the last bug to the underside of the parts chair in the backroom. Everything was ready. He stepped into the alley, locking the door behind him.

"We're in the eavesdropping business." Don nudged Justin.

"In business to put Bryce out of business," Justin added.

Chapter 13

Patti held the wood-framed photograph of her father at arm's length. He was smiling, something he rarely did when a camera was around. Her mother found the picture while searching for one to accompany Paul's obituary. Patti's mind drifted back to the scene captured in the black and white photo. Headstrong and determined, Patti convinced her dad to take four teenagers back-country camping on Mount Rainier. They had had a wonderful time hiking through old-growth forests, climbing steep rock faces, and swimming in unimaginably cold lakes.

The photo of the tall, husky man with four girls was taken by a park ranger who came upon them while patrolling the alpine campsites. Patti and her father got to know Steven Kubic over the years and frequently met him on the mountain. Ranger Kubic joined them on their last trip into the wild; ten months before cancer stole Paul's life. Patti remembered hugging the uniformed teddy bear after her father's casket was lowered into the ground. They both cried.

Growing up, Patti was the consummate tomboy, playing baseball and soccer and running track. In grade school, boys wanted Patti on their team. In high school, they wanted to date her, but she'd have none of it. She decided early on she wanted to be a cop, specifically a detective. Boys and men were distractions she kept at bay. She was thirty-six and had had two love affairs of sorts, both ending badly. One boyfriend demanded she move in with him, and the other wanted to move in with her. Neither got his wish. Both were now happily married. Their time with Patti had been a learning experience.

Patti had no regrets and rarely wondered how things might've turned out if she'd been a little less focused. When she did wonder, she couldn't imagine an alternative life that satisfied her as well as the one she had. Everything had been *just fine* until she encountered the guy at Evergreen. Now she found herself thinking about him often. Physically, the figure in the dark attracted her. Attitudinally, he intrigued her. Emotionally, Bart, or whatever his real name was, confounded her. She was more than a little saddened to think she'd never get to know him. The phone rang, shocking her into the moment.

"I'd be glad to help." Patti hung up. "Bill, I've got to go to Rochester. The sheriff wants another set of eyes on a murder or murder-suicide. Want to tag along?"

"Let me think. No!" came a response from the other side of the partition. "You volunteered. I want nothing to do with those woodhooks."

"That's no way to talk about the folks in Rochester." Detective Linder attached the holster to her belt.

"Who said anything about them? I was talking about the deputies."

Patti shook her head. "You're so bad. I'm going to tell them what you said."

"Go ahead. I tell them that every time I see the little bastards."

Patti laughed, got her coat, and headed to the door. "Living the dream."

An hour later, she pulled up to a burned-out mobile home. Deputy Jack Ogden opened her door. "Detective Linder, what brings you out to the boonies? City cops don't get out here very often."

"Sheriff Knutson said you had three barbequed people and could use a little help. Here I am. What do we have?" Patti didn't like Ogden. Nobody on the OPD liked him. He was arrogant, obnoxious, and considered himself a ladies man.

"As you can see, not much. The fire was intense, and the trailer was old. Not a good match. Pun intended."

"Cute." Linder looked over the scene. "How do you know it was a homicide?"

Ogden pointed to a body. "Scissors sticking in that one's chest, dead give-away."

"Jack, you've got to stop with the jokes. It's too early, and they aren't funny. There were three bodies? What about the other two? Signs of violence?"

37

"Hard to say. The fire incinerated them. The medical examiner will earn his pay on these three. Only the first one looks pretty straight-forward. Scissors to the heart usually gets classified a homicide."

"Was the fire set?"

Ogden kicked a charred hot water tank. "These make great rockets when you superheat them. It's hard to tell if it was set. Trailers this old burn like flash paper. If anyone had been alive, they had minutes, maybe seconds, before the place was engulfed. I hope they were dead before this fire got to them."

"I agree. Being burned alive would be the worst." Patti was surprised by his empathy. "The woman was in the bedroom. Where were the other two?"

"In the front of the structure; probably the living room." Ogden walked towards the remnants of the trailer. "I almost lost it when I got here. I've seen a lot of gruesome things, but extra-crispy bodies are the worst. It'll take dental records to figure out who they were. No fingers left on anybody."

"Who was supposed to be here?" Patti caught up to Ogden.

"Mickey and Elizabeth Thomlinson, brother and sister. They owned the place. A neighbor thinks a guy named Harvey might be the third victim. He was the girl's boyfriend. We're checking the casino where Mickey works to see if anyone knows where he is. Chances are, he's right over there." The deputy pointed to two blackened skeletons.

Other than charred appliances, nothing remained above the frame. Firemen were finishing off hot spots sending mud and debris flying. Patti saw something move. "Hold it, guys. I need to get in there."

"It's pretty much out but be careful," Ogden warned her. "I don't want to have to call the ambulance back."

The detective went to the middle of the structure and crouched. At her feet was a badly damaged revolver, its wooden grip burned away. The weapon was cold and wet. No danger of a round going off accidentally. She couldn't open the cylinder latch, so she turned the gun around, pointed it at her head, and looked down the barrel: five spent cartridges in the cylinder. The lab would have to determine if they'd been shot or went off because of the fire.

"Jack, can you bag and tag this? Note that we found it in the kitchen."

Ogden didn't like taking orders, especially from a female who'd repeatedly turned down his advances, but he got a plastic bag from the cruiser and deposited the weapon. Then Ogden, Patti, and two other deputies combed the ruins. Eventually they found the barrel of a shotgun.

"Hey Patti, Jack. Come here." A deputy was standing by the Saturn. The side facing the trailer was blistered, and all four tires were flat.

"What do you have, Dan?" Jack asked.

"The tires were slit. I'm sure the ones on the other side were. It's harder to say about these," the deputy said.

"Somebody didn't want them to leave," Ogden agreed.

"Looks like an inch and a half puncture." Patti pushed her fingers through the slit. "Hunting knife probably. And the guy who did it was strong. Shoved the blade right through the sidewall."

An hour later, the ME removed the bodies, and the sun peeked out from behind the clouds. It was going to be a long day. She'd have to visit the casino and interview people who worked with Mickey Thomlinson. Somebody might know something, and that information would force her to drive to some other godforsaken place in the south county. She thought back to the night she bagged two punks. That was what she was meant for, fighting, hand-to-hand, if necessary. For the next seven hours, she'd be chatting with people who had no love for cops and plenty to hide.

A white SUV with bright red lettering pulled into the cul-de-sac. A very official looking woman got out and walked straight to Patti. "Detective Linder? I'm Deirdre Woods, State Fire Marshal's Office, arson investigator."

"Nice to meet you. You have your hands full with this one. Not much left to the trailer. I mean mobile home." Patti shook the fire-cop's hand.

"You were right with *trailer*. Looks like a pre-1986 singlewide. They burn hot and fast. Lots of people die in these pieces of crap. Can't get out fast enough."

"Looks like three homicides or a murder-suicide. Let me know what you find, okay?" Patti handed Deirdre her card.

"I'll have a preliminary report later today. I'll shoot you a copy when the chief says I can release it. It'll be nice working with a woman."

"I hear that, but most of the guys are okay. Only a few are sexist pigs."

"Especially that one." Deirdre let Patti know Ogden's reputation preceded him.

❖

Andrei was not looking forward to explaining how an easy assignment turned into a cluster-fuck. Not only was Jenkins out thousands of dollars in cash, he'd also lost the service of a very promising young woman. All because an imbecile let a woman assault him with scissors. He entered the sparsely appointed office.

Jenkins greeted him, "Andrei, have a chair."

Andrei sat with his back against the wall in case Jenkins had a surprise for him.

"I understand we had bad luck last night. Ms. Thomlinson's dead, as are Mickey and her boyfriend."

"That's true." Andrei tried to get comfortable. "We encountered an unfortunate set of events."

"I see. It's best I don't know the details. Plausible deniability is always a good thing. How much did you get from Thomlinson before the *unfortunate events?*"

Andrei handed Jenkins an envelope. "There's $3,600. Far less than we expected."

"This is unfortunate." Jenkins put the money on the table.

"As I said, events overwhelmed us."

"Those things happen. I am disappointed, Andrei, not only with the cash, but also with losing Ms. Thomlinson's services."

"I'm prepared to make up the difference any way you see fit."

Jenkins smiled. "This is what I like about you, a man of integrity. You're taking the fall for what I assume was a misstep by one of our associates."

"It's good to work for you. Things should've turned out better." Andrei began to relax.

"Then we agree. You owe me for Mickey's marker and lost revenue from his sister."

Andrei wasn't surprised by Jenkins' lack of humanity. Liz was a commodity. Her forced prostitution would've brought him a specific amount of income. The impact three months in a brothel would've had on her meant nothing.

"You'll forfeit your fee, and you'll cover all expenses." Jenkins circled the room.

"Absolutely." Andrei had anticipated that requirement.

"Did you get the names of Thomlinson's associates?"

Andrei checked his notes. "Sarah Geld and Charles Coley. They live in Oakville, fifteen miles from Thomlinson's house."

"Excellent. They could cover a substantial part of your debt. When you find the woman, convince her to take Liz's place. That'd square part of the loss. We may be all even when you're done with them." Jenkins sat on the edge of his desk. "You need to find them quickly. Do what you want with the guy, but don't fuck up again with the girl. I want her in Portland."

Andrei was somewhat surprised by Jenkins' reasonableness.

"This pittance doesn't help me at all." Jenkins tossed Andrei the envelope. "I have another assignment for you. There's a barber in Olympia who's operating in my world without my permission. You're going to convince him to join my team. He seems to be doing quite well referring clients to our local burglars."

"Does the barber have a name?" Andrei stuffed the money in his jacket.

"Todd." Jenkins smiled, sure the Russian would miss the allusion.

"His first name is Sweeney, and his shop is on Fleet Street?"

Jenkins was surprised and a little irritated. "Most Russians would've missed that connection. His name's Bryce Williams. His shop's on Fourth Avenue."

Andrei sensed Jenkins dissatisfaction with him knowing the play. "I'll get right on this. Is there anything else?"

"I'm sure we'll have more business in the future. I intend to keep you busy."

"One last thing." Andrei stood up. "Are the two *associates* expendable?"

"They're purely muscle for hire. I have plenty more."

"Then I can take care of a couple of loose ends?"

"Absolutely."

In the police station on the other side of town, Detective Linder closed the Thomlinson file. Hours of interviewing Mickey's co-workers had produced little. He was a non-descript kind of guy. He suited and showed up better than most, didn't cause waves, and wasn't connected with anyone. Nobody had anything bad to say about him. Most didn't know where he lived or that he had a sister.

Two co-workers recalled a man asking questions about Mickey a month or so ago. Neither remembered much about the man except he was white, average height, slender, and dark hair. Both said he was *all business*. He had pictures of a man and a woman and asked if they'd been at the casino. The male employee remembered the woman, especially a specific part of her.

If the mystery man had focused exclusively on Thomlinson, he might've been an old buddy or a relative. But his interested in two other people caused Patti to wonder. *Did the mystery man murder Thomlinson? Burn the trailer?* More questions, no answers.

While Patti chased wild geese at the casino, two unauthorized crime fighters were exploring the world of high-tech eavesdropping. Justin settled into his chair. "Let's see what the airwaves brought us."

Don poured his friend a soda and watched him signal the machine on Mottman's roof to transmit. With the computer's acquisition-mode set to maximum, seven hours of information was relayed to Don's computer in three minutes. When the transmission ended, Justin commanded the Mottman machine to return to receiver-mode. Justin engaged filters to eliminate ambient noise and highlight louder, more intense, and possibly more valuable sounds. With the filters working at their optimum, it took fifteen minutes for Justin to pinpoint two events: a fight in the alley and a motorcycle being kick-started.

"You didn't expect more than that, did you?" Justin bit into the cheese toast. "Hey, this is great cheese. Vermont?"

"Burlington's best. The Army knows how to treat its assistants."

"Assistant my ass. Without me, you'd be holding a glass to the wall." Justin took another bite. "I'll need the address. White cheddar's the best."

"Glad you like it. I'll pack some for the road and give you the address. Remind me or I'll forget." Don put the cheese back in the refrigerator.

"Getting old sucks, doesn't it?" Justin loved reminding Don the Ranger was almost a decade older than him. "You're electronics are all set. Got to love surveillance without the risk of getting caught or spending hours in a cold car needing to pee."

"If Patti was there, it might not be so cold."

"You have to grow a pair, or you won't be sharing any time with her." Captain Clarke, retired, grinned. He'd miss Don. It was like old times, except without mortar bursts, tracers, and men screaming for medics or their mothers. They'd gone through hell together. Justin wandered into the past.

He was twenty klics north of Fahlaya, bringing artillery fire down on an Imperial Guard position. Marine command ordered him and his spotter to withdraw, leaving the rest to the Air Force. They were delighted to oblige, got to their rally point, and waited. Jets screamed in and dropped their payloads. A huge shock wave washed over them.

Justin's partner, Jimmy McGlin, pointed out that waiting much longer in the middle of the desert in broad daylight might not be such a good idea. Justin agreed, and they moved south to their backup point, closer to Fahlaya. They hadn't gone far when an Iraqi sniper put a bullet through Jimmy's thigh. After taking cover, Justin tended to the wound joking that a little higher and Jimmy wouldn't need condoms anymore. Pinned down, alone, and with limited ammunition, the Marines called for support but got no response. The dune sheltering them from the sniper also blocked their transmission.

The terrain was barren, giving the sniper a full field of fire. They were stuck until the Iraqi killed them or they killed him. Justin knew sooner or later more Iraqis would arrive and turn the place into a shooting gallery. The sniper was dug in, well protected, and fairly good at his trade. The standoff continued for an hour, until a truckload of Iraqis arrived. Seven soldiers dispersed along the hillside. Justin estimated he and Jimmy had fifteen minutes before they were killed or captured.

Someone on the hill shouted, and bullets plowed sand all around them. Capture was obviously not the Iraqis preferred option. The guys on the hill were pissed off and taking it out on two Americans trapped behind a sand dune. The Marines clung to the earth. Given they hadn't been hit; the small hill provided adequate protection. Adequate as long as the Iraqis didn't move fifty-feet in any direction. During a lull in Iraqi gunfire, Justin stuck his M-16 over the top of the dune and fired several rounds in the general direction of the sniper. He didn't expect to hit anything, just letting the bastards know they were dealing with Marines who intended to fight.

His gesture brought intense return fire.

Jimmy decided to piss them off a little from his side of the berm. He lifted his rifle and pressed the trigger. Almost immediately hell erupted on the hill: explosions, screaming, more explosions, automatic weapons fire, more explosions.

"What the hell did you hit?" Justin asked. "The gas tank? Ammo pack?"

A voice came from the hill, "Hold your fire. Rangers are up here."

"Not Rangers! I'd rather be shot than have those grunts save me." Jimmy laughed.

"Do you need help? Anyone wounded or have their panties in a knot down there?"

"Knock it off, soldier. Get down there and make yourself useful." The Ranger leader ended the taunting.

Justin was grateful, especially for the one giving the orders. He'd never forget the man's voice. When he looked up, there was Don standing on the crest of the hill, bald head glistening, looking a lot like John Wayne. Justin expected to hear, *Well pilgrim, we best get moving.* When Don sauntered down the hill, the image of John Wayne became more vivid.

The Special Ops team had heard gunfire and, like the old west's Seventh Cavalry, rode to its sound. The Iraqis were focused on eradicating the Marines and didn't notice the Rangers until grenades rained down. Most of the Iraqis died in the first few seconds of the Rangers' attack. The others lasted only a few more.

Two large men carried Jimmy to their Humvee hidden a hundred yards behind the sniper's hill. Don kept vigil while his men checked for maps and weapons on the bodies and in the remnants of the truck. The Rangers respected the dead but left nothing, including boots, for the enemy. Bodies were put side-by-side with faces covered. They'd fought well and deserved the dignity afforded a foe that died honorably. Don taught his men even in war respect had its place.

They loaded up and moved out. Justin suspected this exceptionally well-trained squad wasn't a scout team. They were on a specific, probably highly-classified mission, and, for Jimmy and him, they'd been in the right place at the right time. Five Rangers and two Marines headed west, deeper into enemy territory, toward Fahlaya. The mission remained unknown to Justin and Jimmy.

When they got near the town, the major ordered them to dismount. Justin thought of John Wayne in any number of westerns. "Looks like we'll have to fight some bad guys, pilgrim," he muttered under his breath, doing his best Duke impression.

Don wasn't amused. Huddled around the vehicle, in darkness one can only experience in the desert, Don briefed the team on their objective. Ultimately, they were robbing a bank.

McGlin would stay with the Humvee, manning its 50-caliber machine gun to cover their retreat. The other six would advance on the town in pairs, focused on getting into a two-story structure fronting the town's square. The bank was directly across from it. The orders referred to the *depository,* but Don dubbed it *the Last National Bank of Fahlaya.* Fahlaya was a commercial outpost, a stopover for cash on its way to Bagdad. British intelligence determined the bank currently held a substantial amount of money. This team was to confiscate or destroy it. Deprive the enemy of resources, a key wartime tactic.

Don boosted Jimmy into the gunner's seat. A box of ammo was fed into the weapon with two more at Jimmy's feet; more than a thousand rounds.

"You know how to use this weapon?" Don asked.

"Sure do, boss. Learnt me real good stateside." Jimmy tore back the bolt.

"Quit joking around, Marine." Don was very serious. "You and this weapon may be the last things between us and a mass grave."

Jimmy sat up straight. "We'll provide sustained cover fire, sir. You can count on us."

With the machine gun prepped, four Rangers oozed like ink into the night. Justin was amazed how quickly and completely they disappeared. His respect for the Army was growing by the minute. Don tapped his arm. "Let's move out. We'll bring up the rear and make sure nobody slips behind our guys. Stay on my six."

The men rallied at a point directly behind the building Don wanted to make the center of operation. They entered quietly through an unlocked door. Combat knives ready, they checked every room on both floors. Empty, not just unoccupied but completely empty: no chairs, beds, or clothes. Don put two men upstairs. From there, they saw the bank had twenty or more Iraqi soldiers around it. Military intelligence hadn't mentioned a company-sized unit guarding the place. The Iraqis apparently wanted to hold onto the money, enough so that they deployed one-hundred men to safeguard it.

"Use the SAW. Take them out quickly. When you're done, move to the back of this building and cover our exit. Don't worry if some are still alive. We'll finish from downstairs. Hit 'em hard and then move." Don went downstairs.

Facing a massively superior-sized force, Don decided blowing up the money was more feasible than stealing it. He positioned a man at each of the two first-floor windows. They would hold fire until the men upstairs completed their fire mission. Then they'd take out anyone still able to fight. Once done, they'd intercept any Iraqis coming from either side of the bank. When the guards were disposed of, Don would sprint across the courtyard, toss an explosive satchel into the bank, and retreat to the building they occupied. After the explosion, everyone would exit and join the SAW-team.

"Justin, help with cover fire," Don said, more a request than an order.

"How about I tag along? Two of us stand a better chance of getting a grenade into that building than one."

Don thought for a moment, agreed, and handed Justin four grenades.

"Don't ask. I know how to use them."

Don smiled. "Roger that. On my count: one, two, three."

The Squad Automatic Weapon, M249, fires 800 rounds a minute, but for this mission, the gunner selected *sustained-rate*, 100 rounds a minute. The courtyard danced in flashing lights generated by the SAW and an M4. The guards across the street were mowed down. Thirty-seconds after they began, the Rangers left their second-story position, ran out the back, and repositioned the SAW one-hundred feet from the building.

The rangers on the first floor had no targets. They redirected their weapons to the approaches on either side of the building. Still nothing. Don and Justin burst through the door zigzagging towards the bank. Don tossed in a C-4 satchel charge, and Justin added two incendiary grenades. They turned and ran for cover, but the explosion sent them sprawling with chunks of brick landing on and around them. Before the blast was completely spent, they were on their feet, sprinting through the building and out into the desert. They stopped at the SAW team's location. Shortly after, the soldiers from the first floor joined them. Behind them shouts and commands could be heard. It'd take a few minutes for the Iraqis to gather their wits and begin the chase.

The Humvee was a half-mile away. At top speed the team could cover the ground in ten minutes; plenty of time for Iraqis in trucks to catch them. Don ordered everyone to run for two minutes. Then he directed the SAW operator to stop, find a suitable position, and provide cover fire. The rest of the group would continue on and set up a second firing base. After engaging the enemy, the SAW gunner would scurry past the second base and set up a third. The second team would provide cover and then retreat to the Humvee. Once the SAW team arrived, Jimmy would provide cover fire for everyone, a textbook leap-frog maneuver.

It took the Iraqis little time to assess the situation and accurately determine the path the marauders took. Some ran after the night raiders, screaming indiscernible epithets. Others, less willing to join the dead who'd been guarding the bank, waited for support vehicles. Ninety-seconds later, eighty Iraqi soldiers who had lost millions of Saddam Hussein's money started their pursuit of Don's unit. Their only hope of surviving Saddam's wrath was bringing him the heads of the men who'd destroyed the money.

The Iraqis weren't Imperial Guard. They were conscripts pressed into service, poorly equipped, and even more poorly trained. The advance-group running blindly after the Rangers encountered the SAW, this time with its setting on *suppression*. Two hundred rounds brought the twelve pursuers to a quick and painful halt. All but one died or was wounded from the fifteen-second burst. It staggered the pursuit and served notice that the men they were chasing were well equipped and disciplined. As the SAW gunner passed his comrades, he indicated all was well and continued on to establish the third base.

We may get out of this alive after all, Justin remembered thinking.

The second wave of Iraqis, also pursuing on foot, focused their guns and grenades on the now-empty SAW nest. Satisfied it no longer posed a threat, they moved past the bodies of their comrades. They didn't find any dead Americans. Now, they'd have to be more cautious and move more slowly.

Witnessing the pursuit's slowdown, Don whistled, and the men at the second firebase pulled back. When they reached the third base, Don said, "No sense waiting for them. Get back to the vehicle. Justin and I. will stay here. We'll make them think again about following us. After we put lead in their shorts, we'll meet at the Humvee. When you hear gunfire, get ready to pull out. Make sure the 50 is ready for action."

The SAW gunner handed Don his weapon, and four men moved out. Don and Justin scanned the dunes through night-vision goggles. Shapes soon appeared along a fifty-yard arc, illuminated brightly by their sweating bodies. Justin would begin on the left. Don would concentrate on the right, moving his stream of fire towards the center. There was no need to hit every target. Those who weren't hit would seek cover.

"Justin, we'll do a double-tap on this group."

"Roger that."

Double-tap was code for a second burst to be fired a few seconds after finishing the first. Don thought the enemy was aware of his leap-frog tactic; one burst then retreat. To overcome that maneuver, the enemy would duck for cover but immediately rise and continue its chase, believing the opposing gunners were also running to the rear. This approach worked well unless the gunners sprayed the field a second time. The double-tap usually caught overly eager troops in mid-step.

The wave of Iraqis made good progress among the dunes, closing rapidly on Don and Justin's positions. Both Rangers saw the officer in charge driving his men. He'd be their intersecting point.

"Now," Don commanded.

46

Two high-powered weapons began their work. Immediately, bullets from the SAW threw three Iraqis into the air. Justin got two on the right with his M60 before the rest dropped to the ground. A few Iraqis gave ineffective return fire by holding weapons above their heads and pulling the triggers. After five-seconds, the Rangers stopped shooting. As Don expected, the Iraqi commander had figured out his tactic. Believing the Americans to be on the run, he ordered his troops forward.

Justin shot the commander in the chest. Don sprayed the dunes with one long burst, taking out several soldiers. The Iraqis were now leaderless and confused. During the lull, Don heard engines. The Humvee accounted for one, but others were audible. He saw the heat signatures of three vehicles racing towards them. "That's not good. Justin, it's time to vacate the premises."

A minute later, Don and Justin arrived at the Humvee. "We've got motorized company coming fast. Let's get out of here. Pronto."

Before they could move, a truck, similar to the one that brought reinforcements to the sniper, barreled over the closest dune. Judging from muzzle flashes, four men were in the canopied bed. McGlin trained the 50-caliber on the truck and fired. The stream of bullets destroyed the vehicle and everyone in it.

Don nodded his approval, and the Humvee raced into the abyss. He brought Command Center on line. "Beta level success. Too many bogies to bring it to Alpha. Will be home soon."

Don brought Justin back from Iraq. "Hey, are you okay?"

"Just spent a few moments back in the desert." Justin looked at the dials. "The bugs are working perfectly. Anyone chatting in the building is going to get recorded. Doesn't matter where they are or how softly they speak."

"Time to ship you back to Margie." Don was going to miss his friend.

"Better saddle up and get us to the airport, pilgrim. We're burning daylight." Justin imitated the Duke.

"You still don't sound like him at all."

Chapter 14

November Saturdays are reserved for Cougar football around Spokane, and Washington State was having a rough season. Tonight they were at home against UCLA. Las Vegas spotted the Cougs eleven points. Bratva offered twelve, and business was brisk. If Matt Dallet, WSU's quarterback, was as sick as Revoldi expected him to be after he and his family dined at a Bratva protected restaurant, then a thirteen-point loss was inevitable. UCLA scored three first-half touchdowns, two off interceptions thrown by Dallet's backup. The Bruins were marching for a fourth when the doorbell rang. Warren Carlisle was on time. Lara was nervous. Maria was watchful. Lara guided him into the family room.

Zoya, the consummate hostess, greeted Lara's friend, "You must be Warren. I'm Zoya, and this is Lara's father, Taras."

"Thank you for inviting me to dinner." The tall, good look young man handed Mrs. Revoldi a bouquet. Lara beamed. She hadn't mentioned a hostess gift when she prepped him for the evening. Warren's mother had taught him well. He was well-groomed and well-mannered. Maria noted the flowers' impact on her mother.

Mrs. Revoldi was delighted with the gift. "Let me find a vase. See if Warren would like a soda." Zoya trotted off with her husband in tow. "You never bring me flowers, Taras. You could learn a thing from Warren."

"I bring you lots of flowers. He's just trying to get on your good side."

"He's done that." She arranged the flowers in the Waterford vase Taras had given her for Mother's Day; the one American holiday she fully embraced. "Set them on the table so we can enjoy lovely flowers while we eat."

"I'll put them up his..." Taras picked up the vase menacingly.

"Now, now. Give him his due." Zoya enjoyed seeing her husband a bit jealous. An hour later, she called everyone to dinner. The flowers reminded everyone Warren had contributed in a significant, though not appreciated by all, way. Taras said the blessing and cut the roast into thick slabs, offering the first to Lara's guest. Warren declined saying he'd wait until the ladies were served. Even Taras appreciated that gesture. The vegetables were passed, followed by homemade dinner rolls.

Warren gave a brief overview of his family. His father owned a sporting goods store, and his mother was a research librarian for the Spokane Bar Association. He had two younger sisters, and he would attend the University of Washington's law school next fall. Taras refrained from interrogating him further.

Everyone enjoyed the meal. The girls cleared the table while Zoya put the final touches on her dessert. Zoya's Vatrushka was a sweet, bread-like cake. The strawberries were fresh, sliced by Lara to her mother's exacting specifications and soaked in berry juice and honey. The topping was heavy-cream blended with sugar, vanilla, and salt. The results were delectable, an excellent end to a fine meal.

"Taras, help me with the dishes. Maria, watch television in my bedroom. Lara, you and Warren may have the family room."

Taras gathered the last of the dishes and followed his wife into the kitchen. "He had you with the flowers, didn't he?"

"Yes, he did. And you have to admit you like him."

"We've taught our daughter well. She can go skiing with him, but one false move and Levi will cut him to pieces."

"You will not have Levi bother them. Lara can take care of herself. And Warren knows if he wants another piece of my Vatrushka, he'd better take special care of my little girl."

"What do I have to do to get another piece of your Vatrushka?" Taras approached Zoya from the back and grabbed his wife's firm buttocks with both hands, bringing a smile to her face.

"Behave yourself. There're children here. You can have all the dessert you want."

"Maybe it's not Vatrushka I'm talking about," Taras said with a glint in his eye.

"Who said anything about Vatrushka?" she smiled. "I said *dessert*."

Just then Lara spoke up, "You two need to get a room. Dad, we're going to change the channel. UCLA clobbered the Cougs, beat them by thirty points."

Taras was elated. "Tell Warren I have lots of guns and know how to use them. Now I have to get your mother up to our room and your sister into hers."

Lara shook her head. "Parents! Can't live with 'em, can't pay for college without 'em. Oh, by the way, Warren loves guns too, practices all the time. He's teaching me to shoot."

Chapter 15

The loaded 12-gauge, double-barreled shotgun lay across Charlie Coley's lap. The Thomlinson murders had unnerved him, and he flinched at every noise. He called Sarah, "Did you hear what happened? They murdered Mickey and burned down his house."

"Maybe they don't know about us. Mickey might not have told them." Sarah offered some much needed reassurance

"Mickey would give up his mother to save his ass. We need to get the hell out of here." Coley went fishing. "Can we crash at your mom's in Flagstaff?"

"No. She's taking care of my sister's kids." Sarah's voice was cold. "It's been a couple of days, and nobody's bothered us. I think we're okay."

"Mickey knew where I live. They would've been here by now, right?" Coley wanted to believe he was out of danger. "When this is over, can we get back together? I'll stop drinking."

"Your drinking was the least of our problems. We're better off going our separate ways." Sarah ended the call.

The conversation left Charlie depressed. He hoped their separation was temporary. He hoped she'd forget about him sleeping with his neighbor. He'd gotten drunk, and the woman came on to him. It was a perfect storm, intensifying dramatically when Sarah came home early. Now he was paying the price for being stupid. Sarah had left, Mickey was dead, and the money was gone. He was alone and terrified.

The rest of the morning dragged; nobody came, nobody called. The afternoon followed with few prospects on television. Game shows and a golf tournament were Charlie's only choices. The clouds broke around three, and his need for chocolate and beer forced him out the door. He crossed Highway 12 to the convenience store, imagining being shoved into the back of a van, but nothing happened. With a case of cheap beer in the fridge and a bag of cheaper candy by his couch, he chose the golf tournament. At six he pulled out the ingredients for a grilled cheese sandwich with no hope of having it taste as good as the ones Sarah made.

Three miles west, Thomas and Jeremy met Andrei at a rest stop. Andrei went over the plan. He needed Coley to be able to speak, but beyond that the men had full rein. Broken bones, missing teeth, and painful balls were all acceptable. Sarah, on the other hand, was to be left unharmed with absolutely no damage to her face. He wouldn't disappoint Jenkins again. Twenty minutes later, the threesome stood outside Coley's house. Andrei signaled Jeremy to go around back. Porch boards creaked as Andrei and Thomas approached the front door. A quick peek through the window confirmed Coley was not in the living room. Charlie had been careless. He'd locked the door but neglected to set the deadbolt. The two men entered as Coley came out of the kitchen.

"Hello, Mr. Coley," Andrei said.

Startled, Charlie turned to run but found Jeremy in the kitchen.

"Thomas, find Ms. Geld."

"She's not here," Coley offered.

"See if he's telling the truth." Andrei picked up the shotgun and took out the shells. "No sense anyone getting hurt."

Jeremy reported, "No sign of her. Found clothes but no girl."

"I told you, she's gone. Left me because I banged my neighbor."

"Ah, it's good to see a woman with standards." Andrei shoved his captive onto the couch. "Where is she, Mr. Coley? She needs to be part of our little group."

"I don't know. She told me to fuck off and stomped out." Coley fought back his need to vomit. "She's probably in Arizona with her mother."

"I don't believe you." Andrei pulled Coley to his feet. "Jeremy, we need some very private time with our friend. Tie him up and gag him. Thomas, bring the car around back. Mr. Coley, you're going for a ride."

Coley wasn't conscious to hear the end of that sentence.

50

In a house thirty miles to the north, the three thugs took an hour to beat Sarah's address from her former lover. Andrei elected to take her by himself. He drove to her house on Mill Street, walked to Sarah's door, and knocked. The porch light came on, and a voice asked who he was and what he wanted. Andre played it straight. "Sarah, I'm Andrei. You and your friends stole money from my employer. I'm here to arrange repayment. You have two choices, talk with me now or have my associates visit you later. May I come in?"

After a moment's hesitation, Sarah opened the door. Andrei wiped his feet and made his way to the living room. "I'm here to make arrangements for you to pay back what you've stolen."

"Did you kill Mickey?"

"I can't discuss that, but Mr. Jenkins has no use for a dead man or woman. Get your things. We have a meeting to get to. Come willingly and participate fully, and no harm will come to you."

"How do I know you're not just saying that so I'll go quietly?" Sarah sighed.

"You don't, but again, Jenkins will be very displeased if you're hurt in any way." Andrei started towards the door. "He only wants his money."

The third member of the Thomlinson crew got her coat, slid on her shoes, and walked to the street. Andrei pointed to his car and motioned to her to get in the passenger side. They drove to west Olympia. Four miles north of Cooper Point Road's intersection with Harrison Avenue, Andrei pulled into the driveway of a house that couldn't be seen from the street.

Perfect place to murder someone, Sarah thought.

Sensing her fear, Andrei said, "This is a business meeting. Be honest and accommodating, and it'll work out well for you." Andrei opened the front door and led Sarah down a flight of stairs. In the middle of the great room, Charlie was tied to a chair, naked. His head hung so that his chin rested on his chest. Black and yellow bruises drew attention to his stomach and arms. Red, crescent-shaped welts appeared on both thighs. He'd been tortured. Sarah gasped and turned away. "You bastards."

Hearing Sarah, Charlie raised his head and opened his eyes. "Babe, they beat your address out of me. They were going to kill me."

"To Mr. Coley's credit, we did exert significant pressure on him. He held out quite a long time." Andrei directed Sarah to a chair.

"Are you going to do that to me?"

"Our employer wants both of you as unharmed as possible. Had Mr. Coley trusted us and cooperated, we wouldn't have laid a hand on him, but he chose to protect you." Andrei patted Coley on the head. "Actually, a rather commendable act."

"Why is he naked?" Sarah asked a question she didn't want answered.

"We had to stop hitting him. So we used water, a car battery, and jumper cables." Andrei pointed to Charlie's crotch. "Testicles are very sensitive."

"Fuck you," Coley muttered.

"Charlie isn't being very respectful. Mr. Welch, apply another treatment."

"No," pleaded Coley.

Smith poured water over Coley while Welch pressed a small racquet-looking device between his legs. Charlie's body twitched, and he screamed.

"Mr. Welch, you caught him in the thigh. That isn't adequate. Please redo it and make sure you get the paddle firmly against his balls."

"No. Please no." Charlie was in tears.

Sarah begged them to stop.

"Charlie, if you close your legs, we'll zap you until you open them. It'd be better if you let this happen." Andrei's voice showed no emotion. "Mr. Welch, proceed."

Coley gritted his teeth, and pain shot through his body. He was weeping after the paddle was removed.

Andrei ran his hand over Sarah's forehead. "I hope you see what happened to Charlie as an object lesson. He chose the hard path. He could've avoided a great deal of pain had he been civil. Learn from his example."

"What do you want?"

"I want $32,000, or something of equal value."

Sarah almost laughed. "I don't have thirty-two dollars, much less $32,000. I'm unemployed."

"I know." Andrei circled. "You dropped out of college, tried your hand at modeling. That didn't work out for you. You met Thomlinson and decided to steal your way to success."

Sarah tried to explain, "I was broke. Mickey told us nobody'd miss the money."

"But it was missed, all $32,000." Andrei patted Coley on the head. "Charlie's giving us his car and ten thousand dollars. That's half. You'll pay the rest."

"I told you I'm broke."

"My employer's willing to have you pay him back in trade." Andrei pulled up a chair next to Sarah.

"What are you mean *trade*?" Sarah was confused.

"Sarah, you're good looking, nice body, young, and energetic. And you said it yourself, *broke*. Starting this weekend you'll entertain men in Portland. For each satisfied customer you'll earn $100 towards your debt."

She shook her head. "You want me to be a prostitute? That's not going to happen."

"I remember having a similar conversation with Liz Thomlinson." Andrei put his hand on Sarah's leg. "If my math is correct, you'd need 170 satisfied customers. If you service five men a night, that's about one month's work."

"What if I refuse?" Sarah held back tears.

"I'm open to any alternative that gets me $17,000 from you tonight, or a guarantee I'll have it within five days."

Charlie couldn't take it any longer. "You motherfucking bastard. You aren't going to turn her into a whore. Let me out of these straps, and I'll kick your ass. And your boss's fucking ass."

Andrei turned to Thomas. "Mr. Welch, Charlie is getting chilled. Warm him up."

Welch pushed the paddle into Coley's groin, but this time he left it. Coley shook from head to toe, puked, and passed out.

"Sarah, those paddles work equally well on women. All the marks are hidden by clothes; once you're able to put some on. Please don't make me go there. In the end, you'll face the same decision but in frightfully more pain. All you have to do is agree to the terms, and tomorrow I'll escort you to Portland. In a month, I'll bring you home. What do you say? Should I have Mr. Welch demonstrate our negotiating technique again?"

"No. I'll do it. I fucking hate you." Sarah began to cry.

"Look at it this way." Andrei's tone softened. "If we prosecuted you, you'd go to prison for five years where you'd be raped almost every day. Caged women are no less animalistic than caged men when it comes to sex. They may be worse. You're exchanging thirty days of relatively pleasant service for those nineteen hundred days of brutality. I'll take you home now; unharmed, as I promised."

They climbed the stairs and left. Sarah was trying to get her head around what'd just happened. She'd considered prostitution before Mickey came along. It wasn't her dream job, but it wasn't abhorrent to her either. "Why Portland?"

"It's less likely you'd run into someone you know. That could be awkward."

"You've thought of everything, haven't you?" Sarah stared out the car's window.

"I try to be thorough. Want something to eat?"

"Just take me home."

"I'll pick you up ten. I need you in Portland by two." Andrei looked at Jenkins' latest acquisition. "Sarah, don't do anything stupid. We have people watching. If you try to leave or contact the police, what happened to Coley will be just the beginning of your ordeal."

"I'll be ready." Sarah was resigned to an uncertain fate.

Andrei pulled up in front of Sarah's house. "I need the name of your landlord so I can pay him your rent."

At the house of torment, Welch revived Coley. Smith offered him a pen and a piece of paper. "Bank account numbers, social security number, and the codes."

Coley complied. He was broke again. When he finished, he asked to get dressed.

"Charlie, you have one more decision. Do you want your left knee broken or the fingers on your right hand smashed?"

Coley was stunned and too weak to fight. He pleaded for mercy.

"Didn't you see *Casino*?" Welch was almost giddy with anticipation. "Charlie, you pay when you steal from the mob. Knee or fingers? Make the call or we will."

Jeremy held a baseball bat in one hand and a ballpeen hammer in the other. "I recommend the knee. One quick shot, and it's over. You'll pass out before you hit the floor. If we do the fingers, it'll take five hits, and I'll have to wake you for each one. You'll puke everywhere. And whoever owns this house is going to hate you."

Charlie didn't make the decision quickly enough. Welch pointed to the knee, and Jeremy swung the bat. The direct hit shattered the bones and ripped apart ligaments and tendons. But Jeremy was wrong. The pain didn't knock Charlie out. He thrashed around the floor in a circle clutching his useless knee, screaming in agony. They wouldn't be able to drop him off like this so Jeremy whacked him on top of the head. The screaming and writhing stopped. Welch was pleased to find a pulse.

Chapter 16

The next morning, Charles Leonard Coley occupied a bed in St. Peter's Critical Care Unit. He was alive thanks to a paperboy who found him in a parking lot nearly naked and completely incoherent. Two medical teams were trying to improve the quality of that life.

"They hit him with a bat in the back of his head. It's a wonder it didn't kill him." The neuro-surgeon put the x-ray on the table. "The swelling in the front of the brain has eased. We'll wait a day and see if he comes around without surgery. He's all yours for the knee replacement."

The orthapod shook his head. He'd never seen such damage. "They used the same bat on his knee. I hope he was unconscious when they did this to him. There's nothing left to the patella. He might not stand again and forget walking."

In his bed, Coley moaned in a drug-induced sleep. The leather restraints prevented him from scratching the scabs forming over the welts on his thighs and genitals. He had been beaten, tortured, and left to die. The nurse summed up his situation as only a nurse could, "He pissed someone off."

At noon, Coley regained a semblance of consciousness. The nurse repositioning his knee realized this when he screamed and nearly yanked the restraints from their mounts. She adjusted his morphine drip, and Coley returned to his stupor. Around six, he woke briefly and asked for Sarah. He stayed awake long enough to beg her not to go to Portland, saying it wouldn't be safe. Then he returned to his nightmare and convulsed.

❖

Sarah's bags sat by the door. She considered running to Flagstaff, but if they found her, they might hurt her mother too. The beating Charlie endured convinced her Portland was her only option.

The doorbell rang. Andrei was on her porch. "Are you ready?"

"I guess." Sarah turned off lights and unplugged the toaster. "I don't know if this is going to work for me."

Andrei tried to be reassuring. "It'll work if you let it work. I've seen a couple of women through this, and they did pretty well. There's always the alternative. Just find me the money."

She locked the house, and Andrei put her suitcases in the backseat. She got in the car, and Andrei pulled on to Mill Street. "You'll be back in no time, before Valentine's Day."

"But between now and then I'm going to have sex with two-hundred men." She fought back tears. "I'm not sure I can do that."

Andrei had to deliver Sarah Geld to Portland. "Let me go over this again so there's no surprise down the road and you back out."

Sarah looked at him. He was cold, businesslike. She shuddered.

"You owe twenty-thousand dollars, seventeen from the casino and three for rent. We'll house you, feed you, and provide you with birth control and medical care. While you're with us you'll pay room and board. Your earnings will cover all of this in about three months."

The next part of his speech was more difficult for him. "You'll service a number of men. They're screened and nothing happens to you that you don't want to have happen. But, the more open you are to the exotic, the more you'll earn. The more you earn, the sooner you leave. Do you understand?"

Sarah found his accountant-like attitude somehow reassuring. This number divided by that number multiplied by another. But the set of figures Andrei didn't mention bothered her. She'd have sex five times a day, almost every day, for months. "I do, but I have questions."

"Mrs. Waite is better able to answer them." Andrei tried to calm her. "Sarah, this doesn't have to be difficult. Waite will get you checked out by the doctor this afternoon and put you to work tomorrow. If you want to leave, I'll come back Tuesday and bring you home. But you'll have to come up with another way to pay your debt by next Friday. Deal?"

"Deal." She was unconvinced she could see it through.

Andrei changed the subject. He asked her about music, friends, places she'd visited, the weather, sports. For two hours he kept her mind off of the topic of sex with strangers. Just after noon, Andrei took exit 13 off Interstate 84, twelve miles east of downtown Portland.

Andrei drove past a school and several churches and eventually parked in the driveway of a three-story Victorian house. Sarah had expected something entirely different, something more brothel-like. There were three high-end luxury cars in the parking area. They climbed a set of stairs and crossed a small deck. Andrei knocked, and an attractive, middle-aged woman opened the door.

Andrei greeted her, "Mrs. Waite, this is Sarah."

"Welcome. Come in. Can I get you something to eat or drink?"

Andrei requested a sandwich and a soda. Sarah asked for a glass of water. Mrs. Waite guided them to a small office off the kitchen and invited them to sit while she got refreshments. Soon she was back with a tray. She handed Andrei his lunch and gave Sarah a tall glass of water and a plate of cheese and crackers. "I know you're nervous, sweetie, but there's nothing to worry about. We're one big family here. It'll be okay once you get to know us."

Sarah sipped the water and took a bite of cheese.

"Andrei, I need to go over a few things with Sarah. Would you mind eating in the kitchen? Sarah, I'm sure you won't be going home today, but I want Andrei to stay until the doctor gives you a physical."

For a moment Sarah thought she'd throw up. Andrei closed the door. Mrs. Waite said, "Stand up and remove your clothes."

A half-hour later, they came out. Sarah half listened as Waite described the layout of the building. Being the new girl, she'd be on the third floor.

Waite turned to Andrei. "I've gone over the details with Sarah, and she understands the agreement. Doctor Jacobs is on his way. I'm sure he'll find Sarah in excellent health. After that, you're free to go, unless you'd like to enjoy one of the girls."

Andrei declined.

Waite put her hands on Sarah's shoulders, "Honey, you'll have to take care of Doctor Jacobs' bill before he'll certify you. You can figure out how to do it."

Sarah went out to the car and got her bags. When she returned, Mrs. Waite took her to her room. A few minutes later, Waite returned. "She's going to do fine."

A BMW Sportster pulled into the driveway. A rotund man of fifty made his way up the stairs. Mrs. Waite opened the backdoor.

"Virginia, good to see you, and you couldn't have picked a better day to have me over. The wife's been out of town for a week. I'm horny as hell."

"Vincent, you crack me up." Waite pointed to her guest. "This is Andrei. He brought Sarah to us and is waiting for you to okay her for work."

"I'll get right to it, I mean her. Is she in Maryjane's room?"

"She is. I'll buzz her and tell her you're on your way." Mrs. Waite took his coat.

The doctor loosened his tie. "Tell her I'll undress her."

"Same dirty old man." Mrs. Waite dialed Sarah's room. "Doctor Jacobs is on his way up. Keep your clothes on."

Andrei was surprised at the sound of the fat man bounding up the stairs. "Amazing what the prospect of sex with a young woman can do for a guy."

"Sex is the fountain of youth." The madam smiled.

An hour later, they heard footfalls on the stairs. The doctor was done. "She's fit as a fiddle."

The doctor left, and, with no hint Sarah wanted to leave, Andrei followed. Sarah watched from her window. The doctor had been thorough, pleasant, and not a horrible john. Andrei had been good to his word. She began to cry.

Chapter 17

Andrei sat in Jenkins' office, more comfortably than the last time. The secretary brought them coffee. Andrei watched her leave, accurately assuming why Jenkins hired her.

"Everything went well yesterday. Nicely done." Jenkins raised his cup.

"Sarah saw the alternative and that convinced her. I made the transition as pleasant as possible." Andrei returned the salute. "She'll do okay, but don't count on her staying past her time."

"Leave that to me. I have ways of convincing women to do what I want." Jenkins sat behind his desk. "You remember Maryjane, don't you?"

Andrei nodded. "The Irish girl? Mrs. Waite said she'd moved out. I assumed she finished her contract and went home."

"Not exactly. She finished her contract. I was paid in full, but while she was with Mrs. Waite, she attracted the attention of a man who has, shall we say, rather odd proclivities. Proclivities he paid handsomely to carry out on Maryjane. Mrs. Waite refused to allow him to engage in such behavior in her establishment. I was a little dumbfounded by Waite's outrage. She's retained some maternal instincts." Jenkins laughed. "I had no choice but to extract Maryjane and deliver her to my client."

"How did Maryjane react?" Andrei asked.

"She wasn't pleased, but a sedative calmed her down. My client has access to plenty of that sort of medicine, but I believe he prefers a little resistance. He showed me her room, very impressive and very sound proof. Strange man, but a very, very wealthy strange man." Jenkins changed the subject. "Tell me about Coley. How did that go?"

Andrei detailed the evening Coley endured, including his resistance to giving up Sarah. "I'm surprised he survived the night. I cleaned out his accounts. We got $10,000 from him." Andrei handed a thick envelope to Jenkins. "Said he was saving the casino money to buy Sarah a ring and take her on a honeymoon."

"He won't need the money for those things now." Jenkins pocketed the money. "He knows what Sarah's doing, doesn't he?"

"He does, and he's angry. You don't have plans to keep Sarah, do you?"

"That option remains open. I'm sure Mrs. Waite has an hour or more of porn starring her. Those tapes usually keep women around until I'm done with them. And my Portland client might need a replacement about the time Sarah's wrapping up her contract. I wouldn't mind pocketing another nice chunk of change in a couple of months."

Sarah's face flashed across Andrei's mind. "You should let her go. This'll be hard on her."

"What I do with my girls is none of your fucking business," Jenkins snapped. "You're a delivery boy, not her father. Sarah gets to leave when I say she can."

The exchange galvanized their impressions of each other. Andrei saw Jenkins as a parasite. Jenkins considered Andrei an arrogant immigrant. Both decided the other had to die.

"It's time you visit Mr. Coley and remind him what happens to someone with a loose tongue." Jenkins ended the conversation.

"I'll make sure he won't tell anyone anything." Andrei got up and left.

A few minutes later, Jenkins put his plan to rid the world of Andrei into action. He called Welch. "How much do you trust Andrei?"

He confessed he didn't trust the Russian at all, and Jeremy shared his feelings. They hadn't been paid and were getting nervous.

Jenkins played on Welch's doubt. "He thinks you're idiots and afraid you'll rat him out. He wants to tie up loose ends, meaning you and Jeremy."

Welch was outraged. "What the fuck? We did everything we were supposed to on both jobs. I'll fucking kill the commie bastard. Can I get rid of him?"

"He's a hired gun. I can find a dozen of them. Do what makes you feel comfortable." Jenkins hung up, his plan was in motion. He made another call.

Chapter 18

Monday passed without Coley noticing. Morphine has that effect. Tuesday, twenty-four hours after his first knee surgery, Coley came around. His pain had subsided, and the morphine drip was removed. The CCU nurse checked his vitals and mentioned to her patient that he had had a visitor earlier. "Andrei wished you a speedy recovery. Said he'd check back when the two of you could chat."

The nurse thought Coley's convulsion was an odd reaction to her cleaning his electrical wound. She continued bolstering his spirits. "It'll be nice for you to have someone who isn't poking or prodding you to stop by."

After the nurse left, Coley tried to leave and fell to the floor. Two nurses responded to the alarm set off by the sensor in his bed. They lifted him onto the mattress. He was borderline incoherent, so they attached him to the bed's four-point restraints.

An hour later, the nurse's station got a call from Bill Dunshee who told the unit clerk he'd be in around two-thirty to get Coley's statement. At two, Andrei got off the elevator and checked with the nurse he'd spoken with earlier. She told him Coley was alert but agitated. Andrei started towards Coley's room, and the clerk caught him. "A cop's coming soon to interview him. You might want to stay."

Andrei thanked her. That was the last thing he wanted to do. He walked into Coley's room and stood over his victim. His timing was perfect. Charlie opened his eyes to find his tormentor looking down at him. He strained against the leather straps, his heart-rate monitor spiked, and he started to speak. Andrei placed a hand softly over Coley's mouth. "Listen and remember. You were attacked by kids. You don't know how many. Didn't get a good look at them. Nod if you understand."

Coley nodded.

"Good. I'll get the nurse. You look like hell." Andrei pressed the service button and left.

A half hour later, Detective Dunshee introduced himself to Charles Coley. "What do you remember about Sunday night?"

Charlie began his story, "Not much. Some kids started mouthing off, and I told them to shut the fuck up. Next thing I know four or five of them are punching me."

Dunshee wrote down a few notes. "Where did this happen?"

"Someplace near a church. I don't remember."

"So what we have is four or five kids, young men I assume, got pissed off when you told them to shut up. And they nearly killed you." Dunshee wrote *bullshit* in his pad.

"That's it. I don't even know if they were white or black. It was dark, and I didn't have a chance to check them out. They hit me on the head, and that's the last thing I remember. You may as well leave."

"This isn't much to go on, Mr. Coley." Dunshee looked over his notes. "And it doesn't explain the burn marks or you being nearly naked. But your memory might improve. Here's my card. Call me if you remember anything else."

Andrei watched the detective exit the hospital. The cop was calm, displaying no sense of urgency. Coley hadn't said anything. Andrei turned his attention to more pressing matters. Welch answered on the first ring.

"Were you expecting my call?" Andrei asked, jokingly.

"No. Just watching *Bones*," Welch replied. "The doctor's hot."

Andrei shook his head. "Is it okay to interrupt with business?"

"It's commercial, so yeah go ahead." Welch missed Andrei's sarcasm.

"I have money for you and Jeremy. Can we meet tomorrow night?" Andrei looked over the map on his lap. "At the quarry off Highway 12, by Oakville?"

"Sure, I need the dough. Was everything okay with the boss?"

"He thought we did a great job with Sarah and Charlie. I'll see you at seven."

Welch acknowledged the meeting time and hung up. Two minutes later, he relayed the information to Jenkins. A few minutes after that, Jenkins left a message: "Seven o'clock tomorrow night, the quarry on Highway 12 near Oakville."

Chapter 19

Ralph and Dennis finished their breakfasts, stuffed their backpacks, and were watching a show about ancient aliens. Anne had already left, entrusting Bryce with readying the boys for school. He'd done well and would reward himself with a latte from the San Francisco Street Bakery on the way to the shop. Even with a threat of showers and possibly snow, he opted for his twenty-seven speed. He pedaled past Roosevelt Elementary hoping to see Anne. Her classroom was dark. She was elsewhere in the building. He rode on disappointed.

Bryce had barbered for twelve years, establishing a large, loyal clientele. Fifteen heads a day earned him twelve-hundred dollars a week, enough to make ends meet. Anne's salary and medical insurance allowed them a better than average home, a pleasant lifestyle, but little else. An occasional visit to Disneyland was possible, but a trip to a World Cup soccer match was out of the question. Out of the question until Bryce discovered a lucrative sideline literally under his nose.

Two years ago, a man waiting for a trim listened to a balding man tell Bryce his vacation plans and, more importantly, the steps he'd taken to keep burglars, such as the man on the couch, out of his house. When it was his turn, the man asked a seemingly innocent question. "What's that guy's name?"

Thinking nothing of it, Bryce gave him the answer. Two weeks later, the man returned, handed Bryce two-hundred dollars, and offered him a deal: ten percent of the take on every burglary set up with Bryce's information. Bryce was surprised at his willingness to take the man up on his offer. He looked at it this way; he'd pick the victims, the locations, and the times. He could make sure nobody got hurt. The coup de gras was convincing himself everything was covered by insurance. The victim was a faceless company, probably in New York City.

His new sideline became so lucrative he had to hide the additional, unexplainable wealth from Anne. Municipal bonds were perfect. He purchased them on line, stashed them in a private account, and watched them generate tax-free income. He invested well and, within a year, was making five-percent on over ten-thousand dollars in bonds. As nest eggs go, his was better than most.

Bryce's ride took twenty minutes. He opened the shop's door for business at precisely eight o'clock and noticed an envelope on the floor. He'd been expecting it ever since the paper reported the Hollander burglary. He stuck it into his jacket. The receiver atop the Mottman building blinked to life as three microphones picked up Bryce's entrance.

❖

The men responsible for the microphones were almost to the airport. Don was surprised at the almost non-existent Tuesday morning traffic. He turned onto the airport's access road much earlier than expected.

A year ago, he found the access route confusing, but now it made sense. It mirrored Sea-Tac's primary landing pattern; taking drivers to an outer marker, turning them one-hundred-eighty degrees, and sending them hurtling or, more often, crawling back to the terminal. Most drivers had enough time to maneuver into the proper lanes. Those failing to heed the signs were doomed to doing it over, sort of a modern day, horizontal Sisyphus situation.

"Justin, you did great." Don pulled over to the curb. "I don't know what'll come of it, but I hope we get some punks off the street."

61

"It was a pleasure working with you, Major, and nobody was shooting at us."

"We may not be so lucky next time, but they'll be worse off for trying. Do you have everything? Margie going to meet you?" Don got Justin's bag.

"I'm good to go, and she'll be there. I'm looking forward to a couple of nice, quiet evenings with her. Hopefully, it'll be just her. Her mother drives us both nuts." Justin slung his bag over his shoulder. "Hey, if the thing with the detective doesn't work out I'll set you up with Kathryn. She's one-hundred-forty-years old. Just right for you."

"I may be your senior, but when it comes to the ladies, I've got teenage blood running through these veins."

"And about the same amount of common sense."

Don hugged his buddy. "Take care of Margie. She's going to need a little R and R after dealing with her mom."

"Keep me posted on what's coming out of Bryce's shop. Going to miss you pal."

"Me as well, slacker. I'll text you as soon as I get anything."

Justin slapped Don on the back and disappeared into the terminal.

Arriving home, Don found Brian over on his porch. "I thought you were leaving the decorations up for next year. Do you or the kids enjoy Halloween more?"

"Definitely me. If they get dressed up and walk around in the rain, the least I can do is scare the crap out of them." Brian stepped off the ladder with a witch in hand.

"Yeah, you really have Frank N. Stein written all over you. Or maybe I should call you Dr. Acula? What did you hand out this year?"

Brian beamed. "Full-size candy bars, not those bite-sized things."

"I should've come over."

"You could've come as a Marine."

"I'm no wussy, Brian." Don asked if Brian had heard from the police about the break-in. He hadn't but wasn't surprised. Brian summed up the situation with a basketball adage, *no blood - no foul*. "If you want to catch someone stealing from you, you have to be there when they break in. And you might want a baseball bat."

"Or a Ruger Magnum," Don muttered under his breath.

"Don, could you hand me the lightbulb? It's on the railing."

Handing his neighbor an *energy-miser* bulb, "You know, plenty of people think you're deranged."

"Truth is, I am. One more thing, can you help me un-rig the doorbell? The scream machine is still on, and it bugs people now that Halloween's over. And by *people*, I mean Deirdre."

"Anything to help a fellow lunatic."

They went inside to disconnect the last vestige of Halloween. Minutes later, Brian pressed the doorbell. An ear-shattering shriek confirmed the wires were still attached.

"Had to hear it one more time. Okay, pull the wires. Bring on the chimes."

Once they were done, Don crossed to his house. Along the way he thought it was probably good the two weirdoes lived next to each other.

❖

As the guys dealt with Halloween paraphernalia, Detective Linder reviewed the ME report. It confirmed Liz was stabbed to death with scissors. Campbell died from a single gunshot to the head. Mickey also died from a gunshot to the head, but he was shot in both knees, presumably before the kill shot. The men died side-by-side. Liz died in the bedroom. Time of death for all was estimated at nine p.m. based on when Mickey left work and the time the fire was reported. Extreme fire damage prevented a more detailed assessment.

The report added nothing to Patti's file. Patti wrote her conclusions in the margin: *Someone, probably two, maybe more, visited the Thomlinsons. They tortured Mickey and murdered everyone. A nine-millimeter pistol was used to kill Mickey and Harvey. Liz was killed with scissors. There were two assailants; the men killed by one, Liz murdered by the other.*

Patti kept returning to Mickey. He paid a much higher price than the others. He was the target, and they were collateral damage. With Mickey, came the casino. He'd worked there for two years. A mysterious man was looking for him just before the murders. Patti wasn't sure how to follow that lead. It'd happened a month ago, and the description of the man fit most males in Thurston County.

She poured another cup of coffee and stared out the window. The morning looked promising, showers but not steady rain. With winter coming, any break in the weather was welcomed. A run and then a bout with the heavy bag would let her burn energy and organize her thoughts; perfect break in the middle of the day.

Chapter 20

Welch and Smith knew too much and had to be eliminated. They consistently made bad decisions; the latest was agreeing to meet him at this quarry. They'd be armed, maybe even expecting an ambush, but Andrei was prepared. Their deaths would extend his life.

Two hours before the meet, Andrei drove his SUV down the quarry's winding dirt road. He hid the car behind a slag pile and climbed the ridge overlooking the road. It'd take Welch and Smith five minutes to get from the entrance to the parking lot, plenty of time for him to get down the hill and ambush the idiots. At six-thirty headlights illuminated the entrance. Andrei grew concerned when the vehicle stopped in the road. The dome light came on and a door closed. Someone had gotten out. After a moment, the vehicle moved forward. A man with a flashlight climbed the hill next to his. They were setting their own ambush. *Maybe they're not so stupid after all.*

With high beams on, the car circled the parking lot. Satisfied Andrei wasn't there, the driver pointed his car towards the entrance and turned off the engine. Only the light above an equipment shed broke the darkness.

"Somebody's been coaching you guys," Andrei muttered. A light flashed on the hill to his left. A responding signal came from the car. Their trap was set but an hour too late. Considering the two men he was dealing with, Andrei concluded Welch was on the hill, armed with the Marlin 336 he talked about incessantly. Jeremy would be the driver, pissing his pants.

Andrei's new plan was to take out the gunman, and then quickly deal with the driver. If Jeremy got to the highway, Andrei Clemmens would have to disappear. Fifty-yards of open ground separated him from his first target. It was dark, and he was behind the sniper. Andrei bet the man didn't have night-vision googles and would be concentrating on the road, not giving a damn about what was behind him. The Russian enforcer waited until the man flashed the light again, then strode rapidly across the open ground and pounced. The sniper could not fend off the vicious knife attack.

Pulling the dead man close, Andrei didn't recognize him. "Who the fuck are you? You two bastards have some explaining to do."

Andrei started his descent when a thought occurred. The sniper probably would signal when he saw Andrei arrive. It was time for that signal. "One flash meant *I'm in place*. Two must mean a car's on its way. Let's see what happens."

Andrei found the flashlight and pressed its switch twice. Almost immediately, two flashes responded from the car. The headlights came on, and Welch got out, gun in-hand. If the sniper failed, he'd finish the Russian.

"You're going to pay for this." Andrei cautiously made his way down the hill. The men would expect a car soon. Andrei had to get two shots off before the driver raced out of the quarry.

Andrei knelt and brought the sniper's weapon to bear on his target. Backlit by the headlights, Welch was a sitting duck. An amateur could've picked him off, and Andrei was anything but an amateur. He zeroed the scope on Welch's stomach. Andrei needed information: confirmation that

Jenkins had set him up. *Best to leave both men alive for the time being*, he thought and pulled the trigger.

The bullet slammed into Welch, propelling the bear five-feet backwards. The wound was mortal, but death would take a while. The second and third bullets tore apart the car's engine. The driver wasted precious time turning over the ignition and pumping the gas pedal. Andrei ran forward, staying out of the headlight's illumination arc. He arrived at the driver's door before Jeremy could get out and run. When Jeremy saw Andrei coming, he locked the doors.

Andrei laughed. "That's not going to help. I'll shoot my way in, and you'll end up dead. Unlock the door and come out. Keep your hands where I can see them."

Jeremy shook his head. He wasn't leaving the security of his car. Andrei's bullet shattered the rear window. "Next time it's the driver's window, and you're right behind it. Last chance to come out before I come in."

Jeremy opened the door. "We were scared you'd kill us. We didn't mean you any harm. Honest."

"Whenever someone says *honest* I know he's lying." Andrei pulled the shaking man from the car. "Come around here, we need to check on Thomas."

Welch was on his back. The slug caught him just below the rib cage. Andrei was sure the exit wound was far larger than the dime-sized hole in Welch's belly. "You're hurting really bad, aren't you, Thomas? Your friend on the hill isn't hurting anymore. He's dead. Almost had his head taken off. It's gruesome."

Welch moaned. "Fucker. He was my brother."

"It's your fault. I didn't invite him to our parley. And I don't appreciate a guy with a rifle on my backside." The Russian tossed Welch's now empty rifle on top of its owner. "Who put you up to this?"

"Fuck you," Welch muttered.

"Thomas, just for that I'm going to let you die for a long time." Andrei picked up Welch's pistol. "Jeremy, have you ever been shot with a .38? Hurts like a bitch. Want to see?"

"Hell no! This wasn't my idea." Jeremy moved towards his car. "I told Thomas we needed to be straight with you."

Andrei grabbed Jeremy and looked him in the eyes. "Who put Thomas up to this?"

"Do I have to tell? If I do, he'll kill me."

"If you don't, I'll kill you, right here, right now." Andrei let the little man go. "Tell me who's behind this and help me pull dipshit's brother off that hill. Then you can leave. That's a good deal."

"I can leave?" Jeremy hadn't expected that possibility.

"You didn't raise a hand against me. Didn't even bring a gun. You were set up by Welch and the mystery man. Give me his name, and let's get on with it."

"Jenkins. He said you were going to kill us."

Andrei walked over to Welch and shot him in the head.

Jeremy gasped.

"He was hurting, and we weren't going to save him. It was the right thing to do. Help me load him into the backseat. His brother will fit in the front."

They labored getting the big man into the car. Andrei secured the body.

"Okay partner, let's go get the other Mr. Welch. He's on top of that hill. Oh, that's right you know where he is, don't you?"

A few minutes later the second body was strapped in the front seat, snug against the door.

"Now Jeremy, get into the driver's seat and buckle up."

"You said I could leave when we were done."

"I changed my mind. If you do as I say, I'll make your death painless. If you don't, then I'll shoot you in both knees, put you in the car, and buckle you in myself. Either way, that's where you're going to end up."

Jeremy began to cry. "Don't shoot me."

Exasperated, Andrei gave into the man. "Okay, Jeremy. I won't shoot you. You're right, no reason to do that. Just get in the car and steer it."

Sensing a change in Andrei, Jeremy complied.

"Put your hands on the steering wheel, at ten and two."

Jeremy took the wheel, and Andrei punched him in the throat. The enforcer secured the misguided man's left hand to the steering wheel. Jeremy, eyes panicking, watched Andrei zip-tie his right hand.

"I'm not going to shoot you, I'm going to drown you."

Jeremy struggled against the straps. Blood oozed down both arms. Andrei got his car and aligned the bumpers. After putting Jeremy's car in neutral, Andrei slowly pushed it over a small rise in the parking lot. Gravity took over. Jeremy and his dead friends slipped into oblivion. Jeremy screamed all the way to the surface of the pond, two-hundred feet below the roadbed. The screaming stopped abruptly.

The second sniper, the one sent by Jenkins, waited patiently for Andrei to complete his chores. Then he brought up his rifle. Light from the shed reflected off the scope's front lens. Seeing the glint, Andrei's brain screamed *sniper*. In that instant, two related events took place: Andrei dropped to the ground, and the sniper pulled the trigger.

The bullet missed Andrei's head by less than an inch. Sprawled behind the car, he was protected for the time-being. Andrei hoped the sniper believed he had either killed or seriously wounded his target. He played possum, waiting for the sniper to come and finish him. He pulled out his

Glock. With a flick of his finger, the safety came off, readying the gun for use. Andrei's taillights illuminated the parking lot softly but thoroughly.

The sniper crossed in front of the car, directly through Andrei's field of fire; an incredibly stupid thing to do. Blocked by the open door, all Andrei could see were the sniper's legs. The man moved cautiously, uncertain of Andrei's condition and unaware of the Russian's marksmanship. Andrei aimed the semi-automatic at the man, and, when less than twenty-feet separated them, he fired four rounds, hoping one would find its mark. The man screamed.

Andrei sprang to his feet and ran at the sniper who was on the ground holding his left leg. Andrei kicked the rifle away and assessed the wounds. A bullet had clipped the right kneecap causing the sniper to collapse. A second found the man's left thigh. Neither was fatal, but both were painful. Andrei checked for weapons and found none.

"Jenkins sent you to clean up whatever was left after the boys and I met. Is that right?" Andrei already knew the answer.

"Fuck you."

"That's all you've got to say? You saw what I did to those other assholes?"

"I did, but you won't do that to me." The sniper glared at Andrei. "I'm a cop, and even a dumb Russian like you knows better than to kill a cop."

Andrei stepped on the wounded kneecap. "I'm one dumb Russian who isn't afraid to kill a cop, but I'm not going to kill you. I'm going to use you to send Jenkins a message. He's a dead man."

"I'm not telling anyone anything for you. Now get me to a hospital."

Andrei thought for a moment. "We'll use your car. I don't want blood all over mine."

"Fine. It's half a mile down the road. You'll have to get it. I can't walk because you fucking shot me in both legs." The cop stuffed a handkerchief into his thigh. "Here are the keys. Hurry, I don't want to bleed out."

Andrei stood over the man wondering how he'd act if he was at the mercy of a man who wanted to kill him. He concluded he wouldn't be as calm or as arrogant as the cop. He admired the man's calmness but hated his arrogance. Andrei shot him in the head. It took an hour to collect the cop's car, load his body, and roll a second car into the pond.

It was abundantly clear, Jenkins wanted him dead. He had sent four incompetent men to kill him. For the next few hours, Jenkins would believe he'd gotten his wish. At any point during that time, Andrei could walk into his office and murder the bastard; pure, unadulterated revenge. But Andrei wanted more than revenge. Maybe it was Jenkins' contempt for him and his Russian heritage or his threat to sell Sarah to the psychopath that convinced Andrei to turn his car eastward, towards Spokane and a meeting with

Apakoh. With the Dragon's approval, Andrei could exact a more interesting and far more devastating penalty on the treacherous pig.

❖

Sunrise erupted over Mount Spokane. Andrei was home. The wind sent shivers through his body. He stored his weapons, called Revoldi, and drove to Apakoh's warehouse. The Dragon greeted him; bear hugs and kisses on both cheeks.

Revoldi guided his man to the office. "Why have you've driven all this way?"

Voytek began, "Jenkins hired me to collect money stolen by an employee. The process went badly because one of the men he saddled me with wasn't cautious. He let a woman stab him, and he killed her. I had to kill her brother and her lover. We got only a small fraction of what was owed to Jenkins. We destroyed the bodies and got away cleanly. I met with Jenkins. He was unhappy but accepted his losses. I agreed to his terms to cover those losses."

Voytek took a breath. "Then I told him the two incompetents were dangerous, and I wanted to eliminate them. He agreed. I set up a meeting with the men, but Jenkins had warned them. They brought another fool, a sniper for protection. I disposed of them, but not before I confirmed Jenkins had set me up."

Apakoh shook his head. "This is what happens with westerners. They don't share our values. Jenkins is not honorable, Voytek. Do you have plans for him?"

"That's why I'm here, but there's one more detail. Jenkins sent a second sniper to kill whoever survived the meeting. He was better than the first, but not as skilled as he needed to be. And he was a cop. I put him down."

"These men, they won't be found?"

"Not likely. If they are, there's no tie to me, to us."

"Good. As usual you were thorough and careful." Apakoh was relieved. "Does Jenkins know you're alive?"

"I assume he does. He hasn't heard from any of his men."

"But he doesn't know if you are aware of his involvement. He may think it, but he can't be sure. If he believes his part is undetected, he may let his vendetta against you simmer. When the time's right, you will have my full support in whatever you do with Jenkins. We'll deal with him the way Bratva deals with traitors." Taras hugged him.

Andrei had what he wanted, the Dragon's permission. Jenkins would regret what he'd done.

Taras extended Andrei a prize. "You're home. It's time to eat and have some comfort. Perhaps you'd like the company of a woman? I have a special lady you should meet. Her name is Charlene."

They drove to an apartment building on the outskirts of Spokane. Revoldi sung her praises the entire trip, "She's stunning, absolutely stunning. And she's getting wonderful reviews from my clients. She is making me a fortune."

Charlene answered the door, letting her employer and his friend into her home. Andrei was instantly mesmerized. Never had he seen such beauty and pure sex-appeal. Revoldi's description failed to do Charlene justice. *Exquisite* was the only word that came to Andrei.

Taras rambled on about his daughter's upcoming ski-trip. Andrei offered to chaperone, but the Dragon declined. Zoya had forbidden him from sending anyone to spy on her child. After what seemed an eternity, Revoldi made his excuses and left.

"What do you do for Mr. Revoldi?" Charlene poured drinks.

"I eliminate problems."

It was early afternoon the following day when Jenkins got Andrei's call. "Mr. Jenkins, we need to meet. Do you have some time later today?"

His men, including Ogden, had failed to neutralize the Russian, but the mad-monk didn't seem to be aware of his role in the ambush. "I'll make time, Andrei. When can you be here?"

"Could we meet at the sandwich shop on the corner in about an hour?" Andrei asked. "I haven't eaten all day, and I'm starved."

The restaurant was perfect for Jenkins, small and very public. "I'll see you there."

Thirty minutes later, Jenkins made his way across the street and found a table in the corner. There weren't many customers, so the meeting would be relatively private. One thought kept rolling through his mind, *he doesn't know. Rasputin doesn't know.*

The lunch rush was long over. The lone waitress asked, "Do you need a menu?"

"I'm waiting for a friend, so we'll need two." Jenkins looked out the window expecting to see Andrei any minute.

The waitress set the table, dropped off two menus, and retreated to her station behind the counter. Not long after, a disheveled Andrei walked in and went directly to Jenkins. "Sorry, I'm late. The last twenty-four hours have been miserable."

"You look like you've been rode hard and put away wet." Jenkins tried to insert some levity into their conversation.

"I'm not sure what that means, but I'm ready for peace and quiet."

The waitress took their order and left them to their conversation.

Jenkins leaned towards his nemesis. "What went wrong?"

Andrei delivered the story he'd practiced over and over on the drive from Spokane. "I got to the quarry early. They were on time. We met, and before I could take out my gun Welch pulls one from his coat. He had me, but he forgot to release the safety. I eliminated him, and before Smith could run, I shot him in the spine."

"Sounds like things went exactly as planned," Jenkins interjected.

"That's when things got all screwed up. They brought a sniper. They were ambushing me, and it nearly worked." Andrei surveyed the room. "I bent over to check Smith when a bullet missed me by an inch. I drop to the ground like I'm hit, and the sniper bought it. He walked right up to the car I was behind. Must have thought I was dead. I sat up and shot him in the chest, twice."

"Did he say anything?" Jenkins asked.

Andrei shook his head. "By the time I got to him his lungs were filled with blood. He gurgled something, but I couldn't understand."

"Who was he?" Jenkins breathed a sigh of relief.

"No ID, probably a friend of those two idiots."

Jenkins relaxed. "What did you do with the bodies?"

"Put them where they'll never be found." Andrei stopped talking while the waitress delivered their meals. "Do you want me to visit the barber?"

The change in subject caught Jenkins off-guard. He stammered, "Yes."

"Tomorrow?"

"That'd be fine."

They finished eating, and Jenkins paid the bill. He walked back to his office confident Andrei was none the wiser. Andrei drove east, confident Jenkins believed his story.

Chapter 21

Bryce got ready to have lunch and watch soccer. He turned on the television and walked to the front door, the *Out to Lunch* sign in his hand. Before he got to hang it, a man came in from the cold.

"I'm closing for lunch, sir." Bryce fully expected the man to leave. "Could you come back in an hour?"

"No." The man brushed by the barber.

"Okay then," Bryce said, a little irritated. "I'll get you cleaned up and on your way. Have a hot date this afternoon?"

"Just the one I have with you. Lock the door and meet me in the back."

Initially annoyed, Bryce was now angry and a bit afraid. "I don't have an appointment with you. You need to leave."

Andrei flashed the nine-millimeter. "Unless you're packing something bigger than this, lock the door and step into the backroom."

"My money's in my wallet. Take it. No need to go into the backroom."

"I don't want your money." Andrei almost laughed. "I want to make you an offer, a damned good offer. Lock the fucking door, and come with me. Don't make me ask again."

Bryce didn't want anything to do with this man but did as ordered.

"Here's the deal, Bryce." Andrei sat in the half-dismantled barber chair. "We know what you're doing, and starting today you're doing it for us."

"I don't know what you're talking about." Bryce avoided the man's eyes.

"You know exactly what I'm talking about, and you don't have an option. This is going to happen."

A while ago, Bryce thought something like this might happen, but with the passage of time he'd dismissed it. The mob couldn't be bothered with his smalltime operation. Apparently, he was wrong. Proof of *how* wrong stood in front of him.

"What do you want me to do?"

"I'm glad you're being smart." Andrei spun in the chair. "It'd be horrible if Anne or the kids got hurt."

"I'm working with you. Don't threaten my family."

"Just wanted you know I'm serious, and I represent people even more serious." The Russian got out of the chair and extended his hand. "I'm Andrei, and I'll contact you with more details soon. Keep this between us. Nothing to your wife, nothing to anyone. Understand?"

Bryce reluctantly shook the man's hand. "I've got it. Are we through?"

"For the moment, yes."

❖

That evening, with a beer in hand, Don brought up the day's recording. He had nine hours to review. Most would be banal, useless drivel: soccer scores, football predictions, problems with women, problems with men, problems with republicans, problems with democrats. He took a long sip and settled in for another boring night.

Bryce's early customers were seniors complaining about the relatives they'd have to endure at Thanksgiving. Next were businessmen complaining about the cost of the dinner, or having to drive the family to some godforsaken part of the state. Don pictured Bryce nodding his agreement with all of them.

At the recording's eleven-fifty mark, silence indicated the shop was empty. Don heard Bryce's footsteps. A clock chimed in the background. It was noon, and Bryce was closing for lunch. Someone came in, and Bryce asked the customer to return later. Don was as surprised as Bryce had been when the man said *no*. Don listened intently to the man threaten Bryce and then offer him a deal. Bryce was the victim of a hostile take-over.

Chapter 22

The six-mile ride to JFK had turned into an hour-long slalom course through rush hour traffic. The airport was busier than McGlin had feared. Thanksgiving's exodus had begun. He checked his luggage and, with boarding pass in-hand, went to Concourse D's security checkpoint. He was amused by the family in front of him. Mom had hijacked dad's business trip, turning it into a Disneyworld outing. The man wasn't as enthusiastic as his kids were about the new plan, but he was being a good sport.

Carrying diamonds from New York to Seattle demanded attention to detail and an ability to react decisively to any threat. Today, his biggest threat was missing the flight. He relaxed after TSA opened a fifth check-stand, and the line lurched forward. He made the flight with minutes to spare. The elderly woman occupying the seat in front of him seemed happy reading *People*, and the young couple sharing his row were arguing politics. The three *Seahawk* fans behind him posed more a threat to the drink cart than to his diamonds.

Sea-Tac was one of his favorite destinations. It was easy to get through, and David usually picked him up. The limousine driver shared McGlin's affinity for scantily-clad women in dark bars. McGlin relaxed. His seatmates turned their attention to banking scandals. *Could be worse*, McGlin thought. *They could be wrestling fans.*

Three thousand miles away, two men sat in a late model Highlander across from Olympia's Windjammer Hotel. When the courier arrived, they were to watch him, assess his skills, and find a weakness. Jenkins told them the courier's name, where he was staying, how he'd arrive, and when to expect him. They had every pertinent piece of information, including the color of his limousine. Throughout the afternoon, they checked the status of the courier's flight and were pleasantly surprised when it landed fifteen minutes early. If traffic cleared on I-5, it'd take the limo an hour to get out of Sea-Tac, pass thru Tacoma, and wind its way through Olympia. The car should arrive around five-thirty.

At five, Mel, the better dressed of the two, went inside and found a seat across from the front desk. From there, he could hear small talk between the clerk and guests. A half-hour later, his phone vibrated. The limo had arrived. He continued to read *The Olympian* and watch the doors. McGlin walked through them at 5:37. *The traffic gods smiled on you*, Mel thought.

McGlin scanned the lobby, fixing his eyes for a moment on Mel. The courier didn't consider him a threat. James approached the front desk and greeted the clerk. The usual exchange took place; credit card and driver's license for a pen, paper, and a plastic key card.

"Room 318, Mr. McGlin. Enjoy your stay."

The man looking at the paper's football schedule wondered if the clerk intended for everyone in the lobby to know the courier's room number. Mel concluded the courier was reasonably skilled with the notable mistake of dismissing him as a threat. Mel wanted to try distracting the courier. He went out to the Highlander.

"Call Jessica. Tell her to come here and wear something nice."

"When do you want her?" Seth asked.

"He'll go to dinner soon, probably Marconi's. He'll come back around seven-thirty, so let's have her here at seven. Tell her get a room. We'll put her at the reception desk and see if he notices her."

"He'd have to be dead not to notice Jessica." Seth dialed her number. "Will she spend the night?"

"Yes. She gets a nice evening in a swank hotel."

Jessica, pleased with the assignment, promised to be on time.

James exited the hotel twenty minutes later and walked north towards Marconi's. His stalkers stayed well behind him. They knew where he was going, so there was little need to stay close. They parked across the street from the restaurant in a poorly lit lot and watched the front door. At quarter to seven, they returned to the hotel and found Jessica in her car. She wasn't hard to spot when she got out. She wore tight jeans, a white blouse, and a leather jacket.

She came over to Mel's car. He gave her instructions. "When he turns the corner, head for the lobby. Make sure he notices you."

"Do you think he could miss me? He'd have to be pretty gay not to notice the girls." Jessica pushed up her boobs.

"You're right there." Mel handed her four one-hundred dollar bills. "Use this to pay for the room and keep the change."

Ten minutes later, McGlin walked through the parking lot. He noticed a young woman pulling a suitcase disappear into the building. He saw her again at the counter and quickly assessed her threat potential as minimal. There was no place to pack a weapon in the clothes she was wearing. Once he concluded she wasn't a threat, he took a moment to enjoy her figure.

Seth summed up the encounter well. "He's not gay."

Jessica turned and smiled at the courier. For a brief moment, James was transfixed. When she turned back to the clerk, McGlin regained his composure, entering the elevator as the doors closed. He was a professional, a horny professional, but a professional nonetheless.

Mel started the car. "We've got him!"

Chapter 23

It'd be Easter before Olympians experienced a warm, sunny day. Don stood on his front porch watching cold mist defy gravity. Brian poked his head out his door, "Hey, neighbor. I want to show you my new shotgun."

Don appreciated weapons and understood the excitement hunters experience when they purchase a new one. He tossed on his sweatshirt and ran over to Brian's porch. The door was open, so he walked in.

"What did you buy?" Don asked, wondering where Brian was.

A distant voice directed him to the basement. Three gun cabinets lined the far wall, each holding its maximum number of rifles and shotguns, not an AR among them. Brian sat on a high-backed stool leaning over a workbench. The lighting was exceptional, bright but not blinding, perfect for detail work. Professional-grade reloading equipment was mounted on the far end of the bench. For Don, guns were tools. For Brian, they were a passion.

Brian was examining a shotgun.

"Is that the new addition?" Don asked.

"I've looked for a graded-class Parker 16-gauge DHE for years. Finally found one I could afford. Got a great deal. It's as good as the dealer promised, maybe better."

Don surveyed Crane's collection. "You could outfit a small army, Brian."

Brian scanned his collection. "Most are hand-me-downs from my father and uncles. I was the only boy. So when they kicked-off, I got their guns. Good memories in those cabinets."

Don flashed on memories of his weapons, most were not very pleasant and some downright terrifying. "You hunted with your dad."

"And my uncles. Mostly up in the Methow, above Winthrop. There're mule and black-tail deer running around in the fall. Some elk, but they're hard to get a tag for. The best is goose season. I'm going up there this December. Want to come?"

"I never knew you were such a gun enthusiast. Sort of saw you as a bit of a bookworm, no offense." Don eyed a classic Winchester 30-30. "I appreciate the offer, but I'm not much of a hunter."

"I don't advertise this part of my life. There are a lot of PETA-prone folks in the senate. I let the gun control debate roll over me and then go hunting. Neither side will ever convince the other to change its position. It's frustrating. What they don't know about me won't hurt me."

"I'd put all this on a need to know basis, with nobody needing to know." Don inspected the new weapon. "This is beautiful."

"Thanks. I've been wondering if that guy you saw was looking for the guns. You scared him off before he got down here. I've got two deadbolts on the basement door, and he'd need cable cutters to get the guns out of their lockers. It'd be easier to steal the woodstove."

"I don't know. When I saw him, he was hanging around your desk." Don studied the reloading press. "Cash maybe, but once they get in, they'll take anything that's not nailed down."

Brian ran a cloth over the barrel. "I'm prepared, and I'm well insured."

"How long have you been hunting?"

"Since I was ten. That's when I got to go shoot with the big boys. Dad taught me to shoot earlier than that but didn't think it'd be safe until I was older. I didn't get my first buck until I was twelve." Brian set the shotgun down. "Senator Bernard and I are going before session. You're welcome to tag along."

"Thanks, but I'll have to pass." Don climbed the stairs. "I'd like you to walk me through your collection, especially the stories behind the guns."

"I'd love to. Could you let yourself out? I want to touch up the bluing a bit."

"No problem. I'll catch you later. Keep your powder dry." Don had seen another side of Brian, a side he admired.

Chapter 24

The day after Thanksgiving found Detective Linder driving back to the White Pine Casino hoping someone would remember something about the man who'd been looking for Mickey. Nothing new had turned up in the ME report or the forensic data Deirdre sent over. Three murders, arson, probably a robbery, and almost certainly a drug deal happened in the span of an hour in the Thomlinson trailer, and she had virtually nothing to show for the hours she'd spent on the case. Not a single lead remained except for the mystery man.

The casino sported a Native American motif with canoes, headdresses, and costumes right out of classic westerns. It lay in wait for gamblers a mile off Highway 12, Washington's highway to the Pacific. It took Patti an hour to get from Olympia to its newly remodeled entrance.

"Going all Vegas aren't you?" she quipped walking through the double doors. Nobody'd mistake the White Pine Casino for Caesar's Palace, but among the cedars, it was impressive. She showed her badge to the receptionist, a young woman with native blood, who phoned the business manager. Mr. Harland met her in the lobby. He looked straight out of Frank Sinatra's *Ocean's Eleven*.

"What can I do for you, officer?" Harland asked, coldly.

"It's detective, Mr. Harland." Patti corrected him. "I need to speak to two of your employees about Mickey Thomlinson. If they're not here, I need their addresses and phone numbers."

"That shouldn't be a problem. Follow me and I'll have the office manager get that for you. She's not terribly bright, but she's the chief's daughter, so we're stuck with her," Harland said, nonchalantly. "She can probably help you, but if not, one of the white girls will."

Patti was floored, but she held her tongue. Walking from the lobby to the office, she assessed the place. It was busy, especially for a weekday morning. A lot of money exchanged hands here, mostly from patrons to the house. And the house, Patti figured, meant the mob. Harland did little to dispel that notion.

Irene Tisdale was at her desk working on a pile of receipts. Harland introduced her and told her to get the detective whatever she wanted. He used a tone that spoke volumes about his disdain for the young woman. He wished Detective Linder a pleasant day and returned to his duties.

Patti gave Irene the names of the two employees who mentioned the mystery man, and Irene retrieved their schedules. Neither was working, so Patti would have to catch them at home. The lovely young woman provided their addresses and phone numbers, and asked, "Do you want Mr. Thomlinson's personnel file?"

Patti accepted, and Ms. Tisdale produced a manila folder with "Thomlinson, Michael" printed on the tab. She handed Patti a form that acknowledged she'd taken the file. Patti signed it and was about to leave.

"Did you want any security tapes?" Irene asked.

After thinking how helpful Irene was being, Patti nodded. "That'd be great."

"They're not actually tapes. They're computer files, easier to store and review." Irene typed commands into her computer.

"Can you pull the tape, or file, or whatever for the night Mickey was killed?"

"Yes, what one do you want? We have one-hundred cameras on at all times."

Patti was quick to answer, "I'd like the one covering his station."

Irene reviewed that night's assignment log. Thomlinson dealt five-dollar blackjack and had been under the watchful eye of camera twenty-three. Ms. Tisdale entered a password and brought up the video files for that day, selected camera twenty-three, punched in the time frame, and a file was identified. Ms. Tisdale looked up from her computer. "I can copy it to a disk or send it to your email."

"How about both?" Patti gave the office manager her email address. A few clicks and Patti had a CD and a message on her phone indicating an email had arrived. Pointing to the screen showing each camera's location, Patti asked, "What's the camera number for the table across from Thomlinson? Looks like it's the other blackjack table."

"They're in sequence going from east to west. So that's twenty-two."

"Can I get the same files for that camera?"

"You sure can." Ms. Tisdale made a few more entries, and Detective Linder received another CD and a second text message.

"Irene you were fabulous. These will help a lot. Many thanks."

"You're more than welcome. I hope you find whoever did that to Mickey and his family. I didn't know him well, but he seemed like a nice guy."

She shook Irene's hand and thanked her again. On her way out, she found Harland and told him what a fine job Irene had done. He glared at her as she walked away.

Kevin A. Harland. The A probably stands for Antonio, Patti thought. *Or maybe just asshole.*

❖

In Olympia, Brian used the day to move his investigation forward. The Capitol Campus was a ghost town, perfect for Brian to work on matters that didn't concern him. He had a history of poking into other committees' business, irritating members, staff, and constituents. Unfortunately for them, Bernard had given him free rein, and today he was exercising that latitude with the Senate Transportation Committee, much to Bernard's dismay. Under most circumstances, a legislator would be delighted to have Brian actively working to support his project, but Crane was the last person Bernard wanted looking into project finances. When Brian mentioned he was *doing a little research* to prove the project was worthy of continued financing, Bernard was hard-pressed to call him off.

Three years ago, Bernard pushed Spokane's North-South Interchange project through the legislature using the time-tested *I scratch your back, you scratch mine* approach. Each year since, he had to get the project more money as it hit overrun after overrun. A month ago, the DOT contract office got word to Brian; the project needed another infusion of cash. It was becoming a boondoggle, one that could end Bernard's chairmanship. While Brian didn't like Bernard, the thought of breaking in a new chair motivated the analyst to dispel the nay-saying.

Initially, Brian believed there were plausible reasons for the project's problems. NIMBY, the *not in my backyard* mantra of suburbanites, certainly was at play. Environmentalists found a marmot breeding ground in the road's path. The cost to relocate the endangered rodents was absurd. Most recently, engineers discovered a granite outcropping. Why highly educated engineers hadn't expected to find granite in the mountains around Spokane baffled Brian.

Even with these factors accounted for, costs were well above projections. Trying to save his boss from embarrassing questions, Brian opened Pandora's Box.

For comparison purposes, he built a massive spreadsheet and populated it with years of road construction cost-data. He spent hours creating and testing inflation-adjustment routines that brought ten-year old cost figures to current-day values. Today, after a month of preparation, Brain ran his predictive model, and no matter how he adjusted the variables, the model couldn't account for the staggering overages. No scenario came close to predicting the project's current expenditure pattern. Brian reluctantly concluded the cause resided in a variable he had no way to estimate, corruption. There was no other explanation.

Brian sent Bernard an email. *There are unexplainable anomalies in the project's budget. I need to go over my findings with you. Should I fly to Spokane or wait to meet you in Winthrop?*

Senator Bernard's computer signaled when an email from his chief-of-staff arrived. Most of Crane's correspondence was mundane, but the message Bernard received on November 27th captured the senator's full attention.

Bernard immediately replied by email. *I was concerned we might have a problem, and you seem to have confirmed it. Please keep this between us for right now. I'm convinced we can get this project back on track. DOT will make a mountain out of this molehill. Their committee chairwoman loves media time. Bring the file to Winthrop. We'll review it and come up with a game plan.*

Then he left Apakoh a message. "The Okanogan project has to be completed."

Chapter 25

Doctor Whitlam paced like a caged tiger. His team might have solved part of the Thomlinson case. Detective Linder pulled into the crime lab's parking lot. Whitlam ran to greet her. "Detective Linder? I'm Rob Whitlam. We have great news for you."

Patti, overwhelmed by the scientist's enthusiasm, grasped his outstretched hand. "It's Patti. And I'm delighted to meet you. Lead the way, I'm all ears."

He opened the security door. "The dealer was skimming, and he had two accomplices."

Patti was stunned. She'd heard Rob and his team were good, but she hadn't expected them to be this good. They took the elevator to the basement and entered the video lab. Whitlam sat at a control panel and brought up camera twenty-three's video file on a huge flat-screen mounted to the wall. Patti was surprised by the picture's clarity. She expected it to be grainy, black and white, and difficult to watch. It was the exact opposite. She was hovering above the table, watching the dealer and players in crystal clear color. "I wasn't expecting this."

"Frankly, neither were we. The casino has world-class surveillance equipment."

Rob moved the control dials and everyone on screen moved at dizzying speeds. He stopped when the display read 3:58 p.m. November 2nd. From the left, a middle-aged man wearing a dealer's uniform strolled into view. He greeted the players and the departing dealer. Patti recognized Mickey Thomlinson.

"Shift change. Right on schedule," Rob said as two men in lab coats joined them.

"Bruce and Isaac will take over. They spotted what the dealer was doing." Rob gave the controls to Isaac.

Isaac stopped the video. "I'm going to synch up camera twenty-two with twenty-three. We'll look at the scene from across the aisle using twenty-two and directly down from twenty-three at the same time. You could get dizzy, but bear with me."

Isaac flipped a switch, and a second screen came to light. He fast forwarded that video until its time and date matched camera twenty-three's.

Bruce warned everyone, "We're going to have to do this a couple of times, but eventually you'll see how Thomlinson's doing it."

Patti looked at the screens, desperately trying to watch both at once. She got a touch of vertigo.

"What did you see?" Bruce asked Patti.

She described the scene she'd witnessed. "Thomlinson dealt cards to three people. The man with a bunch of chips won. A young woman sitting to his left hugged him. Thomlinson paid out chips, and the game continued."

"That's right, and Thomlinson pocketed four chips, twenty bucks." Bruce smiled.

"What? How?" Patti asked. "I didn't see that."

"Let's watch it in slow motion," Rob said. "It's cool how he's doing this."

The technician replayed the video. Patti was at a loss. "I still didn't see anything."

Rob patted her on the back. "That's not surprising. Mickey did it very quickly. Let's go to stop-frame mode, Isaac."

The scene came to a stop as Thomlinson dealt the winning card to the man who was about to win. "Count the chips in the man's wagering circle," Rob said to Patti. "He has eight, right?"

She confirmed eight five-dollar chips were in the circle. Isaac moved the file forward. The man won, was hugged by the woman next to him, and received his winnings.

"How many chips did Mickey add to the pile?" Isaac asked.

Patti nearly shouted, "He only gave him six chips!"

The next frame showed Mickey sliding two chips from the man's circle back with him. "He was supposed to give the guy eight chips, but he only gave him six and took two from the circle. He stole four chips," Bruce exclaimed. "We caught him."

"Wait," Patti looked at Mickey's hand with chips under it. "Why didn't the guy complain?"

"He was too busy looking at the girl's...um, breasts." Rob's face turned red. "Isaac, pan out on camera twenty-two, and we'll show you."

The camera showed Mickey's table from the side. Isaac provided color-commentary to the replay. "As the dealer declared the man a winner, the woman pulled him towards her, her cleavage holds his undivided attention. For twenty bucks, he got flashed and hugged. If he protested his winnings, he'd be shown his circle contained six chips, matching the number Mickey gave him."

Rob gave his assessment. "It isn't sophisticated, but it's effective. The gambler didn't even check his winnings, just placed another bet."

Bruce wrote $250 on the whiteboard. "We watched Mickey's entire shift, and he pocketed five-hundred dollars. If he earns twenty bucks an hour, his job paid him about a hundred bucks take-home that evening. If he split the scammed money down the middle, he nearly tripled his pay."

Rob introduced another key component. "They had a third member roaming the tables watching for good marks; middle-aged guys betting four chips or more and interested in the female anatomy. Isaac, move to the 7:38 mark on camera twenty-three. The third member shows up then."

Patti listened intently to Rob. "The guy in the Mariner shirt is the mark. This guy in the baseball cap sits next to him. The mark bets four chips, and our guy bets one. Now watch from the left. Here she comes, right on cue. The cap guy gives her his seat. Mickey pulls the rip-off five times on the Mariner guy, and the mark never notices. There's your team: Mickey, the woman, and ball cap guy."

Isaac adjusted the resolution to show the ball cap man's face.

"Can you print that?" Patti asked.

"Absolutely. Do you want a photo of the woman?" Isaac hit Print.

"You could give her one from your collection." Bruce jabbed. "Isaac has a crush on the girl, or at least a particular part of her."

"I do not," Isaac protested.

"Just busting on you." Bruce handed the photo of the man to Patti. "Here you go. We'll find a good one of the girl and get it printed."

"Can you email them to me?" Patti slipped the photo into her file.

"Not a problem. I hope this was helpful." Rob guided Patti to the exit.

"More than you know, Rob. Could the folks at the casino figure out what was going on?"

"If they looked, they'd have figured it out pretty quickly. That being said, he could've gotten away with it for a while. I doubt they review the tapes unless there's a problem."

Patti thanked Rob and got into her car. Had the guys come up with the motive for the murders? Had the mob made an example of Mickey? Why kill the others?

"A little harsh," she said to herself. "If they cleared three hundred a night, which is probably high, they pocketed a thousand bucks a week, two thousand tops. Three people don't get murdered for a thousand dollars a week. They get beaten up, a leg broken, but not murdered. The mob wants its money back."

❖

Six miles south of the patrol's crime lab, Bryce was closing the shop for lunch when Andrei walked through the door. "Good morning, Bryce."

"Are you here to threaten me again, Andrei?" Bryce locked the door.

"No threats, just business to discuss."

Bryce shook his head. "I'm out of business. Nothing for two weeks. Have you shut me down?"

Andrei pulled Bryce's coat off the rack. "That's the last thing I want to do. You're going to be my best asset. It'll just take time. I want to discuss some details about our arrangement, and I'm hungry. How about that Korean restaurant up the street? Let's make it a business lunch. I'm buying."

❖

"Fuck!!!" Don screamed at his computer. "Andrei finally shows up again, and they leave the damned building."

Don fast forwarded the audio file. An hour later, Bryce returned alone. The afternoon was highlighted by Sidney Polska's announcement that his gall bladder was acting up. Last week it had been his spleen and the week before his kidneys. He was falling apart, except for his hair which grew at an alarming pace. Don moved on to the next day's recording. Bryce opened at eight, and business was steady. At 2:15, a customer's arrival brought Bryce from the storeroom.

"What do you know, Lawrence?" Bryce sounded delighted to see an old friend.

Lawrence gave a report on the upturn in business around Olympia.

"Any plans for the holidays?" Bryce asked.

"We're taking the kids to Disneyland."

"When?" Bryce turned on the shaver.

"The weekend after next. We got a great package deal. The kids miss two days of school, but they'll be fine. Nancy visits the spa, and I ride my ass off."

Don's thoughts probably mirrored Bryce's; long weekend, nobody home, perfect target. Lawrence had unwittingly provided all the necessary information. Don yelled at his computer again, "I need a last name."

A few minutes after wishing Lawrence a happy holiday, Bryce made a call. "Andrei, this is Bryce. Lawrence Martin heard good things about your services and was wondering if you're available the weekend after next."

Don was elated for Bryce's help. "Thank you Bryce, thank you. Now where does Lawrence Martin live?"

Don pulled up Thurston County's *White Pages* and typed in *Lawrence Martin*. The target's address came to the screen. With a little research, Don learned Mr. Martin worked for Thurston Federal Savings, was married to Sheila, and had two kids.

Mapquest couldn't find 1411 Cheshire Road in Olympia and asked if he meant 1411 Cheshire in Tumwater. Irritated, Don typed *yes,* and hit the Enter key a bit harder than needed. A map of Covington Estates appeared. The subdivision south of Olympia was bordered by Littlerock Road on the east, the Capitol Forest to its south, and the Black River on its northern and western boundaries. Don zoomed in until the map transformed into a photo of the Martin house: a mid-sized home on a well-groomed lot with its backyard butted up against the Capitol Forest. As he zoomed out, the image revealed a long driveway connecting the house to Cheshire, which in turn, connected to Wilmington Road.

"The game's afoot." Don made his initial entry into his *Martin File.* "Time to visit 1411 Cheshire and the woods behind."

From years of experience doing reconnaissance, Don was certain whoever planned to rob the Martins would start in the woods. They'd check the back of the house and maybe find a convenient point of entry. Don called Justin to discuss an intervention plan and pose a question.

"Hello Major." Justin greeted his friend. "What's going on?"

"We got our first lead." Don was glad he got through. "A burglary's happening sometime next weekend. I know the target, but I don't know when or by whom."

"We should've put in a camera." Justin sat back in his chair.

"Wouldn't have helped. I got most of this from a phone call Bryce made. I need to walk through what I'm planning. Do you have a few minutes?"

"Margie's running errands, so you've got at least an hour." Justin chuckled.

Don laid out his plan. Justin asked questions and offered suggestions. Don adjusted the plan. "Don, you really didn't need my help. It's a pretty good plan." Justin was concerned Don hadn't told him everything. "Do you want me to come out?"

"No, I've got this one, but I may need you if something bigger comes along." Don finally got to his question. "Should I bring Patti in on this?"

"Remind me? Patti is the pretty blonde cop with bodacious tatas?"

"What do you know about her tatas? She was wearing a coat." Don smiled.

"I have a vivid imagination, and you've got to love my *Top Gun* reference?"

Don shook his head. "Really? *Top Gun*? That's where you think the line's from?"

"Exactamundo, big guy. *Top Gun*. Tom Cruise talking about Kelly McGinnis."

"It's from an *Officer and a Gentleman,* and it was Richard Gere's friend, David Keith, pointing out Debra Winger's friend's assets." Don knew his movies.

"Hmm? You might be right, but no way do you involve Patti." Justin gave Don the only reasonable answer. "She'd have your nuts in a vice. Cops don't like amateurs mucking around in their business."

"You're right, but it'd be a lot more fun with her on the stakeout."

Justin became emphatic. "Keep Patti out of it!"

"No way to bring her in?" Don wouldn't let go.

"What part of *no* didn't you understand? The N or the O?" Justin shook his head.

"You're right, but I just can't stop thinking about her."

"Which head is doing that thinking?" Justin poured on the advice. "Fight crime with me. Date Patti."

"Roger that. Damn it." Don wasn't surprised, but he was a bit disappointed.

"Gotta go. Margie just pulled in and her rear end, I mean the car's rear end is dragging."

"Okay pal, thanks for everything. I'll keep you posted." Don thought about Justin's advice, concluded it was spot-on, and ignored it.

"Olympia Police Department: How may I help you?"

"Detective Linder, please." Don became nervous. The operator transferred his call.

A businesslike voice broke the silence. "This is Linder. How can I help you?"

"This isn't Detective Helen Keller?" Don grasped for an opening line. "Were you using an assumed identify at the college?"

"This must be Bart." Patti sat upright. She hadn't expected this call.

"It is. How are you?" Don struggled. Chatting with women was not his strong suit.

"I'm doing well. Is this a social call?"

"Depends on your answer to my next question. Is it okay if I call you Patti?"

"That'd be fine as long as I get your name."

"Fair enough. I'm Don."

"What's the question?" Patti tried to be as quiet as possible.

"I'm not very good at this, so I'm just going to put it out there." Don shrugged and asked, "Are you married, engaged, or exclusive?"

Patti burst out laughing. "Exclusive? What the hell does that mean? Are you thirteen?"

"Don't make this more difficult than it is: married, engaged, or seeing someone? How's that?"

"Better, but none of your business." Patti was delighted with the question, but she wasn't going to let Don know. She had him flapping in the breeze. "Why do you want to know?"

Don jumped right in. "I want to ask you out, but I don't want to cause waves."

"In the forty seconds we were together you decided you wanted to go out with me. On what did you base that decision?" Patti was having way too much fun to stop.

"Just a feeling, I guess. I liked the way you handled the situation." Don had to add something personal. "And you seem like a nice person."

"I seem like a nice person?" Patti's smile radiated across her face. She had all the cards. "I was yanking a guy's arm off his body to beat him with it, and that makes me *nice*? You hang with a tough crowd."

"I used to." Don circled his living room. "Patti, I can't explain why I think we might get along well, but I know we would. Or at least I'd like to meet you and see if you think so. Am I making any sense or just rambling?"

Patti sat on her desk. "Don, this is the clumsiest attempt by someone to ask me out, ever. And for some unknowable reason, I want to meet you...Hello? Are you still there? I said yes."

"I know. I wasn't expecting you'd say *yes* right away. My friend told me you'd probably keep me guessing for a while."

"You have a smart friend. I'm not sure if he has one." Patti needed to give Don a bone. "And, even though I didn't need your help the other night, I appreciate what you did."

"My pleasure." Don grabbed on and ran with it. "How about dinner tomorrow night? Wheelhouse Grill out by the marina at six-thirty?"

"You don't waste time, do you?"

"I don't want you to change your mind." Don pumped his fist in the air. "By the way, I'm not married, engaged, or anything."

"Good to know." Patti looked at her calendar. Tomorrow night was wide open, "Tomorrow won't work. How about Sunday?"

"That'd be perfect; six-thirty at the Wheelhouse?"

"Make it seven." Patti had him right where she wanted him. "How am I going to recognize you?" Patti nodded to her partner who walked into her cubicle.

Don scrambled. "I'll wear a blue sweater with white flecks."

Patti asked, "How will you recognize me?"

"You'll be the woman every man is staring at." Don smacked one out of the park.

Patti liked the answer. "I'll wear my tan jacket with a dark brown collar."

"I'd recognize you if you weren't wearing anything." Don knew immediately that came out all wrong.

"You aren't going to see me naked on Sunday, probably not ever."

Dunshee nearly lost his mouthful of coffee.

"I'm sorry. I didn't mean it that way." Don smacked himself in the head.

"You go with that," Patti continued without missing a beat.

"Do you eat much?" Don shoved his foot deep into his mouth.

"Why would you ask that of a woman, of anyone?"

"That didn't come out right either. You looked kind of skinny." Don tried to regain his composure but failed miserably.

"You do know the first step to getting out of a hole, don't you? Quit digging! And I don't eat much, and I'm not skinny."

Dunshee had to sit down.

"A bit touchy about your weight. I'll make a note of that." Don finally pulled out of his tailspin.

"You're a wiseass." Patti gave Bill a thumbs-up.

"But I'm an entertaining wiseass. You're smiling right now, aren't you?"

She was, but he wasn't going to know.

Don was elated. "I'll see you at seven Sunday evening at the Wheelhouse. I'll be in a blue sweater, and you'll be wearing a tan jacket."

"Don, this has been an interesting conversation, but I have to get some work done. I'll see you at seven. Don't be late."

"I'll be on time. It's one of my most endearing traits."

"You have endearing traits?" Patti continued her harassment.

"You're still smiling."

"Don't be too sure of yourself. I pack a Glock and know how to use it." Patti patted her sidearm.

"So do I, on both counts, but we won't need them. Maybe next weekend, but definitely not this Sunday." Don raised an arm over his head. Victory was his.

"What about next weekend?" Patti asked.

"If our date works out, I'll fill you in." Don didn't know how to end the call. "Now get to work. Taxpayers expect you to earn your keep. Bye."

The dial tone replaced Don's voice. Patti hadn't expected that, and she was surprised at her disappointment.

"So you're going on a blind date with a guy who might be stalking you?" Dunshee asked.

"It's not a date. I'm collecting information. Let's consider him an informant."

Dunshee nodded knowingly. "Are you buying?"

"No fucking way. He asked me out." Patti straightened Bill's collar and tie.

He was happy Patti had a date. "Do you want me to stake out the place?"

"No. He seems like a nice guy, but he'll probably have warts or a uni-brow." Patti composed herself. "Bill, please don't check on me. I'll be fine."

Bill left and Patti turned her attention to the Thomlinson file. Pictures of Mickey's two accomplices were on top of the few notes she'd put together on the triple homicide. Forcing herself to concentrate, Patti called Jack Ogden to see if he'd come up with anything. She dialed his direct line and got voice mail. She hung up and called the sheriff's business phone.

"Good afternoon, Sheriff's Office, how may I help you?"

"Diane? This is Patti Linder. How are you?"

"I'm doing great. Who do you need?"

"I want to see if Ogden has anything more on the Thomlinsons."

The dispatcher's voice showed concern. "Jack isn't here. He's missed work, and we haven't been able to find him. It's just not like him to go AWOL."

"He's missing?" Patti asked.

"He is. We checked his house and called his sisters. Nobody's seen or heard from him. The sheriff's pretty angry."

"I wouldn't want Knutsen pissed at me." Patti closed the Thomlinson file. "The guy's a hard ass, probably a Marine."

"Marine nothing. He was a Jesuit." Diane laughed. "Smart as hell and mean as a snake. Can somebody else help you?"

"No, I just wanted to check in with Jack. Tell him I called."

Chapter 26

Mel and Seth were pleased. Jessica had exposed the courier's weakness.

"That was brilliant. Jessica told us a lot about him." Jenkins congratulated his men. "Will he recognize her if he sees her again?"

"I doubt it. He didn't spend much time looking at her face." Seth chuckled.

After his associates left, Jenkins turned his attention to the next diamond shipment, the one he'd steal. It'd been pure luck that he learned about this shipment. A casual conversation with the limo driver, the jeweler's nephew, gave him everything he needed. It was time to put Bryce to work. Jenkins left a message for Andrei. "We need to meet today."

❖

Across town, Don started his Martin-mission. He drove to the mini-market on Littlerock Road, a mile south of Covington Estates. After parking the Jeep among the commuter cars, he jogged to the access road and entered the forest. An adrenalin rush hit him. He'd grown to like crime-fighting.

He found no footprints or tire tracks in the muddy trail. After a short walk Don stood in the forest behind the Martin house. A three-foot high tangle of shrubs and bushes made access to the backyard impossible for anything larger than a person. It eliminated the service road as a viable route for the thieves. They'd have to use Cheshire. When he turned to leave, fresh footprints in the soft earth caught his attention. The thief had been right where he stood. Doing what he was doing. The size and shape of the footprints surprised him. They were small and narrow and didn't depress the ground much. The thief was a woman, a small woman.

He followed her trail through the forest back to Littlerock Road. She braved blackberry thorns and tree limbs to avoid the muddy roadbed. The woman was smart, experienced, and willing to work hard for what she wanted. He lost her trail when she got to the sidewalk. Don returned to the mini-market in an exceptionally good mood. He'd ruled out the access road and picked up a valuable clue about the thief.

He wondered if his luck might hold. The thief would have to check out Cheshire sooner or later. If it held, he might catch a glimpse of her surveilling the area today. Don took magnetic *ARC Telecom* signs from the cargo area and stuck them on the doors of the Jeep. Don believed the person raising the least suspicion is the one being the most conspicuous. He put on a reflective vest and a bright yellow hardhat. After parking his vehicle at the corner of Wilmington and Cheshire, he set up a tripod at the intersection. The spot provided a panoramic view of the street, ideal for the camera mounted below the sextant.

Over the next two hours, only seven cars ventured down Cheshire. Six stayed somewhere on the street. The one making a round trip was driven by a heavy-set man with three kids in the car. On the way in, Don thought he looked frazzled. On the way out, the man looked like he'd won the lottery. The absence of children probably had a lot to do with the change. Around three, it began to drizzle. Don started to load his equipment. A blue Suburban turning on to Cheshire delayed his departure. It disappeared around the curve, but four minutes later the SUV returned. Don hid behind the tri-pod and took several photos of the young female driver.

"Gotcha!" Don said quietly.

Chapter 27

At their first meeting, Sarah had tried to comprehend what Mrs. Waite told her about transactional sex, but the only thing that registered was she had become a prostitute. Over the past three weeks, Sarah learned what that meant. She'd had sex almost seventy-five times with almost as many men. According to Waite, half of her debt had been paid. Waite wanted to celebrate. Sarah wanted to jump off Portland's Steel Bridge into the freezing cold Willamette River.

Sarah regretted many things but what she regretted most was missing Thanksgiving with her older sister, Gloria. They'd been inseparable through the one father, two step-fathers, and several *uncles* their alcoholic mother had brought home. When Gloria turned sixteen, they ran away, moving in with a girlfriend who had her own apartment. There they became familiar with trading sex for things they wanted, but the trade had always been on their terms with men they chose. Eventually, Gloria met a man. They married and moved to Arizona. Gloria invited Sarah to join them, but she'd met Coley who refused to leave the Pacific Northwest. So she moved in with Charlie, and the rest is history.

Looking out her bedroom window, Sarah made a promise. When this chapter of her life ended, she'd start over in Arizona, get a GED, and attend a community college. After, she'd get a normal job and find a guy who wanted her for more than sex. Her sister had, and she was happy. Why couldn't she expect the same? The wind whipped rain across the parking area. Tears began to flow.

❖

The season's first Pineapple Express slammed into the Pacific Northwest. Don thought about the Martins who'd be enjoying dry, sunny

California in a week. Disneyland sounded pretty good as he collected the newspaper.

"Any plans for tonight?" came a voice from next door.

Don looked over at Brian. "Actually, I have a date. How about you?"

"Deirdre and I are going to Portland to do some Christmas shopping."

"Should a state employee be avoiding our sales tax?" Don asked.

"Probably not, but we all do it." Brian picked up his paper. "The Weather Channel says this is going to blow through and the rest of the day will be beautiful...if you can believe them."

"They can't predict yesterday's weather all that well." Don climbed his stairs.

"I hope they're right. It'd be nice not to need raingear." Brian headed for shelter. "My fingers are crossed."

"Same here. Have fun. I'll keep an eye on your place." The men parted company.

The paper's weather report confirmed Brian's information. The seven-day forecast showed rain throughout the week with clearing on Saturday. Storms returned Sunday. Don was even more convinced. *They'll hit the Martins on Saturday.*

After finishing the paper, Don dressed and checked his things-to-do list. On one side of the sheet were tasks to get ready for the Martin-mission; on the other, things to do to get ready for the date. No matter how much he tried to focus on the mission, he dwelt on the date.

Don thought a change of location might help, and he retreated to his basement. The gear on the table mimicked what he'd taken to the Hansen's. The dosage in the darts posed the biggest challenge. They'd all been the same for the Hansen-mission. He'd prepped for relatively large men, and, that's who showed up. A small woman would be at the Martin's, and a full dose could paralyze her or worse. The last thing Don wanted was to kill someone trying to stop a burglary.

He checked the photos of the woman and estimated her size, a half dose should work. It wasn't scientific, but it was the best he could do. He prepared two darts for her and six for her friends. He didn't know how many people were coming and wanted to have enough to go around. He secured the ready-bag in the Jeep's hidden compartment.

Don turned his attention to his date. He didn't own designer jeans or shirts. He was a throwback, not prone to fashion trends. He put on a pair of khakis, a white shirt, comfortable shoes, and, finally, the blue sweater. Not trusting western Washington weather, he grabbed his North Face jacket. At six-thirty, he left for the restaurant. He wanted to be early, affirming his self-proclaimed *most endearing trait.*

The Wheelhouse was built in the late 1980s and did well until it fell on hard times in the early 2000s. In 2008, two enterprising brothers bought

89

what had become a derelict building along Olympia's north shore and turned it into one of the best eateries in the Northwest. It was open and airy, modern with a hint of an old-style lodge. The parking lot was nearly full when Don arrived.

The hostess looked up Don's reservation. "With the festival going on, every night's been wicked busy. Would you like a booth or a table by the window?"

Don enthusiastically chose a table and wanted one as far from the bar as possible. She offered him a seat in the waiting area, but he opted for the bar. The only empty stool was next to a guy having a beer. "May I sit? I'm waiting for my date."

"They're always late," the man answered. "Get comfortable."

"Thanks." Noting the man's attire, Don asked, "You a cop?"

Before his bar-mate could answer, Don's attention was drawn to a woman approaching the hostess station. She was wearing a tan jacket with a dark brown collar. It was exactly seven. The hostess greeted her and after a brief chat, pointed to Don. Don waved, so did Bill.

"She your date?"

Don nodded. "She your partner?"

"Tonight she's my friend who's meeting a stranger." Bill sipped his beer.

The men smiled uncomfortably at each other and then at Patti. She was pleased to see Don, not so much to see Bill.

Patti walked up to the men. "Comparing notes?"

Don offered Patti his seat. "I just got here. I don't even have a drink. And I'm Don."

"Nice to meet you, Don. And what do you have to say for yourself, Mr. Dunshee?"

"Was in the neighborhood." Bill smiled, sheepishly.

"In the neighborhood, huh? You live twenty miles from here. Your favorite bar is two blocks from your house, and the beer costs about a third what it does here." Patti got the bartender's attention. "Margarita, blended with salt."

"Make that two, and freshen my friend's beer," Don added.

She turned to Bill. "Don's the guy who helped me with those two punks at the college, then disappeared, like you're going to in a few minutes."

Shortly after their drinks arrived, Don announced, "Looks like our table is ready."

The hostess came their way. She asked if there'd be a third. All three said no. Patti and Don followed her to a table on the other side of the room. It was as private as possible. Bill remained seated, nursing his six-dollar beer.

Patti wore a black, figure-hugging skirt. The two-inch heels made her almost six-feet tall. Don helped her out of the tan jacket, revealing a lacy white blouse with pearl buttons, the top two left undone. From the look on Don's face, she'd selected well. She watched Bill leave. "We're alone now."

"Except for the other two hundred people here, I'd say you're right. I like your choice of drinks. Margaritas suit any occasion."

"It's my favorite." Patti was nervous. She looked at Don: tall, strong, purposefully bald, dressed conservatively. He was as imposing a figure as she remembered. "Do you bring all your dates here?"

"You're my first. Actually, you're my first date in quite a while." Don fidgeted.

"Do I make you nervous?" she asked.

"Yeah, I guess so. I'm not good at this dating thing."

"You seem pretty good at it. I'm here, aren't I?" Patti slid back in her seat.

"Yes you are, and you're even prettier than I remember." Don fumbled for the right words.

"You're sweet talking me, but thanks."

"Seriously, you're gorgeous." Don put his napkin in his lap and shuffled his feet.

"You're carrying it a little too far." Patti opened her menu. "What looks good? Besides me."

He lifted his margarita and offered a toast. "To a delightful evening and an even more delightful woman."

Patti met his glass with hers and took a sip to seal the toast.

"You look fabulous, Patti. That outfit is perfect."

"Thank you. I don't dress up very often. Feels kind of nice."

The waiter suggested the salmon or the spaghetti puttanesca and moved on to another table.

"Ah, the whore's pasta." Don clasped his hands.

"What?" Patti didn't understand what he meant.

Don explained, "Pasta Puttanesca, the whore's spaghetti. During World War II prostitutes in Italy were like sisters, some of them were sisters. When times were tough, they'd bring whatever food they had and blend it into a pasta dish. So now when a chef has a bunch of leftovers, he makes spaghetti puttanesca."

Patti looked at the menu. She considered the spaghetti, but the steak looked more inviting. The waiter set a basket of flat bread on the table, and Don told him they were ready. Patti wanted the ribeye, medium well, garlic mashed potatoes, and a dinner salad with raspberry vinaigrette. Don told the waiter he'd have the spaghetti but hold the whores. The waiter had no idea what he was talking about, adding to Patti's amusement.

Don asked his date, "How about some wine? A merlot will go great with your steak and my spaghetti."

"I'd have a glass."

Don added a bottle of merlot.

"Where did you learn about the whore's spaghetti?"

"When I was stationed in Italy. I took a week off and went to Cinque Terre. What a wonderful place." Don recalled one of his favorite vacations. "Built for mountain goats, but it was incredibly beautiful. A restaurant had it on the menu. I knew puttanesca meant whore."

"Of course you did. Every soldier would know that." Patti laughed.

"I took Italian in high school." Don defended an indefensible group of men. "Anyway, I saw it on the menu and asked about it. The waitress was got embarrassed and called the chef. He came out of the kitchen, hands waving, and explained the concept. I asked him what was in his pasta puttanesca, and he told me he couldn't tell me. I'm not sure if he wouldn't give out an old family recipe or just didn't know."

"Did you have the spaghetti?"

"I did, several times. They were all different." Don offered Patti some bread. "If I'd stayed much longer, they'd have needed a crane to get me out. The chef loved me, so did the waitress."

Patti dipped her bread in the olive oil and balsamic vinegar. "Did you tip well?"

"That could be part of it." Don followed Patti's lead with his bread. "I don't like chintzy tippers. I waited tables back in the day. It's hard work and the pay sucks."

"I hear you on that. Worked my way through Evergreen waiting tables."

For two hours, they got to know each other. Don enjoyed the spaghetti, but it didn't compare well with the dishes he had in Italy. Patti finished her dinner, set down her fork, and asked, "What do you think? Did I eat a lot?"

"You have a healthy appetite, but you're still a little skinny."

Patti enjoyed putting Don in difficult positions. "Skinny in a good way?"

"You're not anorexic, so I'd go with good." He weathered another storm.

Patti leaned forward. "Great. Then I want some dessert. Want to share?"

"I'd love to share. Did you see anything on the menu?"

"I didn't look, but I'd like something with chocolate, lots of chocolate." She excused herself and headed to the ladies room. Don asked the waiter for the dessert menu and picked the chocolate-raspberry cake. A soldier walking to a table caught his eye. He had corporal stripes on his sleeve with the Ranger insignia above them. Don thought he and his date might be celebrating something, an anniversary perhaps. After they were seated, Don asked his waiter to find out what brought the couple to a relatively expensive restaurant. A few minutes later, Patti returned. Soon after, the waiter showed up with cake and two spoons.

"They're celebrating their first baby. She's due in six months," the waiter reported to Don. "He's deploying next week and won't be here for the birth. So they're celebrating tonight."

Patti looked a bit perplexed.

"Tell them dinner and dessert are covered. But don't tell them it's me. That's between us, okay pal?"

"I'd be delighted to, sir. Since they're at my table, I'll throw in the tip."

"No you won't. I'll take care of that too. Just make sure they don't know who's doing this. I don't want a scene, okay?"

"Got it. And thank you." The waiter beamed.

"Why are you thanking me?"

"I wanted to do that, but I couldn't afford to." The waiter went away, smiling.

"That's a very nice thing you're doing." Patti picked up her spoon and signaled Don to do the same. "You're a good man, aren't you?"

"I try to be, at least most of the time. The corporal's working his ass off for three bucks an hour. He's spending all his extra money on this dinner, money he needs to put aside for the baby. A corporal doesn't make shit. I mean, he isn't paid well."

"You can say *shit*. I grew up with three brothers. I've heard worse. I've said worse. Shit, I've said worse today."

They enjoyed the cake and chatted about Italy, her brothers, the military, police work. The waiter brought their bill and the one for the other party. Don noted they'd been very conservative with their meals. Don added a twenty percent tip. He was signing the credit slip when the soldier's wife appeared at the table. She was in tears.

"I don't know how to thank you. Patrick couldn't afford to bring me here, but he wanted to celebrate our baby." She took Don's hand. "Why did you do this?"

"He's a fellow soldier. How did you know I did it?" Don tried to look unruffled.

"Patrick knew. When we first got here, he said you might be an officer. When the waiter told us someone bought our dinner, Patrick said it had to be you." The young woman smiled from her heart "Thank you for making this a very special night for us." Her husband gave him a quick salute. Don nodded.

Looking at Patti, who was crying, Don said, "Wow, that didn't go well." He handed her a napkin.

"You have no idea how well that went," She said through her tears.

Don thought the meal was ending on a high note, which was odd since Patti was crying. Hand-in-hand, he led her to her car.

"How did you know this was my car?" Patti asked.

"Look around. Every driver pulled into a slot face-first. You backed in, ready to race off to the next crime scene. Only cops park this way."

"Am I that predictable?"

"You're anything but predictable, Patti. I wasn't expecting those tears."

"I wasn't expecting a knight in shining armor."

"I'm glad I made you feel that way." Don took her in his arms and kissed her. She kissed back. "I'd like to see you again. Could you put up with me one more time?"

"I'd love to put up with you, Don. Next dinner is on me. I won't be a kept woman."

"Shit howdy!" Don laughed. "I'll take you up on that. What night works best?"

"Wednesday? I'd say sooner, but I've got a messy homicide I need to work on for the next couple of days."

"Wednesday it is. Should I meet you or pick you up?"

Patti pulled a notepad from her purse and wrote her address and home phone number. She began to hand it to him and stopped. As he reached for it, she pulled it back. "One question. What's your name?"

"Don Rowland. When you look it up, and I know you will, the system will say there are three guys with that name. I'm the one with the file that has almost nothing in it. You'd need Eyes-Only clearance to access the real dirt on me."

"Oh great! I find a guy who's not a total loser, and he's CIA."

"Worse, Army Ranger - Special Ops. That's all the system will tell you." Don pointed to a car pulling out of its parking slot. "You should wave goodnight to Bill. He's probably cold."

Patti waved as Bill left. Bill flashed his lights.

"Well, you weren't the only driver to park facing out; nice to have a partner who has your back." Don kissed her again and then opened her door. "Better get some sleep. You look tired."

"It's been a tough week, but this has been a wonderful night. Thank you. Pick me up around six. Dress casual."

Patti was anything but tired. Sleep wouldn't come easily tonight. She hoped Don would have the same problem. He did.

Chapter 28

Senator Bernard studied the newly restored Havendell Hotel from his office window. Its refurbishment sparked major upgrades to buildings on both sides. His building benefitted from this unexpected burst of urban renewal, and, now, all but one office was occupied, mostly by lawyers.

Taras Revoldi arrived at ten-thirty. Shortly after, Andrei joined them. As soon as the coffee was delivered and the receptionist closed the door, Apakoh started, "Crane is snooping where he shouldn't be."

Bernard replied, "He's a pit-bull. Once he bites into something, he doesn't let go, and he doesn't care whose flesh it is. Boeing, Microsoft...he's bitten them all. And judging from his email, he's convinced our project is tainted."

"Show me the email." Andrei moved to the senator's desk.

After reading the word *anomalies* in the opening sentence, Andrei nodded. "He's closing in on us. Has he told anyone?"

The senator shook his head. "Unlikely. He keeps things close; doesn't like to share credit. He only has statistical evidence the books are being manipulated. He hasn't put a name with the *anomalies*."

"Not yet." Revoldi shifted in his chair. "If he's as close as you think and as smart as you say, it won't take him long to find Reice and Waters. Once he does, the plan unravels. We can't have it unravel."

"My thoughts exactly," the senator added. "I told him to keep me posted on everything he finds, and I've made sure his regular work keeps him exceptionally busy. It should distract him for a while."

"Good, we have time to do this right. Senator, you mentioned a hunting trip later this month?" Revoldi walked to the window.

"Right after Christmas, Crane and I are going hunting up in the Methow. Brian says the area is very isolated."

"It must look like an accident." Revoldi pointed at Andrei. "If he dies suspiciously, they'll investigate, and we can't be certain he hasn't left a trail. People have hunting accidents all the time."

"Do I have to be there?" Bernard asked.

"No. It's better if you aren't," Revoldi declared. "When the time's right, make an excuse and stay here, but be sure he's already there. Crane doesn't leave the valley alive. Senator, work with Andrei on dates and places. Andrei, I'll leave it to you to handle this. Unless we have other business, our meeting is over."

After his visitors left, Bernard watched a couple enter the Havendell and wondered how Andrei would kill Brian. He wasn't happy about that decision, but Brian had brought it on himself. If he'd have stuck to his job and stayed out of other people's business, he wouldn't be having a hunting accident in three weeks.

❖

In an office overlooking the Capitol, Danielle Weaver explained her plan to Jenkins. "The best time is Saturday around two-thirty in the afternoon. The Seahawks are playing the Packers. Everybody'll be glued to their sets. I could drive a semi up to the front door and nobody'd notice."

Jenkins agreed, "You're right, and Saturday's the driest day of the week. We'll go then. Focus on jewelry, electronics, and cash. How many guys do you want?"

"Two would be great; one to keep watch and the other to load." Weaver had thought the project through.

"Mac and Bernie are available. Mac's small but packs a punch. Bernie's solid muscle and takes orders well."

"Shouldn't need Mac's punch; nobody'll be home. There's no security."

Jenkins liked Weaver: competent and aggressive, bold but not reckless. "Plan to meet them about one. You know Mac don't you?"

"We worked together once. He got the job done."

"I'll pay them. They're my insurance policy."

"That's generous, Mr. Jenkins, and I'll take you up on it. I'm short on cash, and Christmas is coming. Need to get my kids a few things."

Weaver left and made her way to the blue SUV. The rain was steady. She was anxious to get home and fix dinner. The open flap of the car's sunglass holder reminded her to hide the license plates she'd *borrowed* from a disabled van. She used them for her drive-by. She smiled as she closed the flap. Her father used flaps, notes, or whatever was handy to remind him he had something important to do. He used them until the brain tumor killed him.

❖

A few miles from Jenkins' office, Don struggled with Justin's admonition to keep Patti out of his adventures. He looked in the mirror and renewed his promise to keep the Martin burglary to himself.

Faced with Patti's directive to *dress casual*, Don went through his entire wardrobe, now strewn around his bedroom. Eventually, he decided on dark pants and a long-sleeve shirt. The stripes made him look thinner, and that was good. Getting ready for the date was more complicated than planning raids in Iraq. He drove to Patti's house and found the porch light welcoming him. A few seconds after ringing the bell, his date opened the door wearing an apron. The aroma of garlic and oregano rushed past him into the night.

"You have to be kidding me." Don smiled. "Is that what I think it is?"

"I hope so. It'll be the second time you've had it this week, but I hope mine's better than the restaurant's." Patti took Don's coat. "There's wine on the table. Mind opening it? I have to finish the salad. Sorry, no margaritas tonight."

Don uncorked the Chianti and poured two glasses. He brought them into the kitchen. "This is way above the call of duty."

She sipped the wine and put her arms around his neck. "So, you're the Donald Rowland who received the Bronze Star and made major in near-record time? The one who told General Bartsom to take his job and shove it?"

"You've done your homework, and you've had help." Don was thoroughly surprised by what she'd managed to find out.

"I know some guys. I have sources." Patti smile and stirred the pot.

"How well do you know them?"

"Not in the way you're thinking, trust me. But if I need intel, there aren't many places I can't go. I know your hat size, your shoe size, and a couple of other sizes I won't mention. All very impressive."

"You should be ashamed of yourself." Don grinned.

"How about being useful and putting garlic butter on the bread and sticking it into the oven."

Don did as directed. Twenty minutes later, dinner was served. An hour later, they were clearing the table.

"That was excellent, but I feel bad I didn't bring a gift or flowers. I thought we were going out." Don put the dishes in the sink.

"I'm glad I pulled it over on you. Keep the spoons for hot fudge sundaes with real whipped cream. Well, it'll be whipped cream if you know how to use a beater." Patti got the heavy cream from the refrigerator. "The blades are in the top drawer over there."

They talked about how life had gotten them to where they were. Each had a few regrets, but both were satisfied they'd done what they'd wanted. As the night wound down, Patti sat up and looked Don in the eye. "You were waiting out there, weren't you?"

"What? Waiting out where?"

"At Evergreen. You were in the bushes waiting for those guys to attack someone? Come on. Give it up. That was no coincidence."

Don started to answer...hesitated.

"Okay," Patti said. "Here's the deal. No secrets between us. Not now, not ever. I don't care if what we have lasts a day or the rest of our lives. I want you to promise me. No secrets. Starting now."

Don nodded. He'd dealt with generals who weren't as direct or compelling as Patti. Her demand came from the heart, not the head. She wanted a relationship based on trust, trust to the core. "Yes. I was waiting. I knew some guys were setting up a hit, and I couldn't let it happen. I waited, and then you came and then they came and then we got into it."

"Why didn't you tell the cops?" Patti took a bite of her sundae.

"Tell them I had a vision some bad shit would go down sometime, somewhere on campus?" Don became uncomfortable. "They'd have laughed me out of the station or had me hauled away in straps. And I couldn't have blamed them."

Patti curled up next to him. "How did you know?"

"I have sources too." Don relaxed and dug into the sundae. "This is marvelous.

"Not an adequate answer, my friend. What sources?"

"Can we just leave it alone? At least for right now."

"Don't you trust me?" Patti asked, somewhat hurt.

"It's the exact opposite. I trust you implicitly. You'll do the absolute right thing, by the book. And I'd probably end up in jail. I need you to let me work this out so I keep me out of prison and you on the police force."

"Really? It's that hush-hush? You tapped into NASA drones?"

"NASA doesn't have the drones. NASA has rockets. NSA has drones. They're probably outside the window right now." Don got up. "Want another sundae?"

"No, and you don't need another one either. You've got a little pudge, major. You haven't been doing as many sit-ups as you should."

"It's your fault. I haven't had fudge like this in my life. How do you get it to firm up on the ice cream?"

"I have ways of firming things up." Patti laughed. "And I'll give you a pass on how you knew to be there. I'm glad you were."

"I don't know why. You could've taken them. Hands down, you'd have kicked their asses without me." Don picked up the empty sundae bowls.

"I know, but I wouldn't be here with you if you hadn't tortured those men at the Hansen ranch now, would I?" Patti walked to the kitchen.

"How the hell did you know that?" Don blew it.

"You just told me, and you have something cooking, Mr. Rowland. Something you desperately want to talk to me about, but you're worried I might have to end your superhero fun." Patti put the last of the plates in the dishwasher. "And you'd be right. Let's leave that topic for another evening. Maybe later this week?"

Don agreed wholeheartedly, reached over, and kissed her.

In her garage fifteen miles from Don and Patti, Danielle inventoried her tools. The lock-picks were essential. She put them in the bucket. Three two-way radios with headsets would make communication among the team effortless. They went into a small valise. Screwdrivers and wire cutters went into the bucket. A pry bar and claw hammer joined them. A ratchet set was the largest item to be included. Headlamps on adjustable straps were dropped into the bucket. Rubber gloves completed the package. She gathered everything and set them in the cabinet under her Navy's Marksmanship Award.

She opened the safe and took out two pistols. The Glock was crafted for someone with small hands. It fired twenty-two caliber bullets, and what it lacked in stopping-power, it made up for in volume. The seventeen-cartridge clip gave the gun a lethal potential, but only if she wanted it. If the situation turned dire, she'd rely on the .357 magnum she had in a police-styled shoulder holster. It was impressive, and, with five quick-load cylinders on the belt, Danielle had thirty hollow-point bullets at her command. She'd invade the house well-armed with plenty of ammunition. She hid the guns behind the bucket of tools and locked the cabinet. All was ready.

She needed to check on homework, pick out a movie, and call Chris. She hadn't found a sitter, but her ex would happily take the girls. They were great kids, and Chris was equally responsible for that outcome. As a dad, he was wonderful, protective, attentive, and dedicated. As a husband, he was boring. Soon after they married, his interest in travel disappeared. After Angela's birth, skiing, mountain climbing, and cave diving vanished. By the time Stacey arrived, his idea of a night out was setting up the telescope and looking for satellites with the girls. Danielle needed more and decided to move on without him. In a few days, she'd leave her girls with *Saint Chris*, pick up Mac and Bernie, and rob a family of everything they owned.

Chapter 29

Don and Patti agreed what the movie lacked in quality it more than made up for in length. "That's three hours of my life I can't get back." Patti slid into the passenger's seat. "Other than a crappy movie, it's been a very nice Friday evening."

"Surprised we had a good time?" Don pulled away from the theater.

"When you're a cop and your date's about to break the law, *again*, it can put a damper on an evening."

Don wasn't looking forward to this conversation. "You can't prove I broke the law, or I'll do it again."

"Call it intuition. Do you want to tell me what you're up to, or do I have to get out the water board?" Patti put her hand on Don's neck and squeezed.

"Ouch." Don feigned being hurt. "Water board is a technique, not a thing. You can't get a water board out of the closet."

"Don't change the subject. You've been lucky, but your luck can end." Patti turned on the charm. "Tell me what's going on, and I'll go easy on you."

"What if I don't want you to go easy on me?" Don smiled at his date.

"You really don't want me pissed off. I'm the cop. You're the civilian. Tell me what you know, and I'll take care of it." Patti chuckled. "Seems simple enough. A man your age should be able to grasp the concept."

"My age!" Don tried to act insulted. "What do you mean by that? I'm barely forty-seven."

"You're way past your sexual prime. Who knows what might not being working. You're probably having *senior moments.*"

Don pulled the Jeep into his driveway. He was laughing. Patti wasn't. "We're home."

"Do the neighbors know they live next to a vigilante?" Patti stepped out of Don's car and quickly checked on her's down the street..

"Crime-fighter to you, and no they don't." Don climbed the stairs. "They think I'm a little weird, but around here, weird is normal. Lot of Evergreen graduates."

"Hey, I'm a Greener." Patti followed him into the warm house.

"Like I said, weird is normal. Want something to drink?"

"I'd love some water. Lots of ice. Please," Patti replied.

"Make yourself at home. If you need, the loo is down the hall on the right."

Patti looked around the living room, sparsely appointed, no knick-knacks. It was clean and orderly, which didn't surprise her. "Don, I'm serious. If you know something, then you have to tell me so I can take care of it. You can't be a one-man anti-crime campaign."

Don shouted from the kitchen. "Let's say, hypothetically, I know a crime's going to be committed. It's a property crime, and nobody's likely to get hurt. I know the victim, but I don't know the criminal. What's the first thing you're going to ask?"

Patti responded immediately, "How do you know?"

"Exactly. You didn't want to know who or when. You wanted my source. And that's where the problem lies."

"What are you talking about?" Patti pulled her hoody over her head. "By the way, thanks for dinner. I love Annie's."

"You're welcome. If I got the information through a less-than-pristine legal process, and I told you, then what?" Don pulled an ice tray out of the freezer and twisted it until the cubes broke free.

"If you beat it out of a guy, I'd arrest you for assault." Patti picked up a photo of two dogs lounging under a tree.

"That didn't happen." Don put some crackers on a plate.

"Oh, you tapped his phone. That's a horse of a different color. The feds get you."

"There you have it." Don put two glasses of water and a plate with cheese and crackers on the coffee table. "So unless I read minds, I'd be screwed, the burglary would happen, and everybody's happy, except the poor schmucks who come home and find everything they care about is missing."

"We'd send a car to the house and prevent the robbery," Patti answered a bit indignantly. "Police cars usually stop people from robbing places."

"The bad guys drive by, see the cavalry parked there, and rob the house on the next block. Only this time, the homeowner *is* there, and they hurt him. You haven't prevented crime, you've just displaced it."

"I'm not sure I like where this is going." Patti folded her arms. "Are you saying we're ineffective or incompetent?"

"Neither. You guys do a great job, but your hands are tied. You risk your lives and they get off on a technicality. It must drive you nuts."

Patti sat in the easy chair. Don, disappointed, sat on the couch.

"Lead on MacDuff." Patti doffed an imaginary cap.

"That really should be *lay on MacDuff*, but I don't want to split hairs," Don smirked. "I love Macbeth, probably my favorite Shakespearean play."

"You have a favorite Shakespearean play? You're full of surprises."

"Well, I'm full of something, but let's play this out a bit more." Don wasn't sure if this was a good idea, but he continued. "If I know about this crime, and I came by that information illegally, and you use it to catch the guys, they'll get off, right?"

Patti thought for a moment. "Only if they find out."

"Their lawyers are going to be just like you, wanting to know that very important detail. And you can't lie." Don thought back to Jacqui Moore. "The system sucks."

"Don. It's not that black and white. If we have reasonable cause to pursue a lead, we can act. We try to prevent crime as much as respond to it."

"I know that, and I love you guys for what you do. Well, maybe not love, but I appreciate it. I want to help."

"You can't break some laws to enforce others. It doesn't work that way." Patti drank her water and tried to divine what the man across the room was thinking.

"I know it doesn't. And I have misgivings about my methods, but in the long run the end justifies the means."

"For crying out loud, you go from Shakespeare to Machiavelli."

"If they've said it best…" Don didn't know where to go. So he spit out the truth. "Tomorrow, there's going to be a burglary somewhere around here."

"You could say that on just about any given night, and you'd be right."

"True that, but I know where it's going to happen, probably know who's going to do it, and how they plan to get away."

"Give me the names and locations, and I'll make sure it doesn't happen." Patti folded her arms.

"That's just it. I want it to happen. If I stop it in progress and then call you guys, bingo, they go to jail. No questions asked." Don stood, picked up her empty glass, and started towards the kitchen.

"Don, that's not how we do things."

He turned. "Isn't it? When you saw those bozos scoping out the library you could've called the uniforms. The cops would've walked around, scared the guys off, and prevented the assault. But you knew they were eventually going to attack someone, maybe hurt them. You prevented a crime by letting it happen, and then stopping it."

"I guess, but that's my job, and my call, not yours."

"I agree, but there's only one of you, and there are hundreds of them."

Patti fidgeted in her seat. "You'd better fill me in. I don't like where this is going or what you think you're doing."

"Patti, you're wonderful. That's why we're having this conversation. Depending on how tomorrow goes, I'll fill you in on everything."

"I should arrest you." Patti was angry, but she couldn't fault Don's logic which made her angrier.

"Did you bring cuffs? I love cuffs." Don tried to lighten the mood. "I don't know where you'd hide them in those jeans."

Patti resisted, but eventually a smile crept across her face. Don was a genuinely nice guy; a very large nice guy. "Okay, I'll go along. No guarantees. Tell me what you're going to tell me."

"I'll settle for that. Tomorrow, two or more people are going to break into a home. Nobody will be there, so no innocent people are in danger."

"Where?"

"Not at liberty to say."

"How do you know this?"

"Can't tell you." Don put a full glass of water by Patti.

"So you have it on good authority a break-in is going to happen tomorrow? A house is going to get ransacked, but nobody'll get hurt?"

Don corrected her. "I didn't say that last part. No innocent person is going to get hurt. The perpetrators may not be so lucky. Depends on how much resistance they put up."

"Resistance? Resistance to what?" Patti picked up the glass but didn't drink.

Don smiled. "To me."

"You're going to stop two or three guys from robbing a place, and they're not going to resist?" Patti slammed the glass onto the table.

"They will a bit."

Patti's ire returned. "Are you going to be armed?"

"Of course, I'd be crazy not to be."

Patti pressed her point. "So, somebody could get killed?"

"Not likely, but I guess so." Don roamed around the room, knowing the conversation was going far worse than he'd hoped.

"And you expect me to sit here and let it happen?"

Don wished he'd listened to Justin. "I was hoping you would. To see if you're on my side."

"Don, this isn't about being on your side. It's about *not* letting you take the law into your own hands."

"You really don't have a choice. I'm sure nobody is aware of the burglary. But if cops show up, I'll let them handle it."

"I'm a cop, tell me, and I'll handle it." Patti stood and picked up her jacket.

"Can't do that. Maybe next time if you're good." Don tried to be charming but failed miserably.

"If I'm *good*?" Patti walked over to Don, her finger pointed in his face. "If I'm *good*? If I'm good, I'll run your ass into jail tonight."

"You won't. I know you too well for that." He wanted to crawl under the couch.

"Oh, you do, do you? What if I decide to follow you tomorrow? In a squad car? Every fucking place you go?"

"That just makes it easier to spot you and lose you."

"So you could lose me? Are you that arrogant?" Patti was beyond angry.

"No, I'm that good, and I knew this'd piss you off. Sorry."

"Sorry? You don't know the meaning of the word. You're telling me I'm incompetent. I can't stop a robbery or tail an amateur. We'll see how incompetent I am. How incompetent the Olympia police are? I'm going home. Don't do what you're planning to do. I'll stop you."

Don grasped at straws. "Patti, I didn't say any of those things. You're very competent. That's why I'm telling you this. You guys need help, and I can give it."

Patti put on her coat. "We don't need or want this kind of help. If you really wanted to help, you'd tell me where this was happening. I'd stake it out and nail the bastards. You just want to keep having fun with guns. Somebody's going to get hurt, Don. Maybe you. Maybe me."

Don tried to convince her. "Nobody's going to get hurt. Least of all one of the good guys. Please, trust me."

"Part of me wants to smack you upside the head with a baton. The other wants me to drive you to the psych ward. No part of me wants to trust you. Understand this. I don't approve."

"I know, Patti. We'll just have to agree to disagree."

103

"I hate that fucking saying. The captain says it all the fucking time, especially when he's fucking wrong. I'm not agreeing to disagree. I'm agreeing to arrest you if you step out of this house armed with anything more than your fingernails. That's what I'm agreeing to. Good night, Don. Think very seriously about what you're planning. It may not end as well as you hope." Patti walked to the door. She looked back at Don who remained in the safety of his living room. "Don, I like you. Don't make me do something I truly don't want to do."

"So, I'll see you tomorrow night?"

"I'm not joking, Don." Patti left the door open behind her.

"Everything will be alright." Don followed her across the porch.

Patti was fuming as she looked back at the house. He waved. She got in her car and drove away.

Twenty minutes later, as Don checked into the Parkside Motel, a grey sedan pulled to a stop three houses from his. The deputies weren't sure what they were looking for, but Patti was dead serious when she asked them to keep an eye on the house for a few hours.

Deputy McIlroy asked his partner "Is the guy married? Cheating on her? Christ, it was just a second date."

Sergeant Fulton shrugged. "Bill says it's her third. I don't know, but she wants a call if he leaves."

Two hours later, Patti pulled in behind the unmarked car and approached her friends. "Thanks, guys. None of this goes on the log, okay?"

"You've got it, Patti. I still owe you." Fulton started the car.

Patti patted him on the shoulder. "Hooking you up with Jane was my pleasure. She's a great girl."

"And an even better mom. Have you seen the photos?" Fulton reached for his wallet.

"Ben, I've seen them on my phone, my computer, your phone, Jane's phone. Hell, I'm seeing them in my sleep."

The sergeant laughed and drove away.

It's nice having friends, she thought. It had already been a long night, and if Don stepped out of his house, she'd be on him, and not in a good way.

Chapter 30

Don woke refreshed but concerned about his future with Patti. Last evening turned out far worse than he'd hoped. She was angry, but she made it clear she liked him. For now, that was all he needed. It would be dark for another couple of hours. He put on his running gear and stepped into the morning chill. Stars dotted the sky. *The weatherman might have gotten it right*, he thought. His run took him past the parking lot where all this began.

Only a few hardy souls were out, walking dogs or doing laps. Don kept to himself and made it back to the motel in under an hour. He hadn't pushed himself. He had a full day ahead and wanted to be at the top of his game. After showering, he decided a good breakfast was in order. The Fifth Quarter served excellent omelets, and it was on the way.

The restaurant wasn't crowded. He ordered, and his thoughts turned to Patti. Don suspected his lady cop was outside his house, probably cold, definitely pissed off. There would be hell-to-pay the next time they got together. Pushing those concerns to the side, he walked through the upcoming day. He would secure the gunnysack near the access road entrance and leave the Jeep among the cars at the mini-market. He'd jog back to the access road, collect the bag, and walk the trail to the Martins. Once there, he'd make sure nobody was home and then get comfortable in the shrubs east of the driveway.

Don stopped and deposited his gear in the brush a few feet off the trail. A half hour later, he was back, stuffing candy bars into the satchel. The sun was rising on what he hoped would be an eventful Saturday. The roadbed showed no new tire tracks or footprints. He was probably the last one to use it. Up to now his hunches had been right. He gave himself a bit of credit for thinking like a criminal. Everything had gone according to plan. He was pumped.

❖

Across from Don's house, Patti was anything but pumped. She'd been in the car for five hours, was tired, and needed to pee. *Don should be up by now*, she thought. Yet there wasn't a sign of life in the house. Something was wrong.

Patti got out and marched down the street. She was serving notice she intended to stop him from doing something stupid and probably illegal. On a hunch, Patti checked the garage.

"Why the fuck didn't I do this three hours ago? He probably left right after I did." She fumed. "What a fucking rookie mistake. Now what do I do?"

"Can I help you?" A man in a bathroom stood on the neighboring porch.

"I'm a cop. Doing a welfare check on Don Rowland. I see he's gone."

"Left last night, around ten." Brian remained a little uncertain about the woman standing in Don's driveway.

"Who are you talking to, sweetie?" The door behind Brian opened.

He turned and greeted his girlfriend. "A police officer, I think."

Surprise erupted on Deirdre's face. "Patti? Is that you? What's going on?"

"Deirdre? I was checking on Don. Do you live here."

"This is Brian's place." Deirdre hugged her boyfriend. "But I have sleepovers. You here on business or personal?"

"A bit of both I guess. I'm worried Don may be up to something illegal."

"Don doing something illegal?" Brian showed his surprise. "Doesn't sound like Don. He's a pretty righteous guy."

"Not so much illegal as just not smart." Patti started towards the street.

"Now, that sounds like Don." Deirdre laughed. "Patti, remember the Titanic themed Christmas display last year? That was Don, but Brian had a hand in it."

Patti nodded. The display was so bizarre, photos of it made the front page.

Brian defended himself. "I merely pointed out his display had the wrong number of smoke stacks. If you're going to go to the trouble, make it historically accurate."

"Patti, want some coffee or breakfast?" Deirdre offered.

Patti knew there was nothing left to do about Don except hope for the best. "Sounds marvelous. Brian, could I use your restroom?"

"Absolutely, down the hall on the left." The three new friends went inside.

The coffee's aroma filled the warm house. After a pit stop, Patti joined them in the kitchen. Deirdre set the table, and Brian finished making buttermilk pancakes.

"Brian gets real maple syrup from the Adirondacks. One of his friends sends it to him every Christmas. It's the best syrup on the planet." Deirdre placed a gravy bowl in the center of the table. "Have to serve it hot or it won't pour. It's liquid candy."

Patti graciously accepted her plate of pancakes and sausages. Their smell was intoxicating. "If he cooks like this, I'd keep him." The first bite of syrup-ladened pancakes exceeded Patti's taste buds' ability to enjoy. "Yep, I'd keep him."

"I plan to. He's all that and French fries." Deirdre came right to the point. "Are you dating Don?"

"Dating may be a bit strong for what we're doing," Patti answered as soon as her mouth was empty. "We're getting to know each other."

"In the biblical sense?" Brian joked.

Patti tried to explain. "You know what I mean? We're checking each other out."

Brian and Deirdre looked at each other and then at Patti.

"Okay." Patti remembered her own advice. "I'll stop digging."

106

Breakfast was highlighted by stories of the funny and kind things the man next door did around the neighborhood. It was nine-thirty when Patti drove home. Don could take care of himself, but she still worried. The best of plans fall apart, and when plans fall apart, somebody usually gets hurt. She didn't want Don to be that someone.

❖

Across town, bacon sizzled at the Weaver house. The girls' bags were packed. All Danielle had to do was get them moving and let momentum take over. At eight, with everything ready, Danielle called them to breakfast. Within minutes, two hungry, adorable little girls were at the table. Angela was nine and towered over her older sister Stacey. They made short work of their waffles.

"Your dad's going to be here soon. Get dressed, and don't turn on the television. You'll have plenty of time for that at his place." Chris was helping a neighbor and would leave the girls on their own for much of the day. As long as they didn't have to help put down sod, they were fine with the arrangement.

Danielle's cell phone buzzed. She didn't recognize the number, indicating it was Mac or Bernie. She let it go to voice mail. A blue Prius stopped in front of the house. Chris's knack for being exactly on-time always baffled and occasionally irked her. Today, she was delighted. Stacey and Angela bolted down the stairs and out the door. They loved their dad. He was a nerd, but he was their nerd. A few minutes later, Danielle waved goodbye. The three amigos were off on their adventure, and it was time for mom to start hers.

"Eight-thirty and all's well." Danielle looked at the blue sky. She hit redial, and Mac answered. The non-descript step van he'd commandeered was parked at a fast food restaurant three miles from her house.

Mac spoke first. "I have the van. Is there anything else we need?"

"Nope, do you have Bernie?"

"He's getting something to eat. Do you want breakfast?"

"Just finished, thanks Mac." Danielle put the tools and weapons in her car. "Meet me in the Home Depot parking lot by the tool rental door in fifteen minutes. I'll hop in and we'll go."

Mac noted the change in plans. "I thought we were going to wait until the game was on this afternoon."

"The early game is as big as the Seahawks' game. It's a revenge match between New England and Denver. Whoever picked these games was a genius and our best friend." Danielle backed out of her driveway. "We can roll in any time after ten and not get spotted. This way we have more time to do a thorough job. Is Bernie back?"

"He's just coming out the door. We're about ten minutes from Home Depot. Give us twenty to get into place."

107

"Okay, park somewhere near that door, and I'll find you. White step van? Right?"

Mac confirmed her description. "Yep. No markings."

"Mac, I like working with you, a true professional."

"See you in twenty. We're pulling out."

Thirty minutes later, the van, loaded with burglars and their equipment turned onto Littlerock Road, ten minutes from the Martin house and Don.

❖

Don was quite comfortable in the hedge running along the Martin's eastern fence line. He had a great view of the driveway and an almost equally good view of the backyard. Though he couldn't see Cheshire Road, he could hear it. An occasional vehicle, several walkers exchanging gossip, and a few dogs were all that had used the road so far. At ten, the distinctive rumbling of a large truck engine piqued his interest. He expected a truck like this, but he expected it much later. He came to attention when a white van drove up the driveway and stopped in front of the house. Three people got out; no hoods, no masks.

"The early bird gets the stereo," Don whispered. He scoped the team with binoculars; two men and the woman he'd seen driving the Suburban. She gave the orders, and the guys eagerly obliged. The woman and the bigger man approached the front door. They didn't bother with a pretext. Thanks to Bryce, they knew nobody was home. She picked the lock. The door swung open. They entered.

The distinctive sound of a cargo door rolling up resonated across the lawn. Soon after, the smaller man walked down the driveway and found a hole in the hedge near the street, perfect for tracking nosey neighbors and cops. His camouflaged outfit blended into the foliage. The communication set on his head indicated these thieves were well organized and well equipped. If he sounded the alarm, the other two would run for the woods. He'd stay hidden, and hopefully go undetected; a simple but effective escape plan.

The former Ranger waited until the lookout got situated; his attention focused entirely on the street. With relative ease, Don moved from bush to shrub towards his prey, stopping every so often to check on his quarry. At twenty-feet out, he stopped, knelt, aimed his rifle, and fired. A few seconds later, the watchman was unconscious, suspended by several stout branches. If his associates looked, he'd appear to be still on active duty.

Remembering the Hansen ranch and quoting his favorite philosopher, Don whispered, "This is deja-vu all over."

He turned his attention to the house. The man loading the truck appeared at regular, almost clock-like, intervals carrying things. He'd heave an item into the van and return to the house. A round trip took forty-seconds. It gave Don thirty-seconds to move up the driveway before taking cover. At that pace, the thief would make three trips before Don got within the rifle's optimal range. He loaded the gun with a full-dose dart and walked briskly toward the house. At twenty-five-seconds, he dropped behind a decorative wheelbarrow. Ten seconds later the thief appeared carrying a rifle. Don stiffened but relaxed when the rifle was placed in the truck.

Don made more progress on the second leg than he expected and was in the open when his internal clock went off. He flopped to the ground and hoped the man wouldn't notice the large human-looking object sprawled on the gravel road. Don readied himself for a shot that'd probably fall short, giving the guy time to shoot or call for help. He didn't want to resort to using his Glock, but if the man came up firing, Don would take him out. Patti's warning echoed in his head, *Somebody could get killed.*

The man returned, struggling with the top of a grandfather-clock. It was heavy and bulky. He swore. Don thought *for as much work as you're doing, you could get a legitimate job*. The man turned back towards the house still upset. Don didn't wait. He ran thirty-feet to the side of the house. The thief came out carrying the clock's solid-wood base. Don didn't have a kill shot, so he waited for the next trip. The dart hit the thief in the neck, dropping him and the box he was carrying like sacks of rocks. Don zip-tied the man's wrists. He looked up and found the barrel of a pistol aimed at his head. "Crap, this is exactly deja-vu."

"Who are you? And what did you do to Mac?" Danielle pushed the toggle switch on her communication set. "Bernie, get up here. We have an uninvited guest."

Being a wiseass, Don answered her questions with a little attitude. "First, I'm the guy who's stopping this burglary. Second, I drugged Mac. Third, Bernie's out of commission too. He looks like he's still in the game, but he's just as unconscious as Mac. Fourth, is now a good time to surrender?"

"Dumb ass." Danielle motioned for Don to get up.

"Oddly enough, you're not the first woman to call me that today."

"You're my new loader. Get those suitcases and that box in next." Danielle waved her pistol towards the door. "There's more stuff inside, so hurry."

"You're the boss, for now." Don complied.

"Before you do anything, load your rifle and give it to me." Danielle tossed Don the air gun. "Don't get heroic. I haven't shot anyone in a while, so I can't promise you I won't hit something important."

Don put a dart in the chamber and handed her the gun.

The woman looked at her partner. "The drug works quickly, doesn't it?"

"Yeah. Takes about two seconds to put you out."

Danielle released the rifle's safety. "Did you plan to use one on me?"

"As a matter of fact I did, but it doesn't look like that'll happen." Don stood next to the woman with all the guns.

"You bet your ass it's not going to happen. Now get moving. Just a couple more things on the porch to load and then Mac. How long will he be out?"

Don put four high-end speakers in the truck. "Three hours, but he shouldn't operate heavy equipment for a day or so."

"Funny guy." The thief was not in a good mood. "Put the television in first. Then that box."

Don did as he was told.

"Get Mac in there. Make sure he doesn't roll around."

Don hoisted Mac into the truck.

Danielle was impressed. "Are you part of a neighborhood-watch thing?"

"Sort of. Trying to keep bad boys and girls from getting away with shit."

"You failed this time, douchebag." She shot the Ranger in the neck.

Don slumped to the ground. Danielle waited a few seconds and then poked him with the gun. Nothing. She tossed the rifle next to Don. She had no use for a toy.

"Fuck! Where did I put the bag of jewelry? The girls love that crap." Danielle walked back into the house. She returned, ready to secure the cargo door but came up short when she saw Don wasn't where she left him. She spun around, but before she could retrieve her pistol, she felt a pinch in her leg. The ground rushed up to meet her. Don answered the question she didn't have time to ask.

"Didn't give myself a full dose. That shot was meant for you."

Don pulled a syringe from his pocket and injected himself with the antidote. He got zip-ties from his backpack and bound Danielle's wrists and legs. Sloppy, but it did the trick. He tossed her into the truck.

Had someone watched him walk down the driveway, they'd have thought he was wrapping up a two-day binge. He staggered to Bernie, dragged him out of the bushes, zip-tied him, and slung him over his shoulder. A few minutes later, all three thieves were secured. He thought about administering the antidote, but he wasn't steady enough to give the injections. Don pulled down the cargo door and dropped the latch into place. "I'm going to call this a success, Beta-level. Beta get the hell out of here. I still crack me up."

Once he got to the woods, he got very sick. That was a good thing. It meant his body was shaking off the drug. After bringing up everything he'd eaten for breakfast and some of last night's meal, he dialed 911.

"Tumwater Dispatch. What's your emergency?"

Don gave the operator the address and a description of the situation. He hung up. The officer checked caller ID, *Danielle Weaver*. Don tossed the phone into the woods. She wouldn't need it for a few years.

❖

As Don stumbled back to Littlerock Road, Deputy Atwater pulled his cruiser behind Don's Jeep. It fit the description the Olympia Police Department had broadcast earlier in the morning. The license plate was a match. He called dispatch. "This is Atwater. I'm at the mini-market on Littlerock. I found that Jeep the Olys want. Nobody around. Nothing in it. What do you want me to do?"

"Hold tight. I'll check with Oly PD. I believe this is just a welfare check."

"Roger that. I'm going into the store to see if the driver's inside." Atwater entered the convenience store and looked around. Except for the cashier, the place was empty. "Hey, Barbara? Do you know who belongs to that Jeep?"

"Not a clue. Probably a jogger. They're always leaving their rigs here."

"Thanks. I'll see you on my late run. Will you have wings out by four?"

"Always do. I'll save you some."

The deputy returned to his car, and his radio barked. "All units in the Tumwater area. All units in the Tumwater area. A reported break-in at 1411 Cheshire Road in Covington Estates. Repeat, break-in at 1411 Cheshire."

Atwater replied, "I'm three minutes out. Any details?"

"Three men involved. They're armed but currently secured. Repeat. Armed but currently secured. We're not sure what that means, so proceed with caution. Full lights and sirens are requested. I have you as responding first Steven. Backup from Tumwater and Olympia are on their way. State Patrol dispatched two troopers. They are about ten minutes out. Proceed with extreme caution." Atwater's siren drowned out her warning.

Don heard the siren but couldn't tell how far away it was. He was a little woozy, but the antidote was working. He'd have a screaming headache for a couple of hours, but he functioned well enough to beat a hasty retreat. Had Danielle hit him with a full dose, he'd still be out cold in front of a looted house with a lot of explaining to do, especially if one of the responding cops was Detective Linder. He deposited his ready-bag in the brush near the entrance. He heard more sirens. As he stepped onto Littlerock, a state patrol car screamed past. An ambulance followed soon after.

Atwater used his cruiser to block the Martin's driveway, passenger side towards the house. He got out and brought up his binoculars.

"Dispatch. I'm at the address. There's a truck parked in front of the house. Can't hear the engine. I assume it's not running."

Neighbors gathered across from the driveway. A little excitement had shown up unexpectedly.

"Folks, you have to disperse. We don't know what's going on here." Nobody moved.

Atwater shook his head, *they'll move fast enough if somebody shoots.* There were a couple hundred feet of lawn between him and the house. Someone with a rifle could easily pick him off. Cruisers from Olympia and Tumwater arrived. A state trooper brought up the rear. Being first on the scene, Atwater had rank and privilege. Until a watch commander arrived, he was in charge. He directed an officer to move the crowd back. Martin's neighbors didn't budge.

Four men in various uniforms scanned the grounds. From two-hundred feet, the truck looked innocent enough. They were too far away to make contact with whoever was in the house. Atwater decided to get closer.

"Beecher, you and I are going up there and see what's happening. We'll work from both sides of the property. Woods, can you put a rifle on that truck?"

Trooper Woods retrieved his rifle. Its scope gave him an excellent view of the scene. He took up position at the rear of Atwater's cruiser and signaled all was clear. The two cops sprinted on tangents away from the squad car. If there was a sniper, he'd be dealing with two fast moving targets. Within seconds, both officers were safely protected by trees on opposite sides of the lawn.

"Atwater, this is Jelsik. Neighbor says the owners are gone. Nobody should be here."

"Great work, Lanny. When I get to the wheelbarrow, I'm going to ask whoever's there to come out peacefully. Get someone around back. If they get to the woods, we'll need dogs to track them."

"There's an access road behind the house." Jelsik had become command-central. "We're sending someone now. You'll have a friend arriving back there soon."

"Good to know, Lanny. I'm moving up." Atwater signaled his partner. They moved forward together. When he got to the wheelbarrow, he saw the other deputy taking up position on his left, drawing a bead on the truck. Atwater got to one knee and yelled at the house. "This is the sheriff's department. We have the house surrounded. Come out with your hands up."

Nothing. Silence. Not a good sign. When the deputy looked back, he saw emergency vehicles clogging the street. Two officers, both wearing helmets and vests, came up the driveway, semi-automatic weapons drawn, moving deliberately from side-to-side. The police now had overwhelming firepower. Atwater rushed to the back of the van. The cargo door was closed and latched. Beecher arrived shortly after and opened the driver's door.

112

Empty. Soon, four law enforcement officers stood behind the truck. More men were making their way up the lawn and driveway.

As the activity around the Martin's unfolded, Don walked unsteadily along Littlerock Road back to his Jeep. Behind him, a state patrol car entered the access road with fully engaged siren and lights. Soon after, he heard a voice coming from the woods. He couldn't make out the words but assumed it had to do with people putting up their hands. Don smiled and, in his best New York City accent said, "You talkin' to me?"

Atwater lifted the cargo door. He wasn't prepared for what he saw: three bodies, motionless, pistols and a rifle stacked on the other side of the bed.

"We just found out what *armed but secured* means." Atwater pointed to the house. Two officers cautiously entered the Martin residence, guns drawn and on high alert. Soon they were joined by more cops. They went room-to-room searching for other *armed but secured* men. They didn't find anyone.

Atwater called for ambulances, and the sea of emergency vehicles parted to let them through. The EMTs checked the vital signs of the truck's occupants. The two men were unconscious but resting comfortably. The woman's heartbeat and blood pressure were significantly elevated.

"They've been drugged, probably darted." The EMT removed the blood-pressure cup.

"Darted?" Atwater asked. "Like the guys who got nailed a couple of months ago?"

"I don't know about those other guys." The lead EMT pointed to the red mark on Bernie's neck. "This wound is too big to be from a needle. They were darted. The docs will know. We have to get them to the hospital."

Three would-be thieves, handcuffed to gurneys, were lifted into the ambulances; the men in one and the woman in the other.

"It's not likely they'll come around soon." The EMT climbed into the back. "Whatever took them out was pretty potent."

The ambulances sped off. Atwater had a moment to think about what had happened. Someone disabled three armed thieves using darts and dope. Nobody got hurt or at least not seriously. It happened in broad daylight, in the middle of an affluent neighborhood. A pattern was emerging. A vigilante was working in Thurston County. He got back to his car and checked in, "We're clear in Tumwater. I'm standing down and returning to the station."

"Great, good work. By the way, Olympia PD wants you to run by the gas station and see if the car's still there."

"Roger that." Deputy Atwater reported the Jeep was gone, and nobody had seen the driver. When he asked for further instructions, the dispatcher said Olympia would handle it. He bought a dozen wings and thought about the mountain of paperwork facing him. "Thank God I didn't fire my weapon."

❖

Sergeant Walden read Bernie Denello his rights, checked his handcuffs, and left the room. Walden had waited three hours for the drug to wear off only to have Denello blabber on about beef patties and special sauce. The cop wanted to know what happened, who'd taken out the thieves, and how he, she or they had done it. Bernie wouldn't answer those questions any time soon. Walden stuck his head into Mac's room. That thief was still unconscious.

Three floors below, the lab worked diligently to identify the neurotoxin found in the thieves' blood and create an antidote. The doctors hesitated applying one without knowing the specific toxin. The wrong formula could have harsh, possibly fatal, effects. When Bernie started coming around, staff was optimistic the drug had a relatively short efficacy period. If their optimism was warranted, MacDougal and Weaver should wake in the next hour. Walden was getting impatient. Hanging around a hospital wasn't his idea of a productive afternoon, especially when all he wanted to know was on whom to pin the medal.

He went to Weaver's room. She was struggling. Her drug was either different, or she'd gotten a significantly greater dose. She thrashed about in her tortured sleep. Staff had secured her with four-point restraints. Her monitors showed elevated blood pressure and heart rate. Her breathing was erratic. The doctors were concerned.

"She going to make it?" Walden asked the attending physician.

"She'll live, but if we can't slow her heart rate she could have a seizure or stroke out. We may have to use an off-the-shelf antidote, but if it's wrong her pressure could skyrocket."

Walden left Weaver's room and spotted Patti Linder at the nurses' station.

Patti saw the concern on Walden's face. "How is she, Stan?"

"Not good. She's not coming around. The guy may have overdosed her. If they can't calm her heart down they're going to give her something that might kill her. They're not having any luck with an antidote. The neuro thing is pretty exotic."

Patti thanked Stan for the update. She walked to the stairwell door and stepped on to the landing. She called her vigilante. "Don, if you get this message you *have* to contact Saint Pete's intensive care unit. The female suspect is struggling. She's not recovering from the drug. I know you did this, and you think you did something good. If she dies, all that good goes out the window. You need to fix this."

Patti was hopeful Don would do the right thing. Coming forward might jeopardize his vigilante work and compromise his anonymity, but if the

114

woman died, he might face homicide charges. After an agonizing fifteen minutes, she decided to drive to Don's house and beg him for the information. She was looking for Walden when a doctor with a tray of syringes and vials rushed into Mac's room.

"What's that all about?" she asked.

A nurse grabbed her arm, hope in her eyes. "We just got a tip. The caller knew what the three people were wearing and the location of their puncture wounds. He gave the lab the antidote's formula. We were close, but what we had wouldn't have worked. The lab modified our material, and we're trying it now. MacDougal's the guinea pig. If it works on him, they'll give it to the woman."

A few minutes later, there was uproar in Mac's room. He'd recovered well enough and quickly enough to make a break for the door. While cops wrestled him to the ground, the doctors went to Weaver's room. Patti stood silently.

"She's coming around. The antidote was spot on." Most of the medical staff left Weaver's room.

Patti went back to her impromptu phone booth, redialed, and left a short message, "Thank you. She's going to be okay."

Walden stood outside a patient's room watching the Seahawks.

"How are we doing?" Patti asked.

"Not so well. We're down six with under a minute to go. I don't know if Wilson has another come-from-behind miracle in his shorts."

"You got to have faith, Stan. You got to have faith." Patti turned back into the hall. "Will you send me their statements, all nice and neat?"

"I will, but why do you want them?"

"I'd like to hear what they remember about their assailant."

"Will do, Patti. Have a great evening."

"Back atcha, Stan."

Patti headed to east Olympia. She had a bone to pick with Donald Rowland and a huge hug to deliver.

❖

Don was about to deal with a woman he had thoroughly pissed off. Patti climbed the stairs, strode across the porch, and banged on the door. "I know you're in there, you miserable excuse for a man. Let me in or I'll take this door of its hinges."

She heard footsteps, and the door opened. "Patti. Hi. Want coffee?"

She burst by him. "What the fuck were you doing? You could've been killed. Those were real guns with real bullets. They could've shot you."

"One of them did shoot me. See?" He pointed to the red spot on his neck. "Nailed me with my gun. She was a pretty good shot."

Patti sat in a kitchen chair. "And you almost killed her."

"Not really, but I'm glad you called. I assume she recovered?"

"She recovered, and she's going to jail." Patti sat at the kitchen table. "Don, you could've prevented this. Just had to tell me what you knew."

"And how I knew. Quoting Bill again, *there's the rub*."

"This is serious. I'm serious. You can't keep doing this shit. You're going to get hurt, either by the bad guys or a cop, maybe by a homeowner, neighbor. Whoever! You're not authorized." Patti was getting worked up, again.

Don thought being a smartass might work. "You could deputize me and then it'd be all good."

Patti was at a loss. "You're not listening to me."

"I'm hungry, and I don't listen well when I'm hungry. I was going to make a grilled Swiss cheese sandwich. Can I fix you one? With tomatoes and basil? Let me cook something for you. You'll be impressed. By the way, the Seahawks won."

Patti shook her head. She couldn't stay angry with him. He was as suave as a hand grenade, but he was genuine. She liked that, but she was still angry.

"I'll stay, but on the condition you tell me how you knew about these crimes."

"No deal. And frankly, you don't want to know. How do you like your sandwich?"

"Crispy." Patti took off her coat. "You made it clear you were getting it illegally."

"Crispy it is. There's a lot of grey around *illegally*. Let's leave it at that." The butter in the frying pan began to sizzle. "Do you want tomatoes and basil?"

"Yes. Do you have any beer?"

"There are *Stellas* in the fridge. Can you get me one?" He prepped the sandwich.

"Don, stop doing this. You could get hurt." Patti opened two bottles.

"You're right about getting hurt. Been there, done that. Poor planning on my part. I'll do better the next time."

"There can't be a next time. You're not Charles Bronson."

"Ah, so you like the *Death Wish* movies too?" Don flipped the sandwich.

"They're not real. It doesn't work like that. Vigilantes don't win in the end."

Don got some cherries from the pantry. "I have, a couple of times."

"I count three."

"The first went well. The second was great because I met you, and now a third notch on the belt. But things got screwed up with this last one."

"What happened?"

Don explained how the woman got the drop on him and then shot him with the half-dose dart. He fended off the drug's effect and hit her with a full-strength dose, knocking her system completely off rhythm.

Patti enjoyed the sandwich, and, as they finished, there was a knock at the door.

Don greeted his neighbors, "Brian. Deirdre. Come on in. Sit down."

Don began introducing everyone when Brian spoke, "We met yesterday when Patti was checking up on you. Deirdre works with her, sort of. We can't stay. Just wanted to be sure she wasn't tazing you or something equally fun. We're heading to Seattle, actually Pike's Place and then having lunch at the Space Needle. Want to join us?"

"Sorry, have to get to the station to wrap up a couple of things," Patti answered first. "Maybe next time."

Don begged off too. He didn't want to be a third wheel, and he wanted to review Bryce's tapes. He hadn't listened to them for two days.

"Maybe the four of us could catch dinner this week?" Deirdre walked to the door.

"That's a date," Don answered quickly. "I'll get my new girl an outfit, and we'll do the town."

"Your *new* girl?" Patti inquired. "There was an *old* girl? Care to elaborate?"

"Nope. I'm pleading the fifth."

"Good luck with that buddy." Brian joined Deirdre. "Cops always get the truth."

"Usually from informants. So Brian, keep your mouth shut."

Brian and Deirdre waved as they got into her truck.

"Nice couple." Don shut the door.

"How many *old* girls have there been, Mr. Rowland?" Patti took a bite of her sandwich. "This is good."

"Maybe one. Could be two. But since I met you I can't remember any of them."

"Smooth. I'll eat, and you tell me how you know about the crimes."

"Speaking of smooth?" Don did his best impression of Dana Carvey doing his George W. Bush impression. "*Not gonna to happen. Wouldn't be prudent. Not today anyway.* Can I interest you in a movie this evening?"

"Hey, that was good. Can you do President Bush next? And yes, a movie would be nice."

"Cute." Don crossed his eyes at her. "Find the movie section and pick one. I'll get the movie, you get dinner."

"That's so not going to happen. You owe me way more than a movie and dinner."

Don was delighted Patti had stopped threatening to arrest him. She picked an action film. It was too soon to drag him through a romantic comedy.

❖

Jenkins expected a call from Danielle by three at the latest. Nothing. At four, he called her cell and got her answering system. He tried Mac. His phone just kept ringing. The five o'clock news anchor answered his question. "Today, three would-be burglars were found bound and drugged outside a Tumwater home."

"Andrei, this is Jenkins. I need you deliver another message."

❖

After talking with Jenkins, Andrei slipped into a pair of navy blue scrubs and hung a hospital identity card around his neck: Joel Herd, LPN. He thanked his elevator mate and got off on the fifth floor. The hubbub from earlier in the day had subsided, and the floor was quiet. Andrei expected guards to be everywhere, but the only police presence was a young officer chatting up a cute nurse at the nurses' station. Andrei entered Mac's room. The man looked like he'd been hit by a truck.

"Do you people have anything for this fucking headache?" The patient sneered at the staff person in the blue scrubs.

"The only pain relief I can offer is this." Andrei exposed the Glock concealed under his smock. "Talk to me again like that, and I'll fix your headache for good."

Mac fell speechless. *Who the hell is this, and what does he want*?

"I have a message. Keep your mouth shut. You'll be out in a couple of days. Understand?"

Andrei didn't wait for an answer. He walked to Bernie's room, repeated the message, and got the same response. Back in the hall, he noticed a considerable amount of activity around Danielle's room. Medical personnel rotated in and out. He needed a diversion. He walked back to Mac's room.

"Hey, I get it. I understand. I won't say a word."

"This is going to hurt." Andrei punched him in the throat and left the room. Alarms sounded. Andrei walked up the hall while real hospital staff raced to Mac's room. He let them pass. The diversion worked. Andrei slipped into Weaver's room. "I have a message. Don't say anything to anyone. We'll have you out in a few days."

Weaver nodded. Jenkins would take care of her.

Andrei walked past Mac's room. A nurse shook her head. "I don't know what happened, maybe a delayed reaction. It was pretty intense. He couldn't seem to catch his breath."

Chapter 31

Gresham's Columbia Street Public Library sits three blocks from its Carnegie Library predecessor and ten blocks from Waites' house-of-ill-repute. It had become Sarah's refuge. Today, with winds howling from the north, Sarah struggled to open its front door. A young man rushed to help, and they soon found themselves tangled up on the warm side of the door.

"Thanks." Sarah shivered. "That wind is wicked."

"Straight from the arctic." The man removed his wool cap. "Are you okay? I didn't mean to shove you."

"I'm fine. If you hadn't shoved, we'd still be out there."

"Glad I could help. I'm George Olcutt." He noticed the stack of books. "Do you need a hand?"

"That'd be great. I should've put them in a bag. I'm Sarah Geld."

George took three textbooks and read their titles aloud, "*Casino Gambling for Dummies; Beginners Guide to Black Jack;* and *How to Deal with Difficult People.* Do you want to be a gambler or a dealer?"

"Maybe both." Sarah walked into the library. "I'm not sure what I want to do."

"First, we get you to the counter."

"Actually, I need a table so I can spread out. I have a lot of notes to take."

"Okay, then a table it is. Lead the way."

They walked through the lobby. Sarah turned down the aisle marked Children's Fiction. George followed. He'd never been in this part of the building and expected short tables with matching chairs. He found three regular-sized tables set against windows overlooking the lawn and what in the spring would be a garden. With thick carpeting and soft ceiling lights, Sarah's sanctuary was very pleasant.

"This is pretty cool." He put her books on the table and took in the surroundings. "I've never been back here."

"No kids?" Sarah quizzed her Sherpa.

"No kids. You?"

"Nope. What brings you to the library on such a crappy day?" Sarah slung her coat over a chair.

"I'm taking a beginners art class. My sisters say I have to expand my horizon and get out more. Stuff sisters say to a recently divorced brother, I guess." George followed suit and took off his jacket. "One of them found this class online and signed me up. I'm glad she did. It's been fun."

"Are you any good? At art?"

"I'm not sure. It's too early to tell. Today we're working on depth perception. That's if we have class. I called earlier and the front desk didn't know if the teacher was going to make it."

"The roads are treacherous. I slipped three times on the way."

"How far did you drive?" George put his coat over his arm.

"I walked. Just a few blocks, but I almost turned back a couple of times."

"I'm glad you didn't."

"Well, I'm glad you made it too. Should you check on your class?" Sarah sat and started to arrange her books. "If it's canceled, come back, and I'll play a few hands with you. If you don't have something better to do?"

"Yeah. I should do that." George was delighted with the offer and hoped class was canceled. "I'll let you know."

Sarah watched him walk off. A few minutes later, he returned. "It's canceled. I'm the only one who made it. I'm all yours."

"Welcome, sir. What do you do for a living, George? The book says I should engage my players. I think they meant victims."

"I'm an investment banker. Kind of a financial advisor." George sat across from the charming young woman.

"What advice do you have for me?" Sarah shuffled a deck of playing cards.

"Don't become a gambler. The house always wins."

"That's very true. Let's start with blackjack, sir. Do you know how to play?" She dealt three hands for him and the dealer's hand.

"Not well, but I know the rules and a little strategy. Don't hit on fifteen. Right?"

"See what the book says." Sarah handed him a textbook. "You get three hands. I didn't bring chips so we'll have to keep track in our heads."

"I'll be right back." George left the table and returned with a box of paper clips, proudly announcing, "Chips. I feel naughty playing poker in the kids section."

"I'm sure worse things have been done here." The dealer flashed a wide grin.

For four hours, as the wind howled outside, they played cards and got to know each other. George was better at Texas Hold 'Em than he let on, but he was horrible at Three-Card Monte. The lights flickered, the library was closing.

"I had a great afternoon, Sarah. Could we do this or something else again soon?"

"I'd like that. I'm free tomorrow, but the library's closed."

"How about O'Reilly's downtown? It's right off the Tri-Met line. Meet for lunch?"

"Could we go to Powell's after? I want to buy a copy of the dummies book."

"It's a date. Can I drive you home?"

Sarah had anticipated that question. "No, I'll walk. The fresh air will wake me up."

George got a bag for her books and escorted Sarah to the street. "Thank you for a wonderful afternoon."

"The pleasure was mine, and you still have all your money." They parted; Sarah towards the brothel and George towards the interstate.

Maybe something good will come out of this horrible situation, she thought. Then she smiled.

Chapter 32

Lara tossed her bag into the BMW and fastened her skis to the rack.

"When's Warren coming?" Maria asked.

"Soon. His dad's dropping him off. We should get to Schweitzer by noon."

"I can't believe mom and dad are letting you spend the weekend with a boy and letting you borrow the car. Are you going to have sex with him?"

"None of your business. But the answer is no." Lara poked her kid sister in the ribs. "I like him but not that much. He'll sleep with the guys, and I'll stay with Christine and Michelle."

Maria was happy. Her big sister had made a good decision.

Warren's dad pulled up and dropped him off just as Taras came out. Revoldi put his hands on Warren's shoulders. "You're taking two of my most precious things. Be sure they return in excellent condition."

Warren assured Mr. Revoldi no harm would come to his daughter or his car.

Zoya hugged Lara and kissed Warren on the cheek. "Take care of my baby."

"I'll take care of myself, thank you very much. We're burning daylight." Lara got into the passenger seat. "Let's see what this can car can do!"

Warren snapped to and started the engine. They waved and headed east.

Levi, parked near the entrance ramp to Interstate 90, let his boss's BMW pass him. The two passengers were chatting, not a care in the world. The Interstate was bare and dry with little traffic, and two cars owned by Taras Revoldi made excellent time getting to Idaho. It was at the border that Levi noticed a grey van on his tail. He slowed, and it passed. He expected it to do the same with the BMW, but it didn't. It fell in behind his boss's daughter and stayed there.

Warren and Lara were oblivious to the car following them, but Levi was on it. He drew close enough to get its license number and called Revoldi. "Apakoh, somebody's following Lara. Could be cops, but I don't think so. I have the license number."

Levi read the number into the phone. Revoldi told him to stay back and watch. He'd run the plate. Ten miles later, Levi's phone rang. "The car belongs to Charlene Morganson. What the fuck is she doing? Is she still following Lara?"

"Charlene's pacing Lara. She's far enough back so the kids won't notice her. She's about a half mile ahead of me. Should I take her out?"

"No. Wait until she does something or they stop."

In the van, Charlene and her ex-husband worked on their plan to kidnap the *fucking Russian's* daughter.

Charlene gestured for Graham to speed up. "We'll get them to pull over on the road to Sandpoint and then take them. There are a lot of empty cabins around there. This'll teach that bastard to treat me like a whore."

"Charlene, are you sure you want to do this. The Russians are mean mother fuckers." Tim Graham slowed to keep enough distance between them and kids. "I've heard stories."

"Fuck the stories. I've seen them in action. But they're idiots. Couldn't find their way out of a paper bag, especially Revoldi. He's dumb as a post. He believed everything I told him. What a peckerwood. He butchered Anton right in front of me. And you know how I felt about Anton. He was the best man I ever knew."

Graham wasn't happy his ex-wife had hooked up with the *commie bastard*, but he knew better than to raise her ire. He'd done that once before, and she got him sent to prison. Graham was sure Charlene had stopped taking her meds, making her even more unpredictable. He drove on, not noticing the car following him.

Charlene studied the Idaho map. "They'll take Route 95 out of Coeur D'Alene. There are plenty of places for us to flag them down. Don't follow too closely. No reason to spook them. We know where they're going. And we sure as hell can't miss that fucking car. Wish there was a way to steal it."

"So, we're doing this to get even with them for killing a man you could have saved?" Graham couldn't help himself.

"If I could've saved Anton, I would've. He knew that, but he kept quiet while they beat him to death. And besides, the Dragon, or whatever the fuck they call him, said he was killing Anton because he tried to rat him out, not because he stole money for me. There was no sense in both of us dying."

"Are we going to kill the kids?"

"Of course we're going to kill the kids. They can identify us. Where the fuck were you when God handed out brains? Pissing in your hat?" Charlene scoffed at her ex.

"Yeah, I guess you're right; can't leave witnesses." Graham caved in as he always did. He followed the BMW when it exited Interstate 90 onto US 95.

"Stay with them. Dammit. Do I have to drive?" Charlene fumed. "Oh, wait, they're pulling into that dinner. Drive past and find a parking spot."

Graham complied. He picked a spot a block north of the Grerson Dinner. He was about to turn off the engine when Charlene ordered him forward. "No reason to wait. There's only one way to Sandpoint. Let's get ahead and find our spot."

The van pulled into traffic. The road sign said, *Sandpoint – 75 miles*, an easy hour and a half drive along Lake Coeur D'Alene. Graham made good time on 95's flat and straight portion, but fifteen miles south of Sandpoint, the road climbed a steep grade and the van struggled to keep pace. Eventually, he pulled to the side of the road, letting a dozen cars pass. The driver of the first car waved a hearty *thank you*. The other drivers weren't quite as cordial, two offering a far different salute. The van's occupants ignored them all.

Morganson turned to her ex-husband. "This is as good a place as any."

Agreeing with her, Graham pulled the van farther off the road, "I'll go down to that curve so I can spot them. When I wave, put up the hood and get the boy to pull over. We'll stash their car in those trees."

Graham took up position about a hundred yards from the van. He had a clear line of sight to Charlene and the mountain curve below. He waited, thankful it wasn't as cold as it could be. Only ten cars passed his hideaway before the BMW cleared the curve. The car was easy to spot and making good progress. He stood and waved. Charlene got out of the van, put up the hood, and practiced her woman-in-distress antics. She decided to tone them down. She wanted to appear in need, not insane.

The ruse worked. Warren pulled over. Charlene thanked her rescuer, pointed at the raised hood, and walked him to the van. Lara waited in the car. A few minutes later, the woman stood outside Lara's door. "Your boyfriend needs you. Can you come over?"

Lara got out and looked for Warren who was nowhere to be seen. "Where is he?"

"On the other side of the van. He wants you to text some friends or something." Charlene and Lara walked quickly to the side of the van where Graham greeted them with a gun. "Get into the van, Lara. Don't argue, just do it."

Lara turned to run. "Do that, and I'll shoot him. Get in and nobody gets hurt."

Lara complied and joined Warren in the van.

Charlene sat next to the daughter of the man she hated most in the world. "Text your father this message, *They have Warren and me. They won't hurt us if you do what they say. They'll contact you soon.* Then give my partner the phone. Graham, make sure she doesn't do anything stupid. I'll be right back."

Charlene concealed Revoldi's car among a stand of pine trees. Lara finished and handed Graham her phone. When Charlene returned, she held the gun while Graham tied Warren and Lara, taping their mouths shut.

Levi watched the scene unfold from a hilltop a half-mile north of the van and wondered what was going on below. Two hours earlier, when the kids and their stalkers stopped in Coeur D'Alene, Levi called Revoldi for instructions. Apakoh directed him to *find out what the hell Charlene was doing.* Before he could get to the van, it pulled away, and he spent the next half hour catching it. By the time Morganson got halfway up Gunderson Hill, he was right behind them with a line of cars behind him. He wanted to stay with the van, but the horde of impatient drivers forced his hand. When the van pulled over, he had to pass. He waved, trying to draw the driver's attention. It didn't work. The man ignored him. Levi continued on until the van was out of sight. He parked his car and scrambled up a hill overlooking Charlene's turnout.

He watched Charlene's partner run a hundred yards down the mountain and hide behind a rock. He was the lookout. Several cars passed him and nothing happened. Then the man got up and signaled. The woman raised the hood and frantically waved at the trees. She stopped, adjusted herself, and tried again, this time far less dramatically. She walked to the edge of the road. Levi saw the BMW come into view, and the woman began her act. Warren dutifully pulled over.

The kidnapping happened quickly. Levi was too far away to intervene. After the kids were forced into the car, the woman lowered the van's hood, moved the BMW out of sight, and jumped into the van's passenger seat. A few minutes later, the van re-entered the highway and struggled to get up to speed.

Levi let it pass then drove hard to make up ground as quickly as possible. Gravity kept the van well below the speed limit, and by the time it reached the top of Gunderson Hill, Levi was behind it again. In Sandpoint, the van made a left onto Highway 2 towards Dover, a small town on the north shore of Lake Pend Oreille. Ten minutes later, the driver pulled into the driveway of a cabin on the lake. Levi drove past noting the cabin's street number and called his boss.

In Spokane, Revoldi threw a chair across the room. Levi had confirmed the ungrateful whore had taken Lara. Hadn't the bitch witnessed what he'd done to Anton? Weren't Anton's screams proof of how brutal he could be? Was the woman insane?

Levi's call calmed him. The kids were okay, and Revoldi knew where they were. Now, Apakoh would rescue them and butcher their kidnappers.

Revoldi told Levi to find out all he could about the cabin; points of entry, best approaches, anything that could help with the rescue.

"Levi, I'll leave as soon as Dimitri and Gustov get here. Find out all you can, but don't do anything to endanger Lara. I know you want to help her but wait for me." Apakoh hung up and jammed the revolver into its holster.

Parked a hundred yards from the cabin, Levi acknowledged the directive and trekked back to the driveway. He scouted the building from the road, but he had to get closer, much closer. The undeveloped property next to the cabin provided the path. He plowed through knee-deep snow. In the fading light, he was confident nobody would see him slither from tree to tree.

A woodpile was situated perfectly next to the cabin's kitchen window. He could peek into the building without being seen. Levi exited the forest, slipped behind the van, and made his way to the woodpile. He smelled the wood fire inside. The kidnappers were comfortable, oblivious to his presence. He looked into the cabin.

Charlene circled the chairs holding her captives, ranting. "Your mother-fucking father is a piece of shit. He's going to pay for what he did to me and Anton. A million dollars ought to leave a mark on the asshole. Are you worth a million bucks to him, sweetie? You'd better hope so." She pointed at Graham. "Let's get this party started."

What happened next infuriated Levi. The man, over six feet tall and weighing in excess of two-hundred- fifty-pounds, raised his hand and struck Warren. The young man, tied to the chair, tumbled across the floor. Blood oozed from the corner of his mouth.

The woman instructed the bull, "Hit the girl. Then the Russian bastard will know we mean business."

Warren pleaded, "Don't hit her. Hit me if you have to, but don't hurt her."

"Okay," the woman said. "Hit the white knight a couple more times. Get him to bleed around the eyes. Then we'll take pictures and send them to Revoldi. Tell him his daughter's next if he doesn't come up with the money."

The big man righted Warren's chair. The first punch caught Warren on the side of his head. The second opened a cut over Warren's right eye and sent him and the chair sprawling into the stone fireplace. Warren didn't move. The blow knocked him unconscious, and a stream of blood ran down his cheek.

Satisfied he'd done enough damage to appease Charlene, the man set Warren next to Lara. Charlene grabbed Warren's hair and yanked his head back to expose the bruises and the blood. She took several pictures with Lara's phone. "That should get your father's attention."

She untied Lara and handed her the phone. "Call your father. Tell him you're sending him photos. Tell him we want one million dollars. If he doesn't deliver it, your face will look like your boyfriend's, maybe worse. Got that?"

Lara nodded and rubbed her wrists. The coarse rope had bitten into her skin. She dialed her father's number. "Dad. I'm sending you pictures. They beat Warren, and they'll do the same to me if you don't get them a million dollars. No, the bitch doesn't want to talk. She wants the money." Lara hung up.

Charlene's ex yanked the phone from Lara and back-handed her. The shot took her to her knees. "We didn't tell you to chat with your old man, just give him the fucking message. Are you deaf? Stupid?"

"Fuck you." Lara staggered to her feet.

Graham set his legs to strike Lara with full force when Levi splintered the back door, driving Graham to the wall across the room. Charlene moved towards the counter to get her pistol, but Lara was quicker and reached the gun first. Charlene stopped, assessed the young woman, then continued at the *Russian princess*, certain the girl wouldn't shoot and desperate to help Graham. Charlene's look of defiance changed to one of disbelief mixed with unfathomable pain. A 45-caliber slug drilled through her chest and exploded out her back.

The gunshot startled Levi. Graham used the distraction to gain an advantage. He pushed the would-be rescuer against a cabinet and extracted a knife from his boot. He drove the double-edge blade towards Levi's throat. Levi was no match for the larger, angrier, and better armed man. Traveling at a thousand feet per second, the bullet from Lara's weapon more than compensated for Levi's disadvantages. A loud thud came from the man's side. He grunted, grabbed Levi's shirt, and slid to the ground, taking Levi with him. He was dead before his hands released Levi.

Lara checked. Charlene was alive. The bullet had incapacitated her, but with quick and proper medical attention she'd live. She'd receive neither. Lara stood over her kidnapper and slapped her hard across the face. Levi was stunned when the little girl he'd watched grow up strike the woman a second time and said, "I'm going to watch you die."

The would-be rescuer straightened up. "Thank you for saving me."

"Thank you for being here. Levi, can you take Warren someplace? The less he knows about what happened, the better. I'll wait for dad."

"I can." Levi checked the boy.

"How soon will dad be here?"

"Probably an hour."

"Call him and tell him we're okay thanks to you. It's best he thinks you did this. Can you go with that?" Lara touched Warren's swollen cheek, and said to the unconscious lad, "Thank you."

126

"I'll tell him I had to because they were hurting you."

Lara rubbed her cheek. The backhand had left a mark. "He'll understand. Time to get Warren out of here."

Five minutes later, Lara's date awakened in Levi's arms outside the cabin. "What happened? Who are you? Where's Lara?"

"I'm Levi. I work for Mr. Revoldi. He had me follow you, and after they took you, I took you back."

"Where's Lara?" Warren repeated.

"She's waiting for her father. We'll meet them later. Now, I must to get you to a safe place. Rest, and I'll see that you're taken care of properly."

Warren nodded and closed his eyes. Soon he was asleep.

Lara looked through the window visualizing police cars screaming to a halt, surrounding the cabin. The fight, two gunshots, and a man carrying another to a car surely had to have drawn attention. But it hadn't. "Apparently, they're used to this kind of ruckus up here," Lara said with a smile.

Soon after Levi left, Charlene moaned loudly and died. Lara covered the woman's face with a towel. Charlene's partner lay in a heap against the far wall. A pool of blood solidified on the floor near him.

Lara made a mental list of the things they'd have to do: remove the bodies, eliminate evidence, stage a break-in. She tidied up the cabin. As darkness fell, headlights illuminated the room. Taras burst in and hugged his daughter. He surveyed the cabin. Charlene was on her back in the middle of the room. A rug covered a large man lying against the wall. Two very large Russians joined them.

Lara suggested, "Maybe we could get rid of them and make it look like somebody broke in and tore up the place."

"A good idea, but we'll do something different." Revoldi issued orders in Russian.

Morganson and her partner, wrapped in sheets, were dumped into the back of their van. Gustov drove it away. Dimitri emptied several gasoline cans in and around the building. A massive house fire would attract the police, fire crews and other emergency responders. There'd be nobody to interfere with the disposal of a van and two carcasses.

Taras kissed his daughter. "Levi told me your friend protected you and took a beating so they'd leave you alone. Warren's a good man."

"I know, Dad. He reminds me of you."

The phone rang. Taras listened and hung up. "Levi has Warren in a motel a few miles from here, and the boy is awake. Send a message to your friends and tell them drunks attacked Warren. You're taking him back to Spokane in case he needs medical attention."

They located bungalow thirteen at the Clover Leaf Cabins and found Levi standing guard outside. The young man inside looked much better than

127

he did in the photos. Levi had bandaged the cut above Warren's eye and had put an ice cold towel on his face. Most of the swelling was already gone.

"Warren," Taras started. "I am proud of you for taking care of my girl. You put yourself in harm's way in the cabin. I don't know how to repay you, but I will. You can be sure of that."

"What was that all about, Mr. Revoldi?"

"The woman's a former employee. I fired her for stealing. She vowed to punish me, but I didn't take her threats seriously. She convinced someone to join her in this crazy plot to extort money from me. They might've gotten away with it if Levi hadn't been with you."

Lara interjected, "Dad, I'm usually angry when you send Levi to watch us, but this time, I'm glad you did."

"What's going to happen to those two?" Warren asked.

Revoldi began his story. "After they knocked you out, they started on Lara. Levi stopped them, and I've dealt with them. They won't bother you or my family again. My men are escorting them out of the area, and they won't be back. I need to ask you a very big favor."

"Whatever you need, Mr. Revoldi," Warren answered, unequivocally.

"You must tell whoever asks that you were assaulted by drunks after you stopped to help them with their car. You protected Lara and were able to get away. You don't remember much about them because you were too busy fighting them off. Can you do this for me?" Taras asked. "If Lara's mother or your mother learns that people who were angry with me kidnapped you, they might not let you see each other again. And that'd be wrong."

Warren nodded enthusiastically. He wanted to remain in Lara's life, and judging from how Lara tended to him, she felt the same way.

"Excellent. Lara, drive Warren home. Stop at a hospital and have someone look him over. Levi fancies himself a doctor, but he's a much better carpenter."

An hour later, a three car caravan retraced the route taken earlier in the day, but this time with far less drama. Warren called his parents and explained the situation as best he could. They were concerned, but more so, they were proud. After a quick stop at an urgent care center, Lara dropped Warren with his parents. She promised to check on him in the morning, a promise she looked forward to keeping.

Chapter 33

Sunday mornings were usually quiet in the Gresham house. The parade of men ended around two the night before, and the first clients rarely appeared before mid-afternoon. Sarah got up early. She was nervous about meeting George; nervous he'd find out what she was doing in Gresham.

"Good morning, Sarah." Mrs. Waite set down her coffee and got right to business. "You're halfway through your stay. I'll give you an exact tally later. Have you given any thought to staying?"

Though the life wasn't as horrible and demeaning as she expected, Sarah wasn't prostituting herself any longer than necessary, but Mrs. Waite didn't need to know that. "Once I'm paid up, I'll probably go home, but I'll think about it."

"Any plans for today?" asked a disappointed Mrs. Waite.

"Going into Powell's. Maybe walk along the river."

"Do you want to borrow my car?"

"No, thanks. I'll take the train. Don't like driving in the city. I'd end up going the wrong way on a one-way street."

Mrs. Waite persisted. "I could run a few errands while you check out the books."

Sarah wanted nothing more to do with the madam than absolutely necessary. "Thanks, but I need some time. I haven't heard from Charlie, and I'm worried."

"Charlie's fine. I asked Jenkins about him last week. He said everything was square between Charlie and him."

"Thanks. Good to know." Sarah went to her room and slipped on an outfit that would hold George's attention and left. Portland trains ran like their European counterparts, but Sarah missed the one she'd intended to take and was now late. She had to forego Powell's and go directly to O'Reillys. She hoped he'd be waiting. At a few minutes past noon, she walked into the tavern. It was quaint, nicely appointed with an Irish theme. Expectantly, she scanned the room. Before she finished a hand touched her elbow.

"I was afraid you stood me up." George spun her around. "I got a booth in the back. In a little while this place will be a madhouse. The Trailblazers are playing the Bulls. We won't be able to hear ourselves think up here. You look marvelous. That's a great outfit."

She thanked him and followed him to the booth.

"George, do you want the usual?" the waitress asked.

"That'd be great, Myra. Do you know what you'd like, Sarah?"

"Um. No. What's your usual?"

"Ginger beer, straight up, no ice."

"I'll have that too." Sarah smiled. "George, nobody puts ice in beer."

"It's ginger beer, not beer beer. Sort of like root beer. You may not like it. It has a kick to it."

"If I don't like it, you can have mine, and I'll get a Coke." Sarah got comfortable in the booth.

"Deal. Did you have any trouble finding the place?" George slid in across from her.

"I've been here before, but I missed the train, almost screwed everything up."

"I'd have waited for you."

Myra brought two sodas and two glasses without ice. "Having lunch?"

George nodded. He was in charge, and Sarah liked it.

They ordered sandwiches and fries. Sarah enjoyed the soft drink and ordered a second. They talked about Portland, the rain, beaches they'd visited, and an assortment of topics typical for a first date. The bar got crowded and rowdy. After lunch, Sarah pointed out their fannies were taking up valuable real estate and suggested they leave.

Outside the tavern, George pointed to the river. "You know that's not the Columbia?"

"Only tourists think that. Smart people know the Colorado runs through Portland."

George laughed. "Okay, that's all I've got. What else do you want to talk about?"

"Tell me about yourself. What does an investment banker do?"

George gladly took up the explanation of his duties. They walked along the river, enjoying the park straddling its western shore. The conversation ebbed and flowed, and soon they found themselves at the park's southern terminus.

"Sarah, I like you. I hope we can do this again. Soon."

"It's been a wonderful day, and I'd love to see you again." Big fluffy flakes floated to the ground. Sarah stuck out her tongue and captured one. George tried, but failed. "Hold your breath, silly, or you'll blow them away. Watch and learn."

She caught another and another. She closed her eyes and let flakes fall against her face. Then George took her hands. She kept her eyes closed and continued to face the sky. She hoped he'd kiss her, and he didn't disappoint his girl from the library. He held her close. She had to see. She had to know if *his* eyes were closed. She peeked. He was kissing her like he meant it. The kiss lasted only a few seconds, but it'd stay with her the rest of her life.

"George, I don't want to go back."

"We can go to a movie and then to dinner," George offered.

"I don't mean just now, I mean never go back. But I have to."

He was confused. "When you're ready, you can explain what you mean."

130

"Thank you. This is about the best day of my life."

"Same here. When can I see you again?"

"Are we done for today?" Sarah asked, hesitantly.

"Are you crazy? We have all evening, but I want to know about the next time." George was ecstatic.

"How about Wednesday?"

"It's a date. I'll pick you up. "

"I don't want to meet there, ever. Let's meet at O'Reillys again?"

"That'd be great. Where next?"

"I need to go to Powell's. Walk me there?" She took his hand, and they walked off together.

Chapter 34

Realizing he wasn't going to get more sleep, Taras rose long before dawn. His side of the bed looked like it had been in a street fight. Nothing had ever upset him like what had happened the day before. Lara could've been killed because he ignored the signs; because he let a woman's beauty and charm dissuade him from doing what he should've done in the warehouse. If Levi hadn't been there, Charlene would've killed his daughter. On the bright side, Warren proved to be a real man, willing to take a beating to protect Lara, and the only reward he wanted was to continue seeing her; a reward Revoldi readily granted.

He told himself things turned out as well as they could have: the kids were safe, the kidnappers disposed of, and all evidence gone up in smoke. But something bothered Taras. It had kept him awake. Levi and Lara's stories didn't make sense. They didn't quite ring true. He had to find out what really happened in Dover, Idaho.

Lara sauntered into the kitchen. "Up early? What's going on?"

"I have some work at the shop. What are your plans?" He avoided the conversation he had to have with his daughter.

"I'm going to see Warren. Mom thought I should bring him flowers, but that's lame. He'd rather have candy. I'll get good stuff at the mall."

Revoldi found his wallet and gave Lara a one-hundred-dollar bill. "Get him all the candy you can carry and get a box for his mother and father. I'm sorry I ever doubted him."

In Olympia, Brian was also up early. Monday usually wasn't his favorite day, but this one was different. He and Deirdre spent the weekend together with no emergency interruptions, a rarity. The Chief-of-Staff was refreshed and ready for work. With coffee in hand, he stared at the five contract files displayed across his dining table. Within them was the proof he needed to call for a criminal investigation, a very rare event in Washington's legislative history.

Every contract far exceeded its budget. Every contract was significantly behind schedule. Every contract included Waters Construction and Reice Facilitation. The patterns were compelling, but they weren't proof. He needed files far more detailed than the ones he had to document the pattern of corruption and identify who was involved. To get those files, he'd need the Department of Transportation's cooperation, an agency that neither liked nor trusted him. Today he'd start his quest. An image of Don Quixote, lance in hand and windmills in the distance, came to mind.

He turned his attention to preparing a healthy breakfast for two. In a few minutes, Deirdre would spring to life, shower, and run off to her office. Brian thought an omelet might entice her to sit for a few minutes. He cubed peppers, onions, and tomatoes and added them to the eggs frying on the stove. Competing and compelling aromas filled the kitchen and wafted up the stairs. Deirdre strode in dressed for work. Without so much as a *how-do-you-do*, she sat down and waited for her crescent-shaped omelet. "You do know how to treat a woman. I hoped you'd do this."

Brian laughed, pleased with himself for getting her to eat a decent breakfast without an argument. "And good morning to you too."

"Oh right, good morning. Did I tell you I'm meeting Don's friend Patti for lunch?"

"Business or pleasure?" Don delivered her breakfast.

"I'd have gone with *business* a couple of days ago, but now that she's dating Mr. Clean, I'll say both. They're a great couple."

"Whoa girl, slow that pony down. They've gone out a couple of times, and you're ready to them marry them off." Brian put his omelet on a plate and joined his girlfriend.

"Oh, stop it. You know what I mean. They're at ease with each other. Like us. That's all I'm saying, but I'll find out more at lunch."

"Where are you going?"

"Not sure yet. It's her call."

They finished breakfast quickly. Both had important things to tend to at work. Brian put the dishes in the sink while Deirdre put leftovers in the refrigerator.

"I'll talk to you later." Brian reminded the yenta. "Don't push Patti too much. Don't scare her off."

"I won't. I'll get all the info I can and tell *you* about it tonight."

"That's my girl." Brian found his coat in the hall closet.

Deirdre asked, "How much of our money are you spending today? Take it easy on us taxpayers, okay?"

132

"I'm not spending money today. As a matter of fact, I found a few places that may have to pay back a bunch of money."

"I like the sound of that. How much are we talking about, fifty bucks?"

"Smart ass!" Brian helped Deirdre into her jacket. "How does three or four million sound?"

"What I could do with three million." Deirdre said. "I could outfit a proper lab."

"Really? You get a huge windfall, and what do you want to do? Build a lab. That is *so* you. How about a trip? A new house? A present or two for me?"

"You don't like presents. Lord knows I've tried. I'll stick with the lab."

They kissed, and Deirdre sprinted out the door and down the sidewalk. She climbed into her *girly* truck; a title Don mercilessly bestowed on it.

The first thing Brian did when he got to his office was leave Senator Bernard an update: *I think two Spokane companies might be jacking up construction costs.*

A short while later, Senator Bernard listened to the message and rightfully assumed Brian was referring to Reice and Waters. He called Andrei and left a terse message. "The trip to the Okanogan is on. Will get you details later this week."

Then he left Brian a message. "Ease off the road projects. I'll explain why when they meet. Get busy on the liquor bill. I need your assessment very soon."

❖

Just before noon, Patti walked into the Flying Tiger Restaurant, Olympia's best Thai eatery. It had been over a month since the Thomlinsons had been murdered and their home reduced to ashes. The homicide and arson investigations began concurrently, achieving the same limited results. Today, the two investigators hoped to move their investigations forward by comparing notes. Patti asked for a booth in the corner. With a window on one side and a wall on the other, the booth shared a common connection with only one table, minimizing the number of people who might overhear them. Deirdre arrived on time and found Patti.

"Hello. Glad you spotted me." Patti greeted her friend.

They ordered lunch from among the lighter fare and got down to business.

Patti began. "You show me yours, and I'll show you mine."

Deirdre laughed. "Haven't heard that since high school, and I don't have a lot to show. The fire was arson. Lab found two accelerants, gasoline and turpentine. Whoever torched the trailer wanted it burned to the frame. Fires were set in the bedroom and the living room, probably wanted to do as much damage to the bodies as possible." Deirdre pushed several photos across the table. "We usually have the outer skin and roof left because they're metal, but this fire was so intense, the metal melted. My guys estimate four gallons of gasoline and a half-gallon of paint thinner were concentrated in the two spots. Once it got touched off, carpet, curtains, furniture, and bodies made it an inferno."

The food arrived. Deirdre closed the folder before the waitress saw the pictures, more to prevent nightmares than protect the case.

Patti began. "I've had some luck. The victims were Mickey and Elizabeth Thomlinson, and Harvey Campbell. They lived and died together in the trailer. Harvey and Liz were involved. Liz was killed with a pair of scissors, buried deep into her chest. The force broke a rib and sliced through her heart. She died in a few seconds. Harvey died from a single gunshot to the head. Mickey wasn't as lucky, shot in both knees, wildly painful. Mickey suffered considerably more than the other two. He was shot in the head also. He's the reason they were murdered." Patti took a bite of her Cobb Salad, and continued, "Mickey was stealing money from the casino. He was a dealer, mostly low-stakes blackjack. The patrol reviewed video tapes of Mickey at work. Those lab guys are very good at what they do. They figured out Mickey's scam and found the man and woman working with him. We're guessing the casino sent enforcers to get the money back and things got out of control."

"Were Liz and Harvey the accomplices?" Deirdre asked.

"No, that would've made this way too simple. I blew up pictures of Mickey's accomplices. The one of the guy is better than the ones of the woman. Both look pretty young. I've got the photos circulating around the office. It's likely they've been in trouble before. I'll run copies out to the sheriff's department later today."

"Why don't you just email them?"

"I want to see what's going on with Jack Ogden. He was the deputy out at the scene when we were there. He's disappeared. Went home for the weekend, and nobody's seen him since. Could be a coincidence, but I think there's a connection. I'll get a better flavor of what the sheriff thinks if I show up in person."

Patti went on, "If I can ID one of the accomplices, then I might be able to track down who killed the Thomlinsons, provided the accomplices haven't met similar fates. How's the chicken?" Patti ended her review.

"Not bad. I really wanted a bacon cheeseburger, but I have to watch my weight."

"You look fabulous. Are you and Brian going away over the holidays?" Patti finished her lunch and pushed the plate to the side.

"I have to go to Everett between Christmas and New Year's. My dad's having surgery, and mom wants me to make sure they don't kill him."

"Not the best doctors?" Patti asked, more than a little concerned.

"Not the best patient." Deirdre laughed. "He snapped his Achilles tendon a couple of years ago. They put him in a cast and told him he'd be in it for eleven weeks. Three weeks later, mom found him in the garage cutting it off. He told her it interfered with his golf game."

"I see. So you'll keep him in line?"

"Not a chance. The old bugger's going to do exactly what he wants. I'll just take mom out for drinks while he's doing it."

❖

Across town in the Senate Office Building, Brian's message light was blinking. He had two messages. He hit Play and a young woman's voice said, *This is the Cattleman's Lodge in Winthrop Washington confirming your reservation for December 26th through December 29th, checking out Saturday December 30th. Two queen rooms without breakfasts, one in the name of Bernard and the other for Crane. If any of this information is incorrect or you need to change your reservation, please call at your earliest convenience. We have a seventy-two hour cancelation requirement and look forward to having you stay with us.*

The second message irritated him. "What the fuck, Bernard? I've just about solved the problem with *your* contracts. Now is not the time to stall me."

Brian checked his calendar. The Lodge was spot on. He tossed the contract files on his desk and brought his computer to life. His weekend efforts generated several new leads which he now had to sit on while Bernard played politics. But the boss wanted the *Booze Bill* ready for session's opening bell.

He dialed the Liquor Board's number. A cheerful voice informed him the director was on vacation. She transferred him to the head of administrative services. Again, he was greeted by a cheerful young lady who told him her boss was out sick. Cheerleaders were apparently substituting for administrative staff. The receptionist connected Brian to accounting. Finally, someone who could help him came on the line, "This is Rick Ward. What can I do for you?"

Brian told the accountant what he was doing and what he needed. He expected to be shuffled off once again. Instead, Ward repeated Brian's request, clarified several points, and told Brian the information would be sent by email later that day. Brian thanked him and sat back in his chair. Things were going surprisingly well. Shortly after, Brian received an email from Ward containing seven large spreadsheets.

❖

In downtown Olympia, about a mile from Brian's office, Bryce arrived at his shop at eight. With less than two weeks until Christmas, every day would be busy. He'd have little time to watch soccer. He unlocked the front door and, with a flick of the switch, the barber pole began to swirl.

"Turn it off and lock the door. We need to talk." Andrei said from the barber chair.

Bryce jumped. "How the hell did you get in here?"

"Really? You think this is Fort Knox? Took me under a minute to unlock the backdoor. You need better security."

Bryce turned off the beacon and locked the door. "What do you want?"

"We want information from this jeweler." Andrei handed Bryce a note. "And you're going to get it for us. Stop by his shop and offer him a free haircut, whatever. Get him into this chair this week. Then find out when his next shipment of gems is coming. Don't make him suspicious. We need to know when and how the jewels will arrive. Did you hear the Martin job got screwed up? All our folks are in jail."

"I didn't have anything to do with that?" Brian turned on the towel warmer.

"If I thought you'd fucked us over, you'd be lying in a pool of blood. If you hear anything, let me know." Andrei got out of the chair, walked across the room, flipped on the beacon, and unlocked the door. "This is your first real test. Don't screw it up."

By noon the floor around Bryce's chair was covered with hair. The last morning customer closed the door, and Bryce put up the *Out to Lunch* sign. The bus to the mall was on time. Fifteen minutes later he stood outside the jeweler's shop. Drary had owned a store two blocks from Bryce's for twenty years. Five years ago, fed up with street people, Drary moved to the mall. His creations were exquisite; owned by the wives, daughters, mothers, and mistresses of governors, legislators, and a host of local dignitaries. Yet, his store was unassuming, almost Spartan-like. Three display cabinets were nearly empty. An uninformed customer might think *Drary's Fine Jewelry* was going out of business. Quite the opposite was true. As the economy recovered, people commemorated their love, celebrated their accomplishments, or rewarded exceptional work with Drary's creations. For the past month, sales climbed steadily. He'd used three-quarters of the stones McGlin had delivered just weeks before. With twelve shopping days left before Christmas, he had little to offer and nothing in reserve for Valentine's Day.

At half past noon, the bell on his door jingled, indicating another customer was browsing. Drary left his workbench and came into the showroom to find Bryce, his former neighbor, hovering over the earring display.

"Hello, Evon. How's business?"

"Bryce, good to see you. Business is beyond my wildest expectations. I had to hire Adam Shaw to get caught up. What can I do for you?"

"Anne wants earrings this year. Thought I'd see what you had."

"The selection's down, but there are some nice pieces. Want me to get them out?"

"You know what? I'm going to have her stop by and browse. If she likes something, put a tag on it. I'll pick it up later."

Drary put his arm around his friend's shoulders. "I'd love to work with her, and I'll put whatever she likes away for you."

"You're looking a little shaggy, Evon. Come over this week, and I'll trim you up. Get you ready for the holidays." Bryce headed to the door. "And it's on the house."

Drary was delighted with the offer. He'd intended to get a haircut but hadn't been able to fit it into his schedule. It'd be good to relax for a few minutes and talk about soccer or something other than clarity, cut, color, carat, and, of course, cost.

"I'll take you up on that. Jill's been bugging me to clean up my act, and there's no better start than a haircut. With Adam here, I can get out for lunch now and then."

"Good. Stop by any time. I'll squeeze you in." Bryce smiled as he left. He liked Evon, but business was business. And Bryce was positive Evon was insured.

Chapter 35

Patti studied the photographs of Mickey's associates. The man was white, late twenties, light brown hair, six feet tall with a slender build. No tattoos or distinguishing features on his arms or neck, well-groomed, wearing Target-quality clothes, no jewelry, no watch. There was nothing remarkable about him. Nothing that'd make identifying him easy.

The photos of the woman were even less informative: blonde, slender, attractive, clothes from sales racks, no tattoos or piercings, mid-twenties. The camera angles and lighting made it impossible to pick up any more detail. Patti had sent the photos to law enforcement agencies in Thurston, Lewis, and Greys Harbor counties hoping someone would recognize them. So far nothing had come back.

Patti looked over the captain's report and noticed the three thieves Don nailed had made bail. She wondered how he'd react knowing all his work kept them off the streets for less than forty-eight hours. He'd be disappointed. She was.

Just hours after making bail, Mac, Bernie, and Danielle sat uncomfortably in Jenkins' office. Their boss wanted to know how they'd been so easily taken out. The two men recounted similar stories: didn't see anyone, felt a sting, woke up in the hospital. They were shot with drug-filled darts. Jenkins let the guys leave after telling them to keep quiet.

Danielle had more information about the vigilante: over six feet tall, muscular but not body-builder size, shaved head, piercing blue eyes. He was calm even when she shot him. Didn't come on like a hero; probably military or former military. Jenkins understood why she hadn't killed the guy. Turning a burglary into murder wasn't reasonable.

"Bernie and Mac will get a couple years at Monroe or Walla Walla. You might get probation." Jenkins summarized his thoughts on the trial. "No matter what, I'll see that the three of you have money and whatever else you need."

After Danielle left, Jenkins began to think about the next order of business, the Drary shipment. He was right about Drary's situation. Nearly all the diamonds McGlin delivered in November had been used.

Evon Drary hit Send. He was excited. This was the largest order he'd ever placed. Three thousand miles east, his broker, Joseph Nogler, would begin acquiring seven-hundred thousand dollars' worth of diamonds tomorrow. A few minutes later, an email arrived from Nogler. "I'm on it. The stones will be ready Monday morning. All the best, Joe."

With the order placed, Evon called McGlin. He was shuffled off to voice mail. Drary left the information James would need to get the gems from Nogler. Nogler and McGlin knew each other, making the handoff much easier. Drary reminded McGlin that unless he arrived in Olympia before four, he had to keep the gems overnight.

His second call was to his nephew. Once again, a machine took his message. "David, James McGlin is arriving at Sea-Tac sometime Monday afternoon, December 18th. Contact him for details. Call me when you've confirmed the arrangements."

Now with a sense of accomplishment, Drary concluded today was perfect to take Bryce up on the haircut. Evon had no intention of stiffing his friend out of twenty bucks. While he'd graciously accept a free haircut, he'd leave a twenty-dollar tip. At ten-thirty, he made his excuses and drove to Bryce's shop.

"Look what the cat drug in?" Bryce quipped as Drary stepped into the barbershop. "I knew a free haircut would get you here."

"You know the saying, *you get what you pay for,* and God only knows what a free haircut is going to look like."

Bryce finished the man in the chair and invited Drary to sit. Bringing the cape around with a matador's swirl, he secured the neck strap and misted the jeweler's hair. "Just over the ears, Evon?"

"That'd be great. The haircutting business still good?"

"Beyond my expectations. It hasn't slowed in a month, and this afternoon, they'll be waiting for thirty minutes. You still busy?"

"Frankly, I'm hoping it'll slow down so I can get caught up. Adam and I have worked our fingers to the bone." Drary scanned the empty shop. "Bryce, I have to tell you. I just put in my largest order, nearly three-quarters of a million dollars. And that's wholesale."

Bryce didn't have to manufacture a surprised look. He had no idea Drary was doing such a land-office business. "Are you kidding? That's a lot of money."

"I'm nearly out of gems, especially the higher quality ones. And Valentine's Day is almost as big as Christmas for me. I have to resupply."

"So you'll get a shipment after Christmas? After New Year's?" Bryce asked, innocently.

"Heavens no, they arrive from New York on Monday, and I have to tap into them right away, especially after you put in your order. I haven't seen Anne yet."

"She'll be in. She's just too busy with school and the kids." Bryce was already calculating his cut. "She hasn't been on her bike since Thanksgiving."

"I'm teasing. Have her come in whenever she can." Evon reached for his wallet. "I have to get back. Thanks for the haircut."

"It's on the house, Evon, and it looks great."

"I know it's on the house, but I'm leaving a tip." Drary put a twenty dollar bill on the counter. "Happy holidays my friend."

Still playing the role of friend, Bryce asked, "Evon, do you want me to ride up the Sea-Tac with you? Monday's my day off, and I don't have much to do."

"For the diamonds? No need. My nephew David is picking up the courier."

After the jeweler left, Bryce called Andrei. An answering machine instructed him to leave a message.

"This is Bryce. I have the information you want. Let's meet for pizza, usual place. I'll be there by six-thirty."

Bryce hung up and put the *Out to Lunch* sign in the door and retreated to the backroom. He turned on a soccer game and wrote the information Drary had unwittingly provided:

- Three-quarters of a million in diamonds
- Coming from New York City
- Arriving Monday mid-to-late afternoon
- Nephew's picking him up

He folded the paper, put it into his shirt pocket, and prepared for a busy afternoon. When he returned to the front, customers were already standing outside his door. *If business were always this good, I wouldn't need my second job.*

❖

Patti checked her email, nothing. "Somebody has to know them."

A patrolman approached her cubicle with a flier in hand. "I know this guy. Last Sunday a kid found him in a parking lot, pretty badly beaten. He was freezing, nearly naked, with a busted knee, burn marks around his balls, and a gash on his head." He handed Patti the flier. "We sent him to St. Pete's. Coley's the name, lives in Oakville. Somebody from your shop must've visited him by now."

Patti recalled Dunshee had been assigned an assault case and tried to remember if she'd shown Bill the photos. She hadn't. Was Coley Mickey's accomplice? Had the mob caught up with him? Bill might have some answers. Shortly after the patrolman left, she found Dunshee and showed him the flier. "Know this guy?"

"I think so. Looks like the naked guy they found outside a church. I interviewed him, but he didn't remember much. Said kids beat him up." Bill retrieved his notepad. "Coley, Charles Coley. None of his story made sense. He's protecting someone, maybe himself."

Patti looked up Coley in the databases. He had a history of minor run-ins with the law, typical juvenile things. Given his reluctance to talk about his assault, she didn't hold much hope he'd open up about stealing money from a casino. If the men who attacked him were the ones who killed Thomlinson, Coley was smart to keep quiet.

On her way to Oakville, Patti stopped by the hospital. They confirmed Coley had been released the day before. They let her look at Coley's records. He was battered and bloodied and definitely her *man of interest.* A blow to the head had concussed him, but the hit to the knee did the real damage. A photo of Coley lying on the ground showed the left leg contorted in a manner that almost made Patti sick. She'd seen mangled bodies, and this injury registered among the most appalling. Photos of Coley's nether-region showed welts on and around his genitals. Angry sores would leave lasting reminders. He'd been taught an excruciating lesson before being tossed out like garbage.

Patti couldn't get the images out of her mind as she drove to Oakville. She found Coley's house a block off the town's main street which doubled as Highway 12. It was small and tidy, without a hint of the holiday season. Patti knocked.

A small, grey-haired woman opened it a crack.

"Who is it, Mom?"

"I don't know, Charles. Let me ask," the elderly lady replied sternly. "May I help you?"

"Ma'am, I'm Detective Linder with the Olympia Police Department. I'd like to speak with Charles Coley."

The voice from the other room was emphatic. "I'm not going over this again. Some punks beat the crap out of me. Leave!"

Speaking past the elderly woman, "I'm not here about the assault, Mr. Coley. I'm here about the casino. We could talk here, or I could take you to the station."

"Good luck with that. You'll need a truck to get me there."

The old lady let in the unwanted cop. A bed was in the middle of the living room. A makeshift tripod suspended Coley's plaster-encased leg. The cast extended from the hip to his ankle, not a signature or mark on it. A blue tarp, serving an obvious duty, lay between the man and the mattress.

Patti sat in the chair next to Coley. "May I call you Charles?"

"You can call me Charlie. What do you want?" Coley barely looked at Patti.

"Charlie, I have a photo of you at the casino. You were playing blackjack."

"I'm old enough to gamble." He shifted his weight, uncomfortably.

"I know, and it appears you were dumb enough to rip off the place."

Coley looked away. This wasn't a conversation he wanted, not now, not ever.

"So you got a taste of what these men will do to someone who steals from them. Believe it or not, you were lucky."

"What the fuck do you mean I'm lucky? I'll never walk right again."

"You're alive. Mickey, Liz, and Harvey aren't."

The names made Charlie twitch. He knew exactly what happened to them. Not from news reports but from graphic descriptions provided by the men who were beating him. "I don't know what you're talking about. I don't know those people."

"I can prove you not only knew *those people* but you were stealing money from the casino with them." Patti continued to play the nice cop. "Isn't it odd the casino hasn't reported any thefts? Not to the cops or to the insurance company. Maybe they've recovered their losses some other way. How did they recover their losses from you, Charlie? A pound of flesh? Beating the crap out of you didn't get them any money. What did they take? What did you have to pay them off?"

"I don't know what you're talking about. I didn't steal from any casino." Coley was becoming agitated. "Now leave."

"Okay, but before I go I need you to tell me who this woman is." Patti handed him a grainy photo."

"Never seen her before." Coley handed it back without looking.

"That's not true. You were sitting at the blackjack table with her, Mickey Thomlinson's blackjack table. You sat with her on a number of evenings. If you were there, she was there. I need to know who she is and where she is."

"I don't know her. You have to leave. Mom has to change my diaper, and I don't want a crowd around to watch."

"I'm leaving, but I'll be back." Patti got up and moved to the door. "Those guys aren't done with you. You should talk to me, and let me protect you."

"That's not ever going to happen. If I talk, then I die, and they'll kill my mother. We're done. Don't come back."

Chapter 36

Lara's 4.0 grade-point-average was a source of pride for her and her family. Only Philosophy 401 stood in her way of becoming Gonzaga's thirty-second student to graduate with a perfect GPA. Brother Jerome prided himself in being the last hurdle to accomplishing this feat. His course had defeated the last ten contenders. Lara was likely to be its eleventh. It wasn't because he didn't like her, quite the contrary. The president of the University found her delightful. She was a worthy challenger, someone whose accomplishments would reflect well on Gonzaga and him.

Eight of the fifteen-hundred graduating seniors signed up for Ph-401. Seven would be grateful for a passing grade. Only Lara sought perfection and was well on her way to achieving it. Today, Brother Jerome threw down the gauntlet, the test that on average reduced every student's grade for the course by one full point. On the board he wrote:

YOU CANNOT DO EVIL SO THAT GOOD WILL COME OF IT.

He stalked the classroom, cassock flowing behind him. Brother Jerome dared anyone to offer a situation that detracted from, much less disproved, the principle. A young man, showing rare bravery and little sense, raised his hand. "Go back in time to before World War II and kill Hitler."

"Ah yes, the *Hitler-Alternative History* scenario, comes up every year. Let's explore it. Mr. Simpson, what's the evil deed and what good comes of it?"

"Killing Hitler is evil because it violates the Fifth Commandment. The good is World War II doesn't happen."

You propose killing Hitler before 1938. At that time, he hadn't committed a capital crime. You'd murder an *innocent* man believing Hitler and only Hitler is responsible for the war, forget the Italians and the

Japanese. And Mr. Simpson, you are aware we aren't yet capable of time travel?"

The class laughed. Brother Jerome pounced, wanting to have the debate he knew he couldn't lose. "Lara, can I kill the fetus to save the mother's life?"

Lara knew this was coming. She'd spoken with him a week ago about abortion, hoping he'd shed light on his position. He told her he'd get back to her on the subject. He was now getting back to her.

He stood beside Lara. "Begin with identifying the evil and the good, and stay away from time travel. Abortions are happening across the country as we speak."

Lara began her response when the bells of St. Aloysius tolled, ending class and the discussion.

Brother Jerome held the class back. "Before you beat feet and think you've escaped this discussion, each of you is to develop a scenario that would challenge or dispel this principle. I want the scenario and your most complete and compelling arguments on my desk by next Friday. No longer than two type-written pages. Ms. Holmes, I'm still reading your last opus. Keep this one under two pages. Lara, do you want to focus on abortion?"

She thought about Charlene sprawled on the cabin floor. "I'm working on a different scenario now."

Striding across the Commons, she decided it was time to discuss her succession plan with Apakoh. Her father, the good natured family-man, would reject it outright, probably denying Bratva's very existence, but Apakoh would embrace it. Even the Lords of the Kremlin didn't pass into their godless eternity without anointing their successors, nor would Apakoh. Lara would be his successor.

Don zeroed the computer in on Bryce's conversation with the jeweler. He needed to glean as much information as possible from the short, one-way conversation.

- Jeweler's first name is Evon. Last name unknown
- Three-quarters of a million in diamonds
- Coming from New York on Monday, probably in the afternoon
- Jeweler's nephew David is picking up the courier
- The courier is staying in Olympia
- Delivering the diamonds on Tuesday

Monday was three days away; little time to sort out where, when, and how a near million-dollar robbery would occur. Don called Justin who agreed to catch the next plane to Seattle. They were confident they could disrupt Andrei's plans.

With a list of questions next to his computer, Don began his research. First, identify the jeweler. Google listed sixteen jewelry shops in Olympia.

The name Evon Drary jumped off the page, and Don scratched question one from the list. If all else failed, they could warn him, and he could bring in the cops.

Item two was far more difficult; identify the courier's flight. Don provided the search engine with the information he had: depart NYC-arrive Seattle. Thirty flights for a dozen carriers from three airports clogged the screen. He limited the search to morning departures, cutting the number in half. By eliminating flights with plane changes or multiple stops, the resulting ten arrivals were spread over nine hours for six carriers at two terminals. Don needed a small army to meet them all, and even if he could meet them all, he was looking for someone being paid well not to be noticed. Hopefully, Justin would have an idea.

❖

In Spokane, Revoldi was delighted to see Lara walk into the showroom. He hugged her. She took his arm. "Dad, we need to talk. Can we go someplace private?"

This was the conversation he knew he needed to have but dreaded. Lara had been kidnapped, had seen her boyfriend beaten senseless, and had watched Levi shoot two people to death. Any one of those events would traumatize a young woman, but all three in the span of a few hours obviously had taken a toll on his daughter. He wasn't sure how he could help her through this, but he was determined to do all that was possible. He pulled her close and told her to wait while he got his coat.

When he returned, Lara and Levi were huddled by the back counter. Levi had his arms around the child he loved like a daughter. Lara needed all the support she could get, and Taras was happy to see Levi embracing her. He slapped his friend on the back and turned his daughter to face him. "Let's go to lunch, baby girl. I know the perfect place." Taras nodded at Levi and guided Lara to the door.

Malnoti's Diner was a pleasant, three-block walk from the shop. The owner, a large Italian immigrant, greeted his old friend with gusto. Revoldi took the man's hand and squeezed. The Italian winced. "Ah, for an old Russian, you have the strength of a bull, at least in the hands."

Revoldi asked for the backroom, and the two patrons were ushered to a small, comfortable area next to the kitchen, away from the dining area. A waitress quickly set the table and poured ice water into two tumblers. She was about to leave menus when Revoldi ordered. "We'll have two calzones; one with sausage and pepperoni and the other with mushrooms and spinach."

Lara nodded her approval, and the waitress scampered off. "I need to talk to you about what happened in Idaho, dad."

Taras braced for a host of questions and probably tears. He didn't know what Charlene had told Lara before Levi killed her. His mind struggled to prepare the right answers and words of comfort if necessary. He took both her hands and held them tightly. "Go ahead, Lara, but I think I know what you're going to tell me."

"You know *I* killed those two? Not Levi?"

It took more than a moment for Lara's words to register. "What? No. Levi didn't shoot them?"

"He was too busy trying not to get knifed in the neck. The woman went for her gun. I got it first, and I shot in her chest. Then I nailed the bastard trying to kill Levi. I didn't have a clear shot at his head, or I'd have put one between his eyes."

Revoldi wasn't sure what astounded him more; what his daughter had done or the words she used to describe it. "*You* killed them?"

"Had to. Levi busted the door down to stop the man from smacking me again. Charlene would've have killed Levi, but I didn't give the bitch a chance. Then the guy pulled a knife out of his boot. The only shot I had was at his heart. The hollow-point pretty much stopped him right then and there."

Is this my daughter? Revoldi thought. *My sweet, innocent little Lara?*

She continued. "The man was dead before he hit the ground. Charlene was still breathing so I slapped her twice across the face. Wanted her to know she'd fucked with the wrong Russian before she went to hell."

Revoldi was dumbfounded, speechless.

Lara completed recounting the story. "Warren doesn't know any of this. He thinks Levi rescued us. And he asked me where I thought your guys had taken Charlene and the guy. I told them to Spokane and put them on a flight to Miami. What does mom know?"

Revoldi wasn't prepared for that question. He stumbled for an answer. "She knows two people tried to steal you, and she thinks Levi got you back. She thanked me for not listening to her. That's a first."

Lara looked at her father. "Apakoh, I know all about the Bratva and what you do. Well maybe not all but a lot. I have for years. And I want to be part of it."

Revoldi shook his head in disbelief. The food arrived giving him time to compose himself, if only for a few seconds.

"I know about the gambling and the protection schemes. And I know about Anton." Lara bit into her calzone. "This is wonderful. Why haven't we eaten here before?"

Revoldi studied his daughter's face. Not a clue to what she was thinking showed.

"I'm glad you don't push drugs, dad, and you have to stop the prostitution thing. It's just not cool." She drank her soda. "I know you've kept mom and us out of it, to protect us. But we can't be kept out of it.

Charlene proved that. You and I can protect mom and sis, but only if you let me be part of the Bratva. Pass the parmesan, please."

Revoldi reached for the shaker but drew his hand back. Lara's words sank in. "You know what I do, and you want to be part of it?"

"I don't want to be part of it. I want to *run* it." Lara smiled. "I still need the cheese."

Revoldi passed the shaker, not sure what to say. Lara filled the void. "In five or ten years, you're going to retire. You hoped Levi would take over, but he isn't interested or capable of leading the Bratva. You know that. You wanted a son so you could pass this on to him. What you don't know is I'm every bit as capable as a son would've been. Dad, there are many Charlenes waiting to strike."

The waitress interrupted with an inquiry about desserts. Taras ordered a cannolo. Lara declined and continued. "I'm not saying I'm ready this instant. I need to prove that I can do this and do it well. I'm proposing we work together for the next few years. You teach me the ropes, and I show you that I'm worthy and able. Levi's seen me in action. I think I impressed him."

Taras mulled over what he'd heard: Lara killed two people, directed Levi to do her bidding, and calmly dealt with Warren, his parents, and Zoya. He couldn't have done better. Now she was negotiating with him, and very effectively. He needed time to think. Zoya would have his head on a pike if he did anything to endanger their daughter, and he could think of nothing more dangerous than having Lara become his successor. But there she sat eating his cannolo. The one person he knew could be the next Apakoh.

"This is good, dad. You should get one." Lara laughed. "By the way, can somebody do something evil so that something good can happen?"

Shocked back into the moment, Revoldi replied, "Good and evil are defined differently by different people."

"So you believe good and evil are in the eye of the beholder?"

"One man's evil is another man's good. History books make the call."

Chapter 37

The tip on Sarah's dresser made her sadder, angrier. Her new attitude, the one she'd developed after her date with George, was affecting her work, at least her outlook on work. Hopefully Mrs. Waite hadn't noticed. Sarah had witnessed the woman rip into girls who were *not into* their jobs. It wasn't pleasant, and Sarah wanted to avoid that chat. At six, she stopped trying to sleep, got up, showered thoroughly, and showered again. She found it interesting she adopted this practice the day after the date. By eight, Sarah was ready to face the day.

"How are you doing, sweetie?" Waite welcomed her to the kitchen.

"Pretty well, but I didn't sleep much."

"I'm sorry to hear that, child. Plans for the day?"

"I'm going into Portland. The Santa Claus run is on, and it should be fun."

Waite nodded. "Do you want a ride to the station?"

Sarah was relieved there wasn't going to be a chat this morning. "I'll walk. I need the exercise. Thanks."

"Be careful. Portland's full of weirdos."

Sarah put on her jacket and left. Knowing what she'd been doing for the past week made it difficult being with George. She'd told him nothing about the circumstances that brought her to Portland. He was interested but not compelled to pry. The other night when they were talking on the phone, she came close to blurting out the entire story, but she didn't, just told him there was more he needed to know about her. His reply had brought tears. "It doesn't matter. Whatever happened brought you to me. We'll make this work. I promise."

Mist collected on the train's windows as it took her across the Willamette River. She'd have an hour to wander the streets before meeting George. But time flew, and she had to hurry to the café. George sat in a booth, two cups of coffee already on the table. He stood and hugged her. They kissed. Sarah slid off her raincoat and sat across from a man she barely knew. They ordered, chatted, ate, paid the bill, and left hand-in-hand. Sarah was subdued. George asked her if she was feeling alright.

"I didn't sleep last night. I guess I was nervous about today."

They were passing the Bonaventure Hotel. George grabbed Sarah's hand, dragged her into the lobby and up to the registration desk.

Sarah was surprised but offered no resistance.

"Do you have a room available now?" George asked.

"Check in is at three, sir." The clerk punched his keyboard. "But I do have a room available."

"I'll take it." George handed him his credit card and driver's license. "All the information is current." In a few minutes, they were in the elevator headed to the seventh floor.

"What are you doing, George?" Sarah asked, sheepishly, almost hopelessly.

"Just doing what a man has to do." He put his finger over her mouth and opened the door to a spacious, well-appointed room. "Get into bed. I'll visit the restroom while you get comfy."

He didn't leave her an option. She undressed and slid between the cool, fresh-smelling sheets. Her heart sank. He'd turned her hope for a romantic day inside out. She wondered how he knew, how he'd found out. She began to cry.

"Are you all settled in there? I'm coming out."

She closed her eyes, disappointment swirled. "How could he do this to me? How could I've been so stupid?" she choked back tears. She waited for the covers to be flung back as a naked man climbed in beside her. She felt his weight next to her. Then a firm, caring hand brushed her hair off her shoulder.

"Why are you crying? What's the matter?"

She opened her eyes, and there he was, fully clothed. She couldn't speak. She reached out and hugged him.

"You're exhausted. You need sleep." George kissed her softly on the forehead. "After I tuck you in, I'll watch Santas turn into jackasses. Not a pretty sight."

"You make me so happy."

"You have an odd way of displaying *happy*." He gathered a tear from Sarah's cheek. "It's about noon. I'll be back at four. We'll catch an early dinner at O'Reilly's. I'll see if anything good's playing at the movies."

George started to close the drapes.

"Leave them open. I like the sunshine."

He opened them as wide as they'd go, walked across the room, and kissed her cheek tasting the salt the tears left behind. "If you need anything, call room service. Sleep well."

He kissed her on the lips. The door closed behind him, and she wrapped her arms around one of the pillows. Now she wished he'd stayed. She hugged the pillow hard as sleep caught up with her. Nobody'd ever shown her this kind of respect, and she'd never felt this way about anyone before. Never this safe.

❖

"Remind me why you own a big-ass whiteboard?" Justin asked.

"We call that a B-A-W in the crime-fighting business. I'm a very visual person, and I like to draw."

"Given what we have, I'm just depressed. We don't know shit. If we can't pull more of this together, we're going to have to warn Drary." Justin looked at the chart with a dozen *unknowns* printed in the matrix. Then an idea crossed Justin's mind. He pointed to one of the cells. "We've been thinking Drary's nephew is doing his uncle a favor, picking up our boy at Sea-Tac. What if he's in the business of picking up people? Drives a cab or a limo?"

"You could have something. We've got nothing else. Let's see if the computer has a Drary in the transportation business."

Don summoned their all-knowing electronic wizard and entered the terms transportation, Drary, Olympia. The search engine popped out a list of

Olympia-based transportation companies. The name Drary wasn't among them. Don was closing the screen when Justin noticed Double D Limo Service. "If you were a kid, wouldn't that name work? Do you know the nephew's first name?"

Don went to his notes, "David. David Drary? We're assuming his last name is Drary. So, Double Ds?"

"Double D Limo is picking up the courier."

"Okay, let's go with that. We're a step closer." Don replaced an *unknown* with *Double D Limo*.

"Roger that." Justin took over. "Let's go through the pickup. The plane gets in mid-afternoon. The airport is crowded, lots of security. Double D is waiting. The courier probably has luggage."

"Why would he have luggage?" Don asked.

"He needs a gun but can't carry one on the plane. He has to check it in his luggage."

Don nodded. "Makes sense. Go on."

"Double D is parked right outside baggage claim. There are a lot of cops on the arrival deck, keeping people from parking. So nobody's going to heist the gems there. Once our boys get on the road, they're safe. Who's going to try a hold up in rush-hour traffic?"

"I agree." Don took over developing the scenario. "They get out of the airport and head to Olympia, an hour drive, middle of the afternoon, almost all interstate. Hijacking a car in broad daylight wouldn't be smart. Too many things can go wrong. The courier's going to be armed. The driver might be too. Why not wait until the courier's alone? The driver drops him off at a hotel and leaves. His job's done."

Justin jumped in. "I can go with that. So the courier's in the hotel alone. He's going to need food, but I doubt he'd walk around Olympia to find a restaurant. He'll order in. He's got to be staying at a hotel with room service,"

"What about delivery: a pizza or Chinese?"

"If you were on an expense account, would you order pizza?" Justin asked.

"Not if I could get a steak and fries delivered to my room, maybe a couple of beers I'll bet he's staying at the Two Sisters." Don went to the white board. "Best hotel in Olympia, with the best food around, if you can afford it, and this courier can afford anything he wants. He's got a jeweler backing him."

"I think you've got it." Justin replaced another *unknown* with Two Sisters.

Don was pleased. "When are they going to take him and the diamonds?"

"That's the sixty-four thousand dollar question, lad. When is he the most vulnerable? When would you take him?"

Don thought for a moment. "When I deliver the food to him. Once he's in his room, the courier thinks he's home safe. So he orders the food, kicks off his shoes, turns on the television, and waits. He's expecting a knock on the door, so his guard is down. The bad guys claim to be room service. He unlatches the door and bingo. They take him."

"But what if he hadn't ordered room service?" Justin tried to defeat the scenario.

"Got that figured out too. The bad guys say Mr. Drary sent the meal, as a thank you. Or something like that. By mentioning Drary, the courier has to assume it's legit."

"Okay, we have a plausible scenario. How do we counter it?" Justin asked.

Don was quick to answer, "We book a room at the hotel and hang out in the lobby. The limo pulls up, we have our courier. The bad guys think their odds get better when the driver leaves but, they get worse. One of us joins him in the elevator and finds out what floor he's on."

Justin completed the thought, "We stake out the hall and when they approach the courier's door, we nail the fools."

"Thank you Mr. T." Don laughed out loud.

Justin wasn't done. "What happens if nobody comes to his room?"

Don shrugged. "They'll have to take him on the way to the mall."

Justin nodded. "The mall's parking lot would be perfect for a smash and dash."

"Smash and dash? You made that up."

"Clever, huh?"

"Right, go with clever. We watch the limo, follow it to the mall. Once the courier gets out, we tail him. If somebody else is tailing him, we tail them instead. When they move, we take them out. Now, let's get some sleep."

Chapter 38

It was nine by the time McGlin arrived at Nogler's on east 48th street. He rang the bell. The broker's disembodied voice greeted him and buzzed him in. The hundred-year old building didn't have an elevator. A few minutes later, the courier opened the office door, thankful it was on the third floor not the seventh. Nogler, a rotund man with blazing red hair, had a drink in hand. The ashtray was full, two butts smoldering.

"You're right on time, James. Want a drink?"

"I'd love one but need to keep my wits about me. If I could get the diamonds, I'll be on my way. Cab's waiting, and JFK's busy."

Nogler moved to the safe. "You're all business. Nervous about the package?"

"There are a lot of people who'd kill for it."

"But nobody knows you have it." The broker placed a small black sack on the table next to McGlin. "We'll inventory them, sign the paperwork, and get you on your way."

Ten minutes later, McGlin was in the cab, the bag of gems nestled in his jacket's hidden pocket. The ride to the airport was faster than he'd expected, and check-in went smoother than normal. The flight left precisely on time, a rare event. Once airborne, McGlin relaxed. He had six hours to enjoy a movie and a meal. Six hours and twenty-seven minutes later, he had his weapon, his suitcase, and a gnawing sense that something was wrong. He dismissed the feeling when he saw David waving from the curb. "To the hotel my friend, and don't spare the horses."

"A quick stop at Club Ambrosia?" David knew the answer.

"Not tonight, but we'll have time tomorrow. My plane's not until ten."

They chatted about football, women, music, women, football, and women. An hour later, Drary deposited McGlin under the Windjammer's portico. Walking through the doors, he scanned the room. The lobby was nearly empty; a clerk behind the counter and a man in the television room reading a newspaper. The clerk made short work of getting him his key. When asked if he'd need a second, James shook his head and passed. This was a business trip, he'd be staying alone. James paid little attention to the unassuming man in the overstuffed chair.

After McGlin entered the elevator, Seth joined his partner outside. Mel picked up his cell. "Hello, Jessica. Get two seats at the bar. He should be there shortly."

At 6:45, James left the warm confines of the hotel, turned left on Columbia, and strolled towards Marconi's, violating the courier's golden rule. He was being predictable.

The restaurant was crowded, and, when James arrived without a reservation, the hostess suggested he wait at the bar. He was delighted to see the only seat available was next to a pretty young woman. He approached and asked if the seat was taken. Jessica told him he was welcome to stay until her date arrived. McGlin ordered a Stella and offered Jessica a drink. She politely declined. They exchanged pleasantries. He was disappointed she was taken, but it helped him to stay focused. Focused until Jessica's phone rang. She listened for a minute and hung up. "The one night I'm in town, and his ex-wife screws it up. The man has no balls."

"You okay?" McGlin asked, hoping she wasn't.

"Yeah, I'm fine. It just sucks. I really wanted a night out, and now I get to go back to the hotel and watch *Survivor* alone. Again."

"This might be a bit forward, but why not have dinner with me? Just dinner. No strings. I'm buying."

Jessica waited a moment. "Just dinner? No strings?"

"Just good food, good conversation, maybe some wine."

"Sure, why not?" Jessica smiled. McGlin had taken the bait.

McGlin changed his reservation to two. Shortly after, the hostess said their table was ready. Jessica was enjoying this assignment far more than she'd expected. McGlin was charming, funny, and good looking. He was single and knew how to spend money. She told him about her made up family, her made up job, and her made up boyfriend. Pieces of each were based in reality, but mostly, she described a life to which she could only aspire. During the conversation, she let it slip she was staying at the Windjammer and seemed pleasantly surprised he was staying there too.

McGlin insisted on paying for her drinks and meal. She agreed when he offered to walk her back to the hotel. Leaving the restaurant, they were greeted by a cold mid-December breeze. Her cotton jacket was better suited for a car ride than a walk. James gave her his coat, and they quickly made their way to the hotel. Jessica pointed out a wine bar and suggested he get a bottle. He was delighted to oblige. She gave him her room number and his coat. He went to get wine; she went to her room where Mel and Seth met her.

"We're set. He's getting wine." Jessica sat on the bed.

"He's probably carrying the stones." Mel closed the kiddy-safe in Jessica's closet. "Jessica, get him to go back to his room and change. He'll stash the diamonds. They'd be hard to explain if the two of you get busy. Make it obvious that's what you have in mind. We'll wait until he gets back to your room before we look through his. You have to keep him here. If he leaves, call his room, and let us know he's coming. What's his room number?"

She gave Mel the number, and the men left. The two thieves entered the stairwell as the elevator delivered McGlin to his fate. James knocked on Jessica's door. She opened it, revealing she was now very comfortable. He handed her two bottles of wine. "I wasn't sure what you liked so here are two options."

"They're excellent. Hey, I've gotten comfy. Why don't you do the same? I'll open these while you're changing." The light behind Jessica made her shirt transparent. McGlin was pretty sure she'd lost her bra.

"Okay. It'll be just a couple of minutes, but go ahead and start without me. I'll catch up quickly. I'll be right back."

His room was one floor below and two doors down from Jessica's. He sprinted the entire way. Once in his room, he yanked off the jacket and flung it on the bed. The dress shirt and pants were exchanged for a polo and jeans. His well-worn cross-trainers felt great as his feet welcomed their old pals. He brushed his teeth.

"How lucky am I?" he asked the mirror.

It responded more like a drill sergeant than a wing-man. *If it seems too good to be true...* He forced the voice to stop. The thought of the blonde-haired woman without underwear on one floor above kicked caution to the wind. But he was stuck. The jacket with a pouch full of diamonds didn't match the new outfit. If he wore it, he'd look like a dork, and he didn't want to explain its real purpose. So he left it strewn on the bed. If someone broke in, they'd likely overlook it. Hiding something in plain sight can work like magic. He secured his pistol under the nightstand and convinced himself everything was fine.

He wished he had time to shower but decided against it. If it got to where a shower mattered, it wouldn't matter. He knocked on Jessica's door and was greeted with a glass of red wine. She had already finished one glass and, with the two gin and tonics at dinner, she was feeling more than a little frisky. When she bent over to pick up the remote, James confirmed her bra-less state. She knew how to get and hold a man's attention. James kicked off his shoes and stashed them out of the way. They shared the couch and began talking about inconsequential things. Soon her hand was on the back of McGlin's neck.

"You know the first time I saw you I thought you were a dweeb."

"Ah, what? When was that? Tonight?"

"Oh, a couple of weeks ago..." She stopped, realizing he was pulling away. She put her arms around him.

"What do you mean a couple of weeks ago? You were here? What's going on?" Then the drill sergeant finished...*it probably is too good to be true.*

"Wait here," he ordered rushing to the door.

She'd fucked up. She dialed and got the front desk, hung up, dialed again with the same result. "Fuck." She gathered her clothes.

McGlin took the stairs in two bounds, raced down the hall, and inserted the card into the lock; red light, upside down. He turned it right-side-up and shoved it in again; green light. The glitch had given Seth plenty of warning. As McGlin pushed his way in, Seth buried a hunting knife in his chest and pulled it out. The courier dropped to the floor, blood pumping uninterrupted from the wound. Seth dragged him in, and the door closed.

Mel announced he found the gems. He told Seth to leave. With the courier's coat under his arm, Mel went upstairs. Jessica was gone. He collected the wine bottles and glasses and left. The men met at their car, sure nobody had seen them. They drove south, glad they had the diamonds. Jessica drove west, glad not to have been caught. McGlin finished dying.

❖

Ten blocks north, the antique clock in the Two Sisters lobby struck nine. Don and Justin had miscalculated. The courier wasn't staying there.

"Now what?" Justin asked.

"I don't know. I was sure he'd stay here." Don looked out at the street. "Should we go home?"

"Let's give it another hour." Don's optimism was ebbing. "Maybe his plane was late, or they stopped for dinner. If he doesn't show by ten, we'll wrap it up." Don sat down, discouraged. "We've got a quiet place so why not plan our next move? Look on the bright side, maybe this courier is so good he doesn't need our help."

Chapter 39

"Mr. McGlin? Maid service. It's nine-thirty." The housekeeper pulled her master key. "Mr. McGlin, I'm coming in."

It took a second for the scene to register with the woman. When it did, Wendy Cole screamed loud enough and long enough to scare the salesman in room 228. He dove to the floor. By the time he gathered the courage to open his door, the hallway was filled with hotel staff and guests. Across the hall, he saw the soles of a man's feet, toes pointed to the floor. The salesman thought his floor-mate had had a heart attack, but when the crowd parted, a dark stain near the body told him otherwise.

By ten o'clock, the Windjammer's second floor had been cordoned off. Guests were in the breakfast room waiting to be interviewed. Room 227 was open, and a gurney waited to transport McGlin to the morgue.

"The maid found him an hour ago." Sergeant Horn looked through his notes. "The front desk got a call from Evon Drary. He's a jeweler, and the guy on the floor is, or was, James McGlin, his courier. When McGlin didn't show, Drary called and asked the clerk to ring his room. He didn't answer, so the clerk sent the maid. This is what she found."

"Thanks, Gerry. Nice work getting this roped off. Did anyone move him?" Detective Linder crouched next to the body.

"No. I checked his pulse when I got here. He's been dead for hours. Should we turn him over?"

"No time like the present." Patti put her hand under McGlin's shoulder and arm. "Gently. You never know what's on the other side."

They rolled him onto his back exposing a large blood pool.

"That's going to be a bitch to get out," Sergeant Horn stated the obvious.

"Really? That's what bothers you about this?"

"Just saying they're going to have to replace the carpet. No way to get that out."

Patti shook her head. She'd never understand men, and that went double for male cops. McGlin's shirt was wet with thickening blood. He had a massive wound somewhere near the heart.

"My guess is a knife." Patti checked for identification. She pointed to the blood trail under the body. "The door wouldn't close so they dragged him in a ways. James McGlin."

"That's who rented the room, checked in last evening alone." Horn closed his notebook.

A uniformed office exited the bathroom. "Nothing in there."

"He didn't die alone. Someone joined him during the evening. Any sign of the gems?" Patti surveyed the room, it seemed small.

"Haven't found anything but personal stuff. He travels light. Not even a razor. Just a toothbrush," reported the officer who'd inventoried the bathroom. "Doesn't look like he showered. The tub's dry, towels are still folded."

"He changed clothes. I've got wingtips and black socks over here, slacks and a dress shirt on the chair. Looks like they got thrown there," Horn added. "Maybe he changed before he went to dinner?"

"Did he go out to dinner? Did anybody see him?" Patti opened a dresser drawer. A new *Gideon's Bible* rested in the corner.

"They're bringing in the crew from last night. The current crew didn't see him. He was long dead before they showed up," Horn speculated.

"Did anyone find sneakers?" Patti flipped through the bible.

"No sneakers, just the wingtips."

"Then where did the boy leave his walking shoes?" Patti pointed to McGlin's stocking feet. "He wasn't running around in socks all night."

"Gerry, go to the front desk and tell them to hold off cleaning the rooms. If any rooms have been cleaned, check to see if the maids found a pair of sneakers."

Gerry hustled out of the room and returned in a few minutes. "They haven't started housekeeping."

"Take two guys and do a room-by-room." Patti sat on the bed. "Look for a pair of sneakers that don't belong. Check any other place he might've taken them off."

Patti looked in the closet. "Where's his coat? Even if he was in cars and planes all day, he would've had a coat? Did anyone find a coat or a jacket?"

155

A murmur of no's came back. She checked the obvious places again. No coat. Did the murderer steal it and his sneakers? Are those where couriers hide jewels?

The coroner arrived and completed a preliminary examination. He confirmed McGlin was dead; while perfunctory it was necessary for the death registry. "He died around ten last night. Looks like a knife got the aorta. He died quickly. It's not much, but it might help the family."

"Thanks, doc. I'll pass that on when I talk with his kin. Sad day. And so near the holidays." Patti patted him on the back.

The body was lifted onto the gurney. Patti watched them wheel McGlin down the hall. The room looked different without a body on the floor and cops everywhere. There hadn't been a struggle. McGlin was ambushed. He'd been somewhere close by, probably another room. Hopefully, the evening-shift could tell her if he'd been with someone and where to find that person. Patti was lost in her thoughts when she was yanked back to the moment by a voice from the other side of the bed. "I found a gun."

The officer was on his knees. "There's a pistol taped to the underside of the nightstand. I should say Velcro'd. Pretty neat set up. He was clever."

Patti replaced the officer and checked the weapon. Wherever the courier had gone, he felt safe enough to leave his gun behind. She stood up, gun pointed at the ground. She removed the clip, worked the slide, and made sure the safety was engaged. "He met someone. And that person was staying here too. Convenient."

Horn returned with a plastic evidence bag. "We found these in room 323. They were tucked under the couch. Whoever cleared out the room missed them."

"Was anyone from the hotel in the room before you guys?" Patti took the bag.

"We got there first. I sealed it. Mallory's keeping everyone out."

"Let's not assume we've found what we're looking for. Not just yet. Great job, Gerry, but have your guys check the rest of the rooms?"

"We're already on it, Patti. No tern left unstoned."

"That joke is so bad." The detective put the shoes with McGlin's belongings.

Patti interviewed staff and customers. Everyone was cooperative, but nobody'd seen anything out of the ordinary.

The evening-shift desk clerk had the most information. "Mr. McGlin checked in at six, went right to his room. He left for dinner shortly after and returned about two hours later with a bottle of wine, maybe two. He was wearing a sports coat and wasn't with anyone."

"Could an escort have joined him later," Patti asked. The clerk assured her nobody of that sort came in on his shift.

The clerk continued, "Cheryl Davidson took room 323. She checked in an hour before McGlin. She was young, attractive, and alone. She mentioned a wedding. Went to dinner and returned a few hours later. McGlin came in a half-hour after with the wine."

No wine was found in McGlin's room. None in room 323 either. Patti noted there were no glasses in 323. Ms. Davidson had cleaned it thoroughly, except for the sneakers under the couch. At six that evening, the team wrapped up their work at the hotel.

Patti was exhausted and hungry. She called Don to see if she could interest him in taking her to dinner. He was delighted and agreed to meet her at seven. He knew a great restaurant on the water that served *medicinal-grade* margaritas. Don asked if it'd be okay if he brought his "dumb-ass Marine friend." Two men to distract her would be great.

❖

In the fading light, Andrei looked through Coley's kitchen window. A frail old woman sat at the table, back to the door. The gameshow blaring in the living room masked his entrance. He waited for Mrs. Coley to put down her coffee cup. Then he drew a length of rope around her neck and pulled. For a few moments her arms rose in protest, but she was no match for the assassin. He held the rope taut until her body slumped.

Andrei left Mrs. Coley upright in the chair and entered the living room. Charlie was engrossed in the television show, rooting for the underdog to get an answer right. He struggled as the rope closed around his neck. Once Andrei had complete dominance over his victim, he eased off. "If you scream, I'll shoot your mother. Do you understand?"

"Yes." Charlie gasped for air. "What do you want?"

Andrei picked up Detective Linder's card. "What did you tell the cop?"

"I didn't tell her anything." Coley rubbed his throat. "But she asked about the casino and who was working with me. I told her I didn't know anything about a casino. She showed me a picture of Sarah and wanted her name. I told her I didn't know."

"I wish I could believe you, Charlie. Your mother's tied up in the kitchen. In a minute, I'm going to stick a knife in her arm unless you tell me everything." Andrei went to the kitchen and opened drawers. "Here's a sharp one."

Coley twisted in bed and yelled, "Don't hurt my mother. I didn't tell the cop a fucking thing. She didn't believe me and said she'd be back."

"Quit crying, Mrs. Coley," Andrei said to the corpse. "Your son's going to make this all better, aren't you Charlie? Your mother looks a little upset. Maybe she doesn't think you'll save her. Which arm do you use more? The right?"

"Don't hurt her. Believe me. I didn't say anything. Mom, I'm telling the truth."

"She can't hear you, Charlie." Andrei came alongside the bed. "She died ten minutes ago. I think it was something she drank. Andrei zip-tied Charlie's hands to the sides of the bed. "Charlie, the less you struggle the better off you'll be."

Andrei forced a plastic shopping bag over Coley's head and secured it around his neck. Coley jerked his head furiously in all directions, to no avail. The bag killed him and contained his screams.

Andrei checked Coley's pulse. Nothing. On his way out, he shut off the furnace and opened windows.

❖

In Olympia, Don and Justin got to Marcy's Pub well ahead of Patti, found a table, and ordered a pitcher of beer.

"This isn't half-bad." Justin held up his glass. "Isn't it brewed here?"

"Yep. Close to the barbershop."

The men finished a basket of chips and a pitcher before Patti found them. "Nice pick on the windows, guys."

Don stood up. "Patti, this is Justin. He's a Marine, so I apologize up front for him."

Justin got up and shook Patti's hand. "Nice to meet you, Patti. Don told me a lot about you. How did you got here without your seeing-eye dog?"

"Oh, this is going to be one of those nights." Patti slid into the middle seat. "Take the boys out, and we'll measure right now."

Don was first, "I didn't bring my micrometer, so we can't measure his."

"I didn't know Rangers knew what a micrometer was." Justin picked up the pitcher. "Patti, we have a local brew, but what would you like? Tonight's on me so you don't have to go with free chips and water like you do when he takes you out."

This was exactly what she needed. "I'll have a beer. As long as it's cold, and there's plenty of it."

"I have it on good authority they have more in the basement." Don squeezed her hand. "You had a pretty rough day?"

"Yeah. One of the worst. A guy got stabbed to death last night. Not much to go on. Can we talk about that later? Right now, I want to find out how a *jarhead* got hooked up with a *grunt*."

The men laughed, a bit surprised she knew the lingo.

"My dad drove battleships. So I know how worthless the other branches are." She pointed at Justin. "He did say something nice about Marines once: for big, fat men, they don't sweat much."

They ordered supper, drank beer, and chatted. Don watched Patti captivate his best friend, impressed with her easy style, warmth, and genuine interest in the back stories of two men she barely knew. Justin was equally impressed.

Patti excused herself and went to the ladies room. "Don, she's damned near perfect. What on God's green earth does she see in you?"

"Not a clue. And I'd appreciate it if you didn't ask her. I'm afraid if she thinks about it, she'll run screaming from the room."

"Don't sell yourself short. She's lucky to have you. You make a great couple."

"Oh fuck." Don threatened his friend. "If you say that, I'll never see her again."

"I'll keep my opinion to myself, but I'm telling you, hold onto her. She'll make a man out of you yet."

Before Don could suitably reply, Patti returned. "Were you talking about me? Which asset is my best?"

Remembering Justin's initial comment about her, Don spoke first, "I said it was the way you deal with difficult people. Justin said it was your tatas."

Justin spit out a bite of hamburger and turned beet red.

"Justin, did I tell you Don hasn't seen my *tatas* and, at this rate, he never will?"

"When did this turn into a pick on Don night? I take you to the best bar in town, and this is how I'm repaid? I'm hurt."

"Okay, we'll stop picking on the poor boy." Patti patted Don's bald head. "But you're still not seeing the twins."

"Damn!" Don said a little too loud. "Okay, tell us about the murder."

"A courier came in yesterday, checked into the Windjammer, and got knifed."

Blood drained from the two men's faces. "Oh fuck," Don said.

Patti sensed the dramatic change in their attitudes. "What's going on? Do you know something about this?"

Don clutched his beer. "Was he carrying diamonds from New York?"

Patti sat up straight. "You'd better tell me everything, and I mean every fucking detail. Or I will make your lives miserable."

Don and Justin told her everything; from the time they'd bugged the barbershop through the Martin burglary to the diamond heist. With each chapter, Patti became more upset, angrier.

"So you guys become vigilantes. You don't help the police. You just try to do their jobs. Caped crusaders? Batman and fucking Robin? This isn't a game. A man is dead because you went to the *wrong* hotel."

Don tried to explain. "I thought about telling you, but I didn't have enough to go on. We knew a few things, guessed at the rest. And, we guessed wrong, horribly wrong. If I'd told you, what could you've done?"

"Warn Drary. Pick up Bryce. I'm damned sure James McGlin would be alive right now."

Justin's head snapped to attention. "Did you say McGlin?"

"That's the courier's name, James McGlin."

Justin reached for his buddy. "Don, it can't be him. Jimmy can't be dead."

"Do you know him?" Patti saw fear in the Marine's eyes.

"Justin served with Jimmy McGlin. He was with Justin when we rescued them."

"Maybe it's a different McGlin." Justin broke in. "My Jimmy is about thirty-five, around six-feet tall, maybe a buck-eighty-five."

"That's him." Patti reached across the table and put a hand on Justin's elbow. "He was ambushed, never had a chance to fight."

The devastation in Justin's eyes eased back Patti's anger. "I wish you'd have told me. Maybe I could've prevented it."

"Don wanted to tell you, but I told him not to. I fucked up." Justin gathered himself. "Nothing is going to change that. How do we catch the bastards who did this?"

Patti went into detective mode. "I need everything you have from Bryce's shop. Maybe you missed something."

She looked at Justin. Her words would have little impact on him, on them. They were in a hell she hoped never to experience. "We'll find them. But by *we* I mean me, the police. Stand down. Stop doing what you're doing. Give me what you have and let me run with it."

There was silence. The men nodded. Finally, Don suggested they leave. They all needed time to think, time to grieve.

When they got to the parking lot, Justin gratefully accepted Patti's hug. He'd let his friend, his comrade, get ambushed and killed. It was on him, all on him. He pulled Patti close and told her, "I won't rest until you get them. I'll do anything you need to make that happen."

She turned to Don. "I'll call you tomorrow. I want everything you have."

"I know you're mad at me. There's nothing I can say to change that, but I'm with Justin. We're going to find the guy who did this and make him pay."

"But we're going to do this by the book, Don. By the book. Do you agree?"

Don nodded, "By the book is okay with me."

Justin got in the car. "Don, do you have any tequila?"

"I don't, but I know where to get some."

Chapter 40

Jenkins shouts echoed around the room, enraged at another botched job. "What the hell went wrong? Were you seen? Did you leave anything behind? How the fuck could you let this happen? And where the fuck is Jessica?"

Nearly eight-hundred-thousand dollars in gems lay in front of him, but they'd come at a price, the real possibility of life in prison. It didn't matter who stuck the knife into the courier; everyone associated with the crime would get the same sentence.

"He showed up early, and Jessica didn't warn us. We'd have been caught if we didn't take him out. It was us or him."

"Mel, I understand why you did it. What I don't understand is why you had to. Find Jessica. I need to know how this got so fucked up. Where is she?"

"We checked her apartment and her boyfriend's. She must be with a friend."

"She's weak and dangerous. She'll give us up in a heartbeat. Find her!"

"We will. When we do, what do you want us to do with her?" Mel dreaded the answer.

"Take her to my cabin. After I find out what happened, I'm running her the hell out of here, maybe to Florida. I have a house there."

Mel was relieved. He thought Jenkins wanted to kill her, not relocate her.

"When we get her we'll call and take her to the cabin." Seth stood and grabbed Mel by the back of the shirt. "Let's get going."

"The key's under a rock next to the stairs. Put it back. Don't make me have to break into my own fucking cabin." Jenkins admonished them as they left.

Jenkins called Andrei. "I have loose ends you need to tie up. Call me right away."

❖

Patti's team had taken over the station's conference room. Its fourteen-foot table held everything they had on McGlin's murder, everything except what Don and Justin told her the night before. Patti couldn't make that information appear out of thin air. For now, she concentrated on what they had legitimately obtained, hoping it would lead to Andrei and Bryce.

A mile away, Don and Justin were parked a block from the barbershop. Patti limited their *assistance* to watching the shop and eavesdropping. They weren't to contact Bryce, and if by some miracle Andrei showed, they were to photograph him, nothing else. Her last words to them were, "Don't do anything stupid."

For the cops, the best lead was the young woman McGlin picked up at Marconi's. The waitress and bartender remembered her being about five-foot-three, blonde hair, nice figure, comfortably dressed. They'd never seen her before. The waitress thought they were a couple, but the bartender was sure the woman was waiting for someone. She connected with McGlin when her date didn't show.

The desk clerk confirmed McGlin came in alone. He recalled a woman arrived about the same time but definitely not with McGlin. The clerk thought it was around nine and identified the waitress's sketch as the woman in room 323. Evon Drary confirmed his shipment had been taken. The diamonds probably had been in the jacket. Drary's inventory was one-hundred forty-seven gems, wholesale value of over seven-hundred-thousand dollars.

Two people were involved in the theft and murder; the woman in 323 and the man who killed McGlin. Judging from various descriptions, the woman was slight, bordering on skinny. She didn't have the strength or size to plunge a knife into McGlin's chest. It took a very strong man with the element of surprise to take out a Marine practiced in the art of hand-to-hand combat. Patti put two pictures on the wall: one the straw figure of a woman, the other a straw figure of a man.

Dunshee walked in and glanced at the pictures. "Her ass is definitely bigger."

Patti shook her head. Even with a guy lying in the morgue, Bill could make her smile. He meant no disrespect; he wanted to lighten the moment.

"You got anything else?" he asked.

"I'm sure there was another guy. I can't tell you why, but my stomach says so."

"If we can't find two, then we may as well look for three. Improves our odds."

"I'll never understand you or your math." Patti sat in front of the evidence.

"That's why I'm a cop and not a rocket scientist." Bill sat across from her. "This may be a difficult one, missy."

Jessica, the woman everyone was looking for, had tossed and turned on Ginger's couch all night. Sleep eluded her. The morning news headlined a story about the robbery and murder. She'd caused McGlin's death. If she hadn't mentioned she'd seen him before, if she hadn't panicked. The *ifs* kept rolling over in her head. She didn't want it to be her fault.

Ginger brought in two cups of coffee. "You had a rough night."

"I'm screwed. I'm the woman the police are looking for."

"I figured that. What happened?" Ginger folded herself in an easy chair.

"Probably best you don't know. I've got to get out of here."

"Do the police know it was you?"

Jessica sipped her coffee. "Cops are the least of my worries. The guys who killed the guy know it's me, and they'll blame me for everything."

"What can I do to help? Do you need money?"

"A few bucks would be great."

"No problem. I'll see how much I can put together." Ginger went into the kitchen.

"Thanks, Ginger. I knew I could count on you. If I can get out of town without Jenkins finding me, I'll be all right. I can go to Denver. I've got family there."

Ginger stood over the sink. "Do you want another cup, and who's this Jenkins? You haven't talked about him before."

"I'd love one. Could I have milk in it? Howard Jenkins is with the mob or something. Not a nice guy."

"He's the one who set this up? The wizard behind the curtain sort of thing?"

"Exactly. We do the dirty work; he takes all the profit."

"Is he up in Seattle?" Ginger gave Jessica her coffee and returned to the kitchen.

"No. Right here in beautiful downtown fucking Olympia. Looks all legit, but isn't anything more than a scumbag."

Jessica went on about Jenkins. Ginger *Googled* him. His name and phone number appeared on her phone. She waited until the drugs took hold and then negotiated her reward with the *scumbag*. A half hour later, Ginger looked in on the unconscious woman. She had no regrets. Three thousand dollars had driven those from her mind.

Jenkins called Andrei. "I need you to pick up a young woman for me. She's unconscious. See that she stays that way. Take her to my cabin. Call me when you have her."

Three hours later, Andrei confirmed he had the woman secured at the cabin.

"Great. We need to talk. Can you stop by my office tonight?"

Four hours later, Andrei knocked on Jenkins' door. He heard floorboards creak as his employer moved across the floor.

"Is Jessica okay?"

"If being drugged and tied to a chair is *okay*, she's fine."

"Good. How did it go with Coley?" Jenkins invited Andrei in to his office.

"A cop visited him, but he didn't tell her anything."

"How can you be sure?"

"He swore on his mother's grave."

Jenkins changed topics. "What about Sarah? She's the last bit of string dangling out there, and that string could unravel this whole thing."

"I assume you want me to take care of her too?" Andrei had hoped Sarah would survive her encounter with Jenkins. That hope disappeared.

"Unfortunately, that's the only prudent course of action. It's a shame to lose her." Jenkins offered Andrei a drink. "Can you take care of her tomorrow? She might hear about Coley and realize she's next."

Andrei declined the drink and affirmed he'd dispose of Sarah.

"Now, about my current situation. My guys killed the courier. They got the diamonds, but fucked the entire operation. They blamed Jessica, but they're all dumb as posts."

"You want me to make sure they don't talk?"

"Yes, and I need you to take care of that in the next day or two also. Can you do it?" Jenkins paced the floor. "This has been a tough week for me."

"I'll be in Portland tomorrow, probably for most of the day. This'll have to wait until Friday. Is that a problem?"

"As long as Jessica doesn't get away, it'll be fine." Jenkins sat behind his desk.

For the next hour they devised a plan to dispose of Mel, Seth, and Jessica. Andrei wondered if Jenkins was being as meticulous in planning his murder.

Jenkins put their plan in motion. "Mel, I've located Jessica, and she's safe. You and Seth meet me at my cabin on Friday night, around eight. Pack a few things and be ready to leave town, probably for a month. I have a place where you can stay until things settle down."

Jenkins sensed relief on the other end of the line. After he hung up, he turned to Andrei. "They'll be there Friday evening. They're expecting me, not you. Mel will be armed. I'm not sure about Seth."

Chapter 41

Justin's urge to confront Bryce was growing exponentially. He could get every piece of information the prick had about Andrei in a heartbeat. He'd been trained. Don knew it was only a matter of time before Justin stormed the building. Finally, Justin broke the silence. "We need to speed things up."

"Patti needs more time," Don answered. "She's good at what she does."

"I hate waiting, especially when someone has exactly what we need. I could get a lot out of that bastard barber if you'd let me."

"If we touch Bryce, we warn the others. They'd bolt. And nothing we'd get from him is admissible." Don checked his notes.

- Andrei organized the attack on Jimmy – assumed
- Andrei killed Jimmy – assumed
- A young woman was bait – assumed
- Bryce can recognize Andrei – known
- Bryce knows how to contact Andrei – known
- They could convince Bryce to help – known
- Patti wanted them to stay out of the investigation – KNOWN

Justin summed up their situation. "All we get to do is run to the end of our fucking chains and bark."

"I may have something." Don was optimistic. "Weaver, the woman from the Tumwater burglary, may know Andrei. He organized that burglary too. Patti told us not to bother Bryce, but she didn't say anything about Weaver. I say we stop by her place and see what she can tell us."

"Anything's better than sitting in this fucking car hoping Andrei magically appears in the barbershop." Justin buckled his belt. "Do you know where she lives?"

"I will in a second."

Justin looked at his friend. "You're not going to tell Patti, are you?"

"No. She's the one who put the chains on us. Let's see if we can do more than just bark." Don turned on his wireless antenna and computer. In seconds, he had Weaver's address. "We need to get our stuff."

They went to Don's house. He took three pistols from his gun safe: a Glock, a Smith and Wesson, and a Ruger Mark 1. The guns and four magazines greeted Justin when he returned from the restroom. "We invading Iraq?"

"Better safe than sorry, lad. You pick: the .09 or the .45? Both feel pretty good to me. You have a carry permit?"

"I'm a Marine, so that's a stupid question."

"Again, better safe than sorry. Which do you want?"

"I'll take the S&W." Justin picked up the weapon. "Do you have a holster?"

"Now, there's a stupid question. Underarm or hip?"

"Always fancied myself a gunslinger, I'll take the hip."

"You'd make a hell of a gunfighter. On a good day, you could've drawn on Wild Bill. Wouldn't have won, but you could've drawn."

Don took the Glock, snapped in the clip, and chambered a round. Justin followed suit. Don inserted a dart into the Ruger. Don put his weapons and holsters in a travel bag. "Have to stop by the bank. They frown when I show up packing."

"What the fuck? We're ready to ride, and you're getting cash for Christmas shopping." Justin climbed the stairs. "Maybe we could buy a turkey along the way."

"I'm riding with one. Just relax. This is something I have to do."

After leaving the bank, they found Weaver's house. Lights in the living room meant she was home. They drove down the alley. A six-foot cedar fence separated them from Weaver's yard. A gate split the fence in the middle. Justin got out and checked the latch. It responded, and the door started to swing open. He grabbed it and slowed its progress. Sticking his head through the opening, he saw all the blinds were shut. He closed the gate and returned to the car.

"We can get in the back without being seen. All the shades are drawn."

"Drive around to the front. Give me five minutes to get the backdoor unlocked. Then knock on her front door." Don picked up the two pistols. "Tell her you're a reporter, cop, or whatever. I need her to go to the front door. Keep her talking."

"What happens if there's a Mr. Weaver or boyfriend?"

"I have the Ruger and two darts. After that it'll be hand-to-hand. Hopefully, she's alone, and you can keep her busy while I get up on her."

Don got out and Justin drove off. When he opened the gate, he smiled. The locks would be easy to pick. As he finished the deadbolt, the doorbell chimed. The bell rang again, generating a harsh response from an irritated female. He waited a few seconds and opened Weaver's backdoor. He looked down the hall. Danielle stood in front of a closed door arguing with Justin.

Don snuck up behind her and shot her in the neck. He rolled her away from the door and opened it. Justin walked in as if invited. Don put a finger to his lips, indicating he wasn't sure if they were alone. He reloaded the pistol and searched the house. Nobody was there. They taped her to a kitchen chair and administered the antidote.

Her first sight was Don standing over her. "Oh fuck, not you again."

"Yes, it's me, and we need to talk. Before we do, I want you to be keenly aware I have another dart with your name on it. If you scream, I'll nail you. If you cooperate, I'll be out of here in a flash. It's up to you."

Danielle recalled the near-death event she had after the last encounter with this maniac and his darts. She nodded. Don pulled up a chair across from her. "Let's talk about Andrei."

Danielle's face turned white. "I don't know anyone named Andrei."

"My associate and I are very, very skilled at getting information from people who don't want to share such information. We know how to do it so there're no marks on the person's body, only her mind. Please, don't make us go there. Help us, and we go away forever. Andrei killed one of our best friends. Stabbed him and left him to die. We intend to see he pays for that." Don stood over her. "We think he set your robbery in motion. So, you know him. Cooperate and we leave. If not, we'll extract the information and then leave. Either way, we're going to get what we need." Don went into the living room.

When he returned, Danielle asked, "How will you stop him from killing me, killing my kids? I know what he can do. I've heard stories."

"He won't know you talked unless you tell him, and, when we're done with him, he won't be able to hurt anyone. I promise. And I'm good for my promises."

"Alright, I'll tell you what I know." Danielle slumped in the chair, her choice truly between a rock and a hard place. These men would hurt her if she didn't cooperate. Andrei and Jenkins would hurt her if she did. But if she helped these guys, she'd have a day to get her family out of town.

"Justin, come in here. We're going to talk."

Danielle began, "Howard Jenkins set up my burglary, not Andrei. Andrei's an enforcer. Jenkins uses him to extort money or payback people when they double-cross him. Andrei works on contract. He's above day-to-day criminal activity so he probably didn't kill your friend, but he probably knows who did. He'd know and so does Jenkins."

"What's Andrei's last name?" Justin peeked out the kitchen window.

"Don't know if he even has one. All I've heard is Andrei."

"What about Jenkins? What can you tell us about him?"

Danielle told them what she knew about the man who'd have her killed for helping the men in her kitchen. Five minutes later, her interrogation was over.

"Grab the kids and go away for a while. It's going to take us some time to wrap this up, and I don't want to worry about you being in harm's way." Don poured the distressed woman a cup of coffee. "Don't warn Jenkins or Andrei. They'd repay you by making you watch them murder your kids."

The warning was unnecessary. She'd already put together an exit plan involving her stepsister in Santa Rosa. Jenkins would never accept her rationale for betraying him. He'd focus on the betrayal. And either he or Andrei would kill her. She hoped these men could make good on their promises. She doubted it. She expected a second dart, but, instead, Don reached into his pocket and pulled out money.

"Don't use your credit cards. Here's enough cash for you to get where you're going. Buy a disposable cell phone. Don't use the one you have." Don looked at a flabbergasted partner. "Leave through the front door in case someone saw you come in. I'll slip out the back, Jack, and meet you at the car."

"You're no Paul Simon. And now I can't get the song out of my head."

After they left, Danielle packed. The girls would be thrilled. They loved Aunt Mary and Uncle Jack. With suitcases and presents loaded in the trunk, she drove off to get the girls from school. With Jenkins' address plugged into the GPS, Don and Justin drove off to the puppet-master's office.

"Now what? Bust in and confront the son-of-a-bitch?" Justin felt the S&W.

"No, that's not going to work. Too many people, too many things can go wrong." Don was thinking. "Right now we have the element of surprise. It may be our only advantage."

"So what do we do?" Justin holstered his weapon.

"We're going to find out everything we can about Howard Jenkins, and we're going to do it quickly. For starters, let's see where his office is."

A half hour later, Don parked the Jeep, and they walked into the Lester Building, climbing the stairs to the third floor. The oak flooring creaked under their weight. Frosted windows in the doors proclaimed each occupant's name and occupation: lawyer, CPA, investment counselor. Jenkins' door read, *Consultant*.

Exiting the building, Justin was subdued. "There's no way to sneak up on anyone in that building. It was like walking on potato chips."

"We'll figure out a way." Don remained optimistic.

"When do we involve Patti?" Justin buckled his seatbelt.

"I don't know. Maybe never."

"That's not a good idea." Justin smacked Don in the chest. "She's going to be pissed, and you don't want to marry a woman who's already pissed at you."

"Who said anything about marriage?" Don pulled into his driveway. Brian was climbing the stairs to his porch. He greeted his neighbors. "What have you guys been up to?"

"Been showing my boy the sights. He's a full-fledge tourist now: the capitol, a couple of micro-breweries, and downtown." Don reported. "Don't want him to tell his wife, Saint Marge, I didn't take him anywhere."

"I liked the breweries, not so much the capitol or downtown." Justin joined Don on the porch

Brian headed inside. "Well, I've got to prep for the hunting trip. I'll catch you two later."

❖

In six days Brian would be hunting geese in the Methow, a welcome distraction from the booze bill and the Spokane contracts. Today it was all about guns and ammo. First, he focused on the Parker. The mint-condition shotgun was suitable for display, but Brian believed a gun was to be used, not just admired. He placed it in a fur-lined, fitted case then in a hard-shelled travel container; no sense taking any risks.

Next, he looked through his collection for the senator's ideal weapon. Bernard wouldn't like a lot of recoil, eliminating his Remingtons. But the senator would enjoy the iconic sound and feel of a slide-action gun. The

Mossberg 16-gauge was perfect; it looked and acted like a shotgun and had little recoil. And it was the gun Brian valued least. He put it in a carrying case and then into a travel container.

Shells, binoculars, and other equipment reminded Brian of his last trip to the valley; two years ago just before session. His golden retriever, Sydney, wasn't doing well, and Brian knew it would be her last trip. She loved the snow and spending time with her guy, but fifteen-years of living life to the fullest had caught up with her. Earlier in the summer Brian promised Syd he'd take her to Winthrop if she beat the cancer in her stomach. She did, and they had a wonderful time. Six months later, the cancer returned with a vengeance, and Brian had to put her down. Tears flowed as he put Syd's picture in with the shells.

"One more time, girl." He climbed the stairs, a shotgun in each hand.

❖

Across the state, Revoldi yelled upstairs to Lara, "Hurry and I'll take you to Warren's."

Lara bounded down the stairs. "I have some ideas about how to get me into the business."

"Your mother would kill me if she knew we were even thinking about this."

"Then don't tell her. Weren't you even a bit surprised how well I shot?" Lara put on her fleece vest.

"You were lucky, and they were close." Taras helped her with her coat.

"She was close, but the guy was across the room holding on to Levi. I wasn't lucky, I'm good. Warren and his dad have been teaching me. I'm a natural. I'm very good with handguns, but rifles scare me. Too noisy." Lara looked for her purse.

Taras was stunned. "I had no idea."

"By the way, Warren and I aren't doing it. Neither of us thinks it's a good idea. Don't want a little Taras running around, now do we?"

Revoldi shook his head at his daughter's off-handed, brazen approach to life. She was just like him. If something needed to be done, she did it, including putting an end to two very evil people.

"Lara, there's a lot you don't know. You may decide it's not what you want."

"That's why I'm not going to Warren's today; I'm coming with you to the office. You can start teaching me."

He knew protesting was useless. She was smart, able to care for herself and others, and had a good heart. He could do worse. The Bratva could do worse. He opened the door and ushered his fledgling lieutenant to the car.

"When do I get *my* BMW?"

Taras shook his head again. "I've created a monster."

169

"No, a dragon, a very cute dragon." She kissed her father on the cheek.

Chapter 42

Patti's thought was unkind but accurate. Don and Justin were doing something they shouldn't be, but she didn't have time to worry about them. The captain wanted an update on the Thomlinson case, a case she hadn't worked since the McGlin murder. She sat with him and explained her thoughts about Coley and an unnamed female accomplice helping Thomlinson scam the casino. The captain thought she'd made significant progress and told her to balance her time between the Thomlinson and McGlin cases. She breathed a sigh of relief when she got back to her desk.

Dunshee looked up from his computer. "Captain okay with where we're at?"

"Oddly enough, yes. I thought I'd get yanked from one of the cases. I guess he trusts me."

"Patti, we all do, but sometimes you need help. We're here for you."

"I know, Bill, and I appreciate it." Don and Justin's disappearance crept into her mind. "More help right now might be a bigger problem than the problem itself."

"That doesn't sound very collegial, Detective Linder." Bill brushed aside the possible slight.

"That's not what I meant. I have a lot of balls in the air, and I'm afraid I'm going to drop one."

"Not likely, Patti. And if you do, I'll catch it before it hits the floor, or the fan, whichever fits."

Patti announced, "Well, it's time to visit Mr. Coley again. At least I'll know he's still in town. Want to ride to Oakville?"

"Can't. Have to take the wife to the dentist." Bill turned off his computer.

"The wife? She has a first name. It's Joyce, in case you're wondering."

"Give it a rest, missy. I'm too old to change, and she doesn't mind, especially since I've stopped introducing her as the first Mrs. Dunshee."

"A major step forward, all the way into the seventeenth century."

Bill signed out on the whiteboard. "If this keeps up, you girls will want to vote."

"Girls?! You asshole. Go get Joyce before you end up wearing a stapler."

"Always resorting to violence. That's why men and women can't communicate." Bill ducked out of the area.

Patti smiled for the first time in days. She grabbed the car keys and followed him to the parking lot.

Eighty minutes later, Patti knocked on Coley's door expecting Mrs. Coley to ask who was there. Nothing. No footsteps, no questions, just silence. Even if his mother was out, Coley would still be there, confined to his makeshift hospital bed. She knocked again, got no answer, and tried the doorknob. Locked. The blinds were drawn so she couldn't see into the living room. She decided to try the back door. On her way, a curtain fluttered inside an opened window. She drew her service weapon and yelled into the empty room, "This is Detective Linder. I'm doing a welfare check. Respond or I'll come in."

She continued to the back of the house. Approaching the door, she saw Mrs. Coley sitting at the table, coffee cup in front of her, but not moving. Patti knocked and got no response. Mrs. Coley remained frozen. Patti tested the knob, and it turned. The door swung open, and Patti saw the cord draped around the old woman's neck. Instinctively she checked for a pulse.

Moving past the corpse, gun in hand, Patti entered the living room. Charlie's head was in a bag; his hands forced back and tied above his head. There was no need to check his pulse. Surveying the scene, Patti thought as brutal as Mrs. Coley's murder had been, she died quickly. Charlie hadn't enjoyed the same fate. A quick check of the house yielded nothing.

Patti radioed the Thurston County Sheriff's office and explained the situation. Because Oakville was outside its jurisdiction, she was patched through to the Grays Harbor County Sheriff's office. The dispatcher assured Patti assistance was on its way. Ten minutes later the first patrol car arrived. Soon other Grays Harbor deputies showed up and were given assignments.

A Thurston County squad car pulled up to the house. "Hi, Patti. The sheriff asked me to liaison on this." Lieutenant Rolf Blanc extended his hand. "Walk me through what we have?"

Patti led him into the house. "Charlie Coley's there in the bed. He was tied up and suffocated, probably tortured. His mother's at the kitchen table. She was strangled." She sat in the chair beside the bed. "Coley was involved with Thomlinson. He was ripping off the casino with Mickey. Somebody beat the shit out of him around the time Thomlinson and his family were butchered and burned. I found him through videotapes the casino had and chatted with him last week. He was afraid and sent me packing. I thought he might have had a change of heart, so I came back today. Someone else thought the same thing."

"Whoever did this knew what he was doing," Patti stood and walked to the kitchen. "Took out mom quickly and quietly. Tied up Charlie. Kept him alive long enough to make sure he hadn't talked to us and then put him out of his misery. The killer's a psycho and smart. Before he leaves, the bastard turns off the heat, opens the windows, and cools down the place, making our jobs harder, less precise. What really worries me is there's a woman out there, actually more a girl, who's next on his list. Maybe she's already dead. She was working with Coley and Thomlinson, and if the killer knew about Charlie, he knows about her, another loose end."

"Do you have any idea who she is?" the deputy asked.

"That's why I came down. Charlie knew her, but he didn't give her up. I have to get my ass in gear and find her. Hopefully, she won't have a plastic bag over her head when I do."

When she got outside, Patti realized it was almost two and she hadn't had breakfast or lunch. Her stomach was growling. "Rolf, how about I buy you lunch? There's a good hamburger stand in Rochester."

"Let me take care of a few of things, and I'll meet you there. Order me a couple of hot dogs and fries."

Patti got to the restaurant, found a booth, and ordered two lunches. Blanc showed up as the food arrived. "How's that for timing?"

"Perfect. Deputies always show up on time when food's involved," Patti joked. She liked Blanc. He was competent, thorough, and a gentleman. "What's the word on Ogden?"

"That's the weirdest thing. He's just gone. Left his house and kept going. His bank account hasn't been touched. No activity on credit cards. He either had a stash of cash or he's lying in a ditch."

"He's wrapped up in this case somehow. Whatever happened to Ogden happened because of the Thomlinson murders." She bit into her fish taco. "This is good."

For the next hour, the two cops discussed what might have happened to Ogden, exploring several theories. None came close to the truth. After lunch they returned to Coley's house.

❖

One-hundred miles to the south, Andrei exited Interstate 5. After crossing the Columbia, he drove to Gresham. He'd eliminate Sarah and dump her body somewhere in the boondocks between Portland and Chehalis. With luck, he'd be back in Olympia by dark. What he hadn't counted on was Sarah not being there.

"Mrs. Waite, call her. Tell her you need her back right away, a customer's demanding her, causing a scene. Tell her you'll pay double."

Waite dialed Sarah's number.

Sarah answered, "Hello, Mrs. Waite. What's going on?"

"You have to come home. One of your regulars is here and wants you right now. Says he's leaving tonight and needs one more session before he goes. He'll pay double if you get here in an hour."

Sensing something wasn't quite right, Sarah asked, "Is it the guy from New Orleans?"

"Yes, it is, feisty little guy." The madam's voice spoke of fear, not of opportunity.

"I'll get the next train, probably an hour or so."

"He can't keep it in his pants." Waite tried humor. "I'll send him to your room."

"Perfect. Tell him to get comfortable."

Mrs. Waite hung up, "She'll be here in an hour. Do you want to meet her here or up in her room?"

"I'll meet her at the station. She's coming with me. Can you pack her stuff?"

Mrs. Waite nodded and went to Sarah's room. When she was done, she brought down two suitcases. "It's not very neat, but I got everything."

"Excellent. I'll go to the station. If anyone asks, tell them she moved to Chicago."

Andrei tossed Sarah's things into the backseat, drove to the station, and parked across from the platform. Nobody got off the first outbound train. *Too early* he thought; *she'll be on the next one.*

❖

Sarah wouldn't be on any train. Instead, she and George were talking about the circumstances that brought her to Portland. She described the casino scam, the Thomlinson murders, Charlie's brutal beating, and her being turned into a prostitute.

"I understand if you never want to see me again." Sarah fought back tears. "But I need a favor. Can you help me get out of the city. I can pull my money from the bank tomorrow, but I have to leave right now. It's not safe here."

"What makes you think it's not safe?"

"The guy Mrs. Waite says is there, went to New Orleans three days ago. She lied. Mrs. Waite's never lied before. Even when she had bad news, she just said it. Something's wrong, I know it."

"You can stay with me. Nobody knows about us, do they?" George took her hand.

Sarah was stunned by the offer. "I haven't told anyone about you. Are you sure you want me around? Now that you know?"

"I know how I feel about you. When we're together it just seems right. I haven't felt this way in a long time. It won't be easy, but we'll work through this. First we have to get you someplace safe. It's either my place or out of town."

"George, you're wonderful. I don't know how to repay you." Sarah wiped a tear from her cheek. "I'm going to call my friend in Washington and see if he knows anything. I want to use a pay phone. Do you know where there's one?"

173

"As a matter of fact, I know where the last payphone in Portland is, and it's on the way. There's change in the ashtray. Take what you need." George pulled up to a convenience store advertising adult videos and toys. Outside was a pay phone.

"Come here often?" Sarah grinned.

"Maybe once or twice, but only to read the articles."

"Right. I'll be back." Sarah was surprised when she got a dial tone. She punched in Charlie's number and deposited eight quarters. The phone rang. "Charlie, it's Sarah."

A female voice replied, "Charlie can't come to the phone. Can I take a message?"

"Who's this?" Sarah asked.

"Sarah, this is Detective Linder. Can I help you?"

"What's going on? Where's Charlie?"

"Charlie and his mother are dead." On a hunch, Patti added, "Much like the Thomlinsons."

Silence.

"Sarah, don't hang up. We need to talk. Take my number and call me when you get your head around this. I can help." Patti gave Sarah her cell phone number and repeated it. "Whoever did this to Charlie is coming for you soon."

"He's already here." Sarah hung up and raced to the car. "We have to get out of here. They killed Charlie and his mother. They'll kill me next; and you. We need to leave."

George spun the car out of the parking lot and drove to his house. She'd known Charlie for years. For a brief time they shared a bed. Mrs. Coley treated her like a daughter. Now they were dead, and she was the last link between Andrei and five murders. A few minutes later, George tossed a suitcase in the backseat and drove out of the driveway. "I know a perfect place for us to hide."

❖

Andrei met every train for two hours. The first ones weren't crowded, mostly last minute shoppers returning from the outlet malls. As the afternoon wore on, more and more commuters got off, making it difficult to be sure Sarah didn't slip past. After the fifth train, he concluded he'd missed her or she wasn't coming. He returned to Mrs. Waite's.

"She hasn't come back or called. Should I call her?" Mrs. Waite asked.

"Yes. Find out what's going on. Just don't alarm her."

The madam phoned Sarah. The call went to messaging. She left a brief note voicing concern about Sarah's welfare and the client's urgency.

Andrei waited, sipping on a soda. His phone rang. Jenkins name appeared on the screen. "Where the hell are you? You were supposed to call hours ago."

"I'm still tending to the Portland matter. I'll be home tonight and will see that everything's taken care of as we planned."

"Okay. Don't screw this up."

"That's not possible. By tomorrow night your problems will be gone." He was going to enjoy killing the bastard on the other end of the line.

Mrs. Waite offered him a sandwich. "Looks like she's run. She's never been late before, and she always calls if there's a glitch."

"Any idea where she'd go? Who she might go to?"

"There's a guy, but I don't know any more than that. She keeps her private stuff to herself. I'll ask the girls, but I doubt they'll know anything."

"I'll hang around another hour and then head north. If you hear from her, tell her the guy left pissed off. Tell her to come home. Call me, and don't let her leave."

At six-thirty, Andrei drove north emptyhanded. Sarah was on the run. She'd be no use to the cops. He'd deal with her later. He had a more pressing assignment. There would be no screw-ups with that one. Then he could concentrate on eliminating Jenkins.

Chapter 43

Bernard listened intently, dejectedly. Brian was well on his way to discovering what had been going on for years. The senator knew once Brian proved the corruption theory, he'd be going to prison for the rest of his life. After his chief-of-staff hung up, Bernard called Revoldi.

Apakoh asked Lara for a moment and took the call. "What's the problem?"

Bernard filled him in on the situation. "Crane's uncovered virtually everything we're doing. He still hasn't connected you or me with it, but it won't be long before he does. We have to wrap this up."

"Your trip with him is still on for next week?" Taras looked over at his daughter.

"Yes."

"Distract him, and I'll attend to everything else. Stay calm. Keep his trust." Revoldi hung up not waiting for a response. "Lara, I'm going to tell you about that phone call, and what I'm going to do. When I'm done, if you still want to be part of the Bratva, I'll make it happen."

Bernard called Brian. "You're on to something pretty dirty, and maybe bigger than we know. I need to snoop around before you go any further. I have a lot of contacts I can trust. Do me a favor?"

Brian was pleased. "Whatever you need."

"Put all of this in an *eyes-only* paper for me. Can you do that? It has to have all the facts, your suspicions, and your theory. It makes sense, but without proof we'll be laughed out of Olympia, and I'll be run out of Spokane. Bring it to Winthrop. We'll come up with a plan."

"Will do. Senator, thank you for taking this seriously." Brian changed subjects. "I have the hunting gear together. How do you feel about a Mossberg 16-gauge, slide action?"

"That's the gun I used when I was a kid. I was never very good at killing things, so you'll have to be patient." Bernard had no intention of ever using that weapon.

Chapter 44

Mel drove down Highway 99. The rain made the forest-lined road feel like a tunnel, darker than usual and foreboding. He didn't put much stock in omens, but earlier in the day a black cat ran in front of him. He couldn't get the image out of his mind.

"Are we almost there?" Seth asked. "I don't want to be late. Jenkins is already pissed at us."

"Don't get your panties in a knot. His driveway is just up the road. Help me find the fire hydrant. His road is right after it."

Seth pointed out a hydrant. "My dad said they should be called fydrants. You know, combining fire and hydrant."

Mel chuckled. "Your dad was brilliant. I like that name." He pulled into Jenkins' driveway. "We're here."

The cabin was silhouetted by the moon reflecting off Lake Vliet. They walked past a black SUV with tinted windows and onto the porch. Mel knocked and let himself into the warm building. He announced their arrival, "Mr. Jenkins, it's Mel and Seth."

A voice directed them to close the door. They walked into the great room. A bank of windows displayed the moonlit lake. A lightbulb illuminated a long wooden dock extending into the lake. A small boat could be seen at the end of the dock. The woodstove's heat embraced them.

"Good evening, gentlemen. I'm Andrei. Have a seat." They turned to see a man pointing a gun at them. The captives moved slowly to the kitchen table. "Mel? Sit in that first chair. Seth, there's rope on the couch. Tie your buddy to his chair. Do a good job."

Mel wanted to charge, but Andrei's reputation and the gun dissuaded him. Seth tied him to the chair.

"Good job, Seth. Now toss this rope over that beam and tie it around your neck." Andrei stayed across the room. "Okay, that looks good. Throw the other end of the rope over to me. Sit in the chair. If you do anything stupid, I'll yank the hell out of the rope and your neck."

Andrei pulled the rope to let Seth know how hanging would feel. He tied the second captive to a chair. Andrei left the room. He returned rolling Jessica before him. She was gagged and bound to a chair lashed to a hand truck. She looked dazed, and her eyes weren't focusing.

"Jessica, can you hear me?" Andrei lightly slapped her face. "The boys and I want to know what happened the other night."

Jessica lifted her head and looked at the man standing over her. She mumbled something.

Andrei went to the kitchen and brought back a glass of water. He put it to her lips, and she did her best to drink some. Andrei poured the rest over her head.

"Jessica, tell us what you did to fuck up the robbery." Andrei sat in the unoccupied kitchen chair.

"Fuck you." Jessica struggled to collect her thoughts. "It wasn't my fault. The guy came to my room ready to party. I said he was cute, but he got all upset. Told me to wait and ran out. I tried to call, but the fucking phone wouldn't work. I kept getting the lobby."

"So something you said tipped him off?" Andrei asked.

"I don't know what it was. He flipped out. It happened too fast."

"You tried to warn your friends, right?" Andrei led the witness.

"Three times," she lied. "I kept getting the front desk."

Andrei tried to help. "Did you dial 8 before the room number?"

"No."

"Stupid fucking bitch," Seth said. "She fucked this all up."

"True Seth, Jessica didn't hold up her end of the bargain, but we got the jewels, and nobody outside this room knows who killed the courier. It's too bad he's dead, but the fortunes of war prevailed."

Andrei picked up a roll of duct tape. "I can't stand screaming or pleading. I'm going to tape your mouths shut."

He and taped Jessica's mouth first. She could breathe but little else. Seth was next and struggled mightily, to no avail. He was gagged as thoroughly as Jessica. Finally, he did Mel.

"You three are loose ends, and Jenkins wants them tied up." Andrei leveraged Jessica off the floor, rolled her out the door, down a path, and out to the dock. He dumped her into a boat, stepped in behind her, bent over for a minute, and then started the engine. The boat eased into the lake. With the moon above the trees, the men had a clear view and cringed when Andrei tossed the chair-bound Jessica overboard. They were surprised how quickly she sank.

177

Soon the boat was tied to the dock, and Andrei returned with the dolly. He secured Seth to it. In terror, Mel witnessed Andrei dispose of his friend. Trying to flee, Mel bounced towards the kitchen but the chair's legs slid out from under him. He was bleeding from a small head wound when Andrei returned. The murderer set Mel's chair upright, got paper towels from the kitchen, cleaned up the blood, and stuffed the towels in Mel's pocket. "Like you were never here."

When he landed in the bottom of the boat, Mel understood why Jessica and Seth disappeared so fast. Andrei fastened cement blocks to his chair. A few minutes and a hundred yards later the madman rolled Mel into the ice-cold lake. Andrei returned to the cabin, called Jenkins, and left a cryptic message. "You need three new chairs."

Chapter 45

Justin put down the cell phone. "Margie said we should go to the police."

Don nodded. "Good advice. If only it was that simple. Danielle gave us Jenkins, but he's just like Bryce, untouchable for the cops. Nothing they have leads to either one of our guys. And we got our information by eavesdropping and drugging a woman. How did Robin Williams put it? *This is not going to look good on our resumes.*"

"Then we go after Jenkins. Make him confess." Justin put the Glock back in its holster.

"I think that's the only way we get him." Don finished making lunch. "I'm just not sure how to do it."

Justin poured his soda into a glass. "I don't want just Jenkins. I want all the bastards who had anything to do with killing Jimmy: Jenkins, Andrei, the woman, and the fucker who stabbed Jimmy. I want them all. We start with Jenkins."

"Let's go get him. Bust in, hit him with a dart, and take him someplace private."

"What if Danielle warned him?" Justin tasted Don's stroganoff. It wasn't bad.

"Even if she has, he won't think we'd take him broad daylight."

"I've got nothing better. If we're going to do it, then we'd better get ready. Is the stuff downstairs?" Justin put an extra scoop of food on his plate.

"It is. All we have to do is put it in the Jeep." Don cleaned his plate. "How's the macaroni and cheese?"

"Macaroni and cheese? I thought it was beef stroganoff." Justin swallowed the last bite of whatever it was Don served. "If this plan works, I'll call you General Donald, *shit-for-brains*, Patton."

They picked through Don's mini-warehouse, packed several bags, and loaded the Jeep. At one-thirty, Don pulled into the alley behind Jenkins' building. With overalls on and toolboxes in hand, they easily passed as workmen. Justin tried the service door. It opened. "That's convenient. You call ahead?"

"If only." Don was pleased with the good fortune. "Let's see if Jenkins is in. If he is, we take him. Awake if possible. If not, we'll knock him out and figure a way to get him out here."

"I'm on your six. If we get away with this, we're buying lottery tickets." Justin joked as they climbed the stairs.

They opened Jenkins' door. The outer office was empty. Their target was on the phone in the next room. Don signaled they'd wait until he hung up. Justin locked the outer door. When the call ended, Don walked into Jenkins' office.

Seeing the tool box, Jenkins said, "You have the wrong office."

"Are you Harold Jenkins?" Don asked.

The man behind the desk nodded. Don pulled out his pistol. "If you do anything stupid, I'll shoot you."

Jenkins sat upright in his chair. "I don't have any cash."

"Not after cash, I'm after you, Andrei, and the fucker who killed the courier. He was a good friend." Don came around to the front of the desk and checked the drawers for weapons.

"You're the bald fucker who screwed up the burglary, aren't you?" Jenkins searched for a way out of the situation. He redirected blame. "I had nothing to do with your friend's death, but I know who did. And they've been dealt with."

Don spun him in his chair. "I haven't heard word one about anyone being caught."

"The police aren't going to catch them. They can't find their asses with both hands and a map. I can show you proof."

Justin walked in and surveyed the situation. "What do we have to lose? He walks out of here with us. No fuss, no muss. He makes a stupid move, you shoot him. When he wakes up, he can say his A-B-Cs, not much more. Where are we going?"

"My cabin, a few miles south of here. It's private, we can talk." Jenkins began to negotiate. "There's no need for torture or threats. I'll explain everything to your satisfaction. I promise. My only stipulation is if you're satisfied, you let me drive away. You can call the police immediately, but you let me leave. Not much to ask for the information I've got."

"What about Andrei?" Don asked.

"Ah yes, Andrei. He actually had nothing to do with the unfortunate event you mentioned, but Rasputin will have to be neutralized. I'll leave the mad monk to you. I doubt you have the wherewithal to catch him, much less take him out. But I'll tell you what I know and that may help. Shall we go?"

"Justin, drive Jenkins to the cabin in his car. I'll follow." The three men descended the stairs, Jenkins in the middle.

"It's the Mercedes." Jenkins pointed to a silver roadster in the parking lot. He clicked the fob, the doors unlocked, and the lights flashed. He handed the keys to Justin. "Fully cooperating, gentlemen."

Don ushered Jenkins to the passenger side of the car. "Hands behind your back. This will be uncomfortable, but you understand. Need to be sure there's full cooperation for the entire ride."

Jenkins complied, and Don buckled him in the passenger seat. "If he gets out of line, slam on the brakes, the dashboard will break his fall. I'll get the Jeep. Once you see me, lead on to the cabin."

A few minutes later, the Mercedes, followed by a Jeep, left the Lester Building. Nobody noticed the black SUV pull into traffic behind them. The trip south took twenty minutes. Jenkins didn't complain about Justin's driving, even though the gears got a significant workout. When they arrived, Don pulled Jenkins from the front seat and cut the zip-tie. Jenkins opened the cabin's door. It was cold inside. Jenkins turned up the thermostat, and the furnace groaned. Soon the fan kicked in and warm air rushed into the room. They sat Jenkins in the lone kitchen chair.

Justin looked around the room. "Where're the rest of the chairs?"

"That's part of what I'm going to tell you. Remember, I have your word. When I'm done I walk out the door."

"Let's hear what you have to say, and then we'll decide if you to get to leave." Justin dragged a stool from the kitchen. "Start at the beginning."

"I'll start with the Thomlinsons and work my way up to today."

The two former soldiers looked at each other. The Thomlinsons weren't on their radar. Don took out a recorder and put it on the table. "Mind if I record this?"

"Not in the least. You may as well get it right. I told you I have a lot to offer."

❖

A half-mile north, Andrei's SUV sat in the driveway of the cabin next to Jenkins'. He'd spotted Jenkins leave his building with two goons. They all seemed very comfortable with each other; chatting and having a good old time. Jenkins even let one of them drive his car. Andrei was sure the two military-looking men were the assassins Jenkins had employed to kill him.

Andrei followed them until it became clear where they were going. He passed and got to his destination the same time Justin pulled up to Jenkins' cabin. The Russian was focused. "In an hour, there'll be more bodies in the lake."

He took out Welch's rifle and attached the scope. For a moment he thought about retrieving the diamonds but decided it was too risky. What he really wanted was Jenkins dead. Then a pleasant thought crossed his mind. Jenkins death would let Sarah live.

Chapter 46

Like an economics professor, Lara explained how the Bratva worked to its leader. "We operate on the law of supply and demand. We supply what people want; various forms of entertainment, protection, enforcement, and a few *socially unacceptable* items. Seems pretty simple, dad."

"On the surface it is simple, but most of it is illegal. And sometimes we have to make very difficult decisions. For instance, what are we going to do about Brian Crane? If he persists, I'll go to jail. So will the senator and a number of men around here. All of us have families. If we go to jail, our community will be destroyed. I can't let that happen. Do you understand, Lara? What should I do?

Brother Jerome's admonition rang in her head: *you can't do evil so that good will come of it.* "We have to silence Crane. Pay him off. Threaten him."

"What if money and threats don't work?" He leaned across his desk, looking directly in his daughter's eyes. "What if nothing works?"

Without batting an eyelash, she said matter-of-factly, "If he won't work with us, we eliminate him. But he'll come around. Most people would, given the options."

Lara no longer surprised him. "There is another person who threatens us, Voytek. He has created far too much turmoil in the west, and he could lead the police to our doors. What do we do with him?"

"If he is beyond salvation, we put him down." Lara sat back in her chair.

Apakoh nodded. "It is a shame, but you are right."

In Olympia, Coley's folder sat alongside Thomlinson's and McGlin's. All three cases were related, but Patti couldn't prove it. Don and Justin had given her information she couldn't use. A guy named Andrei had probably murdered them all. And a local barber was helping the madman.

Patti hadn't heard from her vigilantes in more than a day, not a good sign. They were up to something and leaving her out, again. She left Don another message and turned to her partner. "Bill, I need fresh air and food. How about I buy you lunch? Teriyaki beef from across the street?"

Bill grabbed his coat. "You had me at *buy*."

It was long after noon and the mom and pop restaurant was empty. They ordered and found a seat. "Bill, I need advice about Don. Can you keep this between us?"

Bill was about to crack a joke about Don's manhood when he saw the look on Patti's face. She was serious, all business. He nodded.

She began, "Don's been snooping around. He's learned Bryce Williams is organizing robberies from his barbershop."

The male detective was relieved. Patti's issue with Don was work related, not about personal stuff. "Get out of here. That hippy can barely organize a soccer match. The most illegal thing he does is bet on the World Cup. No way."

"It's true. Bryce found out the courier was coming to town and worked with a guy to set up the robbery." Patti was searching for the right words. "Bryce knows who killed the courier, but I can't talk to him because of how I know. Bryce would walk; the killer would walk; everyone would go free. What do I do?"

"Have you thought about talking to Bryce off the record?" Bill offered a plausible out, "Then if he comes forward and asks to talk to you officially, you just take his statement. That'd be admissible."

"Would he go for it?" Patti's demeanor improved dramatically.

"Can't tell until you ask him. Murder is a far cry from burglaries. Bryce is in over his head, and he may be looking for a way out. All you have to do is show him the door. You could mention that maybe the D.A. would offer him a deal. Clearing five murders might get Bryce off with probation."

"Thanks Bill. I wish I'd talked with you sooner."

Their lunches arrived. Patti dug in relieved she may have a solution to her issue with Don. Her phone buzzed. Dispatch was forwarding an urgent call. Patti hoped it was her crime fighter.

"Detective Linder?" a woman asked, hesitantly.

"This is Linder. Who's this?"

"It's Sarah. We talked a couple of days ago when you were at Charlie's house."

"I'm glad you called, Sarah." Patti motioned to her partner this was a critical call.

Sarah's voice was calm, resolute. "You told the truth about Charlie and his mom. They're dead, and I'm next."

"You don't have to be," Patti said.

"The guy who killed them came for me. I ducked him, but he'll be back because I can identify him."

"I can come get you. Bring you here. We can protect you."

"Nobody's coming to get me. If you can find me, so can Andrei. When he finds me he'll torture me, just like he did Charlie. Charlie told him everything, and Andrei still zapped him in the balls. Then he turned me into a Portland whore."

Patti jotted down some notes on a napkin. "Sarah, I need to hear what you know about Andrei."

"Talk to Howard Jenkins. He hired Andrei. He'll know where to find the bastard. And when you fry Andrei, go ahead and fry Jenkins."

"I won't be able to fry either of them without your help. We need to meet." Patti was growing insistent.

"Not now. I'll stay in touch if I can. Get Jenkins. He'll give you Andrei."

"Where can I find Jenkins?"

"He's in Olympia." The line went dead.

"What was that all about? Who's Jenkins?" Bill asked.

"It was Sarah, the girl working with Thomlinson and Coley. She says Andrei's hunting her, and Howard Jenkins is behind all of this."

"I think you just got a legit way of knowing about Andrei. You may not need Bryce now. Does this Andrei have a last name?"

"Doesn't seem so." Patti put the napkin in her pocket. "Do you know a Howard Jenkins? Sarah says he's in Olympia."

"Can't say I do, but there're a lot of folks I don't know."

"I can forget about Bryce now and concentrate on Jenkins. If she's right, Andrei's killed five people in less than two months."

"Do we have a serial killer on the loose?" Bill grabbed the bill. "I owe you."

"A homicidal maniac is more like it. Let's get back to the station. And thanks for everything."

Chapter 47

Don and Justin listened to Jenkins describe the plan to take the diamonds. Step one, Jessica would distract the courier and get him to leave the gems in his room. That part worked perfectly.

"Women were always Jimmy's weakness, especially ones with nice boobs." Justin looked at the lake remembering several strip clubs.

"I assure you, Jessica had world class boobs. Now where was I? Oh yeah. The courier was in Jessica's room, but she fucked up and tipped him off. He ran out and got to his room right when Mel found the stones." Jenkins joined Justin by the window. "Horrible timing, if you ask me. Your friend crashes in and gets stabbed by Seth. None of that was supposed to happen. I just wanted the diamonds."

"How does Andrei fit into all this?" Justin asked.

"He was my go-between with the barber. Bryce found out when the gems were arriving and told Andrei. I put the team together, and they fucked up."

Don stared at Jenkins. "Andrei had nothing to do with Jimmy's death?"

"I'm not saying Andrei isn't capable of, maybe even predisposed to murdering someone, but he didn't have anything to do with the courier's death. But he made those three pay dearly."

"What do you mean? How did Jessica, Mel, and Seth pay for what they did?" Justin opened the refrigerator. "Don, want a beer?"

Jenkins perked up. "How about we all have one? Then I'll tell you how Andrei avenged your friend's death."

Don agreed. There was no hurry. Jenkins would fill in the missing pieces, and they'd let him go. Turning him loose probably wasn't the best thing to do, but Don was sure Patti and her team would catch him quickly.

While Justin searched for a bottle opener, Andrei approached from the north carrying Welch's rifle. He moved quietly and got to the tree line fifty-yards from the cabin. He used the scope to peer into the room: three men drinking beer and talking about how to murder him. Andrei liked Welch's scope. He could count the threads on his target's shirt.

Jenkins sat and put down the beer. "Now where was I? Oh yes, Andrei's retribution. My kitchen table has only one chair. The other three are in the lake; occupied by Mel, Seth and…"

A shot rang out. The window shattered, and a loud thump emanated from Jenkins' chest. The force of the bullet wedged the chair and the victim against the wall. Don and Justin dove to the floor; years of training and combat experience prevailed. A second shot exploded from the north with a corresponding thud in Jenkins. Whoever was out there wanted to be sure Jenkins was dead. After thirty-seconds, Don sprinted across the room, Glock in hand. Justin was on Don's heels.

"Justin, he may be waiting for us to come out."

"Or he's running back to his car. I say we bust through the door, roll into the parking lot, and come up shooting."

"Sounds good. Open the door, and I'll go."

"Oh, for Christ's sakes Don, you thrashing around out there would be like fish on a hot dock." Justin burst through the door and tumbled into the parking area. Nothing. Don followed remaining on his feet. They arrived at the Jeep at the same time.

"Has to be Andrei," Don surmised.

"What did Jenkins' mean about the chairs?" Justin brushed off his pants.

"Andrei killed them, tied them to the chairs, and dumped their bodies in the lake." Don found the sniper's lair. "He policed his copper. He's thorough, and not a bad shot. About sixty-yards through a window. He put two into Jenkins' chest."

"The second was unnecessary." Justin looked around the lair. "He'd already blown out Jenkins' heart. Did you see the blood splatter? It was like a watermelon. "

Don called Patti. "Hey, it's me. Justin and I are at Lake Vliet. There's been a shooting. We're okay, but a man named Jenkins is dead. Yes, I said Jenkins. He was filling us in on Jimmy's murder. We were about to call when all hell broke loose. You'd better contact the sheriff's office and get their divers here. Do you want the address ...Oh, okay. We'll see you in a bit. We'll wait right here. Won't move. Bye."

"That sounded a bit odd," Justin noted.

"Patti's in Jenkins' office. She'd just got this address from his secretary."

"Patti figured out Jenkins was behind Jimmy's murder?" Justin scratched his head.

"No. She figured out Jenkins was behind Thomlinson's murder. She's good."

"This Andrei guy gets around. He's a one-man *murder incorporated*. What's he up to...six?" Justin did the math. "More like ten, maybe a dozen."

"Why didn't he go for us?" Don kicked stones across the lot.

Justin had the answer. "Jenkins was his problem, not us. He made sure that problem went away and then got the hell out of Dodge."

They heard sirens in the distance. After stashing their weapons, they sat on the porch waiting for the patrol car. When it arrived, they put their hands up, knelt, and were handcuffed. Jenkins waited inside, anchored to his chair, unbelieving eyes looking for an explanation.

❖

Andrei had no trouble getting back to his car undetected. He drove north on Highway 99 keeping to the speed limit. Halfway to Olympia, he let a speeding southbound sheriff's car pass. He relaxed. Jenkins was dead. Coley was dead, and Sarah was running scared. Four fools were rotting in the quarry's pond. Jessica, Mel, and Seth were doing the same in the lake. It had been a busy month. He had one more person to attend to, but he needed something to eat first.

❖

At the cabin, Don and Justin were talking with a Tumwater cop when Patti and Bill arrived. She approached the threesome. "Is Jenkins inside?"

"Yeah. He's not going anywhere. The sniper hit him twice in the chest. He probably doesn't have a back," Justin answered.

Don explained, "Jenkins said he wouldn't tell us anything until we got here. No police; just the three of us."

Patti sat on the steps next to Don and Justin. Bill entered the cabin. She turned to Don. "What did he tell you?"

"Andrei didn't kill Jimmy. The team he put together to steal the diamonds did. There were two guys and a woman."

"I *knew* there were three," Patti interjected. "Sorry, go on."

"The woman hooked up with Jimmy. Somehow he discovered she was a diversion and went to stop the robbery; broke in on the guys in his room. One of them stabbed him. They took the diamonds and split." Don stood up trying to remember the details. "Jenkins had Andrei meet the three dirt bags here and kill them. Justin, how did Jenkins say it?"

"They paid *dearly*." Justin filled in the missing word.

"Jenkins didn't say it outright, but he indicated the thieves are out there in the lake tied to his kitchen chairs." Don sat back down.

"Where are the diamonds?" Patti asked.

"We didn't get around to that question. He went to his grave without saying," Justin replied, somberly.

"Did he mention Bryce in any of this?" Patti hoped for the right answer.

"Bryce got him the information about the delivery." Don returned the conversation to the events at Lake Vliet. "Somehow, Andrei found out Jenkins was talking and shut him up. And he did a thorough job."

"I'll take it from here, guys." Patti opened the cabin's door. "Jenkins and a terrified girl in Portland were the last links we had to Andrei. Now there's just Sarah."

"Wait, there's Bryce." Don moved towards the Jeep.

"Dammit! When is this going to end?" Patti clicked her walkie-talkie. "Dispatch, this is Linder. Send an officer to Bryce Williams' barbershop on Fourth Avenue and stay with him. Williams is in danger. Nobody in until I get there. Thanks."

The Thurston County Swift-Water Rescue Team rolled into the parking area. A six-foot-seven Adonis in a wetsuit exited the van. "Where can I find Patti Linder?"

Don pointed to the woman coming towards them. "She would be Detective Linder."

"Hello, Deputy." Patti turned towards the lake. "There may be three people on the bottom out there tied to chairs. Can you take a look?"

"It'll be dark soon, ma'am, but we'll search as long as there's light."

Patti turned to Don. "Don't say a word; not one fucking word. The next person who calls me ma'am is going to eat my flashlight."

Three divers paddled out fifty-yards and dropped anchor. Soon they were in the water. Their voices came over a loudspeaker in the back of the van. "I have something; a man tied to a chair. I need inflation bags to bring him up."

A few minutes later, another voice confirmed a second body; this time a woman, and finally, a third confirmation came from the lake. A deputy drove a motorboat out to the raft and used a small winch to bring up three bodies and the chairs holding them. The medical examiner arrived and took charge of the macabre scene. Jenkins' body was loaded into an ambulance. The other three, still in their chairs, were covered and placed in a police service van. Patti shivered.

"They were alive when he put them in the water," Bill said.

"How do you know?" Don asked.

"No reason to gag a dead man. They were screaming when he paddled them out; screaming when he pushed them overboard, but nobody could hear. And he made sure they all saw what was going to happen." Bill shook his head. "We're dealing with one very, very sick individual."

Patti, Justin, and Don sat with Bill on the porch. "What do we know about Andrei?"

"He was Jenkins' enforcer. He killed four people here, three at Thomlinsons, Charlie Coley and his mother. That's nine people for sure." Patti cringed.

"He's shot them, drown them, suffocated them. Short of hanging somebody, he's used about every method there is to kill." Bill put away his notepad.

Patti corrected her partner. "He strangled Mrs. Coley, so you can add hanging to the list, sort of."

Justin wrung his hands. "He kidnapped Sarah and sold her into prostitution. Add trafficking to his offenses."

"He's also the middleman. He intimidated Bryce into setting up the diamond heist." Don added to the list.

"I'd better get Bryce into custody, probably his family. No telling what this maniac will do." Patti got up and walked to her car. "Bryce is our best bet. If we offer him a deal, he might give us what he knows about Andrei."

Patti turned to Don and Justin. "You two go home. Occupy your time, but stay off the streets. You may be on his list."

"I'm sorry this all happened," Don started, but she cut him off.

"This was going to happen no matter what you did, or didn't do. Andrei was wrapping things up. You're lucky he didn't wrap you up along with Jenkins."

Bill came over. "You don't need me for Bryce, do you? I'd like to finish here and get home. Deputy Sar can drop me off at the station."

"It's about time you start considering Joyce a little. Take off, and I'll fill you in tomorrow. And you two, go home. That's an order." She pulled out and turned on her emergency lights.

187

"Roger that," Justin said.

"Really?" Don poked at his friend. "We're not in a *Clancy* novel."

"We may as well be for all the good we've done." Justin got into the car. "Where do you think Jenkins was going?"

Don thought for a moment. "Mexico? South America? He had a plan and about a million dollars in diamonds. What do you suppose happened to them? The cops didn't find them in the car."

"Good question. Maybe they're at the office?" Justin offered.

"He wasn't going back to town and definitely not back to the office. My bet is that they're still in his car. He could've stashed them anywhere in there," Don said.

"Should we mention this to Patti?" Justin suggested.

"What a great idea. We'll drop by the barbershop and tell her. Maybe help her a bit with Bryce." Don smiled at his good fortune.

Chapter 48

Bryce didn't pay any attention to the police car parking in front of his shop, but the hair on the back of his neck rose when the officer came in and announced he was there to protect him.

Bryce masked his fear. "Protect me from what?"

"I don't know. All I've been told is to have you lock up and wait for Detective Linder. So, if you don't mind, lock this door."

Bryce did as directed. Noise from the backroom caught the cop's attention. He reached for his sidearm. "Who's back there?"

"Nobody." Bryce put away an electric shaver. "That's the soccer match between Real Madrid and FC Barcelona. I was watching between customers."

"Who's winning?"

"It's tied; nothing to nothing." Bryce pointed to the chair. "Would you like a haircut while we wait?"

The officer accepted. Bryce cut the cop's hair and started to shave his neck when a roar erupted from the television. "I've got to see what happened. Don't go away."

The television was small and old. Without turning on the light, all Bryce could make out was chaos on the field but couldn't tell which team had scored, or even *if* a team had scored. He approached the set and squinted to see the information banner. "Madrid you lucky bast…"

Andrei's hands slid around Bryce's throat preventing the barber from completing his thought. In a matter of seconds, Bryce went limp and slumped to the floor.

"Hey, what happened? Who scored?" the officer asked, not really caring.

"Madrid." Andrei answered.

The cop eased back into the chair.

Andrei wanted to know what Bryce had told the officer so he had to keep him alive, but the cop had to die. He came up behind the unsuspecting patrolman who was very comfortable and ill-prepared for the assault. Andrei slung the razor strap around the officer's neck and yanked down with all his strength. He heard the windpipe snap. The cop was no longer a threat. Andrei had done it so fast nobody could've noticed. He applied a handful of shaving cream to the dead man's face and returned to the unconscious barber. A glass of water brought Bryce around. "Wake up, Bryce. We need to talk."

Bryce opened his eyes and rubbed his throat. The television reflected off the knife in Andrei's hand. The barber was pissed. "Are you fucking insane? There's a cop out there, and he'll shoot your ass."

"He isn't going to shoot anyone ever again, and it's not a good idea to threaten me. Now what did you tell him?"

"Not a thing. He didn't ask. He was protecting me."

"Didn't do such a good job, did he? I told you the backdoor needed improving." He stabbed the barber in the leg; immobilizing him. Bryce tried to fend off the next five thrusts, but each hit a mark on his body. Andrei was convinced the man on the floor hadn't told the officer anything, and, even if he had, that cop wasn't going to pass it on to anyone. Now he just wanted Bryce to suffer. Andrei was about to strike again when a sound from the shop stopped him. He looked into the salon. A woman was tapping on the glass. *Another cop*, he thought correctly.

She knocked on the glass again, expecting the officer to rise and open the door. Nothing. Then the door behind him closed. Patti broke out the glass and opened the door. The patrolman's unseeing eyes told her everything she needed to know about the situation. Andrei was at work in the barbershop.

"This is Detective Linder. Come out here with your hands up." She yelled at the door. "I'm coming in."

Patti pushed the door open. Light from behind her illuminated a shadowy figure retracting a knife from the chest of a person on the ground. Uncertain who was doing the killing, Patti held her fire. "Drop the knife."

It clambered on the floor, and the man stood up. She moved closer, gun aimed at the assailant. Her mistake was glancing down at the victim. When she did, the man in front of her sprang and knocked the gun from her hand.

His punch glanced off her shoulder. She moved to her left, away from her adversary. He was between her and her weapon and only a few feet from the knife. He picked it up.

The television screen backlit his muscular frame. He'd win if he caught her. She moved left, towards the door to the shop. If she could get the officer's gun, she had a chance. The man wasn't going to let that happen and forced her back towards the shelves. He brandished the knife in slow, menacing arcs. Patti found herself boxed in by storage shelves and the wall. The figure lunged. She ducked, but the knife sliced her arm. Patti was surprised it didn't hurt. She kicked out, catching her assailant in the thigh, backing him up. He moved towards her, positioning for the kill. The crowd roared for Real Madrid.

For a moment, a brief moment, Andrei considered opening the backdoor and leaving, but he'd tasted blood and wanted to finish the cop who'd interrupted his fun. If she hadn't come, he'd still be torturing Bryce. She ruined it, and now she'd pay.

Patti searched for something to stave off the next attack. She couldn't see in the darkness and fumbled around with her hands. She found a broom handle. It wasn't much, but anything would help. Blood dripped from her sleeve on to the handle and made it slippery. She grasped it as best she could.

Andrei circled, knife always aimed at his prey. The television reflected in Patti's eyes, reminding him of the flash he'd seen in the quarry. He thrust. Patti was ready and brought up the broom. It caught him square and took his breathe away. He was staggered, but not out. And he was angrier.

Andrei thought about throwing the knife but decided against it. It gave him a huge advantage; one he'd press forward. Patti's broom became an unwieldy weapon. Her arm throbbed and blood flowed down her fingers to the ground. She was wounded worse than she originally thought. If she fainted, she'd die. She propped herself against the concrete wall and waited for the next onslaught. She didn't wait long

Andrei muttered something in Russian and attacked. Patti commanded her arms to lift the broom, but they failed to respond. She felt his hand grasp her shoulder, searching for her neck. Patti lifted up, trying to shove him off her, but she'd lost too much blood, too much strength.

"Ah, you little bitch. You are going to die like a sow." Andrei raised his knife.

Light flooded the room. Andrei turned to see something huge in the doorway.

"How about trying a Ranger, asshole?" Don came at the Russian. Andrei stood and prepared for battle.

"Don, he has a knife." Patti kicked at her assailant.

"I see that." Don had dealt with unfavorable odds before. "He should drop it before I use it on him. Are you okay, Patti?"

The two men faced each other across the defunct barber chair.

"I'm going to needs some stitches, but I'll live," Patti replied, sounding a little drowsy. "He stabbed me."

Rage replaced Don's calmness, and with a scream reminiscent of Boudica, the Celtic Queen who fought the Romans, the former Special Operations commander lunged at Andrei. The chair prevented Don from crushing the coward.

The banshee call was unnerving. Andrei knew this was not a battle he could win. He had the blood of the man's woman on his knife. His adversary would be relentless. Andrei opted to fight another day, found the door, and bolted down the alley.

Don had a choice: chase the madman or tend to Patti. He made the right decision.

Patti protested, "He killed Bryce. Get him. I'll be fine."

Don knelt beside her. "We'll catch him. Count on it."

Justin turned on the overhead light illuminating a gruesome scene. Bryce lay in a pool of blood; dead. Don's hands and Patti's clothes were covered in blood.

"This is going to need stitches, girl; lots of stitches." Don asked Justin. "How's the officer?"

Justin shook his head. "He's dead. I used his set to call for help. They're coming."

Patti looked at Don. "Do you ever do anything I tell you?"

"No." He smiled.

She smiled back. "Thank goodness for that."

Chapter 49

Sarah peeked out at the motel sign framed by the rising sun. Cascade Locks Motor Lodge was forty-five miles east of Portland. The village overlooked the Columbia River, ten miles upstream from the *Bridge of the Gods*. George paid cash for the room, which didn't surprise the clerk. Truck drivers and a few locals paid that way to avoid accountants and wives.

George rubbed sleep from his eyes. "I'm going for coffee. Want breakfast?"

"It's too early. I'll shower and get dressed. We should leave soon."

"Sarah, we're safe. Nobody'll look for us here. It's just a sleepy little town. There won't be a hundred people downtown today. I'll be back in a few minutes. Deadbolt the door after I leave."

Sarah followed his instructions, sliding the bolt and then the chain into place. She wedged a chair against the door for good measure. If someone wanted in, they'd have to break down the door, but there was the window. She'd wait until George got back to shower.

She turned on the television. A Portland station greeted her with news about a howling cold front approaching from the northeast. Roads would be hazardous with ice and blowing snow. Interstate 84 might become impassible. The weatherman sent the show back to two well-dressed people sitting behind a desk. The woman declared it was time for local and regional news. A fire in downtown Portland took up most of the airtime, but news about a grizzly set of murders in Olympia transfixed Sarah.

"One man was shot and three others drowned south of Olympia." The camera showed a cordoned-off driveway. "Two other murders, including that of a police officer, in downtown Olympia might be connected. A spokesperson for the sheriff's office said the only victim to be identified so far was Howard Jenkins, a local businessman."

The reporter added a few words about conspiracy and promised viewers to stay on top of the story. Sarah sat on the edge of the bed, shaking. Jenkins was dead. Three or four others had been murdered. Andrei was cleaning house. She was a loose end, maybe the last one. The knock startled her. George confirmed it was him. She moved the chair and unbolted the door, falling into his arms.

"If it wasn't for you, I'd be dead. Andrei's killed everybody who knew him."

"How do you know? You didn't call anyone, did you?"

"It's all over the news. Five, no, six people got murdered yesterday in Olympia. Jenkins was one of them." Sarah spoke so fast George had trouble keeping up. "Andrei worked for Jenkins. If Andrei can kill Jenkins, he can kill me. Us. He'll kill both of us." Sarah collapsed on the bed, now equally worried about George. "What are we going to do?"

"Exactly what I said. Stay here until Andrei's captured or killed. Once we get situated, I'll run back to Portland and get my stuff. Andrei doesn't know where we are. We'll be fine."

Sarah slung her arms around her knight. She didn't know why he cared so much for her, but he made her feel safe. They showered and dressed.

"Time for breakfast." George opened the door. "There's a diner a couple of blocks up Main Street."

"I'm not sure I can eat anything. I'm still shaking."

"Your appetite will come back."

They walked to the diner and stepped in out of the cold, a variety of aromas welcomed them. They had to wait to be seated. "I was wrong. There're more than a hundred people right here." George looked at a menu. "Says something for the food." The waitress seated them in a booth overlooking the street. They chose pancakes with eggs on the side.

Sarah's appetite had returned; she was feeling better. "I can help them find Andrei. Getting him killed is the only way I can stay alive."

"That's what I think, but you have to be okay with it. Let's finish breakfast and then go to the drug store. They'll have disposable phones. You can call that detective and tell her what you know."

"All I know is what he looks like and the kind of car he drives."

"That's probably more than they have right now, and, you'll be doing something to get through this." George continued to encourage her. "That should make you feel better, more in charge of your life."

"You're right, it's a good plan. You're sure nobody can trace the call?"

"I'm sure. After you call, we toss the phone. We disappear."

The refugees bought two disposable phones. George used one to get the Olympia Police Department's business number. "It's ten o'clock on Saturday. Linder might not be in. If she isn't there, tell them you'll call back at noon. Then hang up."

Sarah dialed.

"Good morning, Olympia Police Department. May I help you?"

"I need to talk to Detective Linder about the murders," Sarah said, breathlessly.

"Detective Linder isn't in. Can someone else help you?"

"No. Just her. Tell her I'll call back at noon. Tell her it's about Andrei." She hung up. Turning to George. "Am I doing the right thing? I don't want to get us killed."

"You have to do it. You'll never sleep if Andrei's on the loose." George guided them to a small park by the river. It was cold and getting colder. The wind picked up from the northeast, a sure sign of snow. Time passed quickly, and George handed Sarah the phone. "They'll try to trace this. Don't chit-chat. Tell her what you know and hang up."

Sarah hit re-dial and the Olympia Police Department switchboard answered. "I want to talk to Detective Linder. You have ten seconds or I'll hang up."

"This is Detective Linder. Is this Sarah?"

"Yes. I don't have a lot of time, listen carefully. Andrei's six-feet tall, about 180 pounds, very dark brown, almost-black hair. He's white but dark-skinned. He doesn't have any tattoos I could see. He has a gap in his front teeth, on the top. No beard or moustache. Hair's short but not shaven. He drives a black SUV with tinted windows. I don't know the license number.

It's a Lincoln, but I don't know the model. He's dangerous. He knew Jenkins. Worked for him. Killed for him."

"How old is he?" Patti continued.

"I don't know, forties or fifties. He's in good shape, so it's hard to say."

"Sarah, we need you to identify him."

"Not unless he's dead. That's all I know. I'll call if I think of anything else." Sarah ended the call and handed the phone to George. He tossed it into the churning waters of the Columbia.

"You did great, and you were quick. No way they got a fix on us." George kissed her. "But we should move east tomorrow just to be sure."

"I've never been to Spokane."

"I was thinking smaller, maybe Hermiston."

Chapter 50

"A few degrees cooler and this turns to snow." The rain made Justin's mood darker. The two friends sat on Don's porch drinking coffee.

Brian stepped out to collect his paper. "Hey guys."

"Hi, Brian." Don greeted his neighbor. "Ready for the big hunt?"

"Guns are in their cases with plenty of ammo and lots of warm clothes. It's getting chilly my friends. This'll be the last morning you'll be sitting out here for a while."

"With enough tequila, I could spend the winter out here," Justin said. "Remind me, where you're going?"

Brian came over and handed Don his paper. "I'm taking Senator Bernard to the Methow Valley, near Winthrop in the north-central part of the state."

"You'll see some pretty cold weather. The weathergirl put an icicle right on top of Winthrop the other day, something about the Fraser River effect," Justin replied.

"That's the place, but the best bird hunting this side of the Dakotas. I have access to six-hundred acres of alfalfa fields bordering the river and a real cozy blind."

"Are you really taking time off?" Don looked in the paper for an update on the murders.

"Just taking one report. Otherwise, it's all hunting. Even with my boss there, it'll be shoot 'em up during the day and good food and beer at night."

"Enjoy yourself, and if I don't see you before you leave, be careful out there." Don began reading the article on Bryce Williams. "Guns and beer don't mix."

Justin added. "Keep your powder dry."

"Thanks, guys." Brian disappeared into his house.

"Speaking of travel, isn't it time you get back to Syracuse? Margie's going to miss you."

"I talked with her this morning. Her mom's not doing well, and she's heading back to Florida. Margie feels like a fucking yo-yo with her mom pulling the string. She'll stay through New Year's and then come home for good. If the wicked witch of the south croaks, so much the better."

"She can't be all that bad." Don laughed.

"She can visit you, then you can tell me how you'd kill her." Justin argued. "Margie's come up with a couple of *accidents*. I tell her we just off her. No court would convict us. Her pharmacist would give us the Medal of Honor."

"Can we let your mother-in-law's murder plan sit for a bit and think about catching Andrei?" Don asked.

"Okay, maybe a hurricane will spin her back to Oz."

"It was a tornado, dipshit, not a hurricane."

"It'd take a hurricane to lift that witch off the ground."

The cold front slammed into Spokane and temperatures plummeted. The forecast had them going below zero tomorrow. Andrei put the SUV into the one-stall garage and attached the heater coil. The walk to the house reminded him of the Russian winters he'd grown to hate, and he wondered why he'd chosen to live in eastern Washington. Once inside, he turned the thermostat to eighty and listened to the furnace come alive. He checked the refrigerator and ordered a pizza.

The sun set as the four o'clock news started. He selected a western Washington station and waited for dinner to be delivered. Brutal murders in Olympia were headlined. He listened intently for any hint the police were making progress. The distraught wife of a local barber begged anyone with information to come forward. When authorities brought out relatives they usually had nothing.

The pizza arrived earlier than promised. Andrei settled in to watch Saturday's edition of Monday Night Football. The Cowboys were playing the much-favored Green Bay Packers. At halftime, with the Packers holding a three point lead, Andrei called Taras. After exchanging pleasantries, Andrei asked if he was needed in the Methow. Revoldi confirmed the assignment. With little else to chat about, the men ended the conversation and retired to their respective chairs. Andrei finished half the pizza and put away the rest for tomorrow's lunch. With the game over, he turned on the late night news. When the station replayed Bryce's wife's plea for assistance, he knew he could rest easy.

❖

Sunday morning brought freezing temperatures and snow flurries to Olympia. Patti was thankful there wouldn't be any accumulation. Tomorrow was Christmas and thousands would be traveling today. Patti, Bill, and cops from four departments would not be among them. They were sequestered in the State Patrol's conference room. Six murders forced them to abandon their holiday plans.

The gun used to kill Jenkins hadn't been located. The knife that took Bryce William's life hadn't been found. No evidence associated with three people tied to chairs and dumped into Lake Vliet had been recovered. The killer was methodical and eclectic in meting out death sentences: two crime scenes, six victims, four methods. Patti and Don were the only people to encounter Andrei and still be alive. Neither had gotten a good look at him. All they could add was he was strong, well trained in hand-to-hand combat, and knew when the odds were against him.

The hastily formed team broke for lunch, hoping food and soda would help. The lieutenant's phone rang. After a brief conversation, he thanked the caller. "We have a fabulous group of guys at impound. They literally dismantled Jenkins' Mercedes and found a bag of diamonds."

"Are they Drary's?" Bill asked.

"We have to check them against the info Drary gave us, but I bet they are." The lieutenant slapped Blanc on the shoulder. "Here's what I think. Jenkins and Andrei didn't want to share with Mel, Seth, and Jessica. They meet their accomplices at the cabin but instead of giving them their cut, they feed the poor slobs to the fish. Then Andrei decides he wants it all and kills Jenkins."

"Why didn't he take the diamonds after he killed Jenkins?" Bill asked.

"He didn't count on those two army guys being there," Blanc suggested.

"One Army guy and a Marine," Patti corrected the deputy, causing Bill to smile. "A gun fight would attract way too much attention. So he packs up and leaves. On the way out of town, he murders Bryce."

Patti moved to the white board. "We have six people involved in the Drary robbery and McGlin's death. Jenkins orchestrated it. Bryce fed them information. Mel, Seth, and Jessica carried it out. Those five are dead; all at the hands of Andrei."

Patti took a breath. "And, according to Sarah Geld; Andrei killed Mickey, Liz, Harvey, Charlie, and Mrs. Coley. Brings his total to ten. With Officer Strack, it's eleven. He's eliminated everybody who can identify him, except Sarah."

The lieutenant asked, "Patti, do you have any idea where she is?"

"No. We couldn't trace her call. She's on the run and that may be the best thing for her."

Bill looked up from his sandwich. "Didn't Sarah say Andrei turned her into a *Portland whore*? If that's true, someone in Portland might know where Sarah is; maybe her pimp."

Patti perked up. "I forgot all about that. Andrei has another loose end in Portland. Jenkins would know the pimp, and maybe he was going to meet the guy when his escape was interrupted. Bill and I'll go to Jenkins' office and see if he has an address book."

❖

Across town, Don paced his living room like an expectant father. Finally, he turned to Justin. "Okay jarhead, time to shop. Want to come?"

"Depends on where we're going." Justin retrieved his jacket.

"Drary's Fine Jewelry. I want to get Patti something very, very nice."

"For keeping us out of jail?"

"No. Well, yes. That too, but mostly because she's my girlfriend."

Don backed out of his driveway and saw Brian loading his car. He rolled down his window. "Getting ready to go? I thought you were leaving after Christmas."

"Deirdre wants to spend the holidays with her mom and dad. So she's leaving this afternoon. I'm leaving first thing tomorrow, trying to avoid the idiots who can't drive in snow."

"I'm sorry you aren't spending the holidays with her." Justin thought of Marge.

"She didn't want to come to Winthrop, and there's no way I'm going to Everett to watch her father watch football. We agreed to an *open* arrangement for the holiday; I get to play with my guns, and she gets to gossip with her mother. Apparently, her sister's pregnant."

"Great. She's going to be an aunt." Don turned up the car's heater.

"Not so great. Good Catholic family, pregnant daughter, no father. Just a sperm donor from sis's office. A married sperm donor, I might add."

"You're doing the right thing. Keep guns away from Deirdre's mother." Justin pointed out the obvious. "And away from Deirdre. She knows how to use them."

"Don't want to be part of a killing spree." Brian shut his trunk. "There's enough of that going on around here."

"True that, lad. True that. Drive carefully and bring us back some venison." Don began to pull out.

"It'll be goose meat." Brian waved and disappeared into his house.

❖

Patti and Bill arrived at Jenkins' office as the sun set on Christmas Eve. The wind made it feel ten degrees colder than the thirty-one degrees displayed by the bank across the street. They went upstairs. Bill pulled the crime tape and walked into Jenkins' office.

"I'll start with the desk. Can you check the credenza and the closet?" Patti sat in Jenkins' high-backed office chair.

Bill opened the cabinet's drawers and found empty folders and magazines.

"I've got gum and note paper," Patti said. "This guy was as much a businessman as I am. You got anything?"

"No. He bought this furniture because it fit; nothing in any of it. I'll try the closet."

Patti started with the desk drawers. "Bingo! Got an address book here."

"Let me know if you find anything under *Portland whorehouse* or something equally classy." Bill grinned.

"Yeah. If only. I'll see if he has any Portland addresses. The book's pretty full. This might take a while."

Bill finished with the closet and moved to the vertical cabinets framing the window. "Nice view of the capitol."

Dunshee opened drawer after drawer, sifting through meaningless papers until Patti exclaimed, "Got one. Not Portland, but Gresham, right outside Portland. Waite - 222 North Devon Street, Gresham. No phone number, just the name and address."

"Better check to see if there're any others. That could be an aunt or a drycleaners for all we know."

"Oh really? Did you pick up on the name? Waite? Begins with *W* which is pretty near the end of the alphabet. You might not remember the alphabet, given how long it's been since you used it."

"Nice. How did I know you began with A? Could've started with Z."

"It's the only Portland address in the book. I'll go tomorrow and visit him."

"I was hoping to spend the day with the wife and grandkids. Can we make it Tuesday?"

"Enjoy the grandkids and the *wife*. I'll let the Gresham cops know I'm coming; see if they have any information on Waite. One of them can escort me." Patti waited for Bill's response to her pun.

"Cute." Bill smiled. "Are you sure?"

"The worst he could be is a pimp. And I'm not even after him. I'm there to warn him Andrei might be coming to kill him. I'll be greeted with open arms."

"Yeah, pimps are always happy to see cops. But I'm going to take you up on the offer. Thanks, Patti."

"I'll let Don know he'll have to surprise me with my fabulous gift the day after Christmas." Patti dialed Don's cell.

Don was delighted to see Patti's name appear on the screen. "I was afraid you weren't talking to me anymore."

"I'm not. Right after you give me a wildly expensive present, I'm cutting you off," she said, laughing. "I have to postpone Christmas. Need to go to Portland."

"You found something?"

"A name and an address, not much but it's worth a trip. If it's Sarah's pimp, I have to warn him Andrei's cleaning house, and he's on the list."

"Just a minute." Don looked at a dozen television screens in the mall's lobby. "There's an update on the Jenkins investigation. The diamonds have been recovered. Hey, we did good."

"What's this *we* shit?" Patti asked. "Need I remind you that you are *not* a cop, and you are *not* working this investigation?"

"No. I suppose you don't, but I did help, and I want to help some more."

"Then ride to Portland with me. I'd like the company. But when it comes to the police work, you sit in the car."

"I'd love to go." Don pointed to Justin and gave him the finger. "And I promise to stay out of the way."

"I'll pick you up at eight. Don't wear crazy Christmas stuff."

"I look good in crazy Christmas stuff."

"If you show up in Portland wearing antlers, I can't guarantee your safety."

"You're right. I'll dress appropriately. Would olive drab work?"

"How about business casual?" She shrugged at Bill.

"I still have no idea what that is, but fine. See you then." Don hung up and pumped his fist. "She loves me! What does business casual look like?"

Justin shook his head. "Just because she hasn't shot you, doesn't mean she loves you. There's still plenty of time to cap you. Give her the present as soon as you can. It might extend your life a couple hours."

The two friends entered Drary's shop and began to wander. Evon Drary stepped from the backroom and greeted his customers. "May I help you?"

Justin and Don turned towards him, and the merchant recognized them. "You're the two who helped recover my diamonds. I'm sorry about your friend, Mr. McGlin. He was a fine man."

The men introduced themselves and thanked the jeweler.

Don looked at necklaces in the display case. "I need a really nice gift for my girlfriend. She's the detective doing the heavy-lifting on the case."

Drary's mood brightened at the opportunity to show his gratitude. "Let me work with you."

Justin pointed to a serpentine strand.

"You have a good eye, Justin," Drary said. "Put a diamond on it, and Don has a wonderful gift."

Don looked at the necklace. It was an intricate lace of thin gold, woven like a DNA helix glistening in the light. "You're right. I'll take it. A diamond seems appropriate, since they got me into all this trouble."

Drary showed them several diamonds he'd already set in gold. Justin preferred the round-cut, but Don picked a flawless, one-carat European-cut stone. Drary retired to the backroom to secure it to the necklace. A few minutes later, the jeweler emerged with two cases. He laid them in front of Don.

Don began to explain he only wanted one necklace, but Drary interrupted. "Justin, I noticed your wedding band and assumed you might like a gift for your wonderful wife. Am I correct?"

"Yes, and you probably saved my life. I haven't gotten her anything yet."

"Don, your lady has the European-cut, and Justin, yours has the round-cut. Both are beautiful, unique, and gifts from me." The jeweler pulled a third case from his pocket. "I'll ask a favor in return. I've crafted a third necklace for the wife, sweetheart, or mother of your fallen friend. Would you please deliver it to her for me and tell her how sorry I am?"

Justin, lost for words, nodded.

Chapter 51

Christmas Day had been especially difficult for Margie. Her mother had fallen and broken her wrist, forcing her daughter to brave Tampa Memorial Hospital's emergency room. The doctor was setting her mother's bones when Justin called.

A few minutes into the conversation, Justin heard foul language in the background and stopped his report. "Is the doctor swearing at your mother?"

"Nope, that's Mom swearing at the doctor. She has a cold, and now she sounds a lot like George Clooney."

"God, I love you. I hope you have that kind of patience when I need it."

Silence, then, "What makes you think you haven't needed it already? Take care of Don, and tell him I hope this thing with the detective works out."

Justin put away his cell. "Margie says Merry Christmas."

"Back at her. They should canonize her for putting up with you for all these years."

"I treat her very well. I get her diamonds. What's for Christmas breakfast?"

"Strawberry waffles, link sausage, juice, and eggs."

"Excellent. I'll set the table."

"Only if you're working at Denny's. Get your coat. I'm buying." Don headed to the door. "Patti's picking me up in two hours, so we have to make this quick. Are you sure you don't want to ride to Portland with us?"

"Not on your life. Spurs are playing the Mavericks, and then there's a special edition of Monday Night Football: Patriots and the Bills. You two have a wonderful time tracking down a pimp."

The folks at Denny's were in exceptionally good moods. The breakfasts were cooked to perfection and served piping hot. The waitress wished them Merry Christmas. They got home just as Patti arrived.

"I'll be right out." Don disappeared into the house.

Justin declined Patti's offer to join them. She hoped he wouldn't come but felt obligated to ask.

Don jumped into the passenger seat. "No squad car? Damn. I wanted to play with the lights and siren."

"Of course you did. That's why we're not taking one. What are you, seven?"

"Doesn't matter how old I am. A guy's never too old to play with a siren."

"Buckle up. We should be in Portland by eleven. I assume you already had breakfast."

"Yep. Just got back from Denny's. Great breakfast there today."

"I imagine they're the only place open."

For the next half hour, they went over what they knew or thought they knew about the murders. "Seems to me, everybody who got whacked sort of had it coming," Don said. "Except Jimmy, of course."

"That's a little cold," Patti admonished. "The others weren't model citizens, but they didn't deserve to die."

"Tell that to Jimmy's mom. She gets him back from Iraq in one piece but has to bury him after he goes to Olympia. Andrei did us a favor taking out that group."

"What about Mrs. Coley and Sarah? Sarah wouldn't think getting killed was much of a favor. She's terrified, and rightfully so."

"You've got a point there." Sensing he'd struck a nerve, Don changed the subject. "Where exactly are we going?"

"Gresham, about fifteen miles east of Portland. I'm meeting Sergeant Erhl at the station. Hopefully he can fill me in on this Waite person. Then we'll run out to the address I got out of Jenkins' book. And by *we*, I mean Erhl and me. You, my friend, will be at the station or McDonalds."

"I'm cool with that." Don played the offended boyfriend. "You go off and have all the fun. I'll just sit on a bench or the floor or wherever they put me."

"I'll suggest a cell, but I'm sure they'll give you a nice, comfortable chair."

Don loved the banter. "It's the least they can do for the guy who broke the case."

"You broke the case? Us cops were just waiting around until you showed up?"

"Not if you put it that way, but I helped."

"Yes you did, mostly by breaking a dozen laws, but you were a big help." Patti patted him on the knee.

"You didn't say that like you meant it." Don pouted. "You hurt my feelings."

"It's not your feelings I wanted to hurt." For a moment she became very serious. "You could've gone to jail, maybe you still could."

Don wasn't done. "I won't do well in jail. I'm too pretty."

"Right. Too pretty. You think rather highly of your little self, don't you?"

"Speaking of pretty, I brought your Christmas present with me. Do you want it now?"

"I need to make a pit stop and check in with Erhl. May as well see what you picked up. Did you get it from the machine at the pizza parlor?"

"Took a bucket of quarters to snag this. You'd better like it."

Patti pulled into a gas station and parked by the convenience store. "All kidding aside, you really didn't need to get me anything, and I didn't have time to get you a present. Sorry."

"You got me a day in Portland with you." Don handed her the box. "I hope you like it. If not, we can return it."

Patti wasn't sure what she thought he had gotten her, but she didn't think it would be jewelry. Her eyes met his as she took the package and gently unwrapped it. When she snapped the lid back, her eyes lit up. "Don. You shouldn't have. It's beautiful. But you shouldn't have. Help me put it on."

"There's a mixed message in there somewhere." He undid the clasp. The necklace hung perfectly around her neck. The diamond pendant sparkled.

"This is way over the top. You really shouldn't have."

"It was a pleasure getting it and even more fun watching you open it." Don loved her smile. "You've put up with me, and I wanted you to know how I felt about you."

Patti blushed, then kissed him, deep and long.

After a moment, she broke away and composed herself. "We'll get back to that later. Right now, I have to get us set up in Gresham. Do you want anything?"

"Well a lot more of that would be nice."

"Later, I promise. I mean from the store. I'm going to get a soda. Want one?"

"Yes, *Mountain Dew*. I need caffeine. And a candy bar." Don was pleased with himself.

"You just ate."

"True, but I didn't have dessert."

"Breakfast doesn't come with dessert."

"It does for me."

"Okay, I'll be right back." Patti returned with two large sodas and several candy bars. "Didn't know what you liked so I got a variety."

"Excellent. This should hold me to lunch."

They talked about a variety of topics; none having anything to do with crime-fighting. Before they knew it, Patti was pulling up to the Gresham cop shop.

"You may as well come in and pick your cell." Patti got out of the car.

"What do you want to do for lunch? Most places will be closed."

"I can't believe you're hungry. You ate four candy bars in the last hour."

"To be accurate, it was three. And I like my next meal or two planned." Don joined her on the steps. "Ask the folks inside where we should go?"

"I'll do that. Along with preventing a murder and hunting down a suspect, I'll squeeze in *What's for lunch* somehow."

Before they reached the double doors, a tall man in a dark suit came out and greeted them. "Detective Linder, I'm Sergeant Erhl. Who's your friend?"

"Don Rowland, meet Sergeant Erhl. Do you have a place where Don can stay while we're running around?"

"Hey, it's no skin off my nose if he wants to join us. Looks like he could lift a car; he might come in handy." The sergeant had suggested the unthinkable.

Before Patti could decline, Don accepted and followed his new partner into the building. "These folks in Oregon are very accommodating," he said as she glared at him.

"Step into my office. It ain't much, but it's private. I've printed out what we have on local prostitution, a person named Waite, and 222 Devon. Oddly enough, they're all connected. Virginia Waite lives at 222 Devon. It's an old Victorian house on the outskirts of town. She has a lot of girls living with her and even more men visiting every day, well mostly at night. She's running a brothel, but it's not been a problem. No complaints. Why are you interested in her?"

"She may be in trouble. She knows the man who killed six people in Olympia, and he's busy getting rid of people who can identify him." Patti looked at Don. "We need to warn her and, if she's agreeable, get information from her. Shall we go?"

"You bet. I've got a car outside. Don, you'll have to sit in the back." The sergeant apologized. Patti stewed.

"As long as I'm not wearing handcuffs, that'll be fine."

"We'll hold off on them until later." Patti didn't realize how the comment sounded.

"Don't want to know what you two do in your spare time but around here that's pretty common." The sergeant grinned ear-to-ear.

"Wait. That's not what I meant..." Patti began but before she could continue all three were laughing.

"Looks like I'm going to have all kinds of fun," Don said.

"Keep dreaming." Patti cut short that conversation. "How far is the house?"

"Five minutes. By the way, Merry Christmas." The sergeant made a series of rights. "I hope Waite's house-of-ill-repute is open."

"Maybe they're offering a holiday special," Don suggested.

"It'd be the only way you'll be getting any," Patti replied. The sergeant tilted his head.

Five minutes later, the Gresham squad car pulled into Waites' empty parking lot.

"Nice place." Patti got out of the car. "Apparently, there's money to be made in the prostitution business."

"Lots and lots of it," Don answered. "Or at least that's what I've heard."

The sergeant led the team to the front door and rang the doorbell. A young woman in lingerie answered. He showed her his badge and asked for Mrs. Waite. The girl disappeared and soon an older woman emerged with two scantily clad women.

"Good morning. I'm Virginia Waite. What can I do for you?"

"It's more what we can do for you. Do you have a private place where we can chat?" Patti showed Virginia her badge.

"Do you want me to wait out here?" Don pointed to a couch.

Patti eyed the young women in the hallway. "Not now I don't."

They entered Mrs. Waite's office. Don smiled at the girls and closed the door.

"I'm going to come right to the point, Mrs. Waite, you're in extreme danger from a man we only know as Andrei. He killed six people, and we suspect him for as many as five other murders. And you're likely on his hit list."

Waite sat heavily into her chair. She began to deny knowing Andrei, but Patti's sincerity stopped her. "You're talking about Andrei Clemmens aren't you? Why does he want to kill me?"

"Sarah Geld works for you. Kidnapped by Clemmens and brought here. She contacted us about the murders and said she could identify him. You also can identify him. If Sarah's in danger, so are you. I came to warn you and get information about him."

"Who did he kill?" she asked.

"Probably the only person you'll know is Howard Jenkins," Patti replied.

"Howard's dead? When?"

"Two days ago. Shot in the chest, twice." Don sat forward in his chair.

Patti shook her finger at Don. "Andrei's tying up loose ends. You're a big one. Tell us what you know about him and then we'll get you to a safe place."

Virginia Waite was shaken. She'd known Jenkins for years and thought of him as a friend. Patti got a recorder from her purse and asked Waite if it was all right to record the conversation. Waite agreed and recalled several instances when Andrei showed up with a woman to be put to work. He'd always been polite and respectful; no show of force or coercion. Waite knew the girls were paying off debts, but she had no interest in that part of the arrangement. As long as they did what they were told, she treated them well.

"Sarah was one of my favorites. Then last week, Andrei showed up looking for her, but she disappeared. I assumed Sarah had run off with one of her clients."

"He was here to kill her. I need you to describe him as thoroughly as you can," Patti said. "Especially anything that stands out: scars, accents, hair color. Anything that could help identify and locate him."

Waite described Andrei and his black SUV in considerable detail. The more she said, the more concerned Don became. Mrs. Waite closed her monolog, and Don asked one final question. "Did he walk with a limp?"

"Yes, sort of, some of the time. When he walked at normal speed, he didn't limp, but the faster he moved, the more he limped. He told me it was because one of his legs was shorter than the other."

Don asked Patti to step into the hall. "Andrei's the guy I saw in Brian's house. The guy limped when he ran, and the car sounds like the one I saw."

"What would he be doing at Brian's? Brian doesn't have a parking ticket much less a criminal record."

"I can't answer that, but it's the same guy."

"Okay. Let's chat on the way home. Now we have to get Mrs. Waite out of here."

Patti wrapped up the session and asked how certain Mrs. Waite was that Andrei's last name was Clemmens.

"He introduced himself the first time we met. He said he had the same last name as the baseball pitcher, Roger Clemens, but he spelled it with two Ms. I'm a Yankees fan, and I adore Roger."

"That's great. Not so much that you're a Yankees fan but you remembered his last name. It's time to get you packed and out of here." Patti stood, ending the session.

Waite was stubborn. She refused to leave or have a cop stationed outside her house. "Not many guys are going to walk past a cop to visit us." She escorted the three visitors to the door. "I have very competent staff who can handle Andrei. I'm going to stay here and take care of business. Christmas to New Years is my busiest time. Lots of lonely guys out there this time of year. What's that old saying, *everybody was feeling Mary, and when she left, they jumped for Joy.* Corny, but it fits the season."

Sergeant Erhl led the group to the car. "There's not much I can do. The captain won't assign anyone to watch her. There's not a credible threat, and if she stays in the house, it's not likely this Andrei character's going to attack her. Not with a dozen girls and their boyfriends hanging around."

"Sarge. Can you run Andrei Clemmens through the system?" Patti asked. "I'd like to know as much as I can before I go north."

"Not a problem. I've got the perfect guy at the shop. He's a geek. We call him Paul, but his real name is Al."

A few minutes later, they pulled into the station's parking lot and strode into the building. "Hey Paul, I've got a job for you."

A young officer emerged from a cubicle and introduced himself. "My name's Al, but you can call me Paul. It's a joke. What can I do for you?"

"We have a name and a description for you to run through the databases. Where do we begin?" Patti wasn't convinced this kid could get the job done.

"Sit over there and let me bring up the servers. This won't take long. How extensive do you want the search?"

"Every database you have," Don interjected. "Can you get into the military's stuff?"

"I have a nearly legal way." Paul chuckled. "Haven't been caught yet."

"I'm not sure I'm happy knowing that, Paul." Patti laughed.

"They tolerate me because I'm coming in through a LEO site."

"Do what you can." Patti looked at Don. "Everybody else has bent the rules on this case."

"Hey, I did you a favor," Don rebutted her insinuation.

Patti gave Paul the information she had. He entered it into the system and sat back. Ten minutes went by and the screen flashed. "No matches."

"Sorry, guys. There's nothing in the systems about Andrei Clemmens. Not with the description you gave."

"Thanks Paul." Patti was disappointed but not surprised. Thanking Sergeant Erhl one last time, they left the station.

"I'm starved," Don announced like it was news.

"Me too. Any candy bars left?"

"Now there's a dumb question. They were gone before we got here. It's either fast food or Denny's. Everything else is closed."

"I could use breakfast." Patti suggested. "How about Denny's? There's one over the bridge in Vancouver."

"You're driving. I'd love a bacon double cheeseburger and fries." Don motioned her forward. "We're burning daylight, babe."

"Don't call me babe. Reminds me of that cartoon pig."

"No offense meant. Just trying to be funny."

"None taken. Denny's it is. I'm buying. So you may as well add a shake."

"What about pie?"

"I'll get you the best pie in Washington. It's on the way home."

"Great. I don't like missing dessert two meals in a row."

Patti shook her head and pushed the accelerator as she entered Interstate 84 westbound. "You could stand to miss a few desserts."

Don thought, *she sort of sounds like a wife. Maybe Justin is right.*

Chapter 52

Brian was delighted when he saw the Cattleman's Inn sign. The six-hour drive had been uneventful. Snoqualmie and Blewett passes were clear and dry with little traffic. As he drove down the main drag, Brian checked out Winthrop's western-themed storefronts. The town had done a marvelous job reinventing itself by turning a disintegrating lumber town into a scene from *Gunsmoke*, bringing tourists and hunters by the score.

"Good evening, Mr. Crane. I hope you had a pleasant trip." The clerk handed him a keycard. "Your room's ready."

"Thanks, Janea. It was fine. I'm going to need supper later. What's open?"

"The Tin Star Diner is until seven. They have a prime rib special. I'd recommend it. My husband and I are going as soon as I get off work."

"That's great. I'll try to save you some, but no promises."

Collecting his suitcase and guns from the trunk, Brian went to his room. It was neat, clean, and warm. Cowboy prints decorated the walls. He turned up the heat and stowed his gear under the queen-sized bed. He stretched out and turned on the flat-screen television. He didn't make it to the first commercial.

Two-hundred miles to the southeast, Andrei readied himself. The only detail he hadn't settled on was how to kill Crane. Revoldi wanted Crane's death to look like an accident and his body found. Several ideas came to mind; an ill-timed shotgun blast, a car accident, a drug overdose, but nothing appealed to him. He had a four-hour car ride to devise a plan. The only thing certain was the *accident* would happen tomorrow.

Andrei pulled out of his driveway. He'd arrive in Winthrop around six. Two hours into the ride, he found himself atop the Grand Coulee Dam. Andrei stopped and photographed the massive structure holding back the Columbia and forming Lake Roosevelt. After an early supper, he pressed on to Winthrop, and checked into a motel outside of town using Mark Stow's credit card. The clerk gave him a key, wished him Merry Christmas, and returned to his primary task, watching television.

Once Andrei settled in, he called the Cattleman's Inn and confirmed Crane was there. He declined the offer to be connected with his target saying they planned to meet later. The evening waned, and Andrei drove to a convenience store and bought a sandwich and a six-pack of wheat beer. With snacks resting in the passenger's seat, he followed the route Brian and he would take in the morning. It was curvy, and, for a moment, Andrei reconsidered a traffic accident. But the road was bare and dry, making an accident unlikely. The information Bernard got about the hunting site's location was precisely accurate. Andrei drove to the gate, turned around, and drove back to town. On his way, he concluded a beer at the Do-Drop-Inn wouldn't compromise his *minimal-contact* rule. He found a booth, and the waitress served him a *Lone Star*. Christmas carols played on the jukebox. Andrei was ready to leave, when several men wearing helmets and spacesuits stomped in and sat at the table next to him.

"The ice is plenty thick enough. It'll save us five miles and at least a half hour." The first spaceman set his helmet on the floor.

"Do you want to crash through the ice?" another one asked. "We won't find your body until May. And even then, it'll still be frozen."

The men laughed and ordered beers. They continued to argue about how ready the ice was for carrying snowmobiles. After a heated discussion, they concluded most of the river had enough ice over it, but there were dangerously thin spots. They agreed to stay on shore for another week. Andrei had discovered how he'd kill Brian. A careless step and Crane would find one of those spots.

When he got to his room he phoned Revoldi and went over the plan. Andrei turned on the last Monday Night Football Game of the year, pleased he'd broken his rule.

Chapter 53

Patti discussed the Waite meeting with the team.

"Can't we arrest her for human trafficking? She's using women as prostitutes to pay debts to a criminal organization," the deputy pointed out. "There has to be something to charge her with."

"That's up to the Gresham police. Waite's not our concern." The lieutenant turned to Patti. "The information corroborates Sarah's input?"

"Waite added to what we know. His last name's Clemmens, and he limps when he walks fast or runs. Sarah didn't mention either of those details." Patti moved to the whiteboard. "There's one more thing. Don, the army guy at the cabin, thinks Andrei's the man who broke into his neighbor's house a couple of months ago."

"Any link between the break in and the murders?" the lieutenant asked.

"Nothing. His neighbor is pretty much a boy scout."

The lieutenant joined Patti. "We'll release the guy's name and description. It may not get us much, but it may get him to leave Sarah and Mrs. Waite alone. No need to shut them up anymore."

❖

While the team considered next steps, Don called Brian.

Brian was getting ready to go out for dinner. "Hey, Don. Hope you're not calling with bad news."

"I'm not sure it's news at all," Don admitted. "The guy who's killing people around here is the one who broke into your house. Does the name Andrei Clemmens ring a bell?"

"Never heard of him. What makes you think he's the one?" Brian turned down the heat.

"Your guy ran with a limp and drove a black SUV with tinted windows. The same as Andrei," Don replied. "I don't see how the break-in fits with the murders or the diamond heist, but I'll bet it's the same guy. Be careful. Clemmens is cleaning house."

"Okay, Don. I'll keep an eye out for a man with a limp driving a black SUV." Brian smirked. "By the way, every vehicle in town is a black SUV. There are about a hundred of them parked outside my door."

"I'm just making sure you don't wind up dead." Don stepped on to the porch and checked Brian's house. "And all is well over here."

"Seriously, thanks for the warning. Remember, I've got my Parker. If anyone fucks with me, *blam-blam*, both barrels to the chest."

"See you in a few days. Good hunting and stay warm."

"That's why they invented rum." Brian hung up.

Andrei and Brian, separated by three miles of snow-covered fields, watched the same Spokane news station. They stopped when the anchor announced the Olympia taskforce reported significant developments regarding the recent murders.

The State Patrol released the following information about a suspect in the murders. His name is Andrei Clemmens, white male, six feet tall, medium build, dark brown hair, with no distinguishing marks. He was last seen driving a dark blue or black SUV with tinted windows. He's considered armed and dangerous. Anyone having information about Andrei Clemmens is to contact the patrol at the number on the screen. A five thousand dollar reward has been posted.

"How the fuck did they come up with that." Andrei asked the mirror and wondered how long before Revoldi contacted him. He guessed wrong. His cell phone rang seconds later.

"Voytek. Have you seen the news?" Taras asked.

"I have. It's unfortunate, but don't worry. Andrei Clemmens no longer exists. I'll take care of my assignment and meet you at your office tomorrow afternoon."

"Given what happened, I need to confirm this with the senator. I'll call you back within the hour. Until then, do nothing. Don't leave your room."

"My friend." Voytek tried to calm his voice. "I'm skilled at my job. I appreciate your advice, but I will go about my life as I see fit."

Voytek hung up, irritated at Revoldi's words and attitude. "Apakoh, you are acting like a schoolgirl. I'm better at what I do than you are at what you do. There was no need to insult me."

He returned to cleaning his weapons, angry at the Dragon. While Voytek stewed, Revoldi called Bernard. The senator had heard the news and was about to call him.

"What should we do?" Bernard asked. "They have a good description of him."

"He's in place and using another name. The description fits half the men in the state. We must proceed. If need be, I'll eliminate our connection with Andrei afterwards."

"Okay. I have faith in you. What the hell was he doing in Olympia? Why did he murder so many people?"

"I don't know. A contract got out of control."

"Out of control!" Bernard exclaimed. "It's worse than the fucking Saint Valentine's Day massacre."

"He's my responsibility, and I assure you all's well. We'll deal with Andrei as necessary." Apakoh hung up shaking his head.

"Is there a problem, dad?" Lara stood in the doorway.

"There're always problems when you have incompetent employees or naïve clients. Today, I have both." Taras hugged his daughter.

"Mom wants you to come downstairs. She has a Christmas movie to watch with you. She says you're working too hard. That's why you need me."

"Your mother worries too much, and so do you, my little sparrow."

"I'm not a defenseless bird. I'm your daughter who loves you very much. A loving daughter with talons. Now come."

"As you command, but before I do, I must make a phone call." Taras hit redial. Two hundred miles away Voytek's phone rang.

"Yes?" Voytek said.

"The plan remains as it was. Be careful, and don't attract any more attention." Apakoh spoke sternly, as if speaking to a wayward child.

"I know my business. You seem to have lost faith in me."

"Not in the least. I want you to return in one piece."

"I'll see to it that I return as I left." Andrei hung up, fuming. "Asshole!"

As Voytek swore, Brian's phone rang. "Good evening, Senator."

"Brian. Good to hear your voice. I've got family issues brewing, and I'll be late getting in, probably not until the afternoon."

"I'm sorry to hear that. Is everything okay?"

"Yes, but I have to go to one of the wife's functions." The senator did what he did best, lie. "Then I'll head to the Methow. You should get a day in without me. You're safer that way. So are the geese."

"Enjoy the function, Senator. I'll be back by two so we can connect."

"Did you bring the files?"

"Yes. They're right here."

"Great. Go out and have a couple of beers."

"Will do boss. I know just the place. Have a nice night."

The senator called the inn and cancelled his reservations, hoping to avoid paying a penalty.

Chapter 54

Brian's wake-up call came while he was in the shower. New, wool-lined waterproof pants waited on the armchair. They'd make Brian's lower-body virtually impervious to wet and cold. He layered his torso with a wicking undershirt, a flannel long-sleeved pullover, and a hoodie. A wool jacket waited in the car. He slid into the pants, pulled on his boots, and connected the two. He was ready for whatever the Methow threw at him.

Outside, the breeze took his breath away. The temperature hovered at ten degrees, with wind chill driving it well below zero. It'd been a year since he'd experienced this kind of cold, and he was glad there was a propane heater in the blind. He stowed the shotguns and ammunition belts in the trunk and pulled onto Riverside Drive. Four blocks later, he slid into the diner's parking lot, found a table, and looked over the menu. Men dressed much like him filled the place.

"What'll it be, sweetie?"

"I'll have the *Hunter's Special* with eggs over easy and bacon. Could you add white toast with butter?" Brian pulled off the hoodie.

"I can get you whatever you want." She wrote the order on her steno-pad. "Coffee or orange juice?"

"Both, please."

"Be right up." The waitress wove her way through the crowd to the order window. She returned with two steaming pots of coffee. "Regular or decaf?"

"Regular. Thanks."

A few minutes later, his order arrived. He ate quickly. On his way out, he asked the waitress to fill his thermos with coffee. He checked the car and found everything in order. No surprise. This was the heart of rural America. He could've left the doors unlocked and the windows down, and nothing would've been stolen. He drove north. It wouldn't warm much during the day. His attire was perfect.

After a fifteen-minute drive, Brian pulled off the road and parked by a gate secured to a massive wooden post. Wilfred had unlocked the chain, making it unnecessary for him to fumble around for a key. After swinging the gate open, he drove through, stopped the car, and brought the gate to its closed position. His friend had plowed a road across the field and made a parking area at its terminus.

"What a guy." Brian did a donut in the freshly created parking lot. "I have to get him the 15 year old Scotch this time."

The snow between the car and the blind was knee-deep, making the first trip difficult. Brian plowed through carrying his shotgun and ammunition. It took five trips to transfer the gear, most of which he'd leave in the blind for the balance of the stay. A propane heater sat on an old shag carpet. *All the comforts of home*, he thought. He lifted the shooting window. A glow in the east told him morning was breaking. The geese sensed it too. Brian felt close to heaven.

Fifteen miles away, Voytek enjoyed a hearty breakfast. After finishing the omelet and sausage, he followed the route Brian had traversed an hour earlier. He was in no hurry and stayed below the speed limit. When he came to the gate, he signaled and inched up to the post. For a moment he was concerned about the lock, but the chain had only been swung over the fence post. He freed the gate, nudged it open, and drove through. He parked and secured the gate. Everything looked just like he'd found it. He hoped Brian wouldn't hear him drive up. Voytek preferred taking his quarry unaware. He pulled next to Brian's car, got out, checked his Glock, and followed Brian's trail. After climbing a small rise, Voytek spotted the blind snuggled among alder trees. It had a clear view of the fields near the river. In the distance, a flock of geese milled about in the snow. Soon they'd start foraging and then lift off to find more food.

Voytek heard the heater's distinctive woosh as he approached the blind. He was about to walk in when the door opened. He watched Brian step into the fresh air, stretch, and turn to pee. Voytek startled his prey. The Russian saw surprise turn to fear when he pointed a gun at Brian. Voytek motioned Brian back into the blind. Inside, he picked up Brian's shotgun, made sure it was loaded, and motioned Brian to leave ahead of him.

Whenever Brian turned around, Voytek pointed the shotgun eastward, motioning his captive forward. The nosy analyst soon found himself on the river's frozen crust, ice creaking under his weight. He spread his legs to displace his weight. "Either shoot me or let me get the hell out of here. I've got to pee." Voytek nearly laughed at the ploy.

He fired the first barrel at Brian's feet, tearing a hole in the ice.

"You fucking made me pee my pants," Brian yelled at the madman. Voytek enjoyed seeing the man scramble to stay alive. He fired the second barrel, this time to Brian's left, shattering the ice on that side of Bernard's chief-of-staff. Voytek watched the ice crumble and his target slip into the river.

When Brian didn't surface, Voytek grew concerned. Part of the play required the victim to be found. He was about to go on to the ice to fish Brian out when the man bobbed to the surface.

"Help me," Brian muttered.

Voytek was relieved. He tossed the shotgun a few feet from the hole in the ice. He watched as two causes of death raced to claim Brian. The river tried relentlessly to drown him, and the bitter cold tried feverishly to shut down the man's vital systems. Brian grasped onto the solid ice sheet, ensuring the river wouldn't win. Voytek had never seen a man freeze to death. He watched with more than a little interest. He knew Brian wanted to know why this had happened and felt an obligation to tell him. He inched his way close and said, "You should have minded you own fucking business."

When Voytek set foot on shore again, he paused a minute to take in the scene. Brian's body would be visible; locked in the ice with its head and hands above the white sheet. Soon the river would freeze around him, and the recovery team would need axes and possibly a chainsaw to free the corpse from the ice's grasp. Anyone coming onto the scene would believe Brian had foolishly fired both barrels while standing on the ice. The recoil drove him into the river like a pile driver. The coroner would declare it an accident. Voytek had met both criteria for success.

Voytek walked back to the blind in the trail Brian made. It was unlikely whoever came for Brian would notice, but he wanted it to look like Brian went to the river alone. Voytek secured the gate and wondered how long it'd be before someone found the body; a day or maybe two. On that count he was wrong. The Russian hadn't gotten halfway home before an ambulance was racing to the river. Wilfred had brought Brian lunch. Getting no response from the blind, he followed the path until he came across the tragic scene. He managed to get the body out and drag it to shore.

He called 911 and gave explicit directions to the site. The operator dispatched a deputy and an ambulance. Wilfred suggested she also send the coroner. He'd barely gotten the gate open when a deputy arrived. They knew each other and shook their heads. Soon after, an Okanogan County Fire and Rescue ambulance arrived, and Wilfred directed the driver to the small parking area. The coroner arrived shortly after.

Five men made their way to the river, obliterating the path in the snow. Brian was pronounced dead at the scene. It took a half an hour to get him to the ambulance, now serving as a hearse. Brian's shotgun and other possessions were secured in Brian's car, and one of the EMTs drove it to town. The procession left the parking area destined for Winthrop. Wilfred locked the gate. It was a sad day. Overhead, a flock of Canada geese flew in victory formation. Wilfred couldn't help but think they might be saluting a fallen foe.

Chapter 55

The coroner entered his preliminary assessment. He returned Brian's body to the cooler.

A deputy met him in the hall. "What do you think, doc?"

"Everything's consistent with an accidental drowning. No wounds or bruises. The only odd thing was his boots were filled with urine. He peed himself before he passed."

"Seems a shame that has to be reported. Can you leave it out?"

"Not if I want to keep my job. It's just a fact of life. Has the family been notified?"

"We found a note from his girlfriend in his motel room. We called the Olympia Police Department and asked them to send someone to talk with her."

"Good. Nobody should hear something like this over the phone."

In Olympia, the captain looked at Okanogan's request for a compassion visit. These were never easy, especially when the victim was young and the person receiving the news would be so ill prepared to hear it. "Patti, can you come in here? Do you know Deirdre Woods from the Fire Marshalls Office?"

"I do. We're working the Thomlinson case together."

"We got bad news from the Okanogan sheriff. Her boyfriend, Brian Crane, drowned earlier today."

"Brian's dead?" Patti gasped and sat hard in the chair. "Don was right. Captain, Brian didn't die accidentally. He was murdered by the bastard we're after. Tell the sheriff I'm on my way."

"What are you talking about?" The captain picked up his phone.

"Two months ago, the guy I'm seeing interrupted a burglary at Crane's house. He thought the burglar fit Andrei Clemmens' description and warned Brian yesterday. But Brian laughed him off."

"Shit," the captain exclaimed. "When the fuck is this going to end?"

"Soon captain, very soon." Patti got up to leave. "I'll stop by Deirdre's office and tell her, but right after I'm going to Okanogan. Can you tell the guys to expect me? Make sure they secure Brian's motel room. Nobody in or out until I get there."

Don answered on the first ring. "Is everything okay? Not like you to call in the middle of the day."

"Brian's dead. He drowned. They're calling it an accident." Patti was in tears. "You were right. Clemmens killed him."

Don was stunned. "Brian's dead, Justin. They say he drowned."

Justin shook his head. "No fucking way, boss. He was murdered by our butcher."

Patti continued, "I'm driving to the Methow. Can you come? If Andrei's still there, you might recognize him."

"If I see him, I'll beat him to death."

"Could Justin take care of Deirdre? I don't want to leave her alone."

Justin volunteered without hesitation. Don hung up, grabbed a backpack, and tossed in a few necessities, the Glock being the first.

"If you get to cap him, put one in his knee first." Justin walked out the door ahead of his friend. "Screw it. Put one in both knees; one for Jimmy and one for Brian."

"If I get the chance, the fucker's going to hurt for a long time before he dies…a long fucking time."

Patti collected Don and Justin then drove to the Fire Marshall's Office. Deirdre knew Patti had bad news when she saw the three of them standing in her doorway. "It's Brian? Is he hurt?"

Patti shook her head. "Brian drowned earlier today."

Deirdre sank into her chair, tears streaming down her face.

"The Okanogan cops think it was accidental, but he was murdered. Don and I are leaving for Okanogan right now. We need to turn it into a murder investigation."

"I want to go with you. I want to nail the bastard."

"Deirdre, that's not a good idea." Patti put her arm around her friend. "Justin's going to stay with you. We'll call when we know something. You two should go over to Brian's and check out what he was working on. Maybe you can find something that connects Brian with Andrei. Will you do that for me?"

Patti knew the best thing was to keep Deirdre busy with something meaningful to do. Deirdre agreed. She handed Justin her keys. "Can you drive?"

Justin put his arm around her, and they headed to the elevator. Outside, Justin helped Deirdre into her car. He hugged Patti and shook Don's hand. Then he hugged his friend. "Don't do anything stupid. I won't be there to save your ass."

"Patti will. We'll be fine. Take care of Deirdre. Keep her busy. If you have to, get her drunk."

"Will do. Be careful guys. Keep us posted."

Patti and Don got into her car. She stuck the police light on the hood and turned it on. It proved very effective; traffic parted like the Red Sea. "They have Brian at the county morgue in Okanogan. Normally takes six hours to get to there. We'll make it in five."

❖

Across the state, Voytek arrived home. While Patti and Don raced to the Okanogan, he gathered everything associated with Andrei Clemmens. There wasn't much, and what there was now rested on his kitchen table. He chopped his driver's license and social security card into small bits. A credit card and a few other documents waited for the scissors. In less than an hour, Andrei Clemmens ceased to exist.

Satisfied with his disappearance, Voytek braved the cold to refill his refrigerator and pantry. When he returned, he saw the answering machine's flashing light. It would be Revoldi, demanding an immediate return call. Voytek hadn't called, mostly to irritate Apakoh. He expected a harsh, cryptic message. He wasn't disappointed.

"Voytek, call me when you get this message. I expected to hear from you yesterday, but I've heard nothing. This is unacceptable. Call me immediately."

"I'll call you when I'm good and fucking ready." The assassin snapped at the machine. Voytek seethed as he made lunch. Fried eggs became scrambled eggs after he smashed the first one into the pan. At a little after noon, he called Revoldi. "I'm back. Do you wish to meet?"

"Where have you been? You were supposed to call when the job was done, not when you felt like it."

"I made no promise about when I'd call. I'm not accountable for your expectations."

"You work for me, so you are very much accountable for my expectations. Why are you acting like a spoiled child?"

The words seared Voytek's psyche, and the tone torched his rage. No one spoke to him like that.

"We have much to discuss, especially about what you've done in the west. Your actions may have consequences for me, for the Bratva. I need to know how you'll remedy this situation. I'll call you when I'm ready to meet." The line went dead.

"You are an old, stupid man, nobody threatens me, nobody."

Four hours and seventeen minutes after leaving Olympia, Patti parked the car in front of the Okanogan sheriff's office. They hadn't stopped, and Don knew they rode the last twenty-miles on fumes. It was almost nine, but the office was in full operational mode. Sheriff Petrich greeted Patti and Don warmly, comrades in arms. A conference room had been prepped for the group he'd assembled.

The coroner was flanked by Wilfred, two EMT staff, the deputy who was first-on-site, the motel clerk who'd registered Brian, and a waitress from the diner.

"Patti, these are the people who saw Brian alive or recovered his body. They want to help," the sheriff said. "We've got coffee and sandwiches; sodas if you prefer."

"Thank you, sheriff, and all of you for coming," Patti began. "First, we have to determine if Brian was murdered."

"He didn't fall into the river." Wilfred spoke first and was adamant. "He's come here for years, and he knew the river wasn't safe. Plus, there's no reason for him to go out on the ice."

"That's a strong argument for him being murdered, but what evidence do we have? Did any of you see him with anyone? Anyone following or asking about him?" Patti checked the room. Nobody spoke.

"Anything unusual at the scene?" Don asked.

The deputy stood up in the corner. "Nothing at all. No sign of a struggle. No blood. Looks like he was set for a day of hunting. Even the blind was warm. Wilfred was there first. Did you see anything odd?"

Wilfred confirmed the deputy's statement; nothing out of the ordinary, except for his friend clinging to an ice floe.

"I have something odd," offered the coroner. "His boots were full of urine, and that bothers me."

"What do you mean? Why does that bother you?" the sheriff asked. "I've heard of people peeing themselves just before they die."

"That's not the unusual part. If the shotgun blasts drove him into the river, the freezing water would've forced the urethra to constrict. Making it impossible for him to pee," the coroner stated emphatically. "He was standing on the ice when he peed his pants: before he went into the water."

"Could the insulated pants have given him enough time to...urinate?" Wilfred tried to be delicate.

"No. Way too cold. The shock would've closed the canal."

Don summed up his thoughts. "The killer shot the ice out from under him, scaring Brian, giving him enough time to pee before he fell in. Probably took both shots to collapse the ice."

Patti asked the coroner, "Will you testify that Brian was on the ice when he peed?"

"Absolutely. I'll check with a couple of my buddies who know more about this, but I'm willing to bet my paycheck it happened the way Don described."

"Okay, doc. Put murder as the cause of death and sign the report. Patti, do you want to go over to Brian's room. We sealed it." The sheriff pointed to the clerk.

The desk clerk confirmed nobody had been in the room.

"Sheriff, Don and I will grab a bite to eat here and then head to Winthrop." Patti got up. "You guys are fabulous."

"We don't like people coming here and fucking things up," the waitress said. "Forgive my French, but I hope you kick this asshole all the way to hell."

"That's our mission," Don added.

"Will you two need a room tonight?" the clerk asked. "I mean two rooms. You know, to stay somewhere while you sort this out."

"Two rooms would be perfect." Patti closed her notepad. The sheriff glanced at an obviously disappointed Don. He waved the clerk over, and in a whisper that only Don and the clerk could hear, "Put the rooms on the county tab and make them adjoining."

The clerk took out her cell phone. Don smiled, nodding his appreciation.

After fast food hamburgers and sodas, Patti and Don made the forty-mile trip to Winthrop in an hour. There was no need for the dizzying speed Patti managed earlier in the day. Don was relieved, given the road crossed Loup-Loup pass.

"When I die, I'm leaving the state money to install freakin' guardrails on these freakin' passes." Don said what Patti was thinking. She pulled into the Cattleman's Inn, got out, and stretched.

"Do you want to check in or go right to Brian's room?"

"I need a few minutes to get my head back on square. Let's freshen up and then see what Brian left." Patti walked towards the building.

They entered the lobby and were greeted by a young man behind the counter. "You must be Detective Lender and Ron Dowland."

"Close. I'm Detective Linder, and he's Don Rowland." Patti handled the formalities of checking in.

"We have you in rooms 265 and 267. Hope you have a nice stay." The clerk caught himself. "I'm sorry. I hope you find the guy who killed Mr. Crane."

"We will. If anyone can, it'd be Detective Lender and Ron Dowland." Don chuckled. "Have a good night."

Patti noted the sequentially numbered keycards and pulled Don aside. "Adjoining rooms? How convenient. Is that what the sheriff whispered to you and the clerk?"

Don began to explain, but before he could blame the sheriff, Patti turned to the clerk. "I need a key to Mr. Crane's room."

"Right, I have that here." The young man handed her another keycard. "There's a cop in there. It was too cold for him to wait outside."

"Makes sense. Thanks again." They exited the lobby and, when they were alone by the car, Patti put her arms around Don's neck. "I knew what you boys were doing right from the start."

"You're not angry?"

"It didn't matter what rooms they gave us. We were staying together tonight. I saw the look on Deirdre's face today. She had regrets. I don't want any regrets."

Don hugged her for a long moment. They took their assigned rooms. Patti gave Don explicit orders to make his bed looked *slept in*. He pulled back the covers and stretched out. A few minutes later, a knock on the connecting door rousted him.

Patti looked the room over. "Nice job on the bed. Brian's room will wait."

For the next half hour, they threw themselves at each other. Patti slapped Don on the leg. "Let's go. Time to check out Brian's room."

Don struggled. The bed was warm and soft. "We can't do this tomorrow?"

The detective walked into her room. "Nope. We have to get back at it. Then we can get *back at it*."

Don got out of bed, reluctantly. "I like the way you think. I'll be over in five."

"Make it ten. You really messed up my hair."

Fifteen minutes later, Patti knocked on the door to Brian's room.

"Nice to give him warning. Let him change the channel to the All-Christian station."

"Don you're so bad. He was probably watching sports."

"Oh. Is that what cops call *Debbie Does Dallas*? Sports?"

"Man, you're old if that's the last porn you watched."

"I watch plenty of modern porn," Don said as a giant of a man opened the door.

"Sounds like a personal problem," the officer said.

Patti laughed and introduced herself and Don. She was tempted to call him Ron but knew the officer wouldn't get it.

The officer let them in to the warm room. "We searched thoroughly; didn't find anything suspicious. Everything's just how Mr. Crane left it. It's mostly paper and clothes."

"Thank you. We'll take it from here." Patti patted the huge man on the back. "They do grow 'em big around here."

The officer laughed and left the room to the city folk.

"Don, start in the bathroom. Collect everything that doesn't belong to the motel. Then put it on the dresser." Patti was used to giving orders. "Please."

Don put Brian's personal hygiene and grooming items on the bureau. "You have to admit, he traveled light."

"Guys usually do when no woman's involved." Patti displayed Brian's wardrobe neatly on the bed. She went through every pocket. "Nothing in the bathroom items or the clothes. All that's left is his computer and briefcase. Would you mind putting Brian's stuff into his duffel bag?"

"Will do, boss." Don gathered the toiletries from the dresser. Soon he cleared the bed of Brian's clothes.

"We won't touch the computer. The patrol will download the files and sweep them for data. Let's break out the paperwork." Patti swung the satchel onto the bed.

Notepads, pens, pencils, and a phone charger came out first, and were put off to the side. File folders labeled with the letters DOT and consecutive numbers made up the rest of the contents.

Patti looked at the items. "We've got eight folders and a notebook labeled *Spokane Contracting Issues*."

"Didn't Brian say his boss was coming from Spokane; some senator or something?" Don asked. "Maybe those contract files got Brian killed. And where's the senator. Is he in the river?"

"You're right. I think they were meeting here today. Oh fuck!" Patti dialed *0* and got the night clerk. She asked if a senator from Spokane had arrived looking for Brian. She wrote something on a pad of paper. "Do you have a phone number?"

She looked at Don. "Senator Samuel Bernard was to join Brian today but cancelled his reservation yesterday. We need go to Spokane and ask him some questions."

"It's after midnight. Can we wrap this up and go back to the room? It's been a long day," Don said. "And we have some *business* to attend to. Again."

Chapter 56

Don slid out of bed. He and Patti had agreed to be on the road by seven, but he let her sleep while he showered and readied himself for the day. The hot water cascaded down his body. He was startled when the shower curtain flew back.

"Thought you'd use all the hot water, huh?" Patti climbed in beside him. "It's nice having the tub warmed up. Shove over and give a girl some room."

Don dutifully moved to the back of the tub, then got out altogether.

When she was finished, Patti wrapped a towel around her body and one around her head. "Could you pick up some coffee while I dry my hair? And find me a toothbrush?"

"Sure. How about breakfast?"

"Let's pick up something along the way. When we stop, I'll call the senator and ask to meet."

"We'll leave when you're ready. I'll be back in ten minutes." Don walked out the door, letting a chilly breeze nip at Patti's body.

"Close the door! I'm naked in here."

"That's what you get when you send me on an errand while you're *naked in there*." Don pulled the door shut and went to the diner. He stopped by the registration desk, and the clerk gave him a new toothbrush. When he got back, Patti was ready. Her hair was down around her shoulders.

"I like the look, not so policewoman-esque." Don handed her the toothbrush. "I got us a couple of bagels for the road."

"No pie?" Patti grinned.

"Wasn't out yet."

Patti thanked the clerk for the hospitality and asked if Brian had received any messages. He hadn't. She nodded appreciatively and joined Don in the car.

"Senator Bernard didn't call." She buckled her seatbelt. "Either he's an insensitive bastard or he already knew Brian was dead."

"Could be both. Politicians are kind of like rock stars. They only care about themselves."

"I'll give him the benefit of the doubt and assume he's just an insensitive asshole."

"That's my girl; always looking on the bright side of things. How about Coulee Dam for breakfast? I've never seen the dam, and we're driving right over it."

"Let's see." Patti did math. "Coulee Dam is about sixty miles from here. We should get there around nine. That'd be perfect. I'll call the senator and see if we can meet this afternoon."

For an hour, they marveled at rock formations and the dense forests lining the highway. They were even more impressed by the wide expanses of flat ground buried in snow. Patti's math proved right. They pulled into the little town by the giant structure as the dashboard clock clicked over to nine. She found a restaurant with a half-empty parking lot.

"Let's order, and then I'll call the senator." Patti opened the door to the warm building. "That smells great."

"You're hungry. My cooking would smell good right now."

"I'm not *that* hungry," Patti snickered. "Just kidding. Given the size of your belly, you must cook pretty well and a lot...and often."

"I still have a six pack."

"Buried under that keg." She patted his stomach. "I'm going to the ladies room. Find us a booth, okay?"

"Right. Say something mean and then just run off."

A few minutes later, Patti returned, greeted by a steaming cup of coffee. An elderly waitress took their order. Patti went outside and used the building to shelter her from the wind. She called Bernard.

"That's one very cold fish," she proclaimed as she sat down. "I told him Brian was dead, and we wanted to talk to him. Said he was busy, but he'd squeeze us in. He didn't ask a single freaking thing about Brian or how he died."

"He may already have the details."

They finished breakfast and got coffees to go. The weather remained particularly good for December in northeastern Washington. With clear and dry roads, Patti got them to the Spokane police department well within the Garmin's predicted two hours. Patti thought it wise to let the locals know she was in town, what she was doing, and why. She was escorted to the watch captain's office and explained she'd be interviewing Senator Bernard about the murder of his staff member.

"I thought they ruled that an accident." Captain Gardener scratched his head.

"That's what they first thought, but we found evidence Mr. Crane was murdered, skillfully murdered. He was dropped into the river and left to freeze."

"What does the senator have to with this?"

"Probably nothing, but he was supposed to meet Brian yesterday and opted out. I'd like to find out why and if he knows what Brian was investigating."

"I warn you. Senator Bernard carries a lot of weight around this town. If you push too hard, I'm likely to get a call to pull you off him. Tread lightly."

"He's not a suspect, but he may know something about who killed Brian. Maybe Brian told him something. We won't know until we ask him a few questions."

"Okay, but I warned you." The captain offered his hand. "Good luck with this. We've heard about the crap over on the west side. Looks like you're up to your ears in alligators."

"Yeah, and all we were supposed to do was drain the swamp." Patti shook the captain's hand. "I'll stay in touch."

Don was waiting in the lobby.

"How about lunch by the river? There's a Mexican restaurant overlooking the falls," Patti suggested.

"Sounds great. I'm buying." Don opened her door.

They found the restaurant and joined a crowd pressing for tables by the windows. "Flash your badge," Don suggested. "They'll seat us right away, by a window."

"Don't be an ass. We'll take what we get. No favoritism."

"Sure," Don agreed. "I'll be right back."

A few minutes later, he returned with the hostess. "That's right, Marybeth. She's Detective Linder, and we're here investigating a murder. We need to keep an eye on that couple by the window."

"That's so cool," the hostess exclaimed. "Right this way. I'll put you in the booth behind them."

"Normally, that'd be a great idea, but we need to listen in if we can. Could you put us at the table next to them?"

"Sure. I'll have to get it cleared off, and then I'll seat you."

"Have you no shame?" Patti asked, as Don smiled at the hostess.

"Nope. Not an ounce. And now we have fabulous food *and* a spectacular view."

Patti shook her head in mock disbelief. This was a man who ran headlong into machinegun fire, so asking for a table with a view was well within his limits.

Voytek turned on the news. After a short, uninformative update on the search for Andrei Clemmens, the anchor reported a hunter had been murdered outside Winthrop.

Questions raced through the Russian's mind. *Murder? How could they call it murder? Nobody was there, nobody saw the man die. What had he missed? What had gone wrong? How did they know?*

On the other side of town, Revoldi asked the same questions. So did Senator Bernard.

Three hours later, at Apakoh's command, Voytek brought his car to a halt in Revoldi's parking lot. He needed to find out what the police knew about Crane's death. This meeting was a waste of time. Walking past the secretary, he entered Revoldi's office unannounced.

Revoldi looked up from his ledger. "What did you do up there? Shoot him down in the street? They're calling his death a murder."

"I did as you asked. Crane is dead."

Apakoh stood and circled his enforcer. "I told you, told you several times, to make it look like an accident. *That* you didn't do. And the news is full of your name and description. Everything you've touched has turned to shit."

"It did look like an accident. I don't know why they're calling it a murder, and me standing here listening to you rant is not helping me find out what they know. As for my name and description, Andrei Clemmens no longer exists. I should get started on learning what the police know."

"You're right." Revoldi calmed down. Voytek made sense. They needed to know what evidence the police had, and, specifically, did any of it implicate Voytek, Revoldi, or Bernard. "Leave me Crane's material and find out what you can."

Voytek looked at Revoldi and shrugged. "I know nothing about *Crane's material.* I don't know what you're talking about."

"The contract files, his computer, whatever he brought to Okanogan to share with the senator. You were to bring it here."

"You said nothing about those things. If you had, you'd be looking at them."

Revoldi flew into a rage. "You ungrateful, stupid man. We've wanted that material from the start. That's why you broke into his office and his home. They're as important as Crane. Maybe more. You knew that."

Voytek restrained himself, discretion being the better part of valor. He let Revoldi fume and shout in English and Russian. Outside the office were a dozen men fiercely loyal to the red-faced man screaming at him. If he wanted to walk out alive, Revoldi's fury had to simmer. Voytek stood in the middle of the room while the Dragon circled him, pointed his finger at him, and stammered in his rage. Eventually, a knock on the door silenced the Dragon.

"Is everything okay, boss?" Levi asked.

Gaining control, Revoldi nodded and asked Levi to leave. Turning to Voytek, "Find out what the police know and if they have Crane's documents. I'll call you later. Do not disappoint me again."

Voytek turned and walked from the room, thankful to be alive and furious at having been reprimanded by the old man, an old man who he'd kill soon.

Taras dialed Bernard's number. It rang once.

"Senator," Revoldi began. "We have a problem."

"I know we have a problem. Olympia cops are coming to see me this afternoon about Crane. Why would they be coming to see me?"

"Have you seen the news? They say Crane was murdered."

"I know. What the fuck did your man do? What do the cops know?" The senator struggled for words in his anger.

"He screwed up the accident, and he didn't get Crane's material. That may be the biggest problem."

Silence. Then Bernard spit into the phone. "You have *got* to be kidding me. Andrei put a noose around our necks. Kill the fucker."

"All in good time, Senator." A plan was forming in Apakoh's head. "Right now, he's our first line of defense. We'll sacrifice him when it does us the most good. Let's meet to discuss our next steps."

"Agreed, but not until tonight. I'll be there at seven. Make sure that asshole is there."

Revoldi hung up, and his office door opened. Expecting Voytek, Revoldi was pleased to see his daughter. "Morning, dad."

"What are you doing here?" Taras hugged Lara.

"We agreed you'd let me work around here this week."

"Lara, today isn't good. I need to deal with a huge problem. I won't have any time for you."

Exuberance drained from her face, replaced by concern. "Are you okay?"

"I will be, but I have to concentrate. A very important deal is falling apart, and I have to salvage it. I'm sorry, but it can't wait."

Lara backed out of the office, closing the door behind her. She'd never seen her father in such a state. He was very worried about something. She found Levi and asked him if he knew anything. Levi mentioned that Voytek had met with her father; there had been shouting and Voytek left very angry. Levi shook his head and went back to polishing a cabinet.

It was late in the afternoon before Revoldi emerged from his den. He found his daughter doing menial tasks for the bookkeeper. He hugged her, apologized, and told her tomorrow he'd spend more time with her and went into the warehouse. Soon he walked back to his office with Levi and two other very large men, Marat and Vlad, in tow. The door closed behind them.

"I have a very, very big problem." The Dragon laid out his plan to assassinate Voytek. Voytek would arrive at seven. With Voytek at the warehouse, Vlad would torch Voytek's house, burn it to the ground. The man from Moscow, an arsonist by trade, enthusiastically accepted his role. Levi and Marat would disarm Voytek and bring him to Apakoh. They'd tie him up and kill him. It'd be quick and merciful. Afterwards, they'd dump his body along with evidence implicating him in the west side murders. With Voytek's death, the Olympia police would leave satisfied their murderer no longer posed a threat; justice had been served, even if it came by an unknown hand.

A few minutes after the meeting ended, Voytek received a text message. Its contents didn't surprise him. He sent a confirming text: *Go along with the plan.*

Meanwhile, Revoldi phoned the senator and made arrangements for him to be at the warehouse at seven to witness how the Dragon dealt with problems. The senator accepted the invitation and excused himself to prepare for his meeting with the policewoman.

❖

Voytek made preparations of his own. He knew exactly how he'd deal with Apakoh and his minion: violently and without pity. "If it's death you want, then death you will get Apakoh; yours."

He secured his ankle holster. The phone rang on cue. "Voytek, I must apologize for my harsh words earlier. I was too hard on you, my friend. Please come to the shop tonight so we can plan our strategy for getting the senator what he needs."

Voytek accepted the apology with the same sincerity in which it had been offered and agreed to the seven o'clock meeting. He slipped his revolver into the ankle-holster and snapped the clasp.

Chapter 57

The senator greeted Patti coldly. "I don't know how I can help, and I thought Brian's death was an accident?"

"The coroner didn't have all the facts. Now he does and confirmed it was a murder." The detective looked around the office.

The senator looked irritated. "Why would anyone kill Brian? He was arrogant but not enough to get murdered."

"The motive might be in the papers he had with him; contracts for projects around Spokane. Were you going to discuss those projects, Senator?"

"As a matter-of-fact, we were." The senator sat behind his desk.

"What do you know about them?"

"Brian was on a wild-goose chase. I never thought he had much to go on. There were cost overruns but that's not unusual." The senator was uncomfortable. He usually asked the questions. "And these are road projects. Brian dealt with buildings; entirely different projects, different contracts, different issues. I'm sure we'd have put it to rest if he hadn't died." The senator shuffled some papers. "Why is an Olympia cop investigating a death in Okanogan. Aren't you way outside your jurisdiction?"

"We followed a killer from Olympia to Winthrop and believe he killed Brian." Patti sat without being invited. "You canceled your reservation the day before Brian died. Why?"

"Family matters. I'm not at liberty to tell you more, but I had to make a tough decision. Brian understood."

"So Brian knew you weren't coming?"

"He did. I talked with him. Told him he should go ahead without me. Maybe if I had gone, he'd still be alive."

"Or you both might be dead." Patti closed her notebook. "I've got the files and when you're in Olympia I'll stop by and go over them with you. Maybe something will jog your memory."

"I doubt it, but you're welcome to visit." The senator ended the conversation, stood, and showed her to the door. Once she was gone, he slammed his palm on his desk. "Fucking bitch."

He called Revoldi. "Are we set for tonight? I want that idiot dead."

Apakoh assured him everything had been arranged and asked if the senator really wanted to witness it. Bernard confirmed he'd be there *to see that it was done right.*

Patti got into the car. "He's an arrogant son of a bitch."

"I wish you'd quit sugarcoating how you feel about the senator. Did he have anything to do with Brian's death?"

"Absolutely. We might not be able to prove it, but he's guilty."

Don needed a plan. "So what now?"

"I want to stay here tonight and see what I can find out about Bernard." Patti pulled into traffic. "You good for another night on the road?"

"I am. I called Justin, and he said Deirdre is doing okay. She wants to come over, but I told him we didn't know what we were doing."

"I feel for her, but she'd only be in the way. What do you want for dinner? Olympia is buying."

"How about steak? Maybe someone at the station could suggest a place?"

"You read my mind. We'll go ask." Patti altered her course.

"Shouldn't we find a room first?" Don asked.

227

"How about the Regal?" Patti suggested. "I hear it's beautiful."

"I'll go for that, and the room is on my U.S. Army retirement account. Maybe they'll give me a discount."

The Regal had been in business for nearly a century and boasted an old world charm. The lobby affirmed its claim. Don booked a room and neglected to fill in the line set aside for the name of a second guest. They strolled through the lobby's high-back chairs and overstuffed sofas to the elevators.

"This must've cost a fortune." Patti boarded the elevator.

"They comp'd me. I'm a high roller." Don smirked as the mirrored doors closed.

"Right. I might've bought that if we were in Vegas."

"I got a room with twin beds. I hope that's okay."

"Only if you're strong enough to push them together."

Don set their meager luggage on the bed.

Patti came out of the bathroom. "You're going to get tired of seeing me in these clothes."

"Already am. You should take them off."

"Hey, I'm hungry. You'll have to keep your pants on for another couple of hours. Then I'm all yours. Let's go to the cop shop and see about a great steakhouse."

"We already found it. Did you smell it the downstairs?" Don asked. "We've got the best hotel and the best restaurant in town."

❖

Voytek walked out into the freezing night air knowing Vlad was somewhere on the street watching him. He backed out of the driveway and drove away. Once around the corner, he pulled into a parking lot and turned off the engine. He ran back and, as expected, saw a car pull into his driveway. Voytek walked back to his house. He entered through the kitchen. The stench of gasoline assaulted his senses. He heard noise upstairs. Vlad was readying the second floor for immolation. Once ignited, the house would burn hot.

Vlad was a particularly thorough arsonist. With a jerry can in hand, he descended the stairs and was surprised by a knife being thrust into his chest. He let out an almost imperceptible moan and died. Voytek replaced Vlad's driver's license with one of his forgeries then turned the body over so it would protect the wallet and license from the impending fire. Before stepping out of his house a second time, Voytek tossed a lit match into the kitchen. Flames erupted across the floor, along the walls, down the hall, and up the stairs. With the fire contained to the rear of the house, it would go unnoticed for some time, allowing the second floor to become fully engulfed long before the fire department arrived.

He closed the trunk of the arsonist's car, started the engine and followed the same route he'd taken fifteen minutes earlier. This time he parked the car at the far end of the lot. He walked back to the corner and saw flames coming from windows on both floors. Voytek thought the house might collapse on itself before the first fire engine responded. He started his vehicle; so far, so good.

The clock on the dash read 7:10 when Voytek drove into Apakoh's trap. He used the warehouse's side door and was greeted by Levi and Marat. Both held guns to his head. Marat took Voytek's pistol and patted him down. Levi led them to Revoldi's office.

Voytek was a bit surprised to find the senator sitting behind Revoldi's desk. "What's going on?"

The senator spoke first, "You arrogant asshole. You fucked up everything, and I'll be the one going to prison because of your stupidity." The senator shouted, "You had enough time to murder half of Olympia, but you didn't have time to get Crane's papers. Are you that fucking incompetent?"

Levi forced Voytek into a chair resting atop a plastic tarp.

"Taras neglected to tell me about the papers," Voytek started but before he could go on Revoldi nodded. Levi hit him in the stomach. The blow knocked the air out of Voytek's lungs. He bent over, gasping. When Voytek came up, he came up shooting. The first shot struck Levi in the leg and sent him sprawling on the floor. The second bullet split the senator's eyebrows. Apakoh stopped in his tracks. Marat shrugged and pointed Voytek's Glock at his now former boss. "Voytek pays better."

Revoldi began to negotiate, "Voytek, there's no need for more bloodshed. We can work this out…as comrades. We've been through much together."

"Yes. I'm sure you want me to surrender my gun and make peace with you. I will offer you the same *peace* you were offering me. Marat, make sure the Dragon has no teeth, and this time check all the hiding places."

His accomplice searched Apakoh thoroughly. He was unarmed.

"Sit in the chair." Andrei was in a mood. "When we're done, we'll wrap you in this plastic shroud and dump you into the river. You and that foul mouthed politician will sink to the bottom together."

He aimed the gun at Levi. "Choose! Stay with Apakoh and die, or join me."

Levi's answer was emphatic. "Fuck you."

"Fine. I'll deal with you as soon as this old man is no longer breathing. Getting rid of three bodies is as easy as getting rid of two. Apakoh, I'm going to shoot you in the stomach and watch you bleed to death." The bullet from Voytek's pistol slammed Revoldi back in his chair. A dark stain grew on the Dragon's shirt. "That must hurt like hell, and it'll take you a while to die. Marat and I will watch and make sure you are in pain the entire time. If you're waiting for that incompetent fool, Vlad, to return, it won't happen. My house is his funeral pyre."

Voytek pulled a chair close to Revoldi. "You won't beg for mercy, for your life? Maybe you are not in enough pain. Maybe I should shoot you in the knee. I have seen firsthand what losing a kneecap does to a man's arrogance."

The mad Russian put the barrel of his gun to Apakoh's left knee. He began to pull the trigger. The office door burst open. He swung around; bringing his pistol to bear on what he expected was another of Revoldi's men. His mouth dropped when he saw a young woman with a gun in her hand. She fired first. The direct hit seared Voytek's shoulder. Pain forced him to drop his weapon. From the corner of his eye, Voytek saw Marat aim the Glock at his adversary's daughter. He smiled knowing she'd be dead in a second. Marat squeezed the trigger. Click. The quizzical look on Marat's face was obliterated by the impact of Lara's second shot. In her best Russian, she told the traitorous pig he'd forgotten to release the safety.

Voytek dropped to his knees and reached for his gun. Before he could get it, another bullet from the Dragon's progeny struck him in the ribs. He looked at the girl who held his life in her hands and pleaded; first in English then in Russian.

"Man up, Voytek." She stood over him and blew off the top of his head. "Dad, let's go to the hospital."

"How do I explain being shot?" Revoldi's head spun from the loss of blood and from what his daughter had just done. "Take me to Doctor Rhinehart's, and we must take Levi. He was loyal even in the face of death."

"You need surgery, dad. Rhinehart's only good at handing out pills. Tell the cops Marat and Voytek tried to rob you. Voytek was running from the authorities. He needed cash." She pulled her father to his feet. "Marat, the pig, was his accomplice. Levi interrupted their plan and was shot in the leg, but he managed to kill both of them."

She turned to Levi. "Are you prepared to be a hero again?"

"Whatever you say, I'll do. I owe you my life, a second time," Levi answered.

"You paid that debt standing with my father. What about the senator?"

Levi stood. He dragged his injured leg over to the senator's body. "We have a very hot and powerful furnace. I'll shove his body through its doors."

Lara joined Levi over the dead man. The senator's eyes were still open, registering disbelief. "The bullet didn't exit. There's no blood. Levi, you have a good plan. Let's move him to the furnace."

"Take your father to the hospital. I'll dispose of the senator."

"But your leg," Lara said.

"It's a small wound, an inconvenience. After you leave I'll call the police. Hurry so Taras will be tended to properly."

"Tell them I arrived after the shooting and took my father to the hospital. Oh yes, you need to fire the gun. That way there's evidence you killed these two."

Lara handed Levi her gun. He put two bullets into the wall behind Taras's desk. Lara went over and moved the painting from in front of the wall safe, completing the staging. A few minutes later, the Dragon and his child drove off. Levi dragged Bernard to the furnace. The body went in without much effort. Levi threw in several bundles of waste material to fuel the fire. As he closed the door, he noticed the body was already burning hot. In a few hours, little, if any, evidence of the senator would remain.

Levi called the police. "There has been a robbery. I am wounded, and so is my boss, Mr. Revoldi. We are at 4267 River Front Road, behind the old mill. I've shot the two robbers, and I think they're dead."

The dispatcher had already used the 911 system to locate the call and confirmed Levi's address. She told him the police and medical assistance were on the way. When the police arrived, Levi was waiting outside with his hands raised. He expected the first officer to take him into custody. The officer did and helped him to the steps and had him sit. The cop apologized as he handcuffed Levi, stating it was protocol. Within minutes a half dozen police cars filled the lot. An ambulance arrived but had to wait for one of the squad cars to move before it could get to Levi.

Levi's leg wound wasn't serious, so the detectives interviewed him while the EMTs bandaged it and made him ready for transport. He told them Revoldi's daughter showed up soon after the gunfight and took her father to the emergency room. He wasn't sure but thought they'd gone to Divine Mercy.

Detectives found the scene consistent with Levi's story. Inside, one man had been shot three times, the other once. The safe was exposed but unopened. The chair surrounded by plastic sheets indicated the assailants planned to torture Revoldi into giving them the combination and then kill him.

The police found Marat's identification but found nothing on Voytek's body. With nothing left to process inside, the detectives turned their attention to the cars in the lot, focusing on the SUV with tinted glass. They decided to wait for a warrant before using the keys they found in Voytek's pocket. Levi was carted off in an ambulance, proud of the service he'd performed. He was prepared to lay down his life for Apakoh. Telling a few lies was child's play, and it would kept Lara's secret.

At Divine Mercy, Lara commandeered a gurney and two orderlies. After a doctor assessed him, they rushed Revoldi to an operating room. A nurse gathered up Lara and brought her into an office. "You're better off in here. The waiting room's jammed with some pretty dangerous people tonight, and the police will be here soon to talk with you. Do you want me to call someone?"

"I'll call my mom. She'll be frantic. My uncle better go get her."

The nurse was impressed with how calm the young woman seemed. She passed it off as a coping mechanism. Like shock, it would allow Lara to function until emotions overwhelmed her. She went back to work.

Lara contacted her uncle first and told him about the attempted robbery, the gunfight, and her father being wounded. She asked him to bring her mother to the hospital. He asked if he should bring a priest. Lara told him to wait until the doctors were done. Then she called her mother and told her Taras had been shot, was in surgery, and Uncle Petrov was on his way to her. Lara expected her mother to break into pieces, but she didn't.

For years, Zoya prepared herself for this call, and, now that it had come, she would deal with the consequences. The only surprise was the call had come from her daughter. As Lara hung up, there was a soft knock on the door. "Sweetie, the police need to speak with you. Can I send them in?"

She sucked in as much air as her lungs could hold and exhaled. She opened the door. In a soft, at times quivering voice, she described the horrific scene, "I got there to pick up my father and drive him home. I thought I'd find dad and some of his men working in the back or sharing a bottle of vodka. It's the vodka that worried my mom. But nobody was around. I heard voices in dad's office. Men were arguing, loudly. It was heated, but I couldn't make out what it was about. It could've been about soccer, a woman, Putin…who knows. They argue about everything. I sat downstairs to let it blow over. When Russian bulls butt heads, it's best to be somewhere else. It calmed down for a minute, then I heard bangs: four or five of them. Loud, not like firecrackers. I ran upstairs and opened the door. Levi was on the floor bleeding. Dad was in a chair holding his stomach. Two other men, Marat, a guy from work, and another I'd seen a couple of times, were lying on the floor. There was a lot of blood, a lot of blood."

"So you didn't see any of the actual shootings," a detective interjected.

"No, it was over before I got upstairs. My dad was bleeding pretty badly and sort of losing consciousness. I had to get him to the hospital. It'd take an ambulance too long to find us. I got him to my car and raced over here." Lara took a breath. "Levi was wounded. How is he?"

The detectives promised to find out and were about to press Lara for details when an enormous man entered the room. A woman and girl rushed past him and hugged Lara. Zoya asked the officers to give them a moment. The detectives exited, giving the mountain by the door plenty of room.

The surgeon walked in, blood splattered on his smock. "Mrs. Revoldi? I have good news; your husband is out of danger. Thanks to your daughter.

Not waiting for the ambulance probably saved his life. He's lost a lot of blood and is going to be weak for quite a long time. But he'll live."

The three women said nothing. Tears expressed their feelings. The doctor washed his hands. "The bullet nicked his spine. I don't think it damaged the nerves, but we won't know for sure if he has complete use of his legs until he wakes up; probably in a couple of hours. I can let one of you sit with him if you promise not to disturb him. He needs rest."

Zoya stood and hugged the man who'd brought her such good news. "I'll sit with my husband. For once, he'll be quiet."

She asked her brother to guard her brood. The Cossack nodded. No harm would come to the girls. Zoya joined her husband, thankful for God's intervention. Lara washed her hands for the sixth time. She was glad nobody wanted to test her hands for gunshot residue. She'd learned a lot from watching *NCIS*.

❖

Spokane's coroner wrapped up his work at the warehouse. Two bodies were loaded into an ambulance and transported to his office. In the building, shell casings were located, bullet holes found, photographs taken, and all manner of evidence collected. Everything was consistent with the story fabricated by Lara and Levi.

Outside, the SUV remained untouched. The detectives confirmed it belonged to Andrei Clayton, a Spokane resident, probably the other man being taken to the morgue. Finally, they were informed they had the warrant and the driver's door was unlocked. What they found astonished them: four semi-automatic pistols, a shotgun, and a fully automatic AK-47. Three sets of identity cards were stashed in a leather pouch under the driver's seat. A stack of money was hidden in a compartment under the passenger's seat.

"This guy was prepared for war," the lead detective pointed out. "He had more firepower than all of us combined."

He called the station requesting Andrei Clayton's address. A few minutes later, a return message gave him the information. With nothing left to do at the crime scene, two detectives drove off. Twenty minutes later they were standing next to a fire truck.

A fireman joined them. "Looks like arson. The house was fully engulfed when we got here, and it took the first truck only six minutes to find the place. There's a body in there, but it's still too dangerous to go in for it. The fire marshal and the coroner are on their way."

"What a night this turned out to be." The detective sat on the truck's bumper. "There's going to be a lot of fucking paperwork."

Chapter 58

Don got up well before the sun; old habits die hard. He visited the bathroom, showered, and shaved. With lights off, he eased out of the room, leaving Patti to a well-deserved rest. Descending the hotel's grand-staircase, he pictured himself as a bald Rhett Butler. He couldn't resist and, when he got to the last step, said, "Frankly, my dear, I don't give a damn."

On the opposing wall were scones, donuts, juice, and coffee enticing guests into an expensive Regal breakfast. The marketing plan was working. Don poured coffee, put a scone with raspberry jam on a plate, and settled into an overstuffed chair to read the morning paper. The headline caught his attention, *Robbery Thwarted – 2 Dead*. Andrei Clayton, the name of one of the dead, shouted at him, "Patti's got to see this."

He finished his coffee, poured two to-go cups, and took the elevator. Patti was in the shower. He put the coffee on the night table and turned on the television. Patti's entrance couldn't have been timed better. The reporter described a heroic standoff by a local construction company employee. He had interrupted a robbery and, though wounded, managed to kill both robbers and save the life of his boss. The reporter went on to say there was a particularly sinister twist to the story in that the home owned by one of the robbers had been burned to the ground, and a third body was found there.

"Were any of them Andrei?" she asked.

"Well, no and yes." Don handed her the paper. "Andrei Clemmens, no. But Andrei Clayton, yes. Clayton tried to rob the place and got killed. And he may've torched his house with a guy in it."

Don did his best to bring her up to speed, but he finally suggested they go to the police station and get the full story. Patti pointed out it was still before eight and unlikely anyone at the station would be able to fill them in on anything. She suggested breakfast, checking out, and then going to the station. Remembering the aromas downstairs, Don fully endorsed the plan.

It was after nine when the valet turned Patti's keys over to her. It was sunny and cold, not unusual for Spokane. They drove to police headquarters. Captain Gardener was meeting with his detectives, and when he heard Detective Linder was there, he invited her and her guest to join them.

The medical examiner spoke first. "The two dead men found at the scene were killed by gunfire. Marat Sandaval was struck once, directly in the head. The other man, Andrew Clayton, was struck three times: once in the shoulder, once in the ribs. Neither was fatal. The third bullet entered the skull just above the right eye socket and terminated the victim's life. The first two bullets came from twenty to thirty feet away. The third came from much closer, probably less than ten. All wounds are consistent with a close-quarters gunfight."

"Thanks George." The captain pointed to his staff. "What do my detectives have?"

"There were two other victims; both wounded. Taras Revoldi, the owner of the business, was shot in the stomach. It was a serious wound, but he'll recover. A second man, whose last name doesn't have any vowels, so let's call him Levi, was wounded in the leg. He's been patched up and sent home."

The detective drank from his insulated cup. "From what Levi told us, Sandaval and Clayton, were friends. Clayton was a nasty character and would, from time to time, visit Revoldi, usually to borrow money. Levi was working late, getting ready for a job. He didn't know what Revoldi was doing in the office, but it wasn't unusual for his boss to work late. Somewhere around seven, Levi heard Sandaval and Clayton arrive. A bit later he heard shouting in Revoldi's office. The door was closed, and yelling could be heard everywhere in the building. It was about opening the safe."

The detective checked his notes. "Levi got concerned, went to investigate, and picked up a pistol Revoldi had in the reception area. He got to the door when he heard a gunshot. He opened it and surprised Clayton and Sandaval. Levi shot first and wounded Clayton in the shoulder. Marat pointed a gun at him but it jammed. Levi shot at Marat and apparently killing him. Marat's weapon still had the safety on when we checked. That's why it didn't fire."

The second detective took over. "While he was shooting at Marat, Andrei shot him in the leg. It knocked him off his feet, and he crawled behind a sofa. He shot three more times blindly from behind the furniture. One of the shots hit Andrei in the ribs, and two got lodged in the wall near the safe. Levi waited a bit and got up to see what had happened. Andrei raised his gun. Levi shot him in the head."

"Where does the girl fit into this?" the captain asked.

Don looked at Patti. "Girl?"

"The girl is Lara Revoldi, the owner's daughter. She's twenty-one. She arrived shortly after the gunfight ended. She's a pretty cool customer. She collected her dad and got him to the hospital. Handled herself very well and may have saved his life. It took the ambulance more than fifteen minutes to find this place. I don't know if Revoldi could've held out that long."

Patti asked, "Do we know why she came to the office?"

"She said her dad had had a tough day, and she came to take him home. Her mother was worried and didn't want him to drive. Apparently, he doesn't see all that well at night, and there may've been vodka involved."

The first detective began again. "We got a search warrant for Clayton's car. We found way more than we expected: weapons, ammunition, fake IDs, and ten thousand in cash."

The second detective took over. "We weren't sure it was Clayton lying in the office with his head blown off, so we went to his house. When we got there, we found it burned to the ground. The fire marshal's calling it arson. And there was a body inside. It was burned beyond recognition but was situated in such a way that the guy's wallet was scorched but not burnt up. It had Andrei Clayton's driver's license in it."

"You're telling me we have two Andrei Claytons," the captain quizzed his detectives. "Both dead."

"On the surface, that's what it looks like, but the real Andrei Clayton is the guy without a skull cap. We think he found a guy about his size, murdered him, and burnt the house down around him. It's likely he was running away from something, needed more cash, and tried to hold up Revoldi."

The coroner shrugged. "Makes sense to me. It all fits with what I've come up with. I have the burn victim on my table right now. We're looking for Clayton's dental records, but we aren't going to find any. He's Russian, and they're very secretive."

"Speaking of Russian, could any of this be tied to the Bratva? There're rumors that Revoldi might be part of it," the detective asked.

Don raised his hand. "Excuse me for being a bit out of it, but what's the *Bratva*?"

The captain stood up. "It's our version of the mafia; Russians who've set up a criminal organization over here. We haven't had much luck getting any farther than that. I've met Mr. Revoldi at church, and it's hard to imagine him being part of anything like that." The captain neglected to mention his meeting with Anton Breshnon several months ago and his subsequent call to Apakoh.

Patti looked up from her notes. "Don and I were tracking a guy named Andrei Clemmens. He's wanted for questioning in close to a dozen murders on the west side. We broadcast his name and description along with that of his car, and it spooked him into running. The guy who tried to rob the place is likely Clemmens. The fact he killed someone to cover his tracks also points directly at Clemmens."

With little else to discuss, the team broke up. The coroner wanted to identify the body from the fire. The detectives would follow whatever leads they had, and everybody, including Patti, wanted to talk to Taras Revoldi. And now she wanted to interview his daughter. It was almost ten when Don and Patti left the station. Patti called the senator's office. A very distressed woman answered. "The senator isn't here. We don't know where he is. The police are here. I have to go."

Patti hung up. "Don, the senator's missing. The police are at his office. We ought to stop by and see what's going on."

They drove to the senator's headquarters. Several police cars were parked outside. An officer stood at the entrance. Patti showed him her badge and was allowed to enter. A woman was sitting in the receptionist chair crying. Patti went over to her.

"I'm Mrs. Bernard," the woman said. "When he didn't come home last night, I thought he might've slept here. He does that now and then when there's a problem. But he's not here. I called his friends, and nobody's seen him."

Patti did her best to console Mrs. Bernard, but in the back of her mind, she expanded the scenario the detectives had laid out. Clemmens extorted money from the senator for killing Brian; probably the ten thousand dollars the cops found. Then he took the senator somewhere and disposed of him. The fire victim came to mind, but the description didn't fit. Next, Andrei took on Revoldi, probably because he needed more than ten thousand dollars to start a new life. That proved to be a mistake.

When she got to the car, she walked Don through her theory. Don nodded. It made sense. Andrei killed Brian on the senator's order, probably to stop his investigation. Patti's scenario filled in the rest. For Andrei, opportunity trumped caution. Andrei covered his departure by torching his home with a body in it. With no evidence to the contrary, the coroner would declare the body to be Andrei's.

"He was counting on us to find his body, to uncover his Spokane identity, and close the case. With money from the senator and Revoldi, he'd be home free. You have to hand it to this guy. He's clever." Don got ready to roll.

"And a vicious murderer. Otherwise, a standup guy," Patti replied, "I still want to talk to Revoldi and his daughter."

"Then let's get something to eat and go to the hospital. I could use a burger, fries, and a shake. Maybe dessert."

"I'm going to weigh five hundred pounds." Patti laughed.

"Oh, I know ways to work off those calories. Lots of fun and lots of sweating."

"You are incorrigible." Patti made a left into a restaurant's parking lot.

Chapter 59

Divine Mercy's waiting-room was like no other Don or Patti had seen. It had seven areas best described as living rooms surrounding an information center. Each area could hold fifteen people comfortably in chairs, recliners, and couches all resting on thick carpeting. Bookshelves held magazines, and toy boxes were overflowing.

"Don, could you wait for me here? Two of us might spook Revoldi."

"Absolutely." He grabbed a magazine. "I'll brush up on NASCAR, says here things won't be the same without Jeff Gordon."

"Thanks." Catching the volunteer's attention, she asked for Taras Revoldi's room number. After thanking Don again, Patti found the elevators and soon was on the med-surg floor. Like the waiting-room, the surgical floor was laid out around a hub, this time the hub was the nurses' station.

"Down and on the left." The charge nurse pointed to her right.

Patti walked past several closed doors before finding Revoldi's room. She knocked. A young woman opened the door.

"I'm Detective Linder from Olympia. I'd like to ask Mr. Revoldi a few questions."

"Dad, it's a detective from Olympia. She'd like to talk to you."

"That's fine, Lara. Show her in."

"He's still weak, so this will have to be quick. Okay?"

Patti nodded and sat beside the bed. "Thank you for seeing me. I know the Spokane police asked you all about Clayton. I'm sorry if I cover some of the same ground, but I'm working on a different case that may involve him. We think the name he used on the west side was Clemmens. Did he ever use that name with you? Do you know if he'd been around Olympia recently?"

Revoldi thought for a few seconds and confirmed Clayton mentioned being on the west side, but the name Andrei Clemmens was not familiar.

"Do you know what Clayton did for a living?"

"Odd jobs, I guess. I didn't know him that well. We met at church years ago. Seemed like a nice guy, down on his luck."

"So you gave him money?" Patti took notes.

"Once in a while. He'd come by and ask for help. I tried putting him to work, but he wasn't reliable. He'd disappear for weeks."

"When he showed up to rob you, were you surprised?"

"Surprised? Yes, I'd say I was surprised. A gun in my face would usually surprise me."

"I mean was it totally unexpected." Patti clarified her question. "Did it ever cross your mind Clayton might rob you?"

"I suppose. He was broke, had a temper, and I knew he owned a gun. I saw it once in his car."

"Did he ever mention Howard Jenkins? Brian Crane? Samuel Bernard?"

"They don't ring a bell, detective. Except for Bernard. He's a local politician; senator I believe."

"Mr. Revoldi. Can you tell me who shot Clayton? And why he was shot three times?"

238

"My good friend Levi put the dog down, after Clayton shot me. I don't know why it took three bullets to stop him. I was focused on staying alive. You should ask Levi."

Using a standard interrogation tool, Detective Linder pivoted. "Was Clayton part of the Bratva, Mr. Revoldi? Is Levi? Are you part of the Bratva?"

"Ah, I see you've been talking with the Spokane police about our mythical Russian criminal organization. I'm Russian, Clayton was Russian, my daughter Lara is Russian. We all must be part of the brotherhood, the Bratva. I don't know about Clayton, but I assure you I am not part of the Bratva, and I don't believe such a beast exists."

Lara inserted herself between Patti and her father. "Detective, you need to leave now. My father's tired and can be of no further help. If Levi ended the life of the man you say was Clemmons, then a good thing happened and your investigation is over. Voytek got what he deserved."

Patti was taken aback by the abruptness of the young woman. "Okay. I have most of what I need. Thank you Mr. Revoldi."

Lara escorted Patti to the door. "Detective, do you believe you can do something evil so that good will come of it?"

Patti was first at a loss for words, but recovered. Thinking back on Don's many transgressions and their results, she said, "Sometimes you have to bend the rules a little to get a good outcome."

"That's sort of what my father said. Thanks for coming by." Lara closed the door.

Three floors later, Patti found Don on a couch entertaining a young girl and her mother with a dinosaur-themed puppet show. He ended the performance when he noticed Patti in the doorway. "The little girl is waiting to go upstairs for chemo. The kid's only five, and this is her second bout with cancer. So, I got Lilly and her mom dinosaurs. Wish I could do more."

"Don you never cease to amaze me. I'm sure the mom appreciated the distraction."

"How did it go with Revoldi?"

"With the *Revoldis*," Patti countered. "I met the daughter, Lara. Got well-rehearsed answers from Mr. Revoldi: hadn't heard of Clemmens, nothing about Jenkins, didn't know what Clayton did for a living. Blah, blah, blah. Thought Clayton could be dangerous. Lara didn't say much."

"What *did* she say?"

"She said something about doing evil and good coming from it. Voytek got what he deserved, and I should leave. She wrapped it up by telling me my investigation was over."

"Who or what is Voytek?"

"Andrei Clayton. Andrei Clemmens. My guess is he's all one in the same person. Voytek is probably Russian for asshole."

239

"It was good she closed the case for you. Didn't know she was in charge."

"Oh she's in charge all right. As soon as she spoke up the interview was over, and I was out the door." Patti braced herself against the westerly wind whipping across the lawn. "I think I just met the current and future heads of the Bratva."

❖

From her father's room, Lara watched clouds mass on the horizon, a storm was brewing. "Dad, Detective Linder might be a problem when we move west."

"There're always problems, but you can deal with her when the time comes."

Four hours later, Zoya took Maria's hand and led her out of the room. The orderlies had arrived to get Taras for the surgery that would restore the feeling in his feet. Revoldi caught Lara's hand, held her back, and signaled the men to leave.

"I haven't told you how proud I am of you," he said in a faltering voice.

"Dad, I wasn't going to let them kill you. I'll leave that to mom's cooking."

"Your mother's cooking is fine, but you must be serious for one moment. Most of the men working for me wouldn't have done what you did. Most wouldn't know how to do what you did."

"They would if someone was threatening their father. I did what had to be done. Will Levi keep our secret?"

"From the authorities, yes. From the men, no. He has already given you a very fitting name. Apakoh Pebehok."

"Dragon Child? I'm not sure I like that."

"Too late Pebehok. I need you to get me a few things from the safe. We have much to discuss if you are to take over in a few years."

She hugged her father.

"Dragons don't cry," Taras whispered.

Lara watched as the sedative took her father. "This one does."

The End

240

Made in the USA
Coppell, TX
29 November 2019

12067274R00134